The
Lost
Madonna

Berkley titles by Kelly Jones

THE LOST MADONNA
THE SEVENTH UNICORN

The Lost Madonna

KELLY JONES

BERKLEY BOOKS, NEW YORK

THE BERKLEY PUBLISHING GROUP
Published by the Penguin Group
Penguin Group (USA) Inc.
375 Hudson Street, New York, New York 10014, USA
Penguin Group (Canada), 90 Eglinton Avenue East, Suite 700, Toronto, Ontario M4P 2Y3, Canada
(a division of Pearson Penguin Canada Inc.)
Penguin Books Ltd., 80 Strand, London WC2R 0RL, England
Penguin Group Ireland, 25 St. Stephen's Green, Dublin 2, Ireland (a division of Penguin Books Ltd.)
Penguin Group (Australia), 250 Camberwell Road, Camberwell, Victoria 3124, Australia
(a division of Pearson Australia Group Pty. Ltd.)
Penguin Books India Pvt. Ltd., 11 Community Centre, Panchsheel Park, New Delhi—110 017, India
Penguin Group (NZ), 67 Apollo Drive, Mairangi Bay, Auckland 1311, New Zealand
(a division of Pearson New Zealand Ltd.)
Penguin Books (South Africa) (Pty.) Ltd., 24 Sturdee Avenue, Rosebank, Johannesburg 2196,
South Africa

Penguin Books Ltd., Registered Offices: 80 Strand, London WC2R 0RL, England

This is a work of fiction. Names, characters, places, and incidents either are the product of the author's imagination or are used fictitiously, and any resemblance to actual persons, living or dead, business establishments, events, or locales is entirely coincidental. The publisher does not have any control over and does not assume any responsibility for author or third-party websites or their content.

THE LOST MADONNA

A Berkley Book / published by arrangement with the author

PRINTING HISTORY
Berkley edition / February 2007

Copyright © 2007 by Kelly Jones.
Cover illustration by Tim O'Brien.
Cover design by George Long.
Interior text design by Stacy Irwin.

ISBN: 978-0-425-21419-0

BERKLEY®
Berkley Books are published by The Berkley Publishing Group,
a division of Penguin Group (USA) Inc.,
375 Hudson Street, New York, New York 10014.
BERKLEY is a registered trademark of Penguin Group (USA) Inc.
The "B" design is a trademark belonging to Penguin Group (USA) Inc.

PRINTED IN THE UNITED STATES OF AMERICA

10 9 8 7 6 5 4 3 2 1

ACKNOWLEDGMENTS

I spent my junior year of college at Gonzaga-in-Florence, an American university year-abroad program in Italy. It was two years after the great flood of 1966, but signs of the devastation were everywhere—in the dark lines on the buildings near the Arno River, in the museums and churches where signs proclaiming *in corso di restauro* marked empty spaces where treasures were once displayed. Being young, eager to take in as much as I could, to travel and explore, I don't believe the gravity of the situation hit me until years later. When I decided to write about Florence, I knew I wanted to write about the flood. Many thanks to Gonzaga University and to my parents, Otto and Mary Alice Florence, for the gift of that experience in Italy, which eventually inspired this story.

For the development of the manuscript that became *The Lost Madonna* I have many to thank. I'm especially grateful to Renie Hays, who, after a thoughtful, honest readings of an early manuscript, turned me around and headed me in the right direction. To readers and writers Coston Frederick, Frank Marvin, Maria Eschen, the late Byron Meredith, David Schneider, Lydia Barbee, and Celeste Killeen, I extend my sincerest gratitude. And a big thank-you to Jan English, Margaret Marti, Catherine Jones, and Paul Shaffer, for generosity, support, and the warm, creative meeting place at The Cabin by the Boise River.

I feel very fortunate to have had the opportunity to work with the late Leona Nevler, and continue to be blessed with the support of Kate Seaver, my editor at Berkley Books. My agent, Julie Barer, has been my literary guardian angel, guiding me with a gentle hand, but also keeping a tough, protective eye out for my best interests. Thank you, Julie.

To my first, last, and most dedicated reader, my husband, Jim, who has often been asked to do an emergency reading at seven A.M. at the breakfast table, again I say thank you.

To the citizens of Firenze, who continue to cherish and share their history and art, *molte grazie!*

For factual information on the Florence flood of 1966, I have relied on articles in the *New York Times*, *National Geographic*, *Saturday Review*, *Reader's Digest*, *Holiday*, *Life*, *U.S. News & World Report*, *Newsweek*, and *Time*. I also found the first-person account in *Diary of Florence in Flood* by Kathrine Kressman Taylor (Simon and Schuster, 1967) extremely helpful. "Masolino, Restored," an article by Guy Lesser in the September 1995 issue of Delta Air Lines's *Sky*, which I'd tucked away in my carry-on and remembered as I was writing this story, inspired me to use Masolino as my underappreciated Renaissance artist. Mr. Lesser's article evoked memories of my first visit to Santa Maria del Carmine back in the sixties. I had, of course, ventured into the Brancacci Chapel to see Masaccio's Adam and Eve. Yet, I clearly remember wondering at the time, "What about the fellow who painted the *pretty* Adam and Eve?"

For reconnecting with that youthful sense of adventure, optimism, and emotional vulnerability I have relied on the journal of a young woman, written during a wonderful, wondrous year in Italy.

PROLOGUE

THE FIRST TIME I saw the painting I knew little about art and even less about life. I was nineteen and off on a journey of discovery, seeking adventure and excitement, dreaming of romance. I found it all. And so much more.

I remember the day the small painting, spotted with oil and mud, chipped and flaking from stress on the bloated wooden panel, was loaded on a truck and transported from the Uffizi to the Limonaia. I can still see the sweet face of the Madonna and the Child reaching up with tiny fingers to touch her cheek. I can smell the pungent odor of the disinfectant sprayed on the surface to prevent the growth of mold and mildew, and I can feel the sense of solemnity as the painting was laid out beside other Virgins, angels, and saints, on the stiff metal bed in the winter greenhouse in the Boboli Gardens. And I remember the thrill of working at Stefano's side, and then the sense of satisfaction as we gradually brought the painting back to life.

After I returned home from Italy, I often thought of the Madonna, and I knew that someday I would return to Florence and stroll through the Galleria degli Uffizi and find it gloriously restored, hanging along with other masterpieces of the early Renaissance. A plaque would reveal its history, attribute it to Tommaso di Cristoforo Fini, a fifteenth-century Italian artist better known as Masolino da Panicale, and note that it had been damaged in the flood of 1966 and rescued.

As the years passed, memories and images filtering through time, I wondered if it had been just as I recalled. The thought of a return evoked a mixture of apprehension and cautious excitement. Yet I knew one day I would find my way back and I would see the painting again.

But when I finally came across Masolino's Mother and Child over thirty years later, it happened in an unforeseen way, under circumstances very different from those I had imagined. And it changed the course of my life forever.

1

1999

IN EARLY NOVEMBER Charley Stover, dean of a year-abroad program in Florence for an American university, called and invited me to come over and teach during the spring semester. Charley and I had met in Italy when we were both very young and wrote sporadically over the next three or four years. We reconnected when I taught at a junior college just outside of Portland, where he was teaching at a university, and then kept in touch when I moved to Boise. It still surprised me when I saw him in his clerical collar and realized he was now Father Charles Stover, SJ. He'd always be Charley to me.

I hadn't seen Charley in almost two years, since he'd taken the position in Florence, and his call was a pleasant surprise. He explained that the woman they'd originally contracted for the year had been involved in an accident—she'd gone over to London for the weekend and been hit by a car as she stepped off the curb. "Looking the wrong way for oncoming traffic," Charley told me. She'd survived and returned home to New York. They'd been able to cover the remaining portion of first semester with existing staff, and hoped that Dr. Browning would return for second semester, but her recovery had been slower than anticipated. "The whole thing, quite a shock, surely for Dr. Browning, and it's also left me rather in a bind. I thought of you, Suzanne, and wondered if you could possibly arrange to come over and fill in for a semester. With your love for the city, having lived here in Florence, you'd be perfect for the position."

"I don't know, Charley . . ."

"Give it some thought, Professor Cunningham," he said with the same affectionate formality I might use in addressing him as Father Stover. "But not too much thought," he added with a chuckle, "I need to know soon."

I'd been thinking about a move, feeling a restlessness I hadn't known in years. I'd contemplated applying for a position at a college in Colorado and looked at an opportunity in Montana.

We were about to enter into a new millennium—the twenty-first century—full of doom and gloom and catastrophe according to the least optimistic. I'd also entered a new time in my own life, the rhythms of my body forever changed. A time when a woman who had produced children and sent them into the world might embrace new possibilities and freedoms. I saw only finality. I needed something new, a challenge, a change of course in my life.

For years I'd known that someday I would return to Florence. Maybe the time was now.

The university in Boise agreed to give me a semester's leave, even on such short notice, and I wondered if the discontent I'd been feeling lately was evident, if my gift for teaching was waning, as was my enthusiasm for the work I'd always loved.

I had no immediate family to consult. My sister lived here in Boise, Dad was still down in Twin Falls, but on the most intimate level I'd been alone since Jerry and I divorced over nine years ago. No one, it seemed, would be entirely lost without me, other than Rousseau—my best buddy, my big old thirteen-year-old puppy.

Charley said I'd be scheduled for two introduction to art history classes and one on women in Renaissance art as an upper-level course. The Virgin would be important in such a study, so I went through my collection of books, pulling out those on the subject. While reading through a bibliography in one, I came across a reference to a book that sounded perfect, and decided to find a copy of *The Madonna in Italian Renaissance Art*.

The book was a collaborative effort by several art historians, many of them familiar and well regarded in the field. It had been published fifteen years ago and was now out of print, so I ended up ordering a used copy from a bookstore in Boston that I found on the Internet.

I called and spoke with the owner of the store, who told me the binding was in great shape with no fading in the text, though the jacket showed some wear. I gave her my credit card number and asked her to send it as soon as possible. I'd be leaving for Florence in less than a month, right after Christmas break.

It arrived in a UPS box. I had come home from my morning class to let Rousseau out and found it waiting on the doorstep.

I carried the box into the house, working it open. Inside, the book was enclosed in a padded envelope, double sealed with heavy, brown plastic tape. I could picture the old woman in the bookstore—a clear image had formed in my mind when I spoke to her over the phone—and I could imagine her taking great care, thoughtfully sealing and taping and boxing, making sure the book was properly packed to make it all the way to Idaho.

"Iowa?" she'd asked when I gave her the address.

"No, Idaho." I wondered if she was a little hard of hearing. "I-d-a-h-o." I spelled it out.

"Oh, potatoes," she said, as if she were describing the population, rather than the product.

"Yes, potatoes," I replied. She chuckled a little, maybe wondering what a potato from Idaho would be doing with a book entitled *The Madonna in Italian Renaissance Art*.

I got scissors out of the kitchen drawer and cut the envelope open and pulled the book out. The smell of old paper, old art, and maybe a little of Boston, escaped with the lift of the first page.

The jacket was slightly faded and discolored with a cup ring—had the previous owner taken the term *coffee table book* literally? But the text and reproductions were wonderful, as if the book had barely been opened. I flipped through the pages, marveling at the paintings, familiar from my many years of teaching college art history. Giotto, Cimabue, Fra Angelico, Masaccio, Piero della Francesca, Raphael. These images could still bring a shiver of delight every time I came across them, and memories of the first time I'd seen many of the originals, though at the time my untrained eye saw them in a completely different light. Stefano had told me that one of the things that made art special was the fact that it was intimate and personal, that each viewer could take pleasure in his or her individual way, and even this singular perception might change and grow and expand over time.

I walked back to the dining room looking for my purse—I thought I'd set it on the buffet—still paging through the book. I'd sit down later and read, but right now I was running late for lunch with my sister, Andrea.

Just as I was about to close the book, pages still flipping through my fingers, an image caught my eye—a flash of pink and blue and gold. Quickly, I leafed back and when I realized what it was, I had to sit. It was the Masolino, reproduced in color, a half-page plate. I stared down at the images of the Mother and Child.

After a moment I could see the colors weren't quite right. These were not the vivid pinks and blues of the Madonna's veil and garments, the white of the Child's robe, the rich gold-leaf background revealed as we had cleaned and restored the panel. A dark patina of soot and varnish tinted the painting.

Rousseau, who had been trailing along as I moved through the house, sat down on the floor against my leg, grateful that I was finally still, though only my legs were still—my hands were visibly shaking as I placed the book on the dining room table. I stared, breathless, my heart hammering, memories stirring deep inside. After over three decades, this small, tender painting brought it all back—the flood, Stefano Leonetti, and my foolish, young, unknowing heart.

The caption read *Madonna and Child, tempera on wood, 28 by 22 cm., fifteenth-century Italian, Uffizi, Florence*, and I remembered how small the painting was—no bigger than a piece of typing paper, a magazine cover. The artist was not identified, though the text itself stated that many art historians believe it was painted by Masolino, an artist best known for his frescoes in the Brancacci Chapel of the Church of Santa Maria del Carmine in Florence.

I sat and read, and then I had to take another deep breath. The painting, according to the author, a Roberto Balducci, had been destroyed in the flood of 1966. I read this sentence over and over, staring down at the words I knew were untrue. The painting had been damaged, but it had been restored. I knew, because I had been there.

BY THE TIME I left the house, it had started to snow and a sleek white blanket covered the street. I didn't realize I was half an hour late for my lunch date until I checked my watch as I pulled into the restaurant parking lot.

Andrea sat, drinking what must have been her third or fourth cup of coffee, her fingers wrapped so tightly around the cup I could imagine it shooting out of her hand. She looked up, and then stood to greet me with a hug. "Where have you been? I thought you were in a wreck or something." There was a mixture of anger, panic, and then relief in her voice. "The streets are terrible."

"I ran home to let Rousseau out," I said. "Sorry. Just fell a little behind."

"You really outdid yourself this time," she said, glancing at her watch. Andrea was always on time. The mother of five, all grown now, she had survived by following a rigid schedule, being punctual and organized.

I stomped the melting snow off my boots, unwound the

wool scarf from my neck, struggled out of my coat and hooked it on the back of my chair, then sat.

Andrea stared at me for a moment. "What's the matter, Suzi?" Her voice softened. "You okay?"

I nodded and a waiter appeared at my side. "Would you like something to drink while you're looking over the menu?" He glanced at my sister, the slightest indication that she'd mentioned to him my habit of losing track of time. "A refill on your coffee?"

"Please," she answered.

"A glass of wine," I said. "Bring a couple." I nodded toward Andrea as her eyebrows rose. "Something white—a Chardonnay would be fine."

"Drinking?" Andrea asked, looking at her watch again as the waiter left. I was sure she was going to say, "Before noon?" but she didn't.

We sat silently for a moment. "You're pale as a ghost," Andrea finally said.

"I think," I replied, picking up my menu, "I may have just seen one."

2

TO TELL THIS story I should begin with what happened long ago in Florence, Italy. Yet a story often begins before it really begins. With a seed of discontent, a yearning.

Imagine a girl—tall, thin, with long muscular legs, dark hair flying. She is alone. She is running. The northern Idaho sky is streaked with vermilion and a light dew sparkles on the grass. The quiet of the early morning is intense, and she can hear her own breathing, the rhythm of her feet as they hit the track. Faster and faster she runs, moving so quickly the sound, the color of the light, the cool morning air, and her own heartbeat merge and blur into one enormous sensation.

And, it comes to her—*I am going nowhere*. What can she accomplish from running round and round a track? She wants to run beyond the oval track, through the moist green field, beyond the mountains, the ocean, the sky. To go someplace. To reach beyond her small little space on this planet. She wants to explore the world!

I, of course, am—or *was*—this girl. At the time I was eighteen, a freshman at the University of Idaho, with no idea what I wanted to do with my life. Being athletic, I'd thought about majoring in physical education and eventually teaching high school P.E. But, in truth, I possessed little in the way of academic ambition.

My thoughts from that morning stayed with me and grew until they filled me so full I thought I might burst. When I went home that summer, I'd made up my mind that I wouldn't go back to school, though I didn't tell my parents until almost the end of August.

My best friend, Roxie Royal—yes, an adventurous-sounding name; and she was—had taken a job right after high school graduation, working as a secretary at a bean warehouse down by Kimberly, a short distance from where we grew up in Twin Falls. She hated the job and was eager for a change too.

I was helping my dad that summer, working in his office at the farm implement store in Twin. Over the next few months Roxie and I hatched a plan and saved our money. But by the middle of August we both knew we didn't have enough to take us far.

Luckily, it was Uncle Trace who managed the trusts Grandma had set up for me, my sister, and our cousins—money my dad always told me was for my education. I knew I could convince my uncle that Europe would be educational, in line with Grandma's intentions, but my parents were a different story. I also knew that when I turned eighteen, it had actually become *my* money.

My mom and dad were not pleased when I told them I wasn't going back to school, that instead I was going to Europe. My mother was especially upset, and I thought, What does *she* know? She'd grown up in this boring little town and had never gone anywhere. She'd married my dad when she was all of nineteen, looking barely sixteen in the black-and-white wedding photo that hung in my parents' bedroom.

In the end, they agreed to let me go, but only after I promised I would finish school when I got back home.

I knew I couldn't do this without Roxie, so I agreed to float her a loan—thanks to Grandma's generosity. My parents wouldn't have approved if they'd known, but they took some comfort in the fact that I wasn't going alone.

In mid-September Roxie and I took the bus to Salt Lake City, then a plane to New York, and caught a discounted student flight to London, though neither of us were officially students. Our backpacks were filled with wool skirts, sweaters, penny loafers, jeans, travelers' checks, and a brand-new copy of *Europe on $5 a Day*. If I'd stuffed in the gumption and naïveté I'd also taken along on the trip, the pack would have been impossible to lift.

I had never flown in my life and I still remember that mixture of anticipation and air sickness that turned my stomach and made it impossible for me to eat until the following morning when the flight attendants came around collecting blankets and pillows, turning on lights, and serving coffee and rolls before our descent into the London airport.

We spent a week in Great Britain, easing into our travels in a country where we spoke the language. We found a cheap room in South Kensington and were served bacon and eggs, tomatoes, and beans for breakfast. We ate fish and chips, lifted a pint or two at the local pubs, hung out with some American kids we met at an unofficial hootenanny in Hyde Park. We did the museum thing—the Tate, the Victoria and Albert, the British Museum—and sent postcards home as proof of our educational experience.

The second week, we took a boat over to the continent and spent four days in Amsterdam. We stayed in a tiny room on the top floor of a narrow little house on Canal Street, where breakfast included enormous chunks of Dutch cheese and delicious breads with fresh butter and marmalade. We rented bikes to explore the city, and did not report home on the hippies and flower children we met along the way, or mention the very liberal attitudes the Dutch seemed to take concerning window dressing at the local brothels just down the street from our hotel.

We purchased Eurailpasses and headed to France, where

we both fell in love with Paris. In Germany we discovered Löwenbräu and Wiener schnitzel. We met other American students along the way, mostly boys, who seemed so much more interesting than the guys we knew back home. We discovered we were quite a hit with the European men. There was nothing more than a bit of flirtation and innocent teasing on our part, but every time I saw Roxie develop more than a little interest in a young man, I'd pull her along—quite literally by the hand—and tell her it was time to move on. We had a whole world to explore.

We visited the Lake Country in northern Italy, and then hopped back on the train and headed to Venice. It rained the day we arrived, and continued through our stay. I had expected water in Venice and found the gray wet skies and murky canals darkly romantic. Surprisingly, neither of us found this depressing, though we saw not one glimpse of the sun for three days.

And then we took the train south to Florence. It was Thursday, the third of November, 1966, and the city was decked out for a holiday on Friday, banners and flags whipping ferociously in the rain-drenched wind. Here I had expected sunshine, but the rain showed no sign of letting up. So much for sunny Italy! But this would not hamper our desire to see the city and sights. We pulled out our guidebook and charted our course for the next day.

Throughout the night the rain pounded on the tile roof of the *pensione* where we were staying just a few blocks from the Duomo, the Cathedral of Santa Maria del Fiore. It beat against the wooden shutters, and I slept little that night. When we woke the next morning, we knew immediately that something was wrong. I flicked the light switch, but nothing happened. Roxie and I made our way down the dim hall and ate our breakfast of panini and jam, served by candlelight with lukewarm juice, no coffee or tea. Chatter among the *pensione* guests was at first subdued, giving way to a slow-moving panic as people stood and gazed out the window. Roxie and I got up and joined them. Though it was no longer raining, a river was moving down the street. I looked at Roxie and didn't say anything, but we both knew things were about to change, though neither of us knew how drastically. We walked down to the street level, thinking we might go out to see what was going on, but already the water was ankle deep and so we returned to the third floor, where we sat like ransom victims, each lost in our own thoughts.

By midday, water outside the pensione door was two feet deep and rising. The middle-aged Italian padrone stood, shaking his head, staring down at the street. It was obvious that the Arno River, three blocks away, had burst through its banks. We watched as battered furniture and children's toys floated by. Trees and other debris bobbed in the muddy water. Automobiles were tossed up against lampposts and street signs. People yelled from rooftops and upper floors of nearby buildings.

That first evening we huddled around a transistor radio in the dining room of the pensione with other guests—Americans, a few Germans, some Italian students from northern Italy. "Florence has become a lake," a dark, young, frightened Italian girl translated for us. The city had been literally cut off from the rest of the world, the highways and rails destroyed, telephone communications and electricity gone. "Three meters of water," she said, "over ten feet, in the Piazza del Duomo."

"And the people of Florence?" an elderly American woman asked.

"*Non so*, I do not know."

"And the art?"

Gradually, over the next days, we learned the true extent of the damage. Miraculously, the total number of lives lost in the city would come to only thirty-five. But many Florentines had been displaced from their homes, little basement apartments filled with the awful *fango*, the mud, which had to be hauled out in buckets. The shops in central Florence were devastated. And yes, the art, oh, the art! Books and paintings and sculptures and frescoes, all damaged and in danger of being lost forever.

The Masolino Madonna had been stored on the ground

floor of the Uffizi, where the overflow from the museum's vast
collection was kept, where the workrooms for restoration and
cleaning were located. Unfortunately there had been little fore-
sight in choosing this site. The sixteenth-century building hous-
ing many of the greatest masterpieces of Renaissance art was
located just meters from the temperamental Arno River.

"THE ARTICLE IN the book," I explained to Andrea as we
sat at the restaurant, sharing our order of chicken nachos,
"claimed the painting had been destroyed in the flood of sixty-
six." I picked at the chips, removing the peppers and lining
them along the edge of my plate. My stomach was too excited
to eat anything so spicy, and I wondered why I had agreed to
split this particular dish. Andrea said she couldn't eat a full order, so we'd asked for an extra plate and divvied them up.

"If it was lost, where did the picture in the book come
from?" Andrea asked.

"Obviously the photo was taken before the flood. It had
that smoky patina—you know, like the Sistine Chapel before
the cleaning." The painting had been scheduled for a cleaning
on Monday, November 7. But then the flood happened and
everything changed. Rather than a cleaning, the painting would
require a rescue and restoration.

Andrea listened, nibbling on the nachos, dipping them in
the sour cream and guacamole, then shaking them off until the
tiniest taste remained. My sister is thin and very careful about
what she puts in her mouth. I have always been naturally thin,
though in midlife I've found it no longer comes without effort.

"So, the picture was taken before you went over there, before the flood?" she asked.

"Yes, I'm sure it was."

"And you're sure it wasn't destroyed?"

"Andie, I was *there*. I spent days, nights, running back and
forth from the station and Limonaia, fetching the mulberry
paper, picking up the humidity meters, the reconstruction
tools, sloshing through the mud in my boots . . ."

As these memories came back to me, a sensation as great as the visual images returned—that putrid, fetid smell. Drums stored in basements and filled with oil for heating homes and shops had been ripped open by the gushing waters. The horrible smelly black oil, the *nafta*, clung to everything—the paintings, the sculptures, the books, our clothes and boots. It destroyed the leather, silk, ceramics, antique furniture, and other merchandise torn from the tiny shops of Florence and piled up in the streets and piazzas in heaps of slime. The smell of sewage and dead animal carcasses, rotting paper and leather hung in the air. *Fango, magro, merda.* Some of the first words to become part of my limited Italian vocabulary—mud, slime, and shit.

I had been there and I knew the painting had survived. How could I forget the sweetness of the Madonna who gazed up at me as Stefano and I shared our first kiss?

"You'll pick up the pies then?" Andie asked, interrupting my thoughts, bringing me back to the more immediate issues of the approaching holidays. "We probably should get an extra this year, with Skip and Stacy and her two." Skip was Andie's oldest and just recently married—to Stacy, a package deal, as she'd come with two half-grown kids.

It was the last week of first semester and Christmas was just over a week away. I knew Andie had a lot on her mind: kids coming—all five of them, plus four grandkids—shopping, gift wrapping, getting dinner set up for almost twenty. She didn't seem to be as interested as I thought she could be in what I was telling her.

"I suppose you'll want dessert too," Andrea said, glancing at my wine, now down to the last drop.

"Why the hell not?" I said, flipping through the little menu perched on the table. "Double devil chocolate brownie," I told the waiter. "Scoop of vanilla ice cream—make that two scoops, two spoons." I glanced at Andrea. She frowned and nodded as the waiter left.

"This lost picture thing," my sister said. "It's really got to you—"

"Painting," I corrected. "And it wasn't lost. At least not in the flood."

THAT EVENING I searched the Internet for the article's author, Roberto Balducci, who was identified as an instructor of art history, University of Rome. The copyright on the book was 1984. The article had originally appeared in an Italian art journal in 1983, reprinted here in translation. Roberto Balducci's name came up on several sites for Renaissance art, but nothing connecting him to the Masolino.

That night I couldn't sleep so I got up and read every piece in *The Madonna in Italian Renaissance Art*, going over Roberto Balducci's article twice. In itself it was no great revelation, basically a study of the bridge between late Gothic and Renaissance representation of the Madonna in Italian art. He mentioned that many art historians had attributed the painting to Masolino da Panicale. I thought it strange that this particular painting was being used to illustrate his view on the subject. And the word *destroyed*—as far as I knew, museum-owned paintings and sculptures were all retrieved in some form or another.

Could something have been lost in translation? Did the Italian article say *damaged* rather than *destroyed*? Maybe I could track down the original article in Italy. Not that my Italian was that good, but I was sure I could find someone to help me.

The following afternoon, I realized I couldn't wait until I got to Italy to discover more. I went back online and finally found a phone number for the university, then glanced at my watch—four P.M., eight hours' difference, midnight in Italy.

After another night of tossing and turning, I rose early and called the university in Rome, and was told that Professor Balducci hadn't been there since '87. I was given a forwarding address in Florence, though no phone number was listed. I knew I was grabbing at the remotest possibilities, but I did another computer search for the phone number of the professor in Florence. There were pages of Balduccis in Florence, several

Roberto Balduccis, none of them at the address given to me by
the university. As I waited for the list to print, I typed in one
more name.

There was no Stefano Leonetti in Florence.

EARLY THE NEXT morning, still unable to push these
thoughts of Roberto Balducci's article out of my head, I got
up, grabbed my list of Balduccis, and picked up the phone.

What was I thinking? That I could call some stranger in
Italy who had written an article almost seventeen years ago
and tell him, *You've made a mistake. This painting was re-*
stored. Yet I couldn't help wonder where this information had
come from, and I couldn't free my mind of the image of Masolino's Madonna. Why had Roberto Balducci chosen to write
about a painting he thought had been destroyed? I'd never run
across a reference to the painting in my many years of studying and teaching art history, and I'd come to believe, sadly,
that it had been returned to the obscurity of the Uffizi storage
rooms, that my visions and dreams of it hanging alongside the
most celebrated creations of the Renaissance were just that—
dreams.

I worked through the Roberto Balduccis on my list. No answer on the first, language problems on the next two, an answering machine with indecipherable Italian on the last. I
decided I'd try one of the Balduccis, non-Roberto, on the street
listed by the university. I spoke with Aldo Balducci, a very nice
man, who insisted on speaking English, though his vocabulary
consisted of little more than *yes*, *no*, *I know*, and *okay.* Somehow we managed to carry on a conversation.

"Roberto Balducci, yes, yes, okay, I know, *mio cugino.*"

I thought he told me he'd have his cousin, Roberto Balducci, call, and I gave him my number in the States. I wasn't
sure that Aldo understood what I'd told him or that Professor
Balducci would call or that he was even the Balducci I was
looking for. But it was the closest I'd come and it was as far as
I would get while in America. If I didn't hear from Roberto

Balducci, I could check out the university's forwarding address when I got to Florence.

ROBERTO BALDUCCI CALLED me at home in Boise two days before Christmas and left a message. He said he'd spoken with his cousin Aldo, who told him I was interested in talking to him about something he'd written when he was teaching in Rome. He wasn't sure which article I was referring to. He explained his cousin didn't understand English that well. Roberto Balducci himself spoke English with very little accent. He had a pleasant voice. He said he was leaving and would be out of town the next three weeks. I could possibly catch him that evening.

I called, but missed him. I left a message, giving him my number at the school in Florence.

I spent Christmas with my sister and her family. New Year's went off without a hitch, despite warnings and doomsayers predicting that the world would fall apart, that computers would crash, sending the universe into a tailspin as we entered the new millennium. I spent the next week finishing up at the university in Boise, skiing once with my nephew and niece, and getting things ready to leave. As I was sorting through boxes, moving personal items to a storage unit—I was leasing out the house, furnished, for six months—I came across some photos from my trip with Roxie, and I just knew I had to give her a call.

She suggested we meet for lunch at the mall, where she worked at the Bon in housewares and fine china. She'd been in Boise for almost five years and, though we talked now and then, we seldom got together. It seemed we had so little in common anymore.

As I waved at Roxie across the food court at the mall, I couldn't help noticing how much she looked like her mother. Over the years she'd put on substantial weight, though she was still very blonde and her hair was styled in the same old sixties-type bubble. We'd made quite a pair when we were young—Roxie, a short, busty, bubbly blonde; me, tall and skinny with long, straight dark hair.

We both laughed as we pulled out our reading glasses to look at the photos I'd brought along, then giggled and reminisced as we sorted through them. There was a shot of me in London, Big Ben in the background, and one of Roxie, which I had taken, grinning with the Eiffel Tower behind her. I'd done that little amateur photographer's trick of lining her head up with the tower so it would look like it was sticking out of her head. Roxie's youthful, unknowing grin, the silliness of the photo, made me smile. Another shot, the two of us in Munich, enormous mugs of Löwenbräu raised in a toast. In Venice we stood in the Piazza San Marco under a dark, overcast sky.

"Remember that Italian fellow who so generously offered to take our picture?" Roxie asked.

"God, yes. It took us hours to get rid of him." I remembered how we had stopped at a bar for cappuccino, to get out of the wet and gloom, and he followed us right inside and sat down with us.

"I think I still have that little Brownie Instamatic," Roxie said, and I remembered that we'd taken all these photos with her camera. "Down at my mom's," she added. "And these same photos. God, we were skinny. And young."

I nodded in agreement. When I'd come across the photos it almost seemed as if I were looking at pictures of someone else.

"Half a lifetime ago," Roxie said.

"More than that, if you're counting."

"Quit counting years ago," she said with a giggle.

There were a few pictures taken in Florence. A couple of the students we met at the National Library—Charley among them, tall and thin. There was one of Roxie and me with a guy named Rick who I remembered she was wild about, a student from Harvard. He was gorgeous with thick wavy hair, a million-dollar politician's smile. The picture was taken at the train station the day Roxie left to go home. Our arms were draped around each other's shoulders—Roxie ready to take off, me showing in no way the fear I could still remember so clearly, the knot growing in my stomach with the realization that I would be on my own now.

"I'd almost forgotten about this guy, what was his name?" Roxie said.

"Rick?" I asked, surprised. I thought she was so in love with him, and she couldn't even remember his name.

"Oh, yeah, Rick," Roxie replied thoughtfully. "He was so cute."

"Yeah, he was."

"What about that hunky art restorer?" Roxie asked as she flipped through more pictures. "What was his name?"

"Stefano," I said, feeling the heat rise to my cheeks.

"Ah, yes, Stefano." Roxie rolled her eyes dramatically. "Maybe you can find him again," she said with a grin.

"Well," I said with a grin of my own, "maybe I can."

THE SECOND WEEK in January Andrea gave me a lift to the airport. We exchanged few words as we drove.

"Having second thoughts?" she asked.

"Just mentally checking my list, making sure I did everything. And thinking about how long I'll be gone. I'll miss you and the kids. Those grandbabies of yours will be half grown by the time I get home."

"I'll send some pictures," she said. "Tony could do them on the Internet."

"Good idea." Tony was Andrea's youngest, our computer whiz. I gazed out the window. The streets were damp from melting snow. "I'm thinking about Dad too. Leaving this long."

"You don't need to worry about Dad. He's healthy as a horse."

"So was Mom," I said, glancing over at Andie.

"If he goes as quick as Mom, it won't matter if you're here or halfway across the world."

"Yeah, I know. You're right." Mom had gone quickly—an aneurysm. By the time I got to the hospital, it was too late.

We pulled into short-term parking and Andie helped me with my bags.

"I guess it's probably Rousseau I'm concerned about," I told her as we walked across the street to the terminal. "In people years she's over ninety." I caught Andie's sympathetic smile as I glanced over.

"She'll be okay. Jerry will take good care of her."

"I hope so." I'd dropped her off with Jerry early that morning. He and I were still tied together because of Rousseau. We'd found her at the kennel years ago and had immediately fallen in love with her. The name Rousseau was a compromise, which didn't please either Jerry or me. I had wanted to name our dog after an artist; Jerry's choice was a literary figure, since he taught literature and poetry. We settled on Rousseau, the only name we could come up with that was both artist and writer. Never mind that the puppy was a girl.

As I'd lifted her into the car that morning, her legs cramped and stiff with late-age arthritis, it came to me, as it often did when I thought about my life, that I was living one that had surely been planned for someone else. I hadn't expected that, at fifty-two, my partner in life would be a dog, that she would be the one I'd anguish over leaving. I loved Rousseau, but somehow I had expected to be sharing my life with a real person too.

As I drove to deliver her to Jerry, she snuggled against my side, her breathing heavy. "Well, old girl," I said, finding the soft spot behind her ear, "think you can make it without me for a few months? You're going to go stay with Daddy." Jerry and I had always referred to ourselves as Mommy and Daddy when we were talking to Rousseau. We did it at first as a bit of a joke. I thought it was ridiculous—those old childless folks who treated their pets like children. But here I was now—one of them.

There were a lot of things I was now that as a young woman I had never imagined. It was not in my plans, my lifelong goals conceived as a young woman, to end up this way. Divorced. No family. A professor of art history, of all things. I had never had the slightest interest in art. Until . . .

As I left Rousseau, then again as I boarded my flight for Italy, a familiar thought kept pushing its way into my mind. Everything in my life—my future, my destiny—had changed its course the day I met Stefano Leonetti.

3

THE FIRST TIME I laid eyes on Stefano Leonetti he was covered with mud and I was ankle deep in it, sloshing through the streets of Florence in a pair of ill-fitting rubber boots, a gift from the U.S. Army. Two days after the flood, trucks from Camp Darby had pulled into the city loaded with supplies for the volunteers.

Roxie and I were on our way to the National Library, where we had been volunteering. Like many of those visiting the city during the flood, particularly the young people, we had become actively involved in the effort to save the treasures of Florence.

We'd spent only one day and night stranded in the *pensione*. Miraculously, the water receded within twenty-four hours after the Arno burst over its banks, and additional help flocked into the city—restorers, art students, government officials—all eager to become involved in the rescue and restoration.

By word of mouth from people we met on the street, we'd learned that immediate help was needed at the Biblioteca Nazionale just off Piazza dei Cavalleggeri. When we arrived at the library we joined others and, without any formal instruction or supervision, began removing damaged manuscripts and books, some reduced to a pulplike mush. Over a million volumes were stored at the National Library, many unfortunately in the basement of the building located on the banks of the Arno. We became part of a human chain, moving books out to be transported to higher ground, where restorers would begin the involved process of drying and treating for mold and bacteria. The stench in the lower levels of the library was unbearable; workers in these areas wore rubber gas masks. The Americans were particularly welcomed, as there was grave concern over the diseases—typhoid, tetanus—that were carried in the mud and gunk. We Americans all had our shots and were ready and eager to work.

The mood among the young people was one of exuberance, rather than fear or defeat. If we were not making history, surely we were saving it. The combination of camaraderie and youthful energy was so thick it was intoxicating, and though we returned to our pensione exhausted, Roxie and I barely slept those first two nights.

It was our third day at the library, and the streets were still thick with mud in places close to the river. Debris was piled in mountains throughout the central city. The first two days we'd taken a more circuitous route, but that day we decided to see if we could walk along the river and check things out. It wasn't the lay of the land, so to speak, we ended up checking out.

A group of men just outside the Uffizi Gallery was loading paintings onto a truck. Roxie and I stood and watched, our eyes—all four of them—locking instantly on Stefano. Then Roxie and I exchanged a quick, telling glance. Over the past month and a half, in the intimacy of our travels, we had established little secret signs and codes, and I knew just what she was thinking when she did that thing—blowing, lifting her blonde bangs up off her forehead, like she was trying to cool herself off.

"Hot stuff," she said in a low voice. She licked her lips. "Now that's one tasty hunka pasta." Roxie was very dramatic. Everything she said or did came with exaggerated facial expressions.

She should have been an actress. "Now that, baby," she added, setting her lips in a silent whistle, "that one rates pretty high on the chart."

"Yes," I whispered. One fine hunka pasta, indeed.

We'd been rating the guys we encountered as we traveled. We had decided the English were a bit too angular and generally too thin, the French too snooty, and the Italians too short. We were extremely discriminating, perhaps feeling we could be picky, as Roxie and I got our fair share of attention.

"Marilyn Monroe and Scarlett O'Hara," a young man we'd met in England had called us. "She's British, you know, Scarlett O'Hara."

That was news to me. As far as I knew she was a southern belle. My coloring was similar to Scarlett's—dark hair, green eyes—but with my long, thin, flat-chested body, I would never have filled out that elegant costume she built from a set of velvet drapes.

As I look back on it now, the fact that we were alone, without chaperone, may have been part of the reason we drew so much notice. It was a novelty in the sixties, two girls unescorted, and I'm sure the boys and men thought we were easy. In Roxie's case, it was probably a little true. I myself was less defined. I'd had only one serious boyfriend, a guy named Jeff my freshman year in college. After dating for six months we slept together. I honestly couldn't see what the big deal was— it was messy and awkward. After the first time, that was all Jeff ever wanted to do. I could tell the relationship was doomed, and I decided I could live without until I met someone who knew what he was doing.

I have to admit Roxie and I generally enjoyed the attention we were getting, though on our part it never went beyond a little flirting. We started a kind of rating system for men, and at times we were rather unkind, as if neither Marilyn nor Scarlett would settle for anything less than perfection. Our tastes were not always in agreement. Roxie preferred muscles; I always went for tall.

But when we laid eyes on Stefano for the first time, even

under the foul Florentine mud, and exchanged glances, it was evident that Roxie and I were in agreement.

He stood directing the transport of paintings that had been damaged in the flood. He didn't notice us at first, he was so involved in his task. But then, he looked over and stared at me for a moment. He was tall and muscular, his damp, muddy shirt and pants clinging to his body. His shoulders were broad like an athlete's and his waist trim. Although there was a chill in the air, he wore no coat or jacket and his shirtsleeves were rolled up, the muscles in his forearms flexing as he hoisted a large painting onto the truck.

"*Bella, bella,*" Roxie and I whispered to each other as we continued trudging through the mud, glancing back now and then at the group outside the Uffizi. We knew the word *bella* meant beautiful. It was a word we'd heard plenty from the men in northern Italy. We weren't aware at the time that the proper term to describe a beautiful man was *bello*, not *bella*.

We continued on to the library, speaking little, exchanging our silly grins, as if neither of us could get the image of this beautiful man out of our minds.

It wasn't until three weeks later that I saw Stefano for the second time. Roxie and I were still working at the library, and he had come over to recruit more volunteers to transport works of art to the Limonaia, a winter nursery generally used to house the lemon and orange trees from the Boboli Gardens at the Pitti Palace. It was a perfect place to lodge the paintings where they could be dried slowly, where the humidity and temperature could be controlled to retard the expanding and contracting of the ancient wood panels. The Limonaia had been quickly revamped—new concrete floor and covering, humidity meters, rows of metal racks to dry the paintings—in less than twelve days.

"You," he said, looking directly at me, "*Americano.*" His eyes were deep set and very dark. His hair was a bit long, curling around his ears and neck.

My heart literally stopped for a moment, I swear it did, then rose and caught in my throat. He had picked me!

At the time I was dressed in blue jeans, boots, several layers of shirts and sweaters under a blue pea jacket, a knit stocking cap on my head. There was no heat in the library, where we worked by candlelight, so we dressed as warmly as possible. I hadn't washed my hair in over a week as we had little water for personal hygiene. I'd put it in a ponytail and twisted it up inside my stocking cap.

And now, I thought, this beautiful Italian man—he was a man, not a boy—must have seen something in me, something even deeper than a physical beauty. It was like a romantic movie.

I didn't learn until several weeks later that he had chosen me because I was tall, and under the many layers of sweaters and coat, I looked fairly sturdy. And . . . he thought I was a boy.

ROXIE AND I had both commented how the leers and suggestive remarks, which we had elicited in Venice and were told by some American girls were typical behavior on the part of Italian men, seemed to have subsided, almost disappeared since the flood. It seemed that in this joint effort, this solidarity, we had become not men and women, just people. People from all over the world joining together with a common goal—to save Florence.

But after a very short time, a charged sense of sexual awareness and flirtation on the part of the men returned. Though my job at the Limonaia was that of an errand boy, I was still a girl, and being one of the few, other than a couple of stodgy women art restorers and museum representatives, I got a fair amount of notice from the men.

Except from Stefano. I decided that I would make myself indispensable and maybe in the process he would notice me. But as I did this, something else happened. I became involved, not with Stefano—that would come later—but with the art, the paintings. Something began to move within me—a curiosity, then a fascination, a devotion, a passion. And an understanding that I had indeed been chosen, chosen to save the treasures of Florence.

Roxie had stayed on at the library. I don't think she gave a damn about the books, but she did about Rick, the tall, handsome Harvard boy, who was also working at the library. There were at least half a dozen American universities with programs in Florence—Stanford, Harvard, Syracuse, Florida State, Smith, Gonzaga—and most of them had dismissed classes for the first few weeks of the rescue. Students from all of them, along with the students who flocked into the city from other Italian and European locations, became known as the *angeli di fango*, mud angels, for obvious reasons, and *angeli blu*, blue angels, for their uniforms of blue jeans.

In the evenings, after our work was finished for the day, we would sit around—at one of the student dorms, villas, or *pensioni*, sometimes outdoors near the station, where the young men who came to help were housed in old railway cars—and we would talk, about the flood, about the work we were doing in the city. Huddled together to warm ourselves in the chill of the winter night, we would pass around a bottle of wine, share a cigarette, occasionally a joint. Sometimes, we would talk about what had caused the flood, what precautions were being taken to prevent it from happening again.

More than nineteen inches, one-third of the area's annual rainfall, had come in just two days. The ill-timed release of water from two dams upriver had sent water surging into Florence, which sat in a geographically vulnerable position within the lowest area on the first plain reached by the Arno River after the confluence of its largest tributary, the Sieve.

"The Italians are fatalists," an American boy said as he pushed his longish hair off his forehead. "The city has flooded every century for the past seven hundred years and they do nothing about it. The land has been raped, trees pulled out along the valley, nature's own defenses destroyed. Did you know, Leonardo designed a system of dams, canals, and reservoirs to prevent such tragedies five hundred years ago, yet nothing was ever done?"

I noticed none of the Italian students came to the defense of their country, although one of the French students said something about how the Americans sent over all the money, then thought they had a right to tell the Italians how to do things, how to conduct the art rescue. We had indeed sent money. A special committee called the CRIA, Committee to Rescue Italian Art, had been formed to collect and send funds for the restoration project. Jacqueline Kennedy had been named honorary chairman.

Mostly we talked about what we were doing to help the city of Florence, and these conversations were filled with an excitement and sense of camaraderie. We were all bursting with youthful energy and a knowledge that what we were doing would truly make a difference. But even these discussions at times became heated debates. Some of us were working in the museums and libraries. Others spent their days digging mud out of the basement dwellings of the poor citizens of Florence, bringing food, water, blankets, and clothing to those who had been displaced. At times we argued about whose work was more important.

"People have lost their homes," a thin young British student said. "They have no food, no water. It is the people of Florence we must save."

"People are vulnerable . . . fragile . . . people die . . . people will always die . . . short life spans," one of the Italian boys said. Almost as if making a joke. "But art, art is forever."

"Ah, but have you seen the Cimabue?" This from one of the Stanford boys. "The art is as subject to nature's whims as man himself."

We had all heard about the Cimabue, a treasured crucifix created by the artist Giovanni Cimabue in the late thirteenth century. The artist is often referred to as the "Father of Florentine Art," and many experts believe his work represents the beginning of western art—the bridge between Byzantine and Renaissance. The crucifix had been battered beyond repair in the church of Santa Croce. The ancient paint had literally washed right off the surface, chips of pigment floating unattached on the sea that had filled the sacristy and museum. The chips had been placed on a plate to keep them safe for the art restorers. One of the workmen, completely unaware, had discarded them and used the plate to eat his lunch.

The discussions would go on into the night, never being resolved.

"We can do both," an idealistic American girl, a student from Gonzaga, exclaimed. "Working together we can save the citizens of Firenze as well as the art."

And we would pass the bottle of cheap Chianti. "A toast to Firenze, her citizens and her art."

A COUPLE OF weeks before Christmas we gathered with a group of students in a *pensione* near San Lorenzo. It was sort of a farewell party for Roxie, who was going home in time for the holidays. Her parents were unhappy that she had stayed this long, and she figured she'd have to work for the rest of her life to pay back what she'd borrowed from me. I hadn't been greatly concerned about the money, as there was still plenty in my "Grandma" account. I'd intended to go back and start second semester at the university, but now . . . I had written to tell my parents I was staying a bit longer. I wasn't sure myself how long. I could still make it home for Christmas, but hadn't completely made up my mind what I was going to do. I had been thinking seriously about staying through the spring, through second semester. Not for Stefano, who, as I said, had paid little attention to me. But for the art.

We drank too much that night. We laughed and cried. Roxie didn't want to leave Rick. He said he didn't want her to leave.

Late the next afternoon Rick and I walked her to the train station. The railroad tracks were already partially restored, the main lines bringing people in and out of the city. Roxie would take the train to Rome, spend the night, then catch a morning flight back to the States.

As we left the station, Rick asked if I wanted to go get a beer—a word he seemed to pronounce without an *r*—as if he were ready to get on with his life after Roxie. Or a glass of wine?

His voice is the thing I remember most about Rick. He

spoke with the smooth, assured inflection of a rich eastern boy. When I try to conjure an image of Rick and Roxie that last day at the station, the picture that forms in my mind is that of one of the Kennedy boys, with their Boston-Harvard way, bidding farewell to Marilyn Monroe.

After I said no, I really didn't feel like a drink, I left Rick outside the station and went back to the *pensione* and sat on my bed gazing out the window at the flood line, a dark ugly brown that hung heavy on the once-golden side of the building across the street. I had never felt so alone and afraid. Had I made a terrible mistake, staying here without Roxie?

I went out to look for a phone—I wanted to call home. My parents were not pleased I hadn't returned yet. For the first few days after the flood telegrams had gone back and forth, then letters. I'M SAFE. . . . COME HOME. . . . I WANT TO STAY. . . . WE MISS YOU. . . . I'M NEEDED HERE.

Somehow I had convinced them this was a noble cause, that I could finish school later. I think they were thinking spring semester. I'm not sure what I was thinking. The idea of school was losing the little appeal it once had. What could I possibly learn cooped up in a classroom, or even a gymnasium, or out on a sports field? The idea of becoming a teacher, particularly of high school P.E., seemed so terribly insignificant now.

I walked blocks, but couldn't find a phone that worked. I returned to my *pensione*, sat down, and wrote a very grownup-sounding note to my parents, wishing them a Merry Christmas in case I didn't make it home, realizing as I wrote it that the letter itself might not make it by Christmas. The Italian postal system wasn't particularly reliable, even without such natural disasters as floods.

THE NEXT MORNING I was up early, climbing the hill to the Pitti, going to the Limonaia. I had, in fact, made myself indispensable. "Send Suzanne. Suzanne will go fetch the blotting paper. Suzanne will go for water, for coffee."

There were few people around, just the art restorer who had been put in charge of this special project and his two assistants.

Stefano arrived an hour later, which was unusual as he was often one of the first ones there. His regular assistant, a young man named Pietro Capparelli, hadn't come in yet, so I was recruited to help. We worked silently for some time, Stefano hunched over a Bronzino. I stood behind him, handing him tools, like a doctor's nurse. He was measuring the humidity, checking the thin mulberry tissue that had been placed over the damp wooden surface of the painting to prevent the paint from cracking and flaking. "I'm going to Santa Croce," he said in English.

He glanced up at me and really looked at me for the first time since the day he had chosen me to move from the library to the Limonaia. And I noticed for the first time that he wasn't quite so perfect. His eyes were a little too close, and there were stray hairs between his dark brows that would have been plucked had he been a woman. But even in this brief moment of reality, this recognition of imperfection, Stefano's gaze still sent a surge of prickly warmth through my entire body.

"Would you like to go?" he asked.

I nodded, but I don't think words actually came out of my mouth.

We walked along the Arno, moving toward the Church of Santa Croce. Piles of debris still blocked the path in many places. It was very cold, but the sky was blue. It had rained off and on since the flood, and there had been days when we feared it might flood again. But today the air was crisp and clear. We spoke little as we walked. There were few people out on the street. He asked my name, and when I told him, he repeated it slowly, his deep voice, the way he said it, pronouncing the z like in *pizza*—SooTS-ann—sent a little electric wave of excitement through me.

He asked where I was from, if I wasn't going home for Christmas.

I can't particularly remember my replies to these questions, I was so stunned that I was here with him, walking through the streets of Florence. Several shops along the way had reopened, although broken windows, filthy stone, and battered doors still marred the ancient buildings. Tinsel, evergreens, holly, and bright red bows hung from some of the doors. Many of the shops displayed hand-printed signs in the windows, proclaiming the coming holiday. *BUON NATALE A TUTTO IL MONDO.* Merry Christmas to all the world.

At the Piazza Santa Croce bulldozers sat idle beside enormous piles of rubbish. The mud had been scraped and shoved to make a path through the square. None of the businesses appeared to have reopened. Buildings were shored up with enormous wooden timbers. Blackened storefronts appeared more as if they had been charred in a fire or hit by a bomb than inundated with water and mud. Stefano stopped and surveyed the square, his eyes moving slowly from shop to shop, taking in the filthy, discolored storefronts. We stood for a moment, and then, as if at the same precise moment, we both noticed it—not something we saw, but a smell—not the putrid stench we had become so accustomed to that it was barely mentioned anymore, but the delightful, delicious smell of freshly baked bread. We looked at each other and grinned. His face was the most beautiful I had ever seen, his lips turned up in a smile both sad and joyful. "Ah, the people of Firenze," he said in a low voice. "Yes, the good citizens of Florence, they will survive."

We followed the scent to a little bakery that looked so battered it was almost impossible to believe it had reopened. But the aroma of fresh bread was unmistakable. Stefano bought a loaf and tore off a piece and handed it to me. It was warm and soft, yet with the good hearty texture of the Tuscan bread. I had never tasted anything so delicious. He handed me another piece and we stood in the piazza until we had devoured the entire loaf like two hungry, happy animals. Then slowly we walked up to the church and went inside.

Santa Croce had been hit worse than any monument in Florence. I knew from the talk at the Limonaia, the chatter among the students and volunteers, that treasures within the church had been heavily damaged. Water had measured over twenty feet the morning of the flood, and we'd heard stories of fish floating around inside several days after. Frescoes had been devastated, and Cimabue's crucifix so severely damaged that many said it was beyond rescue.

It was dark inside and it took several moments for my eyes to adjust. Candles flickered against the gray stone walls. Several men, some dressed in smocks—the uniform of the restorers— some in everyday clothes, stood about inside the church, not really doing anything. This was my first time in Santa Croce. I knew it was famous, not only for the art, but because it was the resting place of many renowned figures of Florence— Michelangelo, Galileo, Machiavelli, Ghiberti, Rossini. There were carvings in the stones set into the floor, ancient words and numbers and names, full-size figures of men, and I wondered if we were walking over the tombs as I stepped carefully, noticing even now small puddles of water still remained in the concave areas of the stone carvings.

The men idling about the church displayed no particular sense of awe or reverence, conversing casually as if they were just finishing up their morning coffee break and contemplating, with reluctance, their return to work. Several sipped out of ceramic mugs. The dank, decaying smell of the flood still lingered in the air, captured within the stone walls of the ancient building.

Stefano said *buon giorno* to the men. They all seemed to know him and were friendly, visiting for several minutes, speaking quickly in their Italian, which I, of course, could not understand. Several of them smiled and nodded and also wished me a good day, and I returned the greeting.

Stefano motioned me to follow him. We walked past several small chapels and stopped for a few moments at each, gazing at the oil-streaked frescoes. Saints in filthy robes and tarnished halos. The men conversed rapidly, with arms rising and falling, pointing, and lamenting. *Gaddi, Giotto,* the names were whispered. Then, silently, one of the men led us through a colonnade surrounding a courtyard, which looked like a big wet muddy yellow sponge, and into another long dark room that I could see was part of the same building, yet not part of the church. Paintings were elevated on makeshift beds constructed of wooden chairs and boards and metal, raising them off the still-damp floor. I knew the Cimabue crucifix was here in the museum of Santa Croce. I also knew it would be moved soon to the Limonaia for further work, although the word among the volunteers was that 80 percent of the surface had been destroyed. There were rumors that the various art restorers who had arrived in the city after the devastation were not in agreement on what should be done with the Cimabue. Some felt it should be left as is, a reminder of nature's havoc. Others said it should be completely restored; areas that had been lost should be repainted. Detailed records and photos had survived, stored in the archives, and it could be restored to look exactly as the original. Re-created actually, and this was where the disagreements came in. What was the point if only 20 percent remained true Cimabue?

As in the church, several men milled about. A boy sat on a pile of boards. He picked up a pad and pencil. I thought he was sketching. A knot of older men stood, smoking cigarettes, conversing. They didn't seem to be doing anything and I wondered why they were here. Perhaps they felt they couldn't leave, as if their absence might result in the tiny remaining portions of the Cimabue disappearing or floating away.

So much of the restoration process, I had learned, was a matter of waiting. Waiting for the paintings to dry out, controlling the rate at which they dried. If they dried quickly, the wooden boards would warp, the paint would crack and peel and flake off the surface. Some of the wooden panel paintings that arrived at the Limonaia were so warped they looked like rippling waves of the ocean, curves of a bow. I knew the Cimabue was waiting for the move to the Limonaia, where the environment could be more easily controlled, the temperature and humidity regulated, shrinkage and expansion monitored.

The men gathered around the largest metal bed. Though I could see nothing but the back of this particular painting, the large wooden board cut in the shape of an ornate cross told me it was the Cimabue crucifix. The boy who was sketching got up and came over. He walked with a limp. Stefano talked to one of the men for several moments, then climbed up on a chair to view the painting. He gazed down at the panel. It lay just above my eye level and I could not see the painted side. I wondered sadly as I peered up, What did Stefano see as he gazed at the crucifix from above? Did he see little more than what I viewed from below?

Stefano stood for several moments, looking silently at the Cimabue. He bit his lip, and then lowered his head as if he were concentrating very hard. Or perhaps praying. He raised a clenched fist slowly to the side of his head and rubbed his temple, then slid his fingers through his thick dark hair.

When he climbed back down, there were tears in his eyes, and I knew this was the man I would love for the rest of my life.

4

I HAD NEVER been without family during the holidays. I remember how I had turned it over in my mind so many times—my decision to stay in Florence or go home for Christmas. Like plucking petals off a daisy—yes, stay; no, go home; yes, stay; no, go home. Looking for signs, messages telling me what to do. By the time I realized I hadn't decided, it was too late to decide. On Christmas Eve I found myself alone in Florence, feeling very homesick, missing my parents, my sister, wondering once more if I'd made a terrible mistake. Early that morning, the padrone at my *pensione* let me use the phone at the desk to call home—he said he'd add it to my bill. It was just after midnight back home, and the call woke my parents, frightening my mother. She cried. My dad said I must be very serious about what I was doing to miss Christmas with the family. I didn't talk to my sister, but I'd received a letter just days before. She said she missed me, but most of her letter consisted of telling me about her life, her latest boyfriend. She was a senior in high school at the time, and wanted to know if I'd make it home for her graduation. She said it was so *cool* what I was doing. She drew little smiley faces in the *o*'s of *cool*! And I thought how sweet and young and childish she seemed.

Later that day I climbed the hill to the Limonaia. The team of restorers and volunteers was down to the bones, as they say. Stefano did not come in. His assistant, Pietro, told me Stefano was spending the day with family. Pietro was especially sweet and attentive as we worked together, and I think a little sad that I was alone. He said he was having dinner with his mother that afternoon, then returning later and staying until about eleven, then going over to the cathedral for midnight mass. Did I know the pope was coming to Florence? Would I like to join Pietro and his mother for dinner? It all came out almost as if a single question. "Yes," I replied. I knew the pope was coming. I had very little formal religious education—we went now and then to my grandmother's Presbyterian church—and only the vaguest understanding of Catholics and their strange rituals. My exposure to Christ and saints and biblical events through my working on the art was far greater than it had been in my entire life until now. I still didn't really understand about the pope, but I could see his coming to Florence was a big deal, and everyone was talking about it, so of course, *yes*, I knew.

Pietro seemed to take my yes as a yes to his second question, and I realized I wanted very much to be included in a family this Christmas, even if it was with Pietro, who was not a particularly close friend, and his mother, whom I had never met. At about five he asked if I was ready to go.

My stomach growled as we left the Limonaia, and visions of Christmas ham, roast turkey, dressing, and gravy danced in my head. A chilly breeze riffled the air as we walked down the hill to a neighborhood in the Oltrarno, which was on the south side of the river. Most of the monuments, museums, and historical sights were on the north side of the Arno. The Pitti Palace, with its Boboli Gardens and Limonaia, was south of the river, but other than this impressive edifice, the fountains, paths, and gardens, the area was truly the "other side of the tracks." Many of the city's artists and craftsmen, the working class of the city, lived in the Oltrarno. The neighborhood had been devastated by the flood. The streets were still heaped with mud and rubbish, the section deemed too depressed to be given priority in the city's cleanup. I think this was the first time I truly realized what the flood had done to the *popolino*, the little people of Florence.

When we arrived at Pietro's home, his mother welcomed us warmly with a look of surprise, then sheer delight. She was short, but fairly wide, and I felt the ample padding of her matronly breasts as she gave me a hug. She wore a faded gingham apron that covered her front completely, and she smelled of yeast and garlic and lilac-scented talcum that only old women wear. She seemed delighted that Pietro had invited me, greeting me as if I were a girlfriend he'd brought home to meet his mother.

I honestly couldn't picture Pietro with a girlfriend. The way he latched on to Stefano, I often wondered if he didn't prefer men to women. He was not a particularly masculine man. He wore thick glasses and spoke with a slow, uneasy voice, stammering and stopping, often repeating his words, as if biding time until he found the next. At first I thought he spoke this way only when speaking English, as if he had trouble with the language. But as I became more accustomed to the Italian banter at the Limonaia, and listened intently, trying to understand the conversations of the restorers and volunteers, I realized that he stammered even in Italian.

Like his mother, Pietro was very short, much shorter than me, and I'd felt rather awkward walking down the street with him. I towered over him by several inches. But I was grateful for this invitation to share their meal on Christmas Eve.

The street level of their home had obviously been flooded. There was still a damp mildewy smell about the place, although even that was being overtaken by something which I could see marinating in a pan on the stove. Something white and bony floating around in an oily yellow liquid.

Fish. *I hate fish.* My visions of a real Christmas dinner evaporated as sure as those visions of sugarplums dancing in the imaginations of eager, expectant children on Christmas

Eve. Those naughty children who end up with lumps of coal in their stockings. I must have wrinkled my nose, which wasn't intentional. I was embarrassed when Pietro said, "I h-h-hope you are not disappointed, Signorina Suzanne. It is tradition, the fish. Italians eat fish on Christmas Eve. I hope . . . I hope you will enjoy it."

"Grazie, grazie," I said. "You are so kind to invite me. You are so kind, Signora Capparelli," I said to his mother.

"Benvenuto. Benvenuto," the old woman said. She looked around the room. The only furnishings in the living area were a battered wooden table with four not very sturdy-looking chairs. Signora Capparelli apologized as she pulled a chair from the table and motioned me to sit. She actually laughed as she told me, *"L'Arno ha rubato tutta la mobilia."*

"The Arno has stolen all the . . . all the furniture," Pietro translated with a good-natured smile. How had they done this, I wondered, how had they survived with such good humor?

The old woman raised her shoulders and grinned, revealing a gap, a missing tooth. *"Ma, siamo vivi, e domani è Natale!"* she exclaimed, throwing her hands in the air triumphantly. I didn't need a translator for that—indeed, we were alive and to-morrow was Christmas!

She brought out a bottle of some kind of sparkling wine, a cheap version of champagne, then another as we waited for the fish to marinate. I hadn't eaten since early morning and the tingly wine made me feel silly and giggly, though Pietro and I seemed to be engaged in a serious conversation about our work at the Limonaia, then about Italian Christmas traditions. He told me that the Italian version of Santa Claus was a witch who came not on Christmas Eve, but on the Epiphany, two weeks after Christmas. Signora Capparelli puttered around in the kitchen, which was actually an extension of the small living-dining room, leaving me to visit with Pietro, even though I had offered to help. He explained that eating fish the day before Christmas was a tradition in many Italian families, stemming back to the religious observation of abstaining from meat on Christmas Eve. Many families would eat a set number of

different fish dishes. Pietro laughed as he made a little rhyme—
"F-f-fish dish." He explained how the number of dishes took
on a religious significance. Three for the Trinity. Seven for the
sacraments. Twelve for the apostles. I gulped another swallow
of wine, hoping I could make it through the Father, Son, and
Holy Ghost, praying I wouldn't have to go for the twelve
apostles.

Signora Capparelli brought out a basket of bread and three
tiny glass dishes, with two shrimp each, and some kind of red
sauce. I had never tasted shrimp. My mother used to serve
shrimp cocktail on very special occasions, but never insisted
Andrea or I eat any. She would give us Velveeta cheese and
Ritz crackers, and 7-Up with cherries, while she and my father ate the shrimp and drank alcoholic beverages out of fancy
glasses. I was sure then, as I was sure now, that I did not like
shrimp. But as the old woman smiled and handed me this little
gift, the shame washed over me—they were sharing their
meager meal with me, as ungrateful as I was. Six little shrimp
divided now not by two, but by three. I couldn't refuse this
kindness. I picked one up, dipped it in the sauce, smiled at
Pietro and his mother, and took a bite. Not too bad. In fact, I
actually liked it. Had my taste buds finally grown up?

Pietro grinned. "It is good, *si*?"

I nodded and smiled again at his mother and thought of my
own mother, which made me both sad and joyful. I missed my
mom, my dad, my sister. But wouldn't Mom be proud of me?
I thought as I eagerly devoured the second shrimp. See, I'm
trying something new. Pietro refilled the wineglasses. Was it
the wine that was making me feel both emotional and silly? I
felt like crying and giggling all at the same time.

The second dish was also served with a red sauce. It looked
like large SpaghettiOs, and I thought it was some kind of pasta,
though the texture was different from the Italian pasta I was
now used to eating. A little bit rubbery, but good.

"What is this?" I asked. "It's delicious." The wine was also
making me feel very adventurous.

"*Calamari*," Pietro said. "I don't know in English." He did

a visual demonstration, which made me laugh. A little performance with his hands, adding three fingers from his left hand
to his right hand, making a puppetlike eight-legged creature.

"Octopus!" I exclaimed, much too loud to be polite. "I'm
eating octopus?"

"No, no." Pietro shook his head and laughed. "I remember
now the word. The word, it is *squid*."

Signora Capparelli laughed heartily too, from where she
was working diligently in the little kitchen area. She called to
Pietro and laughed, saying something I couldn't understand.

"Isn't that the same thing?" I asked. "Octopus? Squid?"

Pietro just laughed and served me more.

The signora was now preparing what I took to be the main
course, the dish that had been marinating. She was working on
a black wood-burning stove that I assumed also provided heat
for their small home. The aroma of olive oil, crackling in the
pan, filled the air, and even when she threw in the fish, it didn't
smell nearly as bad as I had imagined. She added potatoes and
olives, seasoned with parsley and thyme and garlic.

"Delizioso," I told Signora Capparelli as I took my first
bite. I didn't love the fish part, but it wasn't awful. With the
help of the wine, I got it down with a smile on my face. The
potatoes and olives were so yummy, I asked for seconds, then
thirds. This especially delighted the old woman. I helped clear
away the plates, despite Signora Capparelli's protest that I
was a guest. Then more food—a sweet Christmas cake filled
with orange-flavored liqueur was brought out—and more wine,
and tea.

Finally Signora Capparelli sat down with us. She spoke no
English, but she was a talkative little lady and had thrown in
the occasional comment while she'd prepared our meal. Now,
as she sat, the conversation went on and on, turning rather
personal as Pietro translated her questions, my answers. She
wanted to know everything about me. Where was I from? Did
I have family? When I told her about my mom and dad, my
younger sister, she patted me on the knee as if she understood
how much I missed them.

She offered more wine, another piece of cake, and I had to hold up my hand. *"Basta,"* I said. *Basta*—the word for "enough." It was the word Roxie and I had been told by some girls we'd met in Venice to use on the Italian men when their attention became too much. They said the word would become essential as we traveled south. It generally came out sounding rather rude, a bit obscene. *"Basta!"* always pronounced with a harsh inflection. But now I said as sweetly as I could, *"Basta,"* then, *"Grazie, grazie. Lei è m-molto gentile."* My words were becoming more and more slurred as the evening progressed, and I think I was actually stuttering—was it contagious?—but I also felt my Italian was improving.

"Stasera, il papa viene a Santa Maria del Fiore," the woman said as she refilled my cup with very hot water, which I could not refuse. It appeared we were allowed one tea bag each, but as much water as needed. This was indeed a precious gift she was offering—clean drinking water, even here in the most depressed section of the city. *"Il papa,"* she repeated. *"Tu vai?"* she asked, using the familiar. Had I become part of the family?

I had heard them talking about the pope at the Limonaia, Pietro asking me if I was going.

"Sì, sì," I answered, dipping my tea bag in and out of the hot water. Yes, I was going out to see the pope. Wasn't all of Florence?

At half past eight, Pietro helped me with my coat. I wrapped my wool scarf around my neck and pulled my stocking cap down around my ears. His mother told us it was too cold and she was too old to go out in the crowds. *"Grazie, grazie,"* I said, giving her a hug. *"Molte grazie."*

As we walked Pietro told me that she had barely left their home since the flood, although she had spent the first two weeks on the upper level, as the mud on the first floor was not removed until some students had come in and shoveled it out. It was still piled in pungent heaps along the street. Pietro told me he had been so busy with the art, he had been unable to do much himself. He explained there was an urgency in the rescue of the art, that his mother understood this was the first priority.

He said he had been at the Uffizi, working as a restorer, for just over a year. At one time he wanted to be an artist, but realized he didn't have the talent and decided he would become a conservator, attending to the paintings of the true artists, ensuring they would be preserved for future generations. When the flood hit the city, of course he became part of the rescue. As he spoke I could detect a passion I'd barely noticed before in Pietro's voice.

He suggested we cross the river and check out the Piazza Santa Croce, as the pope was supposedly going to make an appearance there before going on to the cathedral to say midnight mass. We had promised the others we would be back at the Limonaia by nine. We encountered few people in the Oltrarno along the river, but when we reached the piazza people were stacked so thickly I wasn't sure how much we would be able to see if the pope did arrive. Children were hoisted on parents' shoulders, and motorcycle police pushed through the crowd. I stood, straining and moving, rising on tiptoes to see if there was anything to see. A frosty moon hung over the city, and smoky candle cups sent out light from the windows and rooftops of the buildings around the square. I still felt a little woozy from all the wine, but I also felt very warm and relaxed and there was a magical feel in the air. Pietro, who could not see over the crowd, kept asking, "Do you see him? Do you see the pope?"

"No, he's not here yet."

About ten to nine, we gave up and headed back across the Arno.

When we arrived at the Limonaia, there was a long white car parked outside, a limousine like you'd see at parades and weddings. Two other cars, these as pitch black as the night, were parked beside it. Two men in dark suits and overcoats, who at the time I thought looked like Italian Mafia, paced back and forth along the cars. What was going on?

Pietro gasped, *"Il papa . . . il papa è qui!"*

We walked inside. There in front of the Cimabue crucifix, which had just recently been brought over from Santa Croce, knelt a small man in crimson robes, a white skullcap covering his head. The restorers and volunteers were all kneeling along the corridor between the racks of metal beds holding the damaged paintings, as if this were the aisle in a grand cathedral, the sacred Cimabue the altarpiece. Pietro crossed himself, mumbling something as he fell to the floor on his knees. I lowered myself, kneeling beside him on the cold concrete. I shivered, not so much from the cold, but with an excitement, a surreal sensation enveloping me as if something mystical was about to take place. I bowed my head, feeling strangely unworthy to rest my eyes upon this scene. When finally I looked up, the fragile man in the crimson robes was coming down the aisle toward me. I couldn't move. I couldn't breathe. My eyes dropped once more, and then I felt his presence as he stopped before me. I looked up, into his kind, warm eyes. What was I to do? Was I supposed to kiss his ring? He reached out with his left hand and placed it on my head. His right hand moved in the formation of a cross as he spoke. *"In nomine Patris, et Filii, et Spiritus Sancti. Amen."* He smiled and continued down the aisle. I remained kneeling until he was gone.

When I finally stood, I felt as if I were floating. I spent the rest of the evening in some sort of a daze, feeling half drunk, the other half transported to some celestial realm.

I didn't go to midnight mass. I didn't want to be part of the crowd. I felt very special. That night, I slept more soundly than I had since my arrival in Florence.

Christmas morning I woke, surprisingly without a hangover. I went to mass at Santa Maria Novella and stood on the cold stone floor, which still smelled of the putrid naphtha oil, tempered only slightly with the scent of candle wax and incense. I'm not sure if the mass was in Latin or Italian. I understood nothing. And yet, I felt so much a part of all this. Of Florence. Of Italy. Of the people. The art. And I truly felt for the very first time that my staying here in Florence had been the right decision. I had been given my sign. I had been blessed by the pope.

5

CHARLEY STOVER MET me at the airport in Rome, having driven down from Florence. In the two years since I'd seen him, Charley had put on several pounds, and his bright red hair, which had become sparser every time I saw him, was barely there and now a rather dull, faded brownish gray. He wore a pair of small, rectangular, black-framed glasses. Trendy, I thought, as were the John Lennon–type wire frames he'd worn years ago.

"You look great, Suzanne," he said, giving me a hug.

He was wearing his collar, and explained he always did in Italy—lots of clout and special treatment around here. Years ago when I first saw him in his priestly attire, it was a bit disconcerting, as I always pictured Charley with a pretty blonde on his arm. "Do I have to call you Father now?" I'd asked.

"Nope, just plain ol' Charley," he replied. "You know too much for me to make such demands," he'd added with a grin.

When Charley and I first met in Florence, working at the National Library after the flood, I liked him right away. He was tall and skinny with longish red hair and freckles. Just seventeen, two years younger than me, he came from a family very different from mine. His mother was an artist, his father a political activist. They'd actually *encouraged* him to take a year off to see the world before starting college. Charley was the kind of guy everyone liked, girls included, but mostly as a friend. He had a series of girlfriends, and none of them lasted long. He liked pretty girls, but it always seemed that they were not quite on his intellectual level. It surprised me when he called a few years after I'd returned home and told me he was studying to be a priest, though the fact that he was going to be a Jesuit seemed like a perfect fit for a bright, thoughtful guy like Charley.

As we drove to Florence, he asked about Roxie, and I told him I'd seen her recently and she still had that old spark of enthusiasm. This made me think of how young we were when we first met. Charley, despite the physical changes over the years, seemed just the same—the way his shoulders bounced up and down when he laughed, the way he kept pushing his glasses up on his nose. I wondered if he saw anything of the young woman I'd once been. I had certainly put on my own weight, not to mention my metaphorical baggage, and my hair was still long, though always pulled up now. In a certain light the streaks of silver were quite evident.

We talked about my classes. I'd have twenty and twenty-four students in my Intro to Art History, just seven in my upper division. Charley said they always had considerable interest in the introduction classes; a good percentage of the students took at least one art class, and my Women in Renaissance Art students were all art or art history majors.

We passed little red-tiled farmhouses, rolling hills dotted with poplar, cypress, and olive trees. The memory of another journey long ago crept into my mind—how the leaves of the olive trees had turned from green to silver in the breeze as I looked out from the train window, traveling in the opposite direction then, away from my beloved Florence, away from Stefano.

But today the winter air was perfectly still. We zoomed down the highway. There didn't seem to be any speed limit, and Charley flowed right along with the traffic. We were in Florence in no time at all.

My heart literally leaped as we drove into the city. I'd returned to Europe twice—to Great Britain on my own, then France for two weeks with a university group as a tour lecturer studying the French Impressionists in Paris and Normandy. One summer I had the opportunity to do a study tour in Italy. I was dating Jerry at the time, and he was reluctant to let me go—he knew about Stefano and thought this was the reason I wanted to do the tour. I told him we would only be in Florence for three days and, as far as I knew, Stefano wasn't there anymore. I'd sent a letter to him at the Uffizi and it had been returned. Of course, I told Jerry, I would attempt to look up an old friend. He'd been my mentor. So, I'd been all set, prepared my lesson plans as well as my heart, knowing I would try to find Stefano. But then my mother passed away the week before I was to leave. Andie said I should go anyway—Mom wouldn't want me to miss this opportunity. But we were all in shock, and Dad was a mess. I knew I couldn't leave, and maybe this was just another sign that Italy would remain bound with loss—my mother's now, the flood, Stefano, and a loss so great I had all but erased it from my memory.

Now, over thirty-three years since I had rumbled into the station of Santa Maria Novella on the train and stepped out into the wet, dark city, I found myself once more in Florence, and I smiled at the blue sky and winter sunshine and pushed all those unhappy thoughts out of my mind.

Every familiar sight brought a quiver of excitement and nostalgia. The narrow little storefronts; the cobblestone streets; the restaurant windows displaying meat, wine, cheese, and vegetables; even the little white-haired woman, frowning as she pulled laundry off the line running along the rooftops and folded sheets and table linen into a basket.

Charley took me up to the Piazzale Michelangelo, where I could get that perfect view of the city—the enormous dome of Santa Maria del Fiore, the Duomo, surrounded by a sea of red-tiled roofs, hovering over a large expanse of gold and ochre in the late afternoon sun. The village of Fiesole nestled in the hills to the north.

We had an early dinner just below the Piazzale. As we ate, I couldn't help but think of a conversation we'd had years ago just after Charley was ordained. We were having dinner then too, and drinking wine. We'd both had a bit too much vino and I surprised us both when I said, "I thought you liked girls too much to become a priest."

He'd considered this for a moment, then replied, "In life, we are asked at times to give up that which brings pleasure."

He delivered this in such a forced somber tone I knew I was expected to come back with something clever. That's how Charley and I conversed, particularly if we'd been drinking, making light of the profound or serious.

"Stepping stones to heaven," I replied, "like giving up candy for Lent."

Charley smiled and nodded, and then I took it one step further, something I'd never have done if I'd been completely sober. "So, how come you never hit on me?"

"I suppose because you were a girl I might have fallen in love with," he said without hesitation.

Well, that had sobered me up, as well as shut me up. I wasn't sure if he was kidding or not, but we never broached the subject again, and it seemed we had reached an understanding about our relationship. Our love for one another was special, but would never reach beyond the intimacy of close friendship. I loved Charley, but not in a romantic sense, and I sometimes wondered if it was his vow of celibacy that had protected our friendship over the years.

We finished dinner and drove down to the city center. Charley parked the car and we walked to my apartment, which was just a block from the Duomo. He introduced me to the manager and then loaded me, along with two of my bags, on the shoebox-size elevator. He took the stairs with my carry-on.

We met on the third floor landing. Charley grabbed my largest bag. "What have you got in here? Rocks?" he teased.

"Books," I replied. I'd sent two boxes ahead, right after

I accepted Charley's offer, but I'd purchased several since, including *The Madonna in Italian Renaissance Art*. "You can't expect me to teach without my books, can you?"

"We're in Florence." He grinned. "You don't need books to teach art in Florence."

I remembered Stefano saying something similar, and it made me smile. "This is going to be fun," I replied.

Charley showed me around the apartment, which was very small. The living room was the bedroom, with a bed that folded out of a closet. There was a tiny kitchen, not that I'd be spending much time in the kitchen, and a small bath with shower only. No tub.

It was a sublease from Dr. Browning and came furnished. Charley told me her son had come over after the accident and cleaned out all her personal belongings. The phone was still hooked up, but when we tried to find it, it appeared the son had also taken the phone. Charley suggested I get a cell phone with a short-term service contract, which reminded me once more that my position here was temporary.

"I'll leave you to get some rest now," Charley said.

"Yes, I think the jet lag is getting to me." I had hoped to go out alone for a walk, but I was tired.

"I'll drop by tomorrow," he said, "and give you a tour of the school."

"That would be wonderful."

"About noon? We'll get some lunch first."

"Sounds great."

I slept in that fitful, weird way you sleep when you've lost eight hours of your life in a single day. I woke in the middle of the night and realized I had been dreaming of Stefano. We were at the Uffizi, standing before Botticelli's *Birth of Venus*. And then I *was* the Venus, naked and exposed on her shell, covering my breasts with one hand, my long hair held with my other hand attempting to cover my body. Stefano was alone, gazing up at me, and then a group of gawking tourists with a guide appeared, commenting that the painting looked nothing

like they had envisioned. "Wasn't Botticelli's Venus blonde?"
one of the tourists asked. "Based on the beautiful Simonetta?"
another inquired of the guide. "Ah, but this is much lovelier,"
Stefano said with a grin. I felt my body grow very warm and I
wanted desperately to step off the shell, but I couldn't move. I
was paralyzed. Then, I jerked out of my sleep, feeling out of
place, wondering for a brief moment where I was, then realizing I was in my new apartment in Florence.

I tried to go back to sleep, but couldn't shake the dream. It
had no time frame, yet Stefano and I were both young, and the
memory of my first visit to the Uffizi came back to me with
great clarity. It was after Stefano had taken me to Santa Croce,
after the Cimabue crucifix had been moved over to the Limonaia, and after I had been blessed by the pope.

I remember vividly those days after our walk to Santa
Croce. I would do anything to be near him, to get his attention. On my way to work each morning, I would stop for coffee and pick up panini or sweet rolls at the bakery for Stefano.
He was always appreciative and polite, but never more than
that.

Other than Charley I seldom saw any of the students Roxie
and I had met at the National Library anymore and, although
I had befriended a couple of English and Italian students
at the Limonaia, our friendships did not extend beyond
this building in the Boboli Gardens. We were all exhausted
after the long days of work. My real focus was on the art. And
Stefano.

When I look back on it now, I was probably a bit of a pest.
When Pietro took off for a cigarette or bathroom break, I
would make myself available to help. One day as we worked
on a thirteenth-century altar panel, measuring the shrinkage,
Stefano asked me, "What will you do when you return home,
Suzanne?"

I didn't like the thought that I would have to go back home.
I liked being here in Italy, working at Stefano's side, being
part of this effort to save the art. I had never done anything so

meaningful, and never felt a part of anything of such significance. I don't remember feeling that I was in the middle of a
tragedy, but rather a wonderful opportunity.

"I'm going to study art history," I said then. "I want to be a
teacher of art history." I had given this considerable thought,
but it was the first time I'd put it into words. I had no clear
plan of how I was to go about doing this. I had completed one
year of college, but had never taken, or even contemplated
taking, a course in art or art history.

Stefano laughed. It was not an unkind laugh, but I felt myself blushing with embarrassment. He smiled at me as if he
were amused, an adult charmed by a child's innocent announcement that he or she wants to be a ballerina, a movie star,
an astronaut. "How can you study art history in America?" he
asked with a teasing grin. "America has no history of art."

I didn't know how to respond. I looked down at the painting before us and realized how much truth there was to what
Stefano said. This ancient panel had been conceived, painted,
and hung before Christopher Columbus set foot in America. I
felt rather foolish to think that I could accomplish such a goal,
in America or anywhere else.

"We will go to the Uffizi today," he said, surprising me.
"You will learn everything about the art here in Florence."

Our trip to the Uffizi that day was the first of many. Until
four days before Christmas all of the museums were closed,
and my work at the Limonaia kept me busy from early in the
morning until late at night. On December twenty-first, with
great fanfare at a reception at the city hall, Mayor Piero
Bargellini announced to the world that Florence was ready to
welcome the tourists once more, that the city of the Renaissance was again reborn and well on its way to being back in
business.

That first day Stefano and I spent hours in the museum, but
covered very little of the enormous collection. I had no idea
there could be so many paintings, so many beautiful creations
presented to the world all under one roof. Although the paintings

on the first floor of the Uffizi, where the workrooms and restoration area were located, had been devastated by the flood, the galleries open to the public on the upper floors had been virtually untouched. Stefano explained that though many works of art had been damaged by the flood, in reality it was less than 1 percent of the total art of Florence. This fact amazed me as there were rows and rows of paintings laid out in the Limonaia to dry. I couldn't imagine how much there was to see and study in the city.

"You are so eager," Stefano said, "so eager to learn." And I was. Eager to learn, eager to please.

After that we went each day to one of the museums, churches, or monuments—to the Uffizi, the Bargello, the Galleria dell'Accademia. I fell in love with the Botticellis in the Uffizi—the *Birth of Venus*, *Primavera*, and his many paintings of the Mother and Child. At the Accademia we studied Michelangelo's *David*, standing high on its pedestal, untouched by the layer of mud and slime that had glazed the floor of the museum when the waters of the Arno spewed forth on the city. Stefano told me how Michelangelo had carved his David from what had been a leftover block of marble ruined by another artist. He explained that Michelangelo felt that the figures he carved from stone had been there all along, that he was simply chipping away to release them. The *David* was beautiful and perfect, but I found the carvings of the roughly hewed *Slaves* lining the gallery equally as beautiful. Yet they seemed as if they were waiting to be finished, as if the artist had quit before he'd completed his project. Stefano said that, indeed, many art experts believed they were *non finito*, unfinished work, but many others believed they appeared just as Michelangelo had intended—still struggling to free themselves from the stone.

We studied the frescoes and watched the restorers working at Santa Croce on Gaddi's *Last Supper*. He took me to the Duomo, the Baptistery, the Campanile, the Medici Chapels.

I was exhilarated, and I could tell that he was enjoying

himself too. I could see how much he loved the art, how much he wanted to share it with me. And I began to believe, as I fell deeply in love with Stefano, that he was also falling in love with me. I had no idea what heartache lay in the future.

6

AT FIVE A.M. I rose, unable to get back to sleep. My stomach rumbled with hunger, but it was too early to go out for breakfast, and when I opened the cupboards, hoping Dr. Browning had left something behind, I found they were empty. I pulled off my nightshirt and stepped into the shower, which looked like an afterthought in the corner of the tiny tiled bathroom—a showerhead attached to the wall. The only form of enclosure was a plastic curtain on a semicircular rod to keep the shower from spraying the entire room. My hair took forever to dry, even with a hairdryer, as the apartment was cold and I couldn't find a thermostat to adjust the temperature. I pulled my hair up with a clip, slipped on my jeans, a sweater, my long coat, stuffed a pair of gloves in my pocket, then took the elevator down and walked out into the crisp, cool January morning.

It was amazing how it came back to me, the lay of the city. I walked down Via dei Cerretani, knowing instinctively where it would lead. I remembered how I'd be strolling down a narrow little cobblestone street then, suddenly, it was looming over me—Brunelleschi's dome, the big red-tiled heart of Florence.

Now as it came into sight I felt a familiar jolt of excitement. For many years I had described the architecture in my art history class and told the story of the competition to complete the unfinished cathedral. The large empty space hovered above the building, begun in the late thirteenth century, for over one hundred years. A contest for a plan to complete the cathedral was announced in 1418. Brunelleschi presented a controversial design—two egg-shaped domes, one inside the other, connected with a common ribbing. I had first heard the story of Brunelleschi's engineering feat from Stefano. And I remembered now how I had found it romantic, the way I read romance into everything then—one dome supporting the other, perfection in the two.

I stopped at the Baptistery and gazed at the golden doors. The originals, ten gold-leafed panels, had been created in the early fifteenth century by Ghiberti and depicted the life of Christ and scenes from the Old Testament. When Michelangelo saw them, he was touched by their beauty. He called them "the Gates of Paradise," a name that stuck. When the flood raged into the city on November 4, 1966, five of these panels were ripped off the large bronze doors as they were whipped back and forth by the overwhelming force of the powerful waters. Dante's Inferno meets the gates to Paradise. All five panels were retrieved and restored. I had never seen them, and even now I knew I was looking at copies—skillfully executed reproductions. The original panels were housed in the Duomo museum, the Museo dell'Opera del Duomo, to protect them from the city's pollution and acid rain. The museum was closed, and I decided I would go see them later that week.

I stopped for a quick coffee and pastry, then headed toward the river and lingered on the old bridge, the Ponte Vecchio, remembering how it had been battered by the flood, how the waters had risen, pummeling the tiny shops lining the bridge, how trees ripped up by their roots, dead animal carcasses, and household furnishings had lodged against it. Yet here it was now, in all its splendor, romantic and medieval like in the picture postcards. Shopkeepers appeared and one by one the shops, like wooden treasure chests studded with brass and bound with black iron belts, opened to reveal sparkling gems and gold.

I strolled the Lungarno, then up to Santa Croce. I thought about going in. I knew the Cimabue had been returned after a lengthy restoration period and was once more displayed in the museum off the cloister, but I wasn't quite ready for that.

I crossed through the piazza to the corner of Via Giuseppe Verdi and Via dei Benci, and looked up at the exterior walls of the buildings where the flood line from over thirty years ago was still visible in places. Beneath a green shuttered window and the sign identifying PIAZZA DI SANTA CROCE, two plaques were attached to the ochre building. IL 4 NOVEMBRE 1966 L'ACQUA D'ARNO ARRIVO A QUEST' ALTEZZA read the highest, at least fifteen feet above street level. A second plaque with similar wording, this one dated 13 SETTEMBRE 1557, hung about two feet below. I stood staring, remembering the day I had come to the piazza with Stefano. Several minutes passed before I could bring myself to move on.

On Via dei Tornabuoni I passed Gucci and Ferragamo, windows filled with shoes and bags and designer clothing. By the time I got back to my apartment, it was almost noon.

After lunch with Charley, we walked to the school.

The university leased the second and third floors of a medieval palazzo in the heart of the city. The building had been owned by the same family for over six hundred years, and they now rented the upper floors to various businesses and kept a small restaurant on the ground floor. Typical of a fifteenth-century Renaissance palace, it looked more like a fortress than a family home. A plain, arched entryway and three small rectangular windows on the first level did little to soften the severity of the stone façade. An ordered arrangement of arched windows on the upper two floors added the slightest ornamentation.

We walked through the courtyard, where plants and miniature trees stood in large terra-cotta pots, then we climbed the massive stone staircase to the second floor.

Charley introduced me to his assistant, Mrs. Potter, a thin, efficient-looking woman who greeted me with a welcoming smile. "Professor Cunningham, nice to meet you. You already have a message."

I thanked her as I took the note she'd written in a precise hand. Roberto Balducci had called. He was sorry he missed me again and would get in touch at the end of the week.

EARLY THE NEXT morning I went to the Uffizi, still unable to dislodge the image of Masolino's little Madonna and Child from my mind, still believing I might find it hanging on the wall. I picked up a guide to the collection, but of course it was not listed. I'd already checked an online guide and found no reference to the painting.

I started through the museum. In the Late Gothic Room, I studied *Madonna dell'Umiltà*, Masolino's *Madonna of Humility*. The dark blue and pale pink garments, the gold background, the treatment of light and shadow, the Madonna's long elegant fingers, her beautiful aristocratic face were similar to the painting we had saved, yet this Virgin appeared somewhat removed as she held her breast for the suckling babe.

With interest I read the history of the painting. Described as an altarpiece intended for a small chapel or bedroom wall of an unknown patrician—imagine that, a Masolino hanging on the bedroom wall!—it appeared on the London art market in 1930. Purchased by a private collector, it was seized by the Germans, then recovered in 1954. Though it was now unanimously accepted that it was a Masolino, for years historians had debated the origin of this Madonna and Child.

I stood for some time before the painting, touched by its beauty, intrigued by the history. I tried to imagine how many different people through the past five centuries had stood before this very painting, and then again, I imagined another painting—a smaller portrait of the Virgin and Child, hanging here in the museum, with its own history of recovery.

As I entered the Early Renaissance Room, a small painting

caught my eye. I didn't remember seeing it before. The information placard identified it as a Masaccio that had come to the Uffizi in 1988, confirming that it had not been part of the collection back in the sixties. The colors were similar to the Masolino Madonna, and there was something very pure and tender in the interaction of the two figures. Entitled *Madonna del Solletico—Madonna of the Tickle*—it pictured the Mother holding the Child and stroking him under the chin, his little hands wrapped around her wrist. The child's expression was so sweet, it appeared as if he were about to emit a delightful little giggle.

I studied *The Virgin and Child with St. Anne Metterza*, attributed to Masolino and Masaccio, picking out the portions I felt were Masaccio, those most likely painted by Masolino.

Then I stopped a guard and asked if there were other paintings by Masolino owned by the museum.

He angled his head in the direction of the St. Anne, then motioned back to the previous room. "Just these."

"Grazie," I said, wondering if he had any idea what might be included in the museum's collection, yet not presently on display. I knew from a long-ago conversation with Stefano that many of the paintings owned by the Uffizi were kept in storage on the first floor, where the restoration rooms were also located. Many of these were minor works. Often the paintings displayed in the museum would be rotated, depending on which particular type of work was currently in style. At any given time, there might be hundreds of paintings not available to the public. There were so many works of art in Florence there wasn't enough wall space in the museums to present them all at the same time. I wondered if my beautiful little Madonna was now in storage, hidden in a pile of minor works. Assumed to have been lost in the flood.

From the beginning I had been drawn to the little painting. As I ran here and there, back and forth from the Limonaia, picking up supplies, then becoming increasingly involved in the actual recovery and restoration work, I fell more and more in love with the beautiful Madonna and Child. There was something about the Mother's face, the way she looked so tenderly on the Child, and yet amazingly, she also seemed to be looking at me as I studied the work, as I stood gazing over Stefano's shoulder.

Stefano explained the painting was early fifteenth century. He pointed out how the figures appeared more human, like real people as opposed to the figures in earlier Italian works that looked more like icons. "The beginnings of the Renaissance," he said.

With his finger he traced the lines of the painting. "The circular motion, a skillful composition."

I followed as his finger moved along the curve of the mother's figure, her arms holding the infant, his tiny hand reaching up to touch her face. "This movement pulls the viewer in and holds them within the painting. The circular shape, repeated in the halos, creates a gentle rhythm enhanced by the colors—the soft lights and shadows of the fabrics. When you look at it," Stefano said, "perhaps you do not realize how skillfully the artist has put all these elements together, but it is all part of what makes this a delightful, very human portrait of a mother and child."

The painting was in far better shape than many laid out at the Limonaia. Stefano told me the paintings stored at the Uffizi had been damaged less than many of the Florentine treasures. The waters had risen slowly in that particular area, seeping into the lower level of the ancient building, so rather than being battered like the Gates of Paradise from the Baptistery, or pummeled like the treasures of Santa Croce, the paintings had, miraculously, floated to the surface and waited patiently for someone to come rescue them. That someone had been Stefano Leonetti. The paintings were all saturated, coated with mud. After carefully removing the surface mud, they were patched with mulberry paper to retain the pigment. They were sprayed with disinfectant, and then carefully checked day after day, shrinkage and humidity measured as the paintings dried. Sometimes we would find a patch of fuzzy mold, in an amazing array of colors—green, black, white, and

pink—that had been missed by the disinfectant. Stefano
would send me for a bottle of nystatin. One day as he brushed
it on the underside of the panel, he explained it was an antibi-
otic that was often used on babies to treat diaper rash.

"Our *bambini*," I said.

Stefano glanced back at me with a smile. "*Sì, i nostri
bambini.*"

I truly began to see these lovely paintings, particularly the
painting of the Madonna and Child, as beautiful babies, and
we tended them with great care.

"Who is the artist?" I asked Stefano one evening as we
worked on the little painting. We were moving through the
racks, recording statistical information on the little white tags.
All of the paintings had tags, like bodies in a morgue. Yet
these bodies would be revived. On the tags we recorded the
moisture content, the percentage of shrinkage from day to
day. The humidity in the room was kept extremely high and
the temperature very low, as this was determined to be the best
way to control the drying, the expanding and contracting of
the paintings. Not a particularly comfortable atmosphere in
which to work, yet I had never felt so content, so useful.

"The artist has been identified only as early fifteenth-
century Italian," he replied, "but I believe it was painted by
Masolino da Panicale, a student of Ghiberti. Many believe
Masolino was the teacher of Masaccio." I knew little of either
at the time, but I was learning. There was a Masaccio at the
Limonaia and I knew from the way the painting was being
treated by many of the restorers—if it had been a person it
would have been a celebrity—that the artist Masaccio was
one of great importance. Stefano had told me he was probably
the most significant artist of the early Renaissance. "One of
the first to display true emotion in his work, to use the princi-
ples of light and perspective." Although Stefano spoke highly
of Masaccio, I noticed that he treated all of the paintings as if
they were of equal value and importance. It was our duty to
save each and every one.

"I am intrigued by this little painting," Stefano said

thoughtfully. "If it is a Masolino it could have great significance. It is my opinion that this painting has been unjustly ig-
nored, but perhaps, perhaps after this is all over..." He
sighed and I guessed he was referring to the restoration. "Do
you know Vasari?" he asked, turning to look back at me.

"Vasari Corridor," I said proudly. The corridor, a long covered walkway, ran from the Uffizi Gallery, which had originally
served as the official governmental offices when it was built in
the sixteenth century, across the Arno River over the Ponte Vecchio all the way to the Pitti Palace, where the Medici family
resided. We'd all heard how paintings from the Uffizi as well as
those displayed along the corridor were carried to safety along
this passageway, over the Arno, even as the Ponte Vecchio
swayed and groaned.

"Giorgio Vasari designed the corridor as well as laid out
the plans for the Uffizi," Stefano explained. "He is known as
an architect of the early Renaissance, and he was also a painter. Not a very good painter at that." Stefano gave off a vague
dismissive snort. "Do you know what it is that has kept Vasari
alive as an important figure of the Renaissance?"

I shook my head, thinking, Oh, I have so much to learn.

"*Le vite de' più eccellenti pittori, scultori, ed architettori.*"

I looked at him blankly.

"Vasari wrote a book," he explained. "Several volumes entitled *The Lives of the Most Eminent Painters, Sculptors, and
Architects.*"

I nodded, feeling I was getting another valuable lesson in
art history.

"Do you know how many pages he dedicated to Leonardo?"

Again my empty reply, a shrug of my shoulders.

"Twenty-eight. And Michelangelo? One hundred forty-
three."

I actually gasped here.

"Vasari lived at the same time and had a great respect, a
worship, for the man. Others—earlier artists, who were not
personally known by Vasari, might have been slighted. Yet his

writing remains one of the most important on Italian artists even today."

I nodded, taking it all in, knowing I must read this book if I was to know anything about the artists of the Renaissance.

"How many pages to Masaccio?" Stefano asked, then after a brief pause in which I did not reply, he answered, "Twelve." He stared at me as if he knew I was hanging on his every word, as if he knew I would believe anything he told me. "And Masolino?"

I shook my head.

Stefano waited.

"Ten?" I guessed.

"Three," he replied.

We both stared down at the portrait of the Mother and Child. "Perhaps not enough," Stefano said sadly. And then with a resigned smile, "This little Madonna and Child should make a full recovery." Now his voice carried the confidence of an optimistic physician. He looked back at me. "We have done well, Suzanne."

"Yes, very well."

"She will be moving soon to the Fortezza da Basso." A workshop had been recently set up at the Fortezza da Basso, and after the paintings were treated for mold and mildew and dehumidified at the Limonaia, they were taken there to complete the restoration. I knew I should be pleased that the Masolino would be moved, and soon returned to its home at the Uffizi. But something about this revelation made me very sad. I didn't know if it was because the little Madonna would be leaving us, or the growing realization that at some point I would leave too. I would have to go back home.

"Ah, Suzanne, you should not be sad." Stefano seemed so in tune with my feelings, often commenting how I appeared happy or excited one day, pensive or melancholy the next. Perhaps I wore it all right there on my face, or my open heart on my proverbial sleeve, so obvious to anyone who would bother to look. And Stefano did look. Always, he looked at me as we spoke. Sometimes I would become aware that he was looking at me as I worked, when we weren't even speaking.

I smiled. "This is good."

"Yes, very good." He stood, as if we were ready to move on to our next patient, and then he did something that took me completely by surprise. He reached over, lifted my chin with his finger, and he kissed me. On the lips. Slowly and delicately at first, but then a full passionate kiss, his lips warm and moist. After, he stroked my cheek and smiled. I stared at him for a moment, speechless, my face growing hot, and then I stared down at the Madonna. The room was very cold, yet I felt as if I were on fire. My hand trembled as I reached for the edge of the metal bed holding the painting.

"We are done for the day," he said.

We worked together almost every day after that, Stefano treating me as if I were an apprentice restorer, insisting that I work with him, often sending Pietro on to assist another restorer. I don't know if Pietro was upset by this or not. I can't say I was filled with great generosity or concern for the feelings of anyone other than myself and Stefano.

I was sure he wanted this closeness we shared as much as I, yet I also wanted more. Didn't he want more too? But there seemed to be something holding him back. Was I too young? Too stupid? Too skinny? Too American? Too aggressive? So unlike the Italian girls, who seldom left their homes alone. A young Italian woman would never be seen on the street without her arm linked through that of an elder or another girl, or one on each arm. And here I was, up early each morning, climbing the hill to the Boboli Gardens, following the path to the Limonaia, all by myself.

One day, when I could no longer bear being without him, I asked him to walk me home. He said yes and we started together down the hill, not touching, barely looking at one another. We spoke of the flood, our work, the art, as we always did. When we reached my *pensione*, I invited him up. He took my hand, which trembled, and we climbed the three flights of steps with our fingers tightly laced. His hand was warm and reassuring. He was the world to me—my mentor, my teacher, my friend, and my first real love.

We undressed each other slowly, conversing only with our touches, our eyes. That night we became lovers. It was May 4, exactly six months after the flood, one month before my twentieth birthday.

7

I HAD FOUR more days before classes would start and I spent my time visiting the museums and churches, fine-tuning my class schedule. Charley had sent the syllabus Dr. Browning prepared for Women in Renaissance Art, but said I was free to do whatever I wished, so I tossed hers and prepared my own. I wanted every paper based on something my students could personally view in Florence. I'd decided to structure the semester's study around five basic themes, though I hadn't yet decided on the order. I knew the most comprehensive unit would be on Mary, the Virgin Mother. I wanted to do one on Eve, another on Magdalene, something on the revival of mythical themes involving a study of Renaissance nudes, and a study of society and portraits.

I made notes and quick sketches of the paintings and sculptures of the Virgin Mary as I went from museum to museum, and picked up books and brochures. In the church of Santa Maria Novella I studied the frescoes in the Tornabuoni Chapel, where the fifteenth-century patron Giovanni Tornabuoni had commissioned artists to incorporate members of his family in biblical scenes. I could see this as a source of inspiration for a paper on the section on society and portraiture. In the Museo dell'Opera del Duomo I examined Donatello's *Magdalene*, and continued my search for Mary Magdalene in the Uffizi where I found her as a haloed saint in the background of a Fra Filippo Lippi, and as a beautiful auburn-tressed woman in a scarlet skirt before the crucified Christ in a Luca Signorelli. She appeared as an innocent young girl in the Perugino at the Pitti, and a repentant woman, arms crossed in supplication, in a Filippino Lippi at the Accademia.

I VISITED THE library at school. The librarian, a tiny compact Italian woman named Signora Balzarro, had, like Mrs. Potter, been working during the break when many of the faculty had taken off. I asked if she could find a copy of the art journal in which Roberto Balducci's original article had appeared.

"We don't have many publications in Italian," she said, her voice small and quiet—the consummate librarian, though I thought that "whispering only" in the library had gone out years ago. "I don't believe this particular magazine is still being published." She studied my note with the title of the article and publication date. "Nineteen eighty-three? Perhaps I can locate a copy—an interlibrary loan with the Library of Florence."

"I would appreciate it so much," I said.

She smiled, pleased to be of help.

ON FRIDAY ROBERTO Balducci left another message at school, referring to our playing "phone tag." He sounded so American. He suggested we meet for a glass of wine and talk about whatever it was we needed to talk about. He laughed and said he'd forgotten what we needed to talk about. He suggested a place at the Piazza della Repubblica. How about five Sunday evening? If that wouldn't work out, give him a call.

Sunday I walked to the restaurant on the Piazza della Repubblica. A sign out front, in English, announced LIGHT

LUNCH, TEA ROOM, AMERICAN BREAKFAST. I wondered if
Roberto Balducci thought I'd be comfortable here because I
was American.

I stepped inside and looked around, wondering how I was
going to recognize him. Small wooden tables with benches
and chairs, crowded with customers, were arranged in the center under a vaulted ceiling. Photos and pencil sketches hung
above a dark wainscoting on the right wall. A glass-covered
bar and pastry case stood to the left.

On the way over, I'd imagined a man with a handwritten
sign like a tour guide meeting someone at the airport—
CUNNINGHAM—printed out in black marker on a piece of
cardboard. We'd left messages back and forth over the past
few weeks, but I hadn't actually spoken to Roberto Balducci. I
had no idea what he looked like, and he didn't have a clue
about me either. I noticed a man waving at me from the back
of the room.

I worked my way over, maneuvering around tables.
"Roberto Balducci?" I asked as I approached. I had expected a
much older man. I guessed he was mid to late forties.

"A pleasure to finally meet you, Professor Cunningham,"
he said as I extended my hand. He didn't stand or attempt to
help me with my chair, which might have been difficult as the
adjacent tables were packed tightly around ours. I nodded an
apology to the woman sitting behind me as I pulled out the
chair and sat.

"Thank you for agreeing to meet with me," I said.

"My pleasure." Roberto Balducci didn't look Italian, not a
trace of Balducci in him. His hair was thick and light brown—
well, almost as much gray as brown—his complexion fair, not
the Mediterranean look I had envisioned. If it hadn't been for
the voice, which I easily recognized, I would have thought I
was meeting the wrong person.

"May I order you a drink?" he asked.

"Yes, please. A glass of Chianti."

He called to the waiter and ordered *un mezzo*.

"Are you settling in?" he asked. "Enjoying the city?" He

wore a dark suit, a nice, expensive-looking silk tie. He dressed like a professional, not an art history professor.

"Yes, very much."

"First stay in Florence?"

"I spent over a year here quite some time ago."

"What is it you teach at the university?" Roberto Balducci had a broad, open face, a friendly face, and a slightly upturned nose, a little bit impish. *Cute*, the word came to me. The type of boy Roxie and I would have called cute. He had a comfortable, approachable look about him.

"I teach art history. I'm doing two basic introduction classes, and an upper division course called Women in Renaissance Art."

"You were a student, then? You studied art in Florence?"

"No, actually, I was here as a tourist. Over thirty years ago. I came in November of nineteen sixty-six."

"The flood," he replied immediately.

"Yes." I nodded. "I arrived in Florence on Thursday, November third."

"A bit of a shock for a tourist. You woke up the next morning and the streets were covered with water and mud."

The waiter delivered a small carafe of Chianti. Roberto Balducci poured me a glass and filled his about halfway.

"The flood definitely changed our plans." I explained I'd come over with a girlfriend, that we'd intended a three- or four-day visit in Florence before heading down to Rome.

"You stayed to help out?" he asked.

"I did," I said proudly. "That's when my interest in art began. I was going to school back home. I'd planned to teach in high school." I didn't mention that I'd wanted to teach physical education. "But it never occurred to me I would teach art history. At the time I had no idea I'd end up a college professor."

"Sometimes our lives take these turns," he said. "A tragedy turns into a revelation or a triumph."

"Yes," I agreed, then asked, "Are you a Florentine?"

"I was born here in Tuscany, as were my father and my grandfather."

I must have looked puzzled, though it wasn't intentional.

"My mother is American," he said. "We spoke English at home when I was young, though my mother decided we must speak *solamente italiano* once we started school." He smiled and I sensed the affection for his American mother who insisted he speak Italian. "So, you see, English is my first language. And I went to school—college—in the States."

"You have very little accent."

"I didn't realize I had any." He looked very serious, as if perhaps I had offended him, but then he smiled. He had a nice smile. Nice teeth. Nice lift to the mouth. Little creases around the corners like he smiled often. *"Parla italiano?"* he asked.

"Non bene." I laughed, embarrassed. "I spent over a year in Italy, but never became proficient." I explained how there were many students and young people in Florence at the time of the flood, and we all pitched in to help at the National Library, using English as our lingua franca as this seemed to be the one language that everyone knew. "When I left the library to work on painting restoration, the restorers, academics, and museum people, who came from all over the world, spoke a variety of languages. Eventually I learned a basic conversational Italian. But, even then, half the time I couldn't follow the conversations. Maybe I was too old to learn a new language or maybe just lacked the talent."

"It is difficult," he said. "Language comes much easier for children."

"It seems to."

"You are teaching at an American school? Classes all in English?"

"Fortunately."

"Yes," he said agreeably, no hint of condescension in his voice. "Now, how may I help you? My cousin Aldo mentioned you were interested in an article I'd written when I was teaching in Rome. I'm afraid he wasn't very helpful with the information. It's been years since I've taught."

"The copyright was nineteen eighty-three."

He shook his head and thought for a moment. He leaned in.

He was wearing a spicy-scented cologne or aftershave, barely noticeable at a distance. "This is a professional inquiry?" he asked. "For your art history class?"

"Yes."

"Not personal?" He spoke softly.

"No," I said, shaking my head, wondering why he would use the word *personal*. I didn't want to explain to a man I'd just met, a man who may or may not know the true whereabouts of the Masolino, how very personal this inquiry really was. "For one of my art history classes."

"Oh, oh." He grinned and sat back in his chair. "I was beginning to suspect you had the wrong Balducci. I think it's my father you want to speak with. He taught art history at the University of Rome. I taught for a few years, but I don't think I'd be of any help."

"What did you teach?" I asked, confused.

"Reproductive medicine. Infertility treatment." He smiled.

"No," I said and laughed, "I don't think you'd be much help. I apologize for this mix-up."

"Not need for apologies," he said kindly. "You must speak with my father. He's in poor health, but on a good day, I'm sure he'd love to talk with you. Maybe you could give me the information on the article."

"I'd appreciate it. The article referred to a fifteenth-century Italian painting, a Madonna and Child, often attributed to the artist Masolino."

"The Brancacci Chapel," he said, "with Masaccio."

I nodded, wondering if everyone in Florence was an expert on Renaissance art.

He took a pen and small pad of paper out of his inside jacket pocket and wrote the words *Masolino* and *Madonna*. He had surprisingly legible handwriting for a doctor. "Nineteen eighty-three?" he asked. "A magazine article?"

"Yes, then a translation included in a book, *The Madonna in Italian Renaissance Art*, the following year."

"Ah, yes," he said as he continued to write. He returned the paper and pen to his pocket. He poured me more wine. He'd barely touched his. It would rise to his lips now and then, but it didn't seem he was drinking.

"You're no longer teaching?" I asked.

"Not for several years. I'm in private practice and research now."

I nodded. What could I say about reproduction and infertility? This subject might have given me a little jolt, a pang of regret, but long ago I'd learned to hide this ache.

"You look familiar to me," he said. "Where did you go to school in the States?" He stared at me like he was trying to remember something. He smiled. Quite sweetly. I wondered again how old he was. Younger than me, I guessed.

"Idaho, then I went to graduate school in Minnesota." He looked directly at me when I spoke, and listened with interest.

He shook his head. "I went to school in Chicago. It just seems we've met." He studied my face as if he were an artist about to begin a portrait painting. His eyes were somewhere between blue and gray. He nodded and rubbed his chin, then the laugh lines around his mouth deepened. "Idaho . . . Minnesota . . . interesting places to study art history." His smile held a touch of curiosity, not a smug or unkind interest, but a desire to know more. "I've never met anyone from Idaho."

"Then, I'm your first," I said.

"Yes, my first Idaho girl." He raised his glass in a toast and so did I.

I felt slightly giddy—was he flirting with me? Or maybe it was the wine. I'd eaten a light lunch and even this single glass of wine—well, he'd topped it off once—made me feel the tiniest bit silly.

"You practice here in Florence?" I asked, attempting to regain my professional voice.

"I've been working on a team, a clinic here in Florence with another in Rome, though I'm in the process of discontinuing my association with Rome."

I tried to think of something I could ask about his work, a subject that made me rather uncomfortable. Gracefully he shifted the conversation, asking about my being in Italy during the flood. We talked about the restoration efforts, the help that had come in from all over the world, the generous contributions made by the Americans, the students and young people who had become involved. He told me his father had taken an active part in the restoration, though he was an art historian, not a restorer. "Anyone with any involvement in Italian art came to Florence those first few months," he said.

Interesting, I thought, particularly in light of his article stating the Masolino had been lost. I was more eager than ever to talk to the senior Balducci.

"Maybe that's when we met," he said, "when you were here working after the flood." He shook his head as if trying to bring something to mind, all the while staring at me as if I held the answer to a puzzle. I was quite sure I'd never seen him before, and yet, there was a familiar ease about him.

Two young men sitting next to us groped around under the table searching for backpacks. With tables tightly packed, they could barely leave without disturbing others at adjoining tables.

"I often went with my father when he was helping out with the restoration," Roberto Balducci said now.

"I spent most of my time at the Limonaia."

"I went there once," he said. "The greenhouse in the Boboli Gardens?"

"Yes." I was pleased that he remembered this. "Just weeks after the flood it was revamped to hold the paintings in the initial phase of the restoration."

Now an older woman at the table on the other side of us struggled with her chair, pushing it back, still sitting. The young man sitting with her couldn't get around to help. Roberto Balducci reached over, attempting to assist her. Finally, she was able to get out and up. She took the young man's arm and they worked their way through the labyrinth of tables.

"Would you like something else?" Roberto Balducci asked. "Something to eat?"

I glanced at my watch, surprised that an hour had passed. "Thank you, but I'm going to a reception at the school this evening at seven. A welcome for new faculty. I guess I'm sort of a guest of honor, so I probably should show up." As I said this I realized I wasn't that eager to leave. I would have liked to visit longer with Roberto Balducci.

"May I extend a welcome from the natives, too," he said warmly, lifting his glass. He waved at the waiter to bring our check. "I hope my father will be helpful in your study. I'll see if we can arrange a meeting."

When the waiter brought the bill, I offered to get it, pointing out it was I who had contacted him in hopes that he might help me. Roberto Balducci refused, then suggested that after I spoke with his father, if the information was helpful, I could buy him a drink. I liked this thought, that I would see him again.

The waiter returned with a receipt and I got my bag from beneath the table.

"Would you like a lift?" Roberto Balducci asked.

"I'm not far," I said. "You probably had to park farther away than where I'm headed."

He agreed, acknowledging Florence was a pedestrian city, and then he reached down as if for a briefcase or doctor's bag—do doctors still carry those little black bags? I wondered.

When he pushed up from the table, I saw it wasn't a briefcase or bag he had reached for. He stood, holding a pair of crutches—sleek silver metal with cuff-shaped bands. The type used by someone with a permanent disability. *Cripple*, the word came to me unkindly. I felt a warmth rise up in me, a mixture of discomfort and embarrassment, and a horrible inexplicable sense that I had been duped, which made my discomfort all the more disturbing.

He said nothing and neither did I as we walked out. I felt the effect of the wine as I stepped unsteadily onto the cobblestones of the piazza. I wondered if that was why he hadn't even finished his single glass—if he was always a bit unsteady. Mentally I admonished myself for such an insensitive thought.

"I'll speak with my father," he said then.

"I'd appreciate it." Without thinking, I reached out to shake his hand.

With ease he adjusted the crutch and took my hand, and held it for a moment. "I'll be in touch."

"Thank you, Professor Balducci," I said, then realized it was Dr. Balducci. In my mind I'd been calling him Roberto Balducci—as if his first and last name were inseparable. "Dr. Balducci," I corrected.

"Roberto is fine, Professor Cunningham."

"Suzanne," I said. "Please call me Suzanne."

We stood uncomfortably for a moment, each of us waiting for the other to speak, neither of us quite ready to leave.

"It's been nice meeting you, Suzanne. I'll give you a call."

"You've got my number?" Silly question, I realized—he'd already left me several messages over the past two weeks.

He nodded yes.

"Then yes," I said, "please call."

8

THE RECEPTION WAS held in a large classroom on the second floor. Desks had been moved away and a table set up with crackers, dips, fresh vegetables, and fruit. Two young men, students, I assumed, served wine and beer at the bar. I nodded to a man and woman as I walked in, then spotted Charley, who waved and headed over and introduced me to Anthony and Jennifer Randolph. "Anthony has also joined the staff this semester as our advanced painting instructor."

He didn't look like a painter. He wore slacks and a cardigan sweater like Mr. Rogers, and he was short and chubby with big bushy eyebrows and a little tic in his eye that kept twitching as he spoke. His wife, Jennifer, was at least three inches taller than her husband and, while not a natural beauty, there was something attractive and appealing about her. She spoke with a British accent, an unlikely match for Anthony, whose voice carried a trace of a southern drawl. I thought they made an interesting couple. And then I wondered if most of the teachers, other than the priests, were married. Would I be the only single woman at the school?

As I visited with Father John McMillan, a philosophy

professor, and Signora Balzarro, the librarian, who told me she had ordered the article for me, I couldn't get my mind off of Roberto Balducci, the art historian, wondering again about the source of his belief that the Masolino Madonna had been destroyed in the flood. And each time these thoughts entered my mind, they were accompanied by the image of Roberto Balducci, the son.

A youngish woman with dark hair walked over and greeted Charley with a smile. "This is Regina Bonaminio," he said. "She teaches our sculpture classes."

I reached out for her hand, which was delicate and fine-boned. She had huge dark eyes and curly black shoulder-length hair, so thick it seemed as wide as it was long. Enormous silver spiral earrings dangled from her ears. Her black skirt with tan geometric designs fell over black leather boots.

"*Benvenuto a Firenze,*" she said. "Father Charles tells me you were here years ago, in the sixties."

"Yes, sixty-six." Everyone I met called him Father Charles or Father Stover. I wondered if I should do the same, but quickly dismissed this idea.

"The year of the flood," Regina said thoughtfully.

"During the flood actually."

"Suzanne helped out with the restoration," Charley said. "That's where we met."

"One of the angels," Regina said with a smile that seemed to engage her entire face. *"L'angeli di fango."*

Mrs. Potter, the administrative assistant, approached and spoke in a quiet voice to Charley, who then said, "Speech time," and excused himself.

"We Florentines have always been extremely grateful," Regina said, "for all the foreigners who came to our rescue during the flood."

"It was a tragic, yet wonderful experience," I said. "It was in Florence that my love for art and the history of art began."

"I'd like to welcome our new instructors," Charley said, standing at the front of the room. He began introductions starting with me, one of the mud angels, a flattering portrait of a woman who had been involved in the salvation of the treasures of Florence, and who had come as a savior of sorts once more.

MONDAY MORNING I faced my first class, my upper-division Women in Renaissance Art. And, as always when I started a semester, I felt both apprehensive and exhilarated. It was important that I offer something to my students, that they accept my gift. I could see the enthusiasm right away and it fueled my own.

I talked about my expectations, then gave my students a chance to talk about theirs, requesting they introduce themselves before they spoke. The only young man in the class, Richard Bennington, was the most talkative and very confident. He was a cute boy with fabulously fake blond hair, darker roots under, sticking up all over the place, a style that seemed to be popular with both the guys and the girls.

A couple of the young women, delighted that a class would place the emphasis on women, spoke up right away. I was pleased with this response, as I could see it meant Richard wouldn't dominate the group.

I handed out a syllabus to each student and we reviewed them together. " 'Mary, Virgin Mother,' " I said, "will be our first and most extensive theme. We'll follow this with 'Back to the Beginning: Let's Look at Eve.' " I continued, reading off the syllabus, " 'Venus, Mythical Revivals and Renaissance Representation of the Nude'; then 'Magdalene, Sinner or Saint'; and our final topic, 'Portrait of a Woman.' "

"I notice there will be five papers due?" This question came from the petite blonde in the front row, Mindy Crandall.

I nodded. "One on each theme."

I saw a few eyebrows go up.

"I'll hand out the list of suggested topics on Wednesday."

One of the girls asked, "What's the required word length?"

"Whatever it takes. First paper will be due two weeks from Friday."

"Suggested topics?" Richard asked. "What if we have some

ideas of our own?" I was getting the impression this young man had plenty of ideas of his own, which was fine with me. I was up to the challenge.

"I'm open for that. Come talk to me. My office hours are Tuesday and Thursday afternoons. Hours posted on the door."

"You've got five test dates on the schedule as well as five papers?" This from one of the girls.

"Is that a question?"

A few of them laughed, a few of them groaned.

"Though we are meeting here three times a week, your classroom is the city. I will expect you to do a personal study of all art you use in your papers."

"Hey!" Richard shouted, raising his clenched fist in a victorious gesture. "Right on. We're in Florence!"

My Introduction to Art History students that afternoon didn't show quite the same enthusiasm, but it was a much larger group without the intimacy of my upper-level course. I would assign just two papers, three tests. I didn't want to be too hard on them or scare them off. I wanted them to have the opportunity to love art as much as I did.

THAT FIRST WEEK I established a morning routine. Each day I rose early, put on my walking shoes, and went out. I walked at least half an hour, generally up to forty-five minutes, sometimes passing through the Piazza del Duomo, at times strolling over to the Piazza della Signoria, where vendors were putting up stalls, placing postcards and little statues of the *David* on shelves. Then I stopped at the same bar each morning, where the owner greeted me warmly with a familiar *buon giorno*. For breakfast I bought a pastry or panino and sat with a cup of coffee or cappuccino. I stopped at the Mercato Centrale near San Lorenzo for fresh fruit—early enough to get first choice—and bread, cheese, and sausage or pastrami or prosciutto, then returned to my apartment, showered, dressed, and walked to school. Often I went for a break with some of the other teachers. For lunch I walked back to my room and made a sandwich or ate fresh fruit from the market. Afternoons, I visited the museums. Sometimes I'd stop at a restaurant on my way home for a quick dinner; otherwise I'd snack on fruit, bread, and cheese at my apartment. I never cooked.

THE MIDDLE OF the following week, I found the article I had requested from Signora Balzarro in my box at school. I sat in my office with my Italian dictionary propped on my desk alongside the English translation of Roberto Balducci's article. As far as I could tell, the translation had been done correctly. The Italian article also said the painting had been destroyed in the flood, a fact I knew was untrue. I wanted to check with someone else—to make sure I was reading this correctly.

I decided I would ask Regina Bonaminio. We ran into each other often as we went back and forth, I to my second-floor classroom, she to her third-floor studio. She was always friendly, taking the time to greet me, to ask about my classes, and visit with me about what I was doing with my free time in Florence. The morning after I found the article in my box, I asked if she had time to grab some coffee.

We walked to a place just a block from the school, a typical Italian bar—much deeper than wide, the space magically expanded by a large mirror that reflected rows of sparkling bottles filled with a rainbow of liqueurs and liquors in back of the counter. A glass case displayed fresh pastries and sandwiches. Chocolates and cigarettes were stacked on shelves behind the cashier. An espresso machine hissed, and an inviting aroma hung in the air. I remembered how, when I first came to Italy in the sixties, I thought it was so cool that the coffee shops were called *bars*—you could get a *drink* there too, without showing I.D. And the coffee wasn't just coffee, but cappuccino, which I'd never even heard of back home, and dark, rich, give-me-a-jolt espresso.

Regina ordered a double espresso, and I got a cappuccino.

Regina was in her mid thirties, young enough to be my daughter, but we talked easily. Her English was flawless, though often filled with phrases and idioms of a generation more in tune with my students' than mine. She told me she'd been an exchange student in San Diego when she was seventeen—how she'd wanted to go somewhere away from home, how her mother and father had both grown up in a little village in southern Italy, and never went anywhere. I thought how much we were alike in that respect. I wondered if she had come to an understanding of her parents, as I had much later in life, years after I returned home. As I matured I could see my mother's joy, her contentment, and I realized she didn't have my restlessness, that she wasn't always searching for a better life, a better place.

Regina was married to a young man she'd known since she was a girl and had two children. She liked to ski and play tennis, though she said she had little time for either anymore.

Finally I told her about the article by Roberto Balducci, how I knew the painting had been restored. "I met with his son because of a mix-up, but haven't heard from him since. The elder Balducci is ill and I'm afraid I won't be able to speak with him. I know what he wrote isn't true. The painting wasn't destroyed in the flood." I pulled out the article Signora Balzarro had obtained for me and handed it to Regina, pointing at the section I was questioning.

Her eyes darted quickly over the text. "Destroyed, yes—annihilated."

"But it wasn't. *Damaged*, yes, but restored. I helped with the restoration."

"What do you think happened to it?" Regina's large brown eyes widened with interest.

"I don't know, but I'd like to. It's definitely not on display in the Uffizi."

"You could contact someone here in Florence from the Uffizi, or maybe someone who worked at the Limonaia. Do you remember any of the names of the people you worked with?"

"Stefano Leonetti." I picked up my cappuccino to grasp on

to something, to steady myself, but the cup shook as I raised it to my lips.

"Contact the Uffizi," Regina said, stirring her espresso. She licked the spoon, put it back in the cup, and stirred again. "What's the matter?" she asked as she looked up.

I set my cup down. "Too much caffeine," I said with a nervous laugh. We had quickly established a rapport, but I didn't feel I could tell her about Stefano. Not just yet. "Well, actually," I said, very calmly, "I tried. I mean I tried looking him up on the Internet, then checked the phone book. He's no longer in Florence." My cappuccino was now down to the white foam. I took my spoon and scooped up the froth.

"Maybe he's not in Florence, but he's got to be somewhere unless he's dead." She shook her head as if she regretted mentioning this possibility. "Giorgio has an old friend who works at the Uffizi in the restoration department. I'll have him check it out with Alberto and see if he knows anything about Stefano Leonetti. Maybe you can find out about both the painting and Stefano."

I was grateful for her offer. "I'd appreciate it."

"Consider it done."

I WAITED, HOPING Roberto Balducci the younger would call, but he didn't. I wanted to talk with his father, but I also realized I wanted to see Roberto again. He'd jumped into my thoughts repeatedly since we'd met . . . well, not exactly *jumped*! I couldn't think of him without picturing him pulling those crutches from beneath the table, feeling uncomfortable and flustered all over again. Did my uneasiness have to do with an unadmitted prejudice—that someone physically challenged has no sexuality? Just as one might think a woman of a certain age has no sexuality?

I realized he could have remained sitting in the restaurant, let me leave on my own, and I would never have known. But it seemed he wanted me to know. And this made me feel there was a certain honesty about him. And I liked him all the more for that. Yet was I reading more into this than I should? Why would he care if I knew? We met because of a misunderstanding. It wasn't exactly as if we'd gone on a date, or that we'd ever see each other again.

I went online and typed in his name along with *reproductive medicine*, remembering how many Balduccis there were in Florence. I found him on several sites, including the clinic in Florence as well as an infertility clinic in Rome whose claim to fame was the successful pregnancy of a sixty-three-year-old woman! When we met at the restaurant, and cleared up our misunderstanding after he'd asked if my interest was personal, I'd wondered if he thought I was young enough to conceive a child. Now I laughed a little, realizing he might have been sizing me up as a potential postmenopausal client.

I remembered several years ago I'd read an article in an American magazine about a clinic in Rome where a woman much beyond the normal childbearing years had been implanted with a fertilized egg and delivered a healthy full-term baby. Now I realized this must have been Roberto Balducci's clinic. At the time I had mixed feelings. It was at a point in my life when I was coming to the realization that my biological clock was barely ticking.

Jerry and I had married when I was thirty-nine, and he knew how important family was to me, that I wanted a baby right away. After the wedding, he suggested we wait a while to adjust to married life, which was ridiculous—we'd been going together for two years, living together for the last. Three months later, when I turned forty, I announced I was going off the pill. Jerry didn't seem to have the same enthusiasm he'd exhibited on the subject of children before we married. After six months, we'd yet to conceive. I cried a lot and Jerry said maybe this was okay, just the two of us. I suggested we think about fertility counseling, and he said if this wasn't happening naturally, maybe it wasn't supposed to. I reminded him we'd talked about this before we married, how difficult conception might be at my age. We fought about every little insignificant thing after that. We hung on for another year, then separated, but didn't divorce for another year. I was almost forty-three.

I thought about doing it on my own, but decided a child needed a father. Maybe I still had time to find someone else. Then I was forty-four, then forty-five—still healthy, but moving closer and closer to a time when I knew a child would be an impossibility. Just weeks before I got the call from Charley with his invitation, my doctor informed me that, medically speaking—since it had been a full year since my last period— I was postmenopausal. My reproductive biological clock had ceased to tick.

ONE EVENING CHARLEY invited me to join him and Father McMillan for dinner at a restaurant on Via del Trebbio. As I walked in down a narrow staircase and spotted the two priests I couldn't help but think, Well, here we are, the three celibates!

Father John rose and pulled my chair out for me. He was a nice man, mid sixties I would guess, and I'd visited with him on several occasions.

As the men studied the menu and wine list, I looked around at the walls and ceiling, which were covered with travel posters, and realized that I had been here before with Stefano. It was one of the few times we went anywhere together other than the Limonaia, the museums, or my *pensione*.

"What about you, Suzanne?" Charley asked, interrupting my thoughts. "What are you drinking tonight? Should we order a bottle?"

"Sure, that would be fine," I answered.

Father John, a man with a rotund figure and a ruddy face, was a bit of a gourmet, and there was much discussion between the two priests over the wine selection. In fact, our conversation, as we looked over the menu, the wine list, and then far into the meal, seemed to center around food and drink, and an enthusiastic discussion of meals they had partaken of in the past, accompanied by great detail of place and time. A wine in Burgundy, produced from the famous Pinot Noir grapes; truffles in Périgord; beans in Barcelona that John had eaten as a young student; then a rather intense debate concerning French versus Italian bread, Father John insisting there was nothing in the world like a fresh loaf from a Parisian *boulangerie*.

All this talk of food and drink made me wonder if one passion might be substituted for one denied. Both Charley and Father John had good appetites and appreciated with vigor each course of the meal.

But everything tasted a bit off to me, like it does when you have a cold and your taste buds and sense of smell are impaired.

After dinner, Charley asked if I'd like a lift home and I said it would be easier and quicker to walk.

"You're sure you'll be fine on your own?" he asked.

"Jeez, Charley," I replied, "I've been doing fine on my own for quite some time." It came out sounding rather rude, so I laughed lightly to take the sting out of the words.

He didn't say anything for a moment, but I could tell he wondered if he'd done something to provoke me. "You okay?"

"Sure," I said apologetically. "Just tired. This teaching business is hard work, wears a girl out."

He offered me a concerned smile and gave me a little peck on the cheek. "See you Monday."

As I walked home alone, I couldn't help but think of years ago when I walked back to my *pensione* from this very same restaurant with Stefano. We had been lovers for several weeks by then, and he often walked me home. Even when he was working at the Fortezza da Basso, he sometimes stopped by the Limonaia about the time he knew I would be leaving.

He was a tender and passionate lover. He knew how to touch me, where to touch me. He guided me with such sweetness, never making me feel inadequate, never suggesting I had no idea what I was doing. For the first time in my young life I felt like a woman. A beautiful, desirable, sensual woman.

Stefano seldom spent the night. Occasionally he would

take me to dinner, on a "real date," though we had little time for such events.

That night was a warm evening in the middle of June. The summer tourists were flowing into Florence, clogging the streets, invading the restaurants and hotels, and I realized how different they were from me. That I was no longer one of them. This had become my city, my Firenze. I had earned the right to claim it as my own. Most of the museums, galleries, and churches had reopened. There were still signs of the flood—heaps of mud piled in some sections of the city, the dark brown lines on the buildings, the bare walls and empty spaces in the museums, where little signs proclaimed *IN CORSO DI RESTAURO*—but there was also great hope in the city. And I was in love.

As we walked home from dinner, I felt warm and content, satisfied after our marvelous meal. Overflowing with love for Stefano. Love for the art we were saving. Love for the city of Florence, for the people of Italy, for everything in my life at the moment. I wanted to shout, and then I did. "I love this country!"

I threw my arms dramatically into the air, and shouted again, "I love Italy. I love everything about it. The art, first, oh yes, the art." I smiled at Stefano. "But the silly little things too. The way you can go into a *ristorante* and sit for hours, no one checking on you every two minutes to see how you're doing, like in America where their real intention is to scoot you out the door so they can fill the table again, sell more food, get more tips. And I love the way Italians eat—antipasto, then pasta, then if you've got enough room, the main course, then even dessert." At home when we ate "Italian," my mother served spaghetti, salad with Thousand Island dressing, and French bread from Safeway all on the same plate. But here in Italy, the pasta was just a warm-up, as were the antipasti, the *insalata*. I loved the Italian food, the way they made an event of each meal.

As Stefano and I continued down the street, I looked up. "I love the way there is a treasure on every corner of the city, right here on the street!" We were at Orsanmichele, a church that at one time had been a granary. I pointed to a statue in a little niche, one of the sculptures by Donatello—St. George slaying the dragon. I had learned from Stefano about the sculptures of Donatello—his beautiful little David in the Bargello, his Magdalene in the Baptistery, half-submerged in the flood and tragically cracked. But that night, these sad thoughts of the flood's destruction gave way to euphoria. "I love Italy!" I shouted again, smiling at Stefano, taking his hand.

We continued to walk, Stefano grinning at me. *"Carina, carina,"* he called me. "Such enthusiasm, such energy."

"And I love how the Italians take a word like *cara*—dear—and make it even sweeter by changing it to car*ina,* my sweet little, dear little sweetheart. I love how the Italian shopkeepers, if they have something better to do, will just plop a handwritten sign in the window: BE BACK IN A MINUTE." I didn't feel the impatience I might have felt back home with such disregard for schedules and rules. I loved this place, where everything seemed to exist for the moment. "Don't you love it?" I asked Stefano. "Don't you love everything about it?"

He looked at me, the way he did, the way that made me feel anything I did was endearing, that I made him happy, made him laugh. He put my hand to his lips and he kissed the soft sensitive flesh of my palm. Then he said, "Oh, there are a few things I do not like."

"Like what?"

"There are—"

"Are what?" I prodded.

"Politica."

"Phooey. Who likes politics? Americans don't like politics. Nobody likes politics." I knew little about politics at the time, particularly Italian politics, though I was well aware of the discontent in America over the war in Vietnam, student protests popping up now and then in Paris. "Enough of that," I said, lightly. "What else?"

"The Church."

"You like the Church, or you don't like the Church?"

"Non mi piace," he answered.

I knew enough Italian to know he said, "I don't like it." And that too I loved—the way the Italians said *mi piace* for I like it, or *non mi piace* for I don't like it. Literally, "it pleases me," or "it does not please me."

"What's wrong with the Church?" I asked. "Italy has the most beautiful churches in the world. There's a beautiful church on every corner in Florence." I laughed again.

"The control," he answered. "The Church controls everything here."

If I had been more aware would I have noticed the slightest shift in the tone of his voice? Should I have sensed we had taken a turn? "Like how?" I asked.

"Divorce," he said. "There is no such thing as divorce in Italy."

We continued down the street, my arms no longer flung in the air. My step had lost its stride. Divorce? I looked at Stefano. I would not ask. My heart dropped. Literally sank.

He walked me home to my *pensione*. I didn't invite him in.

How had I not known? There had been so many signs. We seldom spoke of the future. When I told him about my mother's letters filled with suggestions, short of demands, that I come home that fall and enroll in school first semester, I had hoped Stefano would tell me what to do, give me hope that he also dreamed of our being together after all of this was over. But he said only that he wanted what was best for me.

There were so many reasons I should have known. The canceled dinners. The picnic we had planned for days up in Fiesole—"Something's come up . . . I have a meeting today . . . maybe we could go some other time." He rarely spent the night. We always made love at my *pensione*, in my bed. Then he would leave, telling me he would never get any sleep if he stayed, and we had a big day ahead of us.

The next day at the Limonaia, I arrived before Stefano and asked Pietro.

"I thought you knew," he said apologetically. "Yes, a wife,

a daughter. A w-w-wife from a very good family from Milano." He rubbed his thumb and fingers together.

A good family? A wealthy family? And a child? I remembered when Pietro had told me Stefano was spending Christmas
Eve and Christmas Day with his family. I thought he meant
mom and dad, brothers and sisters. I had no idea he meant wife
and child. I felt so very foolish. And very angry. At myself, or
Stefano, or Pietro, I wasn't sure. I stared at Pietro for a moment,
saying nothing. I honestly wanted to push him right off his chair
and smash his stuttering little four-eyed head into the cold concrete floor. I didn't speak to him for the rest of the day.

When Stefano came in, he acted as if nothing had happened, as if everything was the same. And yet, everything was
different. As I watched him, and I did very carefully, he
seemed almost relieved.

We did not speak of his wife or the child.

Although I say Stefano was the same, acting as if nothing
had happened, something changed after that. The work at the
Limonaia became more intense, the lovemaking more desper-
ate, at times even rough. Neither Stefano nor I could get enough
of each other. We both knew one day it must end.

9

I SAT IN my office reading test papers my students had turned in that morning. I'd intended to take them home. My plans for the weekend included grading tests, and a trip to the Brancacci Chapel to study Masaccio's and Masolino's Eves, since a comparison of the two figures would be a topic for our next paper. But I had started reading a test, then another, and was simply amazed at my students' abilities and insight. I finished a second, then placed the remaining in my briefcase. Just as I was about to leave, the phone rang.

"Hello, Suzanne. It's Roberto Balducci."

It had been almost two weeks since our meeting, and I had begun to suspect he was not going to call. Regina had invited me for dinner the following week to meet with her husband's friend from the Uffizi, and I'd decided this would be my most likely source of information on the Masolino.

"Are you busy this evening?" he asked. "I apologize for calling with such short notice, but Papa has had a good day, the first in weeks, and he asked to see you. We can't plan much ahead with him. It's more or less day by day."

"Could I meet you somewhere?" I asked.

"If it's okay, I'll drop by for you. About five?"

"I'll be at the school." I asked if he knew where we were located, and he said yes. We agreed to meet in the courtyard on the first level.

I went down early—it was one of my Florence resolutions, to abandon my habit of tardiness, and I wanted to be waiting for him when he arrived. I didn't want him to have to climb the steps or navigate the tiny box of an elevator. He showed up just before five, moving surprisingly fast along the stone floor of the courtyard.

"I must apologize again," he said, "but I just heard from my daughter Maria—Papa is staying with her family—and I'm afraid he's too tired to see you. He was doing well today, but sometimes he seems to wear himself out just thinking about company."

"That's fine," I said, disappointed. "Maybe some other time."

"I hope you didn't cancel other plans."

"Not really." I was a little embarrassed to admit my biggest plans for the weekend involved grading tests.

"Could I offer you dinner?" he asked.

"Isn't it a bit early for dinner? Italians don't seem to eat as early as Americans."

"Well, I'm only half Italian. But we'll find something else to do until dinnertime. I do have the imagination of an American."

He had a van equipped with hand devices for acceleration and brakes. He drove through the late afternoon traffic like any Italian driver, swerving in and out, around cars, responding to a raised fist now and then with one of his own.

We were soon out on the highway. "Where are we going?" I asked. "When you said dinner, I assumed you meant in Florence."

"I thought since it's early, maybe we could go for a drive before dinner. Have you had a chance to get out of the city since you've been here?"

"There's plenty to keep me busy in Florence."

He nodded. "How about Rome?"

"Rome's three hours away."

He looked at his watch. "Perfect. We'll be there in time for dinner."

I didn't protest. And we kept driving.

We headed out through the city, onto the autostrada, picking up speed, passing a few slow-moving vehicles. I looked over at Roberto. He smiled. "Nice evening for a drive," he said.

"You're not kidnapping me, are you?"

"Could I get a good ransom?"

"Probably not."

"No rich relatives?"

"No."

"Tell me about your family."

"My sister, Andrea, lives in Boise. Dad's in Idaho too. He still lives in Twin Falls, the town where I grew up. Andrea and her husband, Michael, have five children, all grown, four grandchildren—well, two of them she acquired through marriage—her oldest son just married a young woman with two teenagers. She's a bit older than he. Andrea was concerned at first, but it seems to be working out." God, did I sound like a babbling idiot or what?

"You've been a career woman," he said. Was this his nice way of saying, no husband, no children?—facts quite obvious from my answer to his question about family.

"I've been teaching since grad school."

"You enjoy teaching?"

"Very much." This wouldn't have been an honest answer just weeks ago, but, yes, I was enjoying it all—my teaching, my students, being here in Florence. "My students are all so enthusiastic," I told him. "It seems young people are much more assured and confident than I remember being at their age. They truly challenge me."

"You like working with young people?"

"Yes, I do." I confessed that I'd been suffering from a bit of restlessness and that coming to Florence seemed to be just what I needed.

"Sometimes we need a change in our lives to give us a little boost," he said thoughtfully, and I agreed.

We talked about my classes, my students, how teaching in Florence was a dream come true for a professor of art history.

"You enjoy your independence?" Roberto asked.

I guess he was talking about my being single, no kids, no commitments. "I have a dog."

"Here in Florence?"

"No, back home. It was difficult leaving Rousseau."

"Your dog's name is Rousseau, after the artist?" He smiled approvingly.

I nodded. I didn't want to explain how Jerry and I had fought over the name. "She's been with me for over thirteen years." My only true family, I thought.

"A pet can be a good friend."

"Yes, a very good friend. And you, Dr. Balducci, you have family, other than your father and daughter?" Was this where he'd confess a wife and five kids?

"Roberto, please call me Roberto," he said. "Five daughters. Two of them in Florence. Three grandchildren. An older brother in Venice. My mother also lives in Venice."

And a wife? I wondered, followed by my curiosity as to why his mother lived in Venice, his father in Florence.

"I lost my wife four years ago." He said no more.

We drove several moments without speaking. The sun had set and it was dark out, other than the light from a nice-sized slice of moon, traffic on the other section of the autostrada, and vehicles coming up behind us, passing now and then. Roberto wasn't letting many of them get around him, and did his fair share of passing. At this rate we'd be in Rome in no time.

"Your mother," I began. "You said she's American? Where was she from?"

"New York, from a big Irish Catholic family. My Irish ancestors emigrated to the States during the great potato famine." He smiled. He had a beautiful smile that made me feel like smiling too. "It's funny how Americans always relate to being from somewhere else," he mused. "But, I guess other than Native American Indians, they always are."

"You're Italian and Irish American?"

"I am," he said, "but for some reason, I've never been hung up on where I came from, but more concerned about where I'm going."

"And where are you going?"

"Right now I'm heading to Rome for dinner." He smiled again. "So tell me, you grew up in Idaho?"

"I did." I told him about the time I spent on my grandparents' farm when I was a child, how I'd always lived in town, but deep down inside I felt like a country girl.

"A country girl, in the big city now, teaching art history?" He glanced over. "Do you feel confined, spending your days in classrooms and museums?"

"Just lucky," I said. "And blessed that I've been given the opportunity to experience the best of both."

"Does your family still own the farm?" he asked.

"My grandmother sold it shortly after my grandfather died. Neither Uncle Trace or my dad wanted to farm."

"You miss it?"

"I do. I have such good memories of the time I spent with my grandparents. But it was actually my grandmother's selling the farm that financed my first trip to Florence and my education. I never thought of my grandparents as wealthy people. They lived in a rather run-down farmhouse, but they were sitting on land that made my grandmother quite comfortable when she sold it. She bought a little retirement home and put most of the money in trusts for me, my sister, and our cousins. I wouldn't be here in Florence today if it wasn't for my grandmother."

"Then I have your grandmother to thank for making your acquaintance," he said with a grin.

"Well, yes, I suppose indirectly that's true," I replied with a laugh.

"And my father too," he added.

"Yes, your father too." I wondered briefly if I'd ever have the opportunity to actually talk with his father.

Roberto asked how his father could be of help and I explained I was going to use his father's writing in my Women in Renaissance Art, which wasn't exactly the truth, but close enough for now. "I worked on the Madonna and Child, often attributed to the artist Masolino, when I was here. It had been damaged in the flood." I didn't mention that his father had written it had been destroyed, and Roberto didn't either. I wondered if he had any idea, if he had any interest or understanding of his father's work.

"And you, Dr. Balducci, *Roberto*," I corrected myself, "how did you become interested in infertility research?" We were halfway to Rome and it seemed we had been talking mostly about me. I could see he had a comfortable way of encouraging people to talk about themselves, and I wondered if he'd acquired this skill as a doctor or if it came to him naturally.

"I started out in obstetrics," he answered. "I wanted to deliver babies, but then I saw young couples come in, heartbroken because they were unable to have children—"

"But, your interest in"—I cleared my throat—"postmenopausal pregnancies?"

He glanced over at me, wondering, I'm sure, how I knew about his work with postmenopausal pregnancies.

"Women these days are very different from our mothers, our grandmothers. Take a woman in her forties, even a woman in her early fifties. With proper nutrition, medical care, exercise, basically a healthy lifestyle, a woman of this age is comparable to a woman in her thirties years ago, many perfectly fit to carry and raise a child." He looked at me as if trying to read something in my face. "How do you feel about this?"

"I'm not sure," I replied cautiously.

"How did you learn about the work we are doing here in Italy?"

I told him I had read something in an American magazine—*Newsweek* or *Time*, I thought. I didn't add that I'd looked him up on the Internet.

"Quite the publicity," Roberto said. "What did you think then?"

"Honestly?"

"Yes, honestly."

"I thought such work was rather, well, rather progressive to take place in Italy."

He laughed. "You don't see Italy as a progressive country?"

I laughed too. "Things do seem to move a bit slower around here." Again I hesitated. "But don't you feel sometimes as if you're playing God?"

"Wasn't it God who gave us the ability to cure disease, to treat the symptoms of many, to provide comfort to those in pain? Surely you don't suggest we abandon medical advancement and let nature, or God, as one might call it, take its course?"

"No, I wouldn't suggest that, but how far can we go and still remain moral?"

"Men are fertile into old age. Why not give women more time?"

"Yes, why not?" My laugh came out a chortle as I wondered how much more time he was suggesting. "I've heard about old men having children," I said, "but it's not exactly as if they are the ones carrying the baby, suffering through the morning sickness, taking care of the child." What did I know about all of this? And did I really want to pursue this discussion? At least Roberto had children. "Your daughters—all girls, five of them? What do they think of your work?"

"They think I'm wonderful," he said. "They think I walk on water," he added with an ironic laughed, a little bit sad, a little bit amused. "Which in my condition is a particularly miraculous feat."

It was the first reference he had made to his disability. I didn't know quite how to react, so in response I said, "Tell me about your daughters."

Maria, he explained, was the oldest, twenty-five, a full-time mother, though she was trained as a nurse. Her husband, Marco, was a pharmacist. They had two-year-old twin boys, a second-generation set, as Roberto's own twins, Anna and

Stella, were twenty-three. He grinned and nodded as if this were a grand accomplishment rather than a quirk of fate or nature. "Anna is still at university in Florence. Stella is married with a three-year-old daughter, studying to be an obstetrician, following in her father's footsteps," he said, an obvious pride in his voice. "Luisa is twenty-one and works at an art gallery in Rome. Bea, the baby, just turned eighteen. Very spoiled. She's the adventurous one, the creative one. I think she's going to be a writer. She's in the States, going to school. That was a hard one to let go. She was only fourteen when her mother died. She took it the hardest. We were close."

He said it in the past tense—we were close—and it made me a little sad.

"You wouldn't believe all the commotion when all five of them were home," he said. "They would bring friends—girlfriends, boyfriends. Things are quiet now."

"You miss it?"

"I do. Although we manage to get together for the holidays."

"I know how it is, all the activity, I mean." I told him how I always spent holidays with my sister and her family, kids and grandkids, my uncle, aunt, and cousins.

We drove a short distance in companionable silence, then he pointed over to the west. "Have you been to Orvieto?" he asked.

"No."

"A beautiful little city perched on the rocks, still maintains much of its medieval character. Maybe we can stop on our way back from Rome."

"Won't that be a little late?"

He raised his shoulders as if to say *we'll see*, then again we were comfortably quiet. I studied the familiar landscape. Now and then the moonlight would reveal an abandoned farmhouse, the silhouette of a row of Italian cypress, olive trees and vineyards undulating along the hillside.

Highway signs announced we were close to Rome. Ten kilometers. Five kilometers. The trip had gone surprisingly fast.

The next few signs identified exits. We pulled off on one marked *CENTRO.*

We went to a place in what appeared to be a predominantly residential section of Rome, to a little neighborhood *osteria* where everyone knew Roberto, addressing him by name—Dr. Balducci. The tables were set with mismatched sets of wooden chairs and red-and-white-checkered tablecloths like you see in the movies. The aroma of garlicky tomato sauce and freshly baked bread filled the small dining room. There were no menus—the padrone stood and visited with us, explaining what his wife had prepared for dinner that evening. We started out with warm minestrone and a basket of bread.

Roberto and I talked about my being in Florence in the sixties, then returning to the States, where students on campus were caught up in political turmoil. I told Roberto how my time away from home had made me aware that the world extended beyond my little hometown in Idaho, the college campus, how my work in Florence made me feel that one really can make a difference.

"I marched with the war protesters, spoke up about civil injustice, demonstrated for women's rights." It was a strange time for me—coming back. I felt an enormous loss, though I didn't go into detail as I told the story, but also a great obligation—to do something, to become something, to take part in something. Maybe I felt I could make up for what I had given up, by doing something grand, though I didn't tell Roberto this. "I think I wanted to save the world then, after I'd saved the treasures of Florence." I shook my head and laughed at such expectation.

"And did you?" he asked with a curious grin.

"Save the world? We're still here, aren't we?"

"Indeed we are."

I told Roberto how I took art classes, both painting and history. "I was terrible—my attempts at painting. But I wanted to know what it felt like to take a blank canvas, to produce a visual statement, to express a feeling, an emotion, a time. It gave me a greater understanding and appreciation, and I felt it was something I wanted to do. I knew I wanted to teach art history, but I felt this was all part of preparing for that."

"I've done some painting and drawing, mostly when I was younger."

"Were you any good?" I asked.

"Perhaps you'll have an opportunity to decide for yourself."

I wondered what he meant by that. During the evening he had made several references to this or that, as if including me in some future activities. Not in an assuming way at all, but I could tell he enjoyed my company, a mutual feeling, something that I hadn't experienced in years, though my dates since Jerry and I divorced had been few and far between. And even now . . . this wasn't exactly a date. But what was it?

"From Idaho, to Italy, to Minnesota for graduate school, then back again?" Roberto traced with his finger along the tablecloth, as if the checkers of the fabric created a map. He had very nice hands and I wondered what it would feel like—his hands touching me. For a brief moment I thought of sterile doctor's hands, bringing new babies into the world, examining women—fat ones, skinny ones, beautiful, shapely ones. I pushed these thoughts out of my mind.

"With a few jogs along the path," I told him. "I taught a couple of years at a junior college in Oregon."

"What made you decide to return to Idaho?" he asked.

"The job offer," I answered, "and family. My sister's husband took a position with a company in Boise." I remembered how I'd moved back to Idaho, thinking it would be temporary. But I'd stayed as much for family as anything. And with Andie it grew and grew. Just when I thought I might move on, she'd produce another little one to get acquainted with, a brand new baby with a wide-open grin.

"And I met someone," I said, feeling I should reveal that I'd been married and divorced. "He was a professor of literature. We married later in life. There were no children." This didn't seem to surprise or offend Roberto, and he asked for no details.

Our *primi piatti*—pasta shells stuffed with cheese and eggplant—arrived at the table.

"And what was it that brought you back to Italy?"

"Again, the job offer, though it's always been my dream to come back to Florence." I didn't explain about Laticia Browning, how this *was* a temporary position.

Roberto and I talked about art, particularly the Renaissance art of Florence. He knew as much about it as anyone I'd ever talked to, including professors I'd had in graduate school.

The padrone delivered our *secondi piatti*, hot and direct from the kitchen—veal and roasted potatoes and zucchini.

"You're very fit, very healthy," Roberto commented as we ate.

I stared at him for a long moment, thinking what a strange thing that was to say.

Roberto blushed. "Forgive me, Suzanne. I sound like a doctor."

I nodded. "You do. You are."

He laughed. "I think what I was trying to say is that you're an attractive woman."

Did I blush now? "Well, thank you." And you are an attractive man, I thought. I wondered if his patients fell in love with him. I'd had a female doctor for the past eighteen years, a switch I'd made after I felt myself falling for my very kind, attentive, very married male doctor.

"Tell me what it is you do to keep in such wonderful shape," Roberto said.

"Mostly, now, I walk." I told him how I walked each morning then stopped for coffee, then visited the market, where I bought fresh fruit and vegetables, arriving early to get first choice. "I eat lots of fresh fruit and vegetables." I didn't mention that I seldom cooked. Then I told him how I missed some of the things I used to do at home. Somehow, I ended up telling him that I skied every winter, tried snowboarding with Andrea's youngest, Tony, how I was a member of a women's softball team in the summer. Roberto told me, without my asking, that he had polio when he was a child, that he'd had a mild case, and was himself often active as a young man. He also explained that he had what they called post-polio syndrome and had been challenged for the past several years. He didn't go into detail, and I wondered if he was speaking of a physical or perhaps even emotional challenge.

Strangely, this conversation wasn't uncomfortable. We shared a bottle of wine, again Roberto drinking very little, me sipping along, feeling little effect, other than a comfortable warmth as we shared our meal, our conversation. Roberto made a fuss over each dish presented by the friendly padrone, who checked on us often. His wife emerged from the kitchen to say hello, kissing Roberto as well as me on each cheek, giggling with pleasure as both Roberto and I professed our delight in the meal she had prepared. I liked the ease and comfort with which Roberto spoke to the padrone and his wife. There was an appealing mixture of kindness, intelligence, and humor in this man, and I found myself thinking I could easily get used to his company.

By the time we ordered coffee and dessert, I was astonished that we had been sitting for almost three hours.

"Grazie, grazie," Roberto thanked our gracious host, who bowed as if he'd just put on an exceptional performance. When we paid the bill—I offered to split, but Roberto insisted; after all, I still hadn't met his father—and got up to leave, we'd yet to verbalize our plans for the rest of the evening. I couldn't help but wonder if he was going to suggest we spend the night together.

A chilly wind whipped through the street as we walked out of the restaurant. I wrapped my scarf around my neck and pulled my collar up.

"It's probably not a good idea, driving back to Florence tonight," he said, almost shyly. He glanced up at the sky. "Looks like it might storm."

I gazed up at the dark, but cloudy, winter night. "Feels like snow," I agreed.

"I've still got my apartment here in Rome. Going back and forth so often from the clinics, it was something I needed. It's small, just one bedroom, but I could sleep on the sofa." He looked at me with a question in his eyes.

I nodded in agreement and soon we arrived at the apartment, within easy walking distance of the restaurant. I wondered for a brief moment if Roberto had planned this all along, if he intended to seduce me. But the place was freezing, not exactly a cozy little love nest. He turned the thermostat up now, explaining he always turned it down when he left for more than a day. The apartment had a tiny living room, a kitchen off that, a small bathroom, which I asked to use shortly after we arrived.

White towels hung from chrome fixtures. A bone-colored ceramic drinking glass and a single green toothbrush perched in a holder set into the cream-colored tile. Everything neat and tidy. I was tempted to look in the medicine cabinet, and then I did. Nothing very interesting. Shaving stuff, toothpaste, a couple of brand-new toothbrushes still in the wrappers, shampoo, Band-Aids, cough medicine. And then, behind the shampoo, a pack of condoms. The box was opened and I looked inside. Two were missing. In his wallet? In the nightstand in the bedroom? Already used?

My God, what was I doing? Snooping through Roberto's personal things, checking out the condoms? Contemplating sex—safe sex or any other kind, for that matter—was something I hadn't done for quite some time. Again I wondered about Roberto's intentions, and then my own.

As I was washing my hands, I noticed two small drawings reflected in the mirror. I turned to examine them. Lovely pencil sketches, the delicate curves of a woman's body created with fine lines and a skillful use of space. Tastefully done nudes. If I'd seen them in a gallery or museum I would have been touched by their subtlety. But in Roberto's apartment, I found them slightly disturbing. Again I wondered what I was doing here. I barely knew this man. I finished in the bathroom. When I walked out, I smelled coffee.

"I thought maybe you could use a cup of coffee," he said. "Takes a while for the heat to kick in." He was sitting on the sofa, his arms resting along the back. We'd hung our overcoats on a wooden rack just inside the door when we came in, Roberto promising me the heat would warm things up soon. At dinner he was wearing a sport coat—more casual than the suit he'd worn that first meeting—and a tie, a bold geometric art nouveau design, a Gustav Klimt, I was sure. I liked the tie and had decided at dinner that I liked a man who would wear such a tie. He'd removed both tie and jacket now and he'd un-buttoned his collar and put on a brown cardigan sweater. It was the first time I'd seen him without a jacket, and for some reason I was surprised by his broad shoulders and thick chest. A thatch of hair was visible in the V of his unbuttoned shirt. I found myself wondering what he looked like without his shirt, then curious about his legs. I thought I could detect the outline of a brace under his slacks. When he made love to a woman was there great caution, in position, in how the bodies came together? I felt a growing apprehension.

"Thank you. Coffee would be nice." I looked around the room. More drawings on the walls, these done in pastels, por-traits of young women. Roberto saw me staring at them.

"My daughters," he said.

"They're beautiful."

"Yes," he said proudly.

I walked over to take a closer look.

"Maria," he said pointing. "The twins, Anna and Stella. They were all about sixteen, at the time each drawing was done, so of course they were done at different times."

I could see a little Balducci in each of them. The cute up-turned nose on Maria and Anna. Three of them were brunette, two blonde. "And this one, it's Luisa, or Bea?"

"Bea."

"Maria and Bea actually look more like twins than the twins."

"Not so much now, but at that age—when Maria was six-teen, yes, I think they probably did. The twins are fraternal."

"Lovely daughters, lovely drawings." I noticed each was signed *R. Balducci*. "You're the artist?"

He nodded.

"You did these?"

"Yes."

"I'm impressed."

"Thank you."

He got up and went into the kitchen. I followed to help with the coffee. The room was tidy, like the bathroom, almost sterile. Obviously a man's, seldom used for cooking. Nothing but a toaster and can opener out on the counters. He poured coffee in two ceramic cups, and I carried them back in and set them on the coffee table. I could hear the heater, sputtering away, trying desperately to warm the place up, but not succeeding at a rapid pace. He sat back on the sofa. I sat in a chair. For several moments neither of us said anything. I was starting to feel uncomfortable again, wondering if this was a good idea. The euphoric feeling, the warmth from the dinner and the wine were wearing off. I was tired. I wanted to be home in my own bed in Florence. I wrapped my arms around my upper body.

"It will warm up, just takes a while. Do you need a sweater?" he asked. "I'm usually the one who's chilly, so I'm not a very good thermostat for others."

"I'm fine." I was wearing a wool skirt and a V-neck sweater over a knit turtleneck shirt, but still felt cold. I thought about getting up and putting my coat back on, but then he might think I was ready to leave, which I was beginning to think might not be a bad idea. I couldn't quite think of what to say or do now, or how to make the situation feel less awkward.

I cradled the warm mug in my hands, attempting to draw warmth from the hot liquid as if it might spread through the rest of my body, wondering if we had used up all our conversation on the drive from Florence and during our long dinner.

"I have something I'd like to show you," Roberto said slowly, almost cautiously.

"Okay," I replied with the same caution.

He grabbed his crutches, which he'd leaned up against the sofa, got up, went into the bedroom, and came back carrying a large manila envelope. He set it down in front of me.

"What is this?" I asked.

He motioned for me to open it.

I picked up the envelope, then slowly reached inside and pulled out a sketchpad, rather dog-eared with several loose pages sticking out. It looked old and smelled musty, like it had been stashed away in a trunk or attic for years. I opened it. The drawing on the first page showed a group of people at a sidewalk café like you see everywhere in Europe. Nothing extraordinary, but okay. "Nice," I said, then looked up at Roberto.

"Here," he said, flipping over several pages until he came to a drawing of a young woman with long, straight, dark hair. She wore jeans and a pea jacket, like a sailor would wear, something popular with girls during the sixties. I remembered having one myself. It was that terrible, heavy, itchy wool that picked up lint like sticky tape and I remembered forever plucking little fuzz balls off that coat. I turned to the next drawing. The same girl. She was slender and had a stance a bit like a model's—exaggerated long, thin legs. She stood, gazing up, her hands in her back pockets. I looked at the next drawing. Just the face now, a thoughtful expression, not quite a smile. My discomfort expanded once more. Again I looked up at Roberto.

"Remember when I told you I thought we'd met before?" he asked.

"Where did these drawings come from?" I shivered. It was so cold.

"I did them years ago right after the flood. My father was working at Santa Croce, helping with the Cimabue. I'd gone over with him—it was late December, just before Christmas. Back then, I took my sketchpad with me everywhere. We were sitting around, waiting, I think for the panels to dry," he said and laughed. "It was all waiting back then, and this art restorer, came in."

Stefano, I thought.

"He was accompanied by a beautiful young woman. She

was American. I knew that right away, from the way she dressed, the air of confidence about her. I did a sketch, then another quickly, to get her expression—she had such a sweetness, yet a determination about her. I saw the way she looked at the man when he came down from examining the Cimabue. I've never forgotten that look." Roberto studied me for a moment before continuing. "I saw the girl once more, at the San Lorenzo market, haggling with a vendor over a pair of gloves. I followed her for a couple of blocks, but never worked up the courage to talk to her. I saw her just those two times, but her image stayed with me. I was at a rather romantic age, just sixteen, very much aware of girls, and I had this idea I was Dante—although as an artist, not a poet. This woman my Beatrice. I knew I'd never see her again, but her image would remain with me. My muse. My inspiration."

I flipped another page. More of the same. My hand shook as I put the sketches back in the envelope. "This isn't where you take me down to the cellar into a room papered with my portraits, is it?" I said it as if I was joking, but my voice quivered.

He shook his head.

"It's so damned cold in here," I said.

"I could get you a blanket."

"No." This single word came out with a force I myself hadn't expected.

He looked at me apologetically, but said nothing.

"Roberto, I think I should probably leave."

"Go back to Florence?"

"I don't know. I just don't think I feel right about staying here."

"I've frightened you?" He looked concerned, but I still felt ill at ease.

"It's just that this is . . . creepy." I couldn't think of a more appropriate word. I wasn't really afraid, but I was definitely unnerved.

"It is you, though, isn't it?" he asked, a kindness in his voice, a doctor's voice, comforting a distressed patient.

"I don't know." But I did. I did know it was me. I had gone over that day with Stefano. I had watched him come down from the Cimabue. I remembered the feeling so clearly, the utter love and devotion I felt that day. And now this. What was the meaning of this strange revelation? That Roberto had been there, at this most intimate moment?

"Would you call a cab for me, please?" I asked. "I'll stay in Rome, but I'd prefer not to stay here tonight."

"Yes, of course, Suzanne. If that's what you want."

I nodded. "It is."

He got up and went into the kitchen. He came back and told me he'd called a cab and booked a room for me at a nearby hotel.

We waited silently for the taxi. I went in to use the bathroom again, because I didn't want to talk to him, and I felt like I might throw up. I didn't, but I sat on the closed toilet seat for several minutes, staring at the drawings on the wall.

When I came out he asked, "Are you okay?"

I nodded, but I didn't feel I could say any more. It was all too much for one night—the drive from Florence, the flirting, the attention, and then the revelation that he had seen me over thirty years ago with Stefano.

"I'll call you tomorrow?" he asked. Again he sounded concerned. "Tomorrow morning? What time?"

"About nine is fine," I replied, offering a faint smile.

The cab driver came up to escort me down, obviously at Roberto's request. He said good night to me and handed the driver some bills.

I turned the heat up in the hotel room and piled extra blankets on the bed that night, but I couldn't stop shivering. Finally, after I was able to clear my mind of Roberto Balducci, I slept. The next morning I got up before eight and checked out of the hotel. When I tried to pay, the man at the desk said it had been taken care of. I wasn't sure how I felt about this, but decided since I was here I'd spent the day alone in Rome. I had seen little of the city during my first trip to Italy. Roxie and I had intended to go to Rome, after Florence. But then—the flood, our plans, *my life* changed. I had left to go home to the States from Rome, but had less than a day to look around.

Now, by this strange turn of events, and the word *strange* played heavy in my mind as I tried to comprehend what had just happened with Roberto Balducci, I found myself once more in Rome. So I spent the day as a tourist. I went to the Trevi Fountain, climbed the Spanish Steps, and explored the Roman Forum. I tried desperately not to think of Roberto. Did he call this morning? I didn't want to talk to him, but I wasn't sure why. I felt in a bizarre way as if I was being stalked, yet it was I who had contacted him initially. He wasn't looking for me. And the sketches had been done by an innocent boy, an infatuated child.

He *was* younger than me—he said he was sixteen at the time. I had been nineteen. It was funny that Roberto said he could tell I was American by the air of confidence. I had never felt confident. Awkward and unsure more likely. Yet that day at Santa Croce, maybe there had been an intimation of confidence, an inner glow that had come from Stefano's invitation to accompany him to Santa Croce to view the Cimabue. Perhaps a confidence that comes to one from being chosen by another.

I went to the UPIM department store and bought a package of underwear. I hadn't planned on spending the weekend in Rome, so I had brought nothing other than the clothes on my back. I always carried a toothbrush and small toothpaste in my purse. I'd thought about using the shampoo at the hotel Friday night—it was a nice hotel and had a little basket of lotion, shampoo, and cream rinse on the vanity—but I was too confused and uncomfortable to consider the chore of washing my hair, so I twisted it into my usual knot Saturday morning and secured it with my clip. I found a room at a cheap *pensione* that night, and spent all day Sunday at the Vatican. I waited over an hour in line to get into the Sistine Chapel, then stood in awe gazing up, amazed at Michelangelo's colors brought forth from the recent cleaning. And I couldn't help but think of the Masolino Madonna, the dark photo in the art book, contrasting so with the vivid colors of the panel restored and cleaned after the flood.

That evening I took the train back to Florence.

10

MONDAY I FOUND a message on my machine from Roberto, checking to make sure I'd made it home safely. I wondered what he had thought when he called the hotel Saturday and found I'd already left. I felt embarrassed about what I'd done, about how poorly I'd treated him, but I wasn't quite ready to return his call.

I went for coffee with Regina Bonaminio. She got her usual, a double espresso, and I ordered a cappuccino, evidence, Regina teased, that I had not acclimated—the Italians drink cappuccino only at breakfast. We sat, paying extra for the privilege rather than standing at the bar where the locals buzzed in and out, gulping down a quick espresso, then continuing on their way.

"We're on for Thursday evening?" she asked.

"I'll be there." She'd invited Giorgio's friend from the Uffizi for dinner Thursday night and I was eager to see if I could learn anything from him about the Masolino Madonna.

"Have you heard from Roberto Balducci yet?"

"Actually, yes." I told Regina about Roberto, a condensed version of how he had set up an appointment for me with his father, but then had to cancel, and how we'd ended up in Rome at his apartment after dinner. "It was fun at first, but then he brought out these sketches he'd done of me years ago, and it got pretty creepy."

"He got creepy?" Regina's huge dark eyes widened with concern. "You knew him from when you were in Italy before?"

"No and no," I answered. "I didn't know him, and he's actually a very nice man. But, the situation just felt creepy. I left and stayed at a hotel."

"And now you regret it?" Regina pushed her hair behind her ear. She was wearing the most fantastic silver earrings—an interlocking series of small raindrops, or maybe teardrops.

I shook my head. "I wasn't ready for that."

"He saves these sketches of you from—what? Like thirty-some years ago?" She dumped a packet of sugar in her cup and stirred it around in that black, thick mud, then another packet and milk from a small silver pitcher. How did she stay so thin? Every time we went for coffee, she'd add a packet or two of sugar. Maybe she needed it to feed that nervous energy. Her fingers were always busy—dumping sugar, stirring, playing around with her napkin.

"I never even met him," I said. "We just happened to be at the same place at the same time."

"Fate!" Regina said with a knowing grin. "Has to be."

"Jeez, Regina," I said, smiling at her enthusiasm.

"It's romantic." She was still young enough to believe in fateful romance. "He must have been in love with you."

"Childish infatuation at the most," I said, then explained how he'd seen me when I went to Santa Croce with one of the restorers I'd been working with at the Limonaia. "He was much younger than I was. Guess he still is," I added with a dry laugh. "He was just a kid. Not that I possessed any great maturity at the time."

"How much?" she asked. "Like how much younger?"

"Three years, I think."

"That's nothing! My dad is four years younger than my mom. Besides, women are younger nowadays. Look at you."

She grinned and waved a hand at me, as if she expected me to take a look. "When you told me you helped out during the flood, I couldn't believe you were that old. I thought you must have been a child at the time." She giggled, but then said, "No, really, I'm serious."

"You're being very generous, Regina." I shook my head. "Roberto Balducci says women *are* younger now, younger than our mothers or grandmothers were at our age. In fact, you won't believe what he does." I told her about Roberto Balducci's research, his work with postmenopausal women. Then, as if I wanted Regina to know everything about him, I even told her he was on crutches.

Regina's eyes widened further, but she didn't comment on the absurdity of pregnant postmenopausal women. "Does that bother you? His being on crutches?"

"I don't think so, though I did wonder . . . I mean when we were in the apartment alone."

We were both silent for a moment. "Call him," she said. "He sounds like an intelligent, interesting person, and you still want to speak with his father, right?"

I nodded. "Yes, I still haven't had that opportunity."

"And his father probably knew this Leonetti."

"Possibly." I picked at my napkin and twisted it, then set it back on the table, smoothing it with my fingers.

"What's the matter?" Regina asked. "That name, Leonetti, you practically leap up to the roof at its mention. Like what's with this Leonetti? You think this guy has something to do with the painting you're looking for?"

"There's more to this story than I've told you," I admitted.

She stared at me, waiting, nodding her head as if to say *I knew it*.

"I was in love with him. Deeply. Madly. Passionately," I said dramatically.

"You're serious?" she asked, as if she couldn't read the truth through the drama.

I nodded. "I was very young, but yes, very much in love."

"What happened?"

"He was married."

She looked at me with a mixture of concern and excitement. "Things change," she offered. "Maybe his circumstances have changed. You need to find him, you know. To see if he knows anything about the painting. And also," she added cautiously, "for yourself."

FOR THE REST of the morning, thoughts of both Roberto and Stefano faded in and out of my mind. A perfect, young Stefano. Then Roberto Balducci, with his infectious smile, his ease in conversation, his less-than-perfect body.

We'd had fun—driving to Rome, dinner at his little neighborhood *osteria*. But then, his revelation about being at Santa Croce the day I went over there with Stefano. As I pulled up that image, I was outside the picture, observing the young woman from Roberto Balducci's sketches, gazing up at Stefano as he studied the ravaged Cimabue crucifix. I kept trying to place a young Roberto in the scene—the boy sitting on the pile of debris, sketching? As this memory shifted and turned, it all merged together—my past mingled strangely with the present, perhaps even my future.

I couldn't explain why these drawings had upset me, because I wasn't sure why they had. In a sense I felt as if I'd come in contact with Stefano again, and at that moment—sitting in the apartment in Rome with Roberto Balducci—I was not prepared for that encounter.

After class I checked my e-mail and found one from Andrea. She'd attached a couple photos of the two youngest grandkids and that made me smile. She said she'd just talked to Dad, he was doing fine, and that my old friend Roxie Royal had called. "What a character," Andie wrote. She said Roxie was down at her mom's in Twin Falls, and she went through a box of old stuff in her bedroom. Her mom still had all her mementos from high school and our trip to Europe. Roxie found some old photos with a double set she'd evidently intended to give to me. They weren't the same ones I'd brought to the mall. She'd called Andrea to get my address.

The next morning I kept thinking about Regina's suggestion that I call Roberto Balducci and tell him I still wanted to talk with his father. I knew I would have to say something about my taking off Saturday before his call. I'd tell him I wasn't feeling well and had left early, apologize for not being there to take his call. Maybe he hadn't even called. Maybe he thought *I* was the weirdo. After all, I'd gone without protest all the way to Rome, to his apartment that night, and then taken off like some kind of psycho. But he *had* called and left a message at school. He was kind enough to be concerned that I'd made it back home. I owed him the courtesy of a call. I phoned and got his machine and left a message, telling him I was back safely in Florence.

After working in my office that afternoon, I walked down to the first floor and found Roberto in the courtyard. "I was just on my way up to see you. Time for coffee?"

We talked of nothing other than the weather as we walked. It was sunny, though still cold. In the daylight I noticed his eyes were a pale blue, with tiny flecks of gold, and there was a hint of auburn in his hair.

We found a bar and went inside.

"I owe you an apology," he said after we ordered. "When I called Saturday morning and you'd already left, I realized I'd had no right to haul you off to Rome, take you up to the apartment, and show you the sketches."

"I'm a grown woman. I went voluntarily," I replied, but I was glad he had apologized first.

"I could see you were frightened by the sketches. I'm not sure why. I found it interesting myself that our paths had crossed once long ago and now again. But, from the viewpoint of a woman, I should have presented my discovery in a less threatening way. I apologize. Thank you for calling today."

That old comfort I'd felt before he took me to his apartment and unveiled the sketches was returning.

"What are your plans for this Saturday?" he asked.

"No plans just yet." I guess that was settled. We were going to be friends again.

"Maria has suggested we come for lunch. She won't tell Papa you are coming, then if he is feeling well perhaps you could visit for a while. You'll enjoy Maria, her husband, Marco, and the twins. They live in the country. It could be an enjoyable afternoon. I would be privileged if you would join me."

He smiled warmly as he said this. *He would be privileged.* "Yes," I said, "I'd be happy to join you."

"Good." He reached out and put his hand on mine. His touch was light and warm, and lingered for only a moment, and I realized it was the first time he had touched me since we shook hands the day we met.

11

REGINA, WHO DIDN'T have a car, had offered to take the bus to come get me Thursday night, but I said I was sure I could find her place if she gave me directions and bus numbers. I started out early, but was still fifteen minutes late.

Giorgio and his friend Alberto Mazzone were sitting in the living room with the children, Giorgino and Donatella, when I arrived. The two children looked very much like Regina—small-boned, with thick, dark curly hair and enormous brown eyes. In fact, Giorgio looked very much like Regina. One of those odd—or perhaps not so odd—couples, perfectly matched, resembling each other so closely they could have been brother and sister.

The children followed us through the apartment as Regina gave me a quick tour. Donatella was five, her little brother, Giorgino, named after his father, was three. They shared a small bedroom with bunk beds. Donatella, the talkative one, explained in detail each item in the room. *"Questo è il mio letto. Questa è la mia bambola."* She bounced up and down with enthusiasm, first on the floor, then on the lower bunk, though she explained that she slept on the top, as Giorgino was too little and he might fall. They were darling children, very outspoken, not the least bit shy—children raised in a creative environment where their opinions were valued. Regina seemed not at all concerned by all the bouncing, jumping, and jabbering, which, of course, was all in Italian, but surprisingly not at all difficult for me to understand. While Regina left for a moment to check on dinner, I sat on the lower bunk with Donatella as she explained her doll had been a birthday gift from her grandmother, and little Giorgino pulled one toy after another from a toy box to share with me. I laughed a little at the thought that I was completely capable of carrying on a conversation in Italian with a five- and a three-year-old.

Regina showed me some of her husband's work. He was a jewelry designer who sold to local retailers, and also in Milan and Rome, she told me proudly. I liked his work. He used mostly silver, and set stones in modern, inspired-by-nature designs. He had a small work area set up in a corner of their bedroom.

Several of Regina's bronze sculptures were displayed throughout the apartment—a near life-size statue of an old man in the living room, a fairy on a goose in the children's bedroom, and an abstract piece composed of a series of interlocking bands, which she called *Immaginazione*, in the master bedroom. I was fascinated by the variety of paintings, photographs, and sculptures on every table and shelf, in every corner, on every wall. Several, Regina told me, were trades with other artists. Even the children's artwork, in their bedroom and clamped on the refrigerator with magnets, which in themselves were works of art—some type of dough the children had sculpted to look like miniature loaves of bread—was interesting. I'm always intrigued by the homes of creative people.

We sat in the living room and visited before dinner. The children had gone to their bedroom to play, an option their mother had offered them, and I turned my attention to Giorgio's friend. Alberto seemed very young, and I doubted he had been here during the flood, but I thought, since he worked in the Uffizi restoration department, maybe he could provide me with some information.

"Giorgio tells me you were here during the flood as a restorer," he said.

"Actually, just a volunteer," I corrected. "I worked first at the National Library, then at the Limonaia."

"Something to drink, Professor Cunningham?" Giorgio offered. "Scotch, whiskey, wine, a soda?"

"Suzanne, please call me Suzanne. Maybe some wine, but I'll wait for dinner."

"What an exciting time," Alberto said. "I wish I could have participated, but I was only two at the time. Of course, I certainly wouldn't want it to happen again."

"No, it was dreadful."

He asked about the flood, what it had been like, specifically what I'd done. I felt like the old soldier retelling battle stories. The young man listened, rapt, filled with a reverence and respect that was almost embarrassing.

"Regina said you are interested in a painting, a Madonna and Child, for one of the classes you are teaching. Something you saw years ago, during the sixties, a painting that may no longer be in the collection."

"Yes," I said, feeling as if Regina and I were coconspirators. I wanted to get access to museum records, but didn't want to share the information that I thought the painting might have mysteriously disappeared after the flood. "Are there records dating back that far at the museum? Something I might be able to take a look at?"

"It was all rather primitive back then." He spoke as if we were referring to something that had happened during the Stone Age. "We had no computers. Records were kept by hand, but, yes, I am sure I could find some."

"Professor Cunningham had an associate," Regina interjected, "a restorer by the name of Stefano Leonetti. Do you know him?"

"Leonetti?" Alberto pressed his fingers together and tapped them thoughtfully to his lips. "Stefano Leonetti? No, I don't recall that name, but perhaps the head of the department, Dr.

Giuliana Garzoni, would know him. She worked as a restorer then, after the flood."

Alberto wrote down the information about the Masolino, including the time period in which it was most likely created, a description, and approximate size, on a pad Regina had placed on the table. He nodded as he scribbled his notes, shaking the pen when the ink started to fade. Regina handed him another.

"Please, if you'll include in your research paintings currently in the museum's collection as well as those owned by the museum at that time," I said, then explained the painting I was interested in might have been painted by Masolino, but most likely not labeled as such. I said nothing about my belief that the painting described as destroyed in the flood had been rescued and restored, and Alberto asked no further questions.

12

THE FOLLOWING AFTERNOON, I finally made it over to the Church of Santa Maria del Carmine to look at the Masaccio and Masolino frescoes in the Brancacci Chapel. The frescoes had been cleaned since I had seen them so many years ago, the colors more vibrant than I could have imagined. The leaves, which had probably been added in the later part of the seventeenth century to cover the nude figures of Adam and Eve—an attempt at censorship by the prudish Cosimo III— had been removed during the most recent cleaning. How society's sense of morality changes over time, I thought.

My first visit to Santa Maria del Carmine had been with Stefano, just a week after our first kiss. Before we became lovers. I remember how excited he was to share Masaccio and Masolino's collaborative work with me.

As we walked, he'd told me that, even though water had entered the Brancacci as the Arno tore through Florence, the frescoes were almost twenty feet above the level of the floor and had been relatively unharmed.

When we entered the chapel, I looked up and my eyes darted from scene to scene—the larger being New Testament

depictions with Christ and St. Peter. The artists had used architectural backgrounds from Renaissance Florence, similar to
buildings still standing in the city to this day. Many of the figures were dressed in Renaissance-type costumes. Artists of
this period often placed architectural structures and even
contemporary personalities in biblical scenes. At the Medici
Chapels on an earlier visit, Stefano had pointed out various
members of the esteemed family of Florence right there in the
scene with the Magi—Lorenzo il Magnifico himself playing
the role of King Kaspar. Under Stefano's influence I began to
see art in so many ways—a visual delight based on details of
color, composition, texture, contrast; a history, often of biblical
and present times all in one painting; a spiritual experience; and
sometimes even a little game—a Where's Waldo–type puzzle
of patrons.

Stefano directed me to the smaller scene on the first wall inside the chapel, Adam and Eve with a sword-thrusting angel
soaring over them. Then, on the opposite wall, another Adam
and Eve, standing next to a tree with a snakelike figure (with a
woman's face, a medieval view of the woman as temptress)
wrapped around it. Stefano asked me to look closely at the figures in these two small frescoes, the first called *Expulsion from
the Garden of Eden*, the second entitled *The Temptation*. I
could see instantly which was the Masolino, which the Masaccio. Stefano had explained on the way over to the church that
the Masaccio was considered a much superior and innovative
work because of the way in which the artist had used a single
light source with defined highlights and shadows, how he had
incorporated perspective and foreshortening, and how he had
used realistic, rather than idealized, human figures.

Masaccio's Adam and Eve in the *Expulsion* looked common to me, and not at all beautiful. Eve with her thick waist
and wide hips. As I gazed up, I thought the face on Masaccio's
Eve homely and distorted. Granted she looked distraught—
after all she'd just been banished from Paradise, who wouldn't
be a bit upset? She covered her body with great shame, her
eyes were pressed into oblique slits, and her mouth hung open

in such a grotesque way one could almost hear her wail as the angel hovered overhead with raised sword.

Masolino's Adam and Eve, on the other hand, looked rather elegant. Noble figures with beautiful faces. Eve's face closely resembled the Madonna's in the painting we had tended at the Limonaia—her delicate, doll-like lips, fine straight nose, beautiful brows, and Botticelli-style eyes. These figures were naked, as were Masaccio's Adam and Eve, but they were not ashamed. Were Masolino's figures so exquisitely rendered because he had captured this moment before the Fall? Adam and Eve still filled with innocence? An innocence soon enough to be tainted by the sin they were about to commit?

I couldn't possibly tell Stefano that I found the Masolino so much more appealing than the Masaccio. Surely this would be artistic blasphemy.

"Eve looks very much like the Madonna we worked on at the Limonaia," I said instead, staring up at Masolino's rendering of *The Temptation*.

"Yes," he replied, "one of the reasons I believe our Madonna and Child is a Masolino."

"And how is our Masolino doing?" I asked, liking the fact that Stefano referred to it as *ours*. I hadn't seen the painting since it had been moved to the Fortezza da Basso, where Stefano now spent much of his time.

"Very well," he said. "Would you like to go visit sometime?"

"Yes, I would."

It wasn't until much later, after we had become lovers, that he took me to the Fortezza. He introduced me to the other restorers and volunteers, some of whom I already knew. Pietro, Stefano's assistant, was also spending much of his time at the Fortezza now.

As we walked through the workrooms, I recognized many of the paintings that had been brought over from the Limonaia. When we came to Masolino's Madonna and Child, Stefano touched me lightly on the shoulder, and then took my hand, which made me quiver. We stood silently. I took a deep breath. The little painting was beautiful, the colors vivid, the mold destroyed, the buckled wooden panel smooth. The patches of mulberry paper had been removed. I looked at Stefano and he grinned as if we shared something very special.

"She's beautiful," I whispered, and Stefano agreed. *"Bellissima,"* he said in a soft voice.

As I studied the panel, I imagined Masolino himself standing back, admiring his work, wet and glistening, the odor of pigment still lingering in the air. And perhaps, because we had saved it, Stefano and I felt a similar pride that afternoon.

And now, over thirty years later as I stood in the Brancacci Chapel, studying the face of Masolino's Eve—so much like his precious Madonna—I had the strangest sensation, and I knew my job was not yet finished.

13

ROBERTO BALDUCCI PICKED me up outside my apartment on Saturday just before noon. It was a gorgeous day, still cold, but the sun was out, the sky a crisp clear winter blue without a single wisp of a cloud.

When we pulled onto the autostrada, Roberto explained again that Maria and Marco lived in the country. "They have a little farmhouse a few miles south of the city. I promise I'll have you home before sunset," he added with a grin.

"No surprises this time?"

"I'll never promise 'no surprises.' Isn't that what makes life worth living, Professor Cunningham?"

"Perhaps you're right, Dr. Balducci." I laughed and we continued a comfortable chat as we drove.

Maria and her husband, Marco, did indeed live in the country, in a small stone farmhouse complete with chickens pecking away at the cold, hard, winter earth in front of an ancient barn. An old tabby cat basked in a patch of midday sunshine, and a friendly Border collie greeted us as we got out of the car and started up to the house. I stopped and stroked her behind the ears as her tail slapped back and forth in excitement. "What a beautiful puppy you are," I said. Oh, how I missed my Rousseau.

"I think she speaks Italian," Roberto said with a tease in his voice.

"I think she understands the ear rubbing." The collie nuzzled into my hands, fully participating in the ear rub, just like Rousseau always did.

The door of the house swung open and a tall dark-haired young woman and two darling little curly-headed blond boys waved as she called out, *"Buon giorno."* Maria greeted her father with a kiss on each cheek. Roberto introduced me as Professor Cunningham. Maria took my hand, and the boys latched on to their grandfather as we all went into the house. Roberto's daughter was a surprisingly tall woman, and Marco, her husband, who soon joined us, was at least six-foot-three. He was very quiet. I didn't think he spoke much English, which we were conversing in, since I'm sure Roberto had conveyed that I spoke little Italian. The twins, Carlo and Leo, were just two years old, chubby little pink-cheeked angels, and very shy, hiding behind their mother and their grandfather, whom Maria called Nonno, the Italian word for Grandpa, when she spoke to the children, and Papa when she spoke directly to Roberto.

Maria said her grandfather was doing well today; perhaps after lunch I could visit for a while. She always served Nonno his meals in the bedroom. It was a bit confusing, these references to Papa and Nonno, as it often is in a household of several generations, where a person plays many roles. As we sat and visited, Maria asking with interest about my work, the two little boys climbed on and off their grandfather's lap, unaware of any disability, then warmed up to me, looking, staring with childlike innocence, examining this stranger who had arrived with their Nonno. I sensed Maria was doing the same, not with the unguarded approach of the children, but she was studying me. I wondered what Roberto had told her.

The smaller twin—I could see they were fraternal, not identical—kept eyeing my purse, then finally he touched it and

whispered something in my ear. He spoke so softly I wasn't
sure what he said.

"Carlo, Carlo," Maria said with a grin, "no." She shook her
finger at him.

Although Carlo was the smaller of the two boys, he was the
more aggressive.

"He's gotten into a very bad habit of asking for gum and
candy," Maria told me. "Whenever he sees a woman's purse,
he thinks there is gum or candy inside."

"Mi dispiace," I said raising my shoulders, and smiling
apologetically at Carlo. *"Non ho dolci."* I remembered that
was the word for sweets, which I thought also included candy.
I couldn't recall the word for gum, but I didn't have any of that
either. Then I remembered I had a box of Tic Tacs. "I've got a
pack of breath mints. Do you mind if I give him one?" I asked
Maria. "Or would it be too strong?"

"No, that would be fine." She laughed. "He'll eat anything."

I pulled them out of my purse. The little boy grinned with
delight. I shook them to make a rattling sound. He giggled. I
opened the plastic container. He held out his hand. His brother
had now joined us. He smiled and held out his hand too.

"Grazie, Nonna," Carlo said.

He was calling me Grandmother.

"No, no," Maria corrected, a little embarrassed, I thought.
"Professoressa Cunningham."

Carlo attempted to say my name, without great success. It
was too much of a mouthful for him.

We all laughed and the two little boys grinned and giggled
even more, attempting to pronounce the words over and over
again, in a singsong fashion, coming out sillier and sillier with
each attempt. "Profo Coonie," little Carlo said, grinning at
me. "Propro Coochie," Leo said, imitating his brother. "Propo
Cuckoo," Carlo came back. Then they giggled some more as if
they'd been tickled on the tummy. I glanced at Roberto, who
had a look of utter delight on his face.

Lunch was served in the country kitchen on a big wooden
table, and I wondered if Maria was trying to impress me. The

meal consisted of antipasto, salad, pasta, and *bistecca alla fiorentina*. Maria seemed a bit nervous, and I heard Marco teasing her in the working area of the kitchen. I'm not sure what he said, but I think it had something to do with the use of the good dishes. Was this just Maria's style? Or had she brought out the fine china because I was a professor? Or because they thought I was Papa-Nonno's prospective girlfriend?

I felt comfortable and welcomed.

For dessert Maria served a beautiful torte, and when we finished, I was completely stuffed and satisfied. She put the children down for a nap, and then she and Roberto took me in to see the senior Roberto Balducci.

The room was small with a single window, the walls bare except for a crucifix above the bed. It was very clean, almost antiseptic, yet an odor permeated the air, a smell that took me back to my grandmother's last days, as if living flesh had begun to decay on the journey toward death.

"*Nonno, Nonno,*" Maria said, speaking in a soft voice, "*la professoressa Cunningham è qui.*"

The old man sat up with some help from Maria and Roberto. "*Acqua, per favore,*" he whispered. A small table with a tray sat beside the bed, filled with an assortment of medications, a box of tissue, a water glass and pitcher, several magazines and books. Maria lifted a glass to his lips and gave him a drink, then wiped his chin.

"Papa"—Roberto bent over and kissed the old man on the cheek—"remember, I told you about Professor Cunningham." Roberto spoke English. "She's interested in knowing more about something you wrote. She was here during the flood."

Signor Balducci nodded as if Roberto were repeating an earlier conversation. "*Sì, sì.*" The old man looked at me— straight in the eye, just like his son. The elder Roberto Balducci's eyes were very dark and his hair thin wisps of white, matted in places, sticking up here and there in others, as one who had been bedridden for some time. Patches of pink flesh showed between the sparse white hair. He held out his hand, which was spotted and veiny.

I took his hand. *"Piacere,"* I said. He placed his other hand over mine and held it for a long moment. Then he motioned for me to sit in a chair next to the bed. Maria had left the room, but Roberto stayed, standing behind me. I thought maybe I should offer him the chair, but when I looked back, he seemed to be reading my thoughts and nodded for me to sit.

"The material I'm interested in was regarding a painting, one often credited to Masolino, a fifteenth-century Madonna and Child," I began tentatively. "It was at the Uffizi, taken over to the Limonaia for restoration."

"Ah, yes, the Limonaia." He spoke slowly, each word an effort. "For the lemon trees, but used to save the art. Rows and rows, the paintings, like the patients in a hospital. And we did. We did save them, so many we saved." He took a rough, ragged breath before continuing. "I told you he would make a good husband, didn't I, Paolina? Five children, he gave you five lovely daughters."

"Papa," Roberto said softly, "this is Professor Cunningham. She's come to talk about the Masolino, the painting. You wrote about it several years ago."

The old man laughed, then coughed. He shook his head as if pushing out the confusion, or perhaps realizing that he had made an embarrassing mistake. He reached for a tissue lying next to him on the bed and wiped his mouth with a trembling hand. "Ah, yes, Paolina is gone, isn't she, Roberto?"

"Sì, Papa."

"Now, what is it again . . . Cunningham—Professor, is it? Yes, now I remember, you are an American? You teach at the university in Florence?"

"Yes," I answered. "The Masolino," I continued cautiously, "you wrote it had been destroyed."

"But many were saved." He smiled, then fell back, resting on the pillow, staring up at the ceiling. "I am an old man. I am dying. But I have had a good life. I have seen what many have not. I saw the destruction of the city. It was November fourth. Do you know they carried paintings that morning? Through the Vasari Corridor, over the bridge. The water rose. So many concerned, not for themselves, but the art. Then people from all over the world coming to Firenze to work with the citizens of Florence." He reached out for my hand again and looked at me intently. "You remember," he said with a raspy laugh, "the smell? The river rose and the putrid smell. Oh, the smell."

"Yes, I remember." I laughed too.

The old man closed his eyes and let go of my hand.

After several moments of silence, I looked back at Roberto. He was staring down at his father, then his eyes met mine with a kind of hopelessness. I glanced back at the old man.

"But he gets lonely," the elder Balducci said suddenly. "He doesn't tell me. But I know." The old man grabbed my hand again, his grasp tight as he pulled himself up, leaned into me, and whispered conspiratorially in his hoarse, strained voice, "My son is a very good man, but he gets very lonely. I know how it is to be lonely." He placed his head back on the pillow now, then looked at Roberto. "Tell Maria I am ready for my nap. If you will excuse me, Professor Cunningham. It is not a pleasant thing to get old and weak." He shook his head. "It is not good when one is so dependent on others, yet it is good because we know we are loved. We know we are loved when we must ask so much of others. Come again, please come again."

I stood. "*Grazie*, Signor Balducci." When I turned, Maria was standing with Roberto.

"Nonno is quite tired now," she said.

"Yes, thank you," I said.

As I started out of the room, the old man cleared his throat. "Professor Cunningham." I turned. "No, no . . . ," he whispered, as if he didn't want me to leave. Then, "no," this time as if a warning. Again he looked me directly in the eye, and pointed one trembling finger. "Stefano Leonetti," he said.

14

IF ROBERTO NOTICED how shaken I was, he didn't show it. He seemed in a light, happy mood as we talked during the drive back to Florence.

"Maria's children are darling," I said, attempting to put the same cheery tone in my voice. "And what a wonderful meal."

"Maria has a way of making her guests feel comfortable."

"She does. Thank you for inviting me."

We drove onto the autostrada and Roberto picked up speed. "I'm sorry Papa wasn't more helpful. With the medication, the pain, his mind is not always clear."

I had been puzzling over the meaning of the elder Balducci's last words since Roberto and I left Maria's. Was he telling me something about the Masolino Madonna? Was he telling me I must contact Stefano Leonetti to find the missing painting? Or in a brief moment of clarity had he retrieved a memory from the past? I wondered if he could possibly have remembered seeing me with Stefano years ago at Santa Croce. That seemed impossible.

"He's dying?" I asked.

"Pancreatic cancer. There isn't much hope. He's been

hanging on longer than his doctors predicted. We try to keep him comfortable. He doesn't want to die in the hospital. I'm not able to care for him, but Maria, ah, Maria is an angel! She studied to be a nurse, but she wants to stay home with the children while they're young. It's a blessing for Papa that she is able to care for him."

"Yes," I said, "a blessing to be cared for by those you love. Maria *is* an angel." I wondered about Roberto's mother now, as I had several times since Roberto had told me she lived in Venice. I was curious why she wasn't with her husband. Was her health fragile too, and would it be too much for Maria to care for them both?

"The children were quite taken with you," Roberto said.

"They're sweet children, and I think you can impress kids if you have a little goodie tucked away in your purse. Those Tic Tacs certainly did the job."

"They want me to bring you back again, Profo Cuckoo." He laughed and so did I.

I thought about little Carlo's calling me Nonna. "Paolina, she was your wife?"

"Yes."

The sky was scattered with clouds now, fluffy and white, casting patches of shadows across the hillsides.

"You like children," Roberto commented.

"Very much," I said.

"Do you ever regret it, not having your own?" he asked as we approached the exit into Florence. I might have found his question unkind or invasive, but I didn't. Maybe because he was a doctor, used to dealing with women on emotional topics, or maybe because I felt we had established some sort of intimacy, which I was sure he felt too.

"I did when I was thirty," I answered, "then even forty, but not so much anymore. I've learned that we don't always get what we want."

He nodded. Surely Roberto knew what it was to be disappointed, to accept what life dealt.

"Quite frankly I'm content now to enjoy other people's

children." I told him about visiting Regina and her family, and how much I enjoyed my nephews' children.

"You could still do it, you know."

"Are you offering me your services?" I laughed and maybe even blushed. "Your professional services?"

"I'm a doctor with ethics," he said with a smile. "I don't solicit. A woman would have to come to me."

I looked over and offered a smile of my own as we pulled onto my street and slowed. There was no parking in front of the building, and I took it he was dropping me off here. I hadn't thought about whether I would invite him up, but he obviously hadn't been planning that either.

As we pulled next to the curb and stopped, Roberto asked, "Could we get together again sometime this week? I have tickets for the opera Friday night. Do you like opera?"

"Well, I . . ." His invitation took me by surprise, though I was hoping he wanted to see me again. "In all honesty, I've never been to the opera."

"*Tosca* is playing." It was the first time he'd offered an invitation that had nothing to do with my interest in his father's work. "Would you like to give it a try?" I detected some caution in his voice, and I wondered if he thought I would decline.

"Yes, I would."

"I'll come by about seven. We could get a light supper."

"Thank you again for taking me to visit your family," I said as I got out of the car. "See you Friday night."

"It's a date," he said.

"Yes, it's a date."

A date, I thought as I went up to the apartment. It had been a while since I'd had a real date. The opera? I would have to get something new to wear. I felt a surge of excitement and then a nervous little throb of warmth on the back of my neck as I climbed the stairs. Nervous about the prospect of a real date with Roberto? Or nervous about what his father had said?

Stefano Leonetti—the old man's raspy voice repeated the words in my head as I put the key in my apartment door. *Stefano Leonetti. Stefano Leonetti.*

Roberto's father knew Stefano, and I had the feeling he also knew what had become of the Masolino.

MONDAY WHEN I went to my office following my morning class, there was a message from Alberto Mazzone, the restorer at the Uffizi. He said he had found several files for paintings possibly fitting the description of the one I was looking for. There was no file with the title Masolino Madonna, but a couple that would have fit the time period. One was presently on display in the museum, one in storage, and the third had been destroyed in the flood. *Destroyed?* Could this file possibly be referring to the Masolino Madonna? Alberto said he would make copies of pertinent information and drop them by my office sometime this week.

I WENT SHOPPING the next afternoon to find something to wear to the opera. I bought a sleeveless black silk dress and a matching jacket with rhinestone buttons—more formal and sophisticated than what I normally wear. I did pause over the buttons for a moment, wondering if they were a bit too much, finally deciding they were not cheap or gaudy. The dress and jacket together were certainly not *cheap*, more than I would normally spend, even for a special occasion outfit. My everyday wardrobe consisted of jeans for casual, long skirts or slacks for school. Retro-hippie, Andrea often called my style. I got a pair of very high-heeled, narrow, pointy-toed black shoes and a little handbag to match. I laughed as I looked in the mirror—the skirt was short and my legs looked rather shapely. Not bad for an old broad, I told myself.

By Friday afternoon I had still not received the files from Alberto Mazzone. I called and left a message graciously offering to come pick them up. I waited for his return call, but finally left to get ready for my date with Roberto.

I'd asked him to meet me at the apartment building *porta*,

just off the street. I didn't want him to have to come up and he hadn't insisted.

I waited. Five minutes. Ten minutes. Then fifteen. He wasn't coming. Had something happened to him? I felt panicky, then angry. He was standing me up, and here I was waiting in my brand-new dress, shoes, bag, and all. I felt like a fool and was about to go back to my apartment when a cab pulled up.

"I'm sorry," Roberto said breathlessly as he got out. "I called your school to let you know I would be late." His eyes swept over me and he smiled—appreciatively, rather than apologetically. "You look beautiful. . . . But you'd already left. You must give me your number here at the apartment. Or a cell phone?"

"I don't have a phone here," I said, apologizing myself. I still hadn't gotten around to buying a phone like Charley had suggested. "Anyone who needs to reach me can leave a message at the school. And I hate cell phones."

"I'm not crazy about them either, though circumstances force me to carry one," he said as he patted the pocket of his overcoat, "in case one of the girls needs to call, particularly Maria. Now that Papa is . . . well, getting near the end, I want to make sure she's able to reach me."

"Yes," I answered. "I was beginning to think you were standing me up."

"Never," he replied, motioning me out to the cab. "The van," he said, "trouble with the van."

The opera was beautiful, and though I could not understand many of the lyrics, I could sense the emotion on stage, in the audience, in Roberto. He took my hand as we sat, and later during the cab ride back to my apartment he explained portions of the performance I did not understand. His knowledge of so many things amazed me.

The cab dropped us off in front of my apartment and I invited him up. In fact, on my way home from work, I had stopped to purchase a bottle of cognac, with the very intention of inviting him up for a post-opera drink, though I hadn't allowed myself to go any further in analyzing my intentions.

When we stepped inside, it struck me suddenly how drab the placed looked. I spent so little time here, and still hadn't gotten around to hanging pictures or photos. Roberto's eyes swept the room quickly, unobtrusively, but he didn't say anything. At least it was clean. I went into the kitchen, which was more or less an extension of the living room and the bedroom, and got the bottle, poured two glasses, and sat down next to Roberto on the small sofa.

He held his glass up. "A toast? Let's see—to the lovely Professor Suzanne, wishing you much happiness and many good times in Florence."

"And to you, Dottore Roberto Balducci, and a lovely evening."

We drank.

"Have you discovered anything more about the painting?" he asked. This was the first time during the evening we'd mentioned the painting, which in a strange way was the very thing that had brought us together. I hadn't told Roberto that I didn't believe the painting had been lost in the flood, or my true intention for wanting to speak to his father, but I sensed he knew.

"The Masolino Madonna?"

He nodded.

"One of the teachers I work with has put me in touch with a restorer from the Uffizi who is doing some research for me."

"You don't believe it was lost in the flood as my father stated?"

"No, I don't. Have you read your father's article?"

"After you gave me the information that first day, I found the book you spoke of to take to Papa, and I read his piece. I'm sorry he wasn't more help. Sometimes he remembers every detail of something that happened years ago, but often he confuses the past with the present."

I wondered again if Roberto's father had remembered seeing me years ago with Stefano, and I thought of his confusion—thinking I was Roberto's wife. "He thought I was Paolina, your wife, didn't he?"

Roberto nodded. "But you look nothing like Paolina."

"Tell me about her," I said.

"Paolina was a good woman, a good wife and mother. She was tall like you, but blonde—Italian, but very blonde. People don't expect that in an Italian."

"Like Simonetta," I said, "Botticelli's Simonetta."

"Yes." He smiled.

"Your daughters. Two of them are blonde, like their mother."

"Stella especially looks like her mother," he said. "Paolina was very pretty, even as she aged. And kind, but she had a stubborn streak." Again, he smiled. "When she made up her mind about something, that was it. But we got along well. We respected each other."

I liked the idea that he had had a happy marriage. A man who has loved well is likely to love again, I've been told. I wondered what he thought of me, a divorced woman who had spent most of her life alone. Was I set in my ways? Difficult to get along with? Too picky and critical of others?

"Papa spoke of a Stefano Leonetti," Roberto said. "Do you know this name?"

Had Roberto noticed my reaction, my near panic when his father said Stefano's name?

"He was a restorer I worked with when I was at the Limonaia." I surprised myself by how calmly, how controlled this came out of me.

"Perhaps you can find him. Papa's mention of his name, maybe he was trying to tell you to contact this Leonetti."

"Yes, I think maybe he was," I said quickly, and hoped he would change the subject.

Roberto sipped the cognac. "You look beautiful tonight, Suzanne."

"Thank you."

"You enjoyed the evening?"

"Very much." I had.

He leaned in and kissed me. His lips were soft and warm and I could taste the cognac, sense his breathing, his heat.

"You're making me feel very, well . . . very young again," he said. "It's been a while since I've felt like this."

My heart was beating, faster and faster. I knew I should respond, say something, but the right words just weren't coming. Were we moving too fast? I liked Roberto very much, but at the same time I felt panicky. Maybe I shouldn't have invited him up. But I wanted to and I had. Were we ready to flip the bed out of the wall? That could be rather awkward—this wasn't exactly the ideal place for romance. But I was feeling romantic, and I was sure he was feeling it too. Talk about feeling younger. I felt about sixteen, especially when he reached up and touched my hair. As usual I had twisted it up and secured it—tonight with a silver hair stick to match my earrings and necklace.

"Your hair, it is very long?" he asked, stroking along my temple.

"Yes."

"Do you always wear it up?"

"Yes, generally."

"When you go to bed?"

I smiled. "No," I answered. "I take it down when I go to bed."

And then, I heard it, from the small closet where we had hung our coats; I heard it, and so did Roberto. The ringing of a phone.

"Do you want me to get it?" I asked.

"No, not really," he said slowly, still touching my hair. "But, yes. I should. It might be Maria."

I got up, went to the closet, dug into the pocket of his overcoat, and brought it to him. By then it had stopped ringing.

"I should check for a message." He put the phone to his ear and listened, breathing heavily, blowing out puffs of air.

I looked at him, his expression somber. "Your father?"

"He's taken a turn. Maria says it will be tonight."

"I'm so sorry, Roberto." I got up to get his coat. He called

Maria to tell her he was on his way, then he called a cab. I walked him down to the street.

"Thank you for a lovely evening," I said. We kissed quickly, and I realized with a pang that I wanted more.

The cab pulled up and Roberto kissed me again, deeper. "I'll call you, Suzanne," he said, and then he was gone.

I WENT TO school the next morning to check my messages, to see if Roberto had called. He hadn't, but there was a large envelope on my desk. It was from Alberto Mazzone. He must have dropped it off late Friday afternoon after I'd gone home.

Eagerly I tore it open. It contained several pages, which appeared to be copies from files of the paintings he had told me about. I started through them. There was a copy of the beautiful little Masaccio I had seen at the museum, with notes stating it had come into the collection in 1988 and was now displayed in the Early Renaissance Room. A smaller photo of a second painting by an artist I had never heard of, a few handwritten notes attached with a paper clip, then a typed notation that the painting was in storage.

And then—a copy of the Masolino!

Quickly I read the last page of the handwritten history sheet, the notation of a cleaning scheduled in November 1966, and then—my hand trembled, my eyes blinked, and something tightened inside my chest.

The last entry—*distrutta dall'inondazione*. Destroyed in the flood, 4 November 1966.

The words themselves could have caused this intense reaction, but I knew it was more—the script, with an unmistakable left-handed slant, a hand I grew to know intimately as I worked at the Limonaia, watched each day as he noted the percentage of shrinkage, the moisture content. Yes, I knew the hand. And then the initials—*S. L.*

15

STEFANO HAD PUT his total energy into saving that painting as well as the others in his care, and I couldn't believe he had been involved in taking it or falsifying the documents. Had someone forged his handwriting, initialed the history sheet to make it appear as if it had been Stefano? But who? And where was the painting? For that matter, where was Stefano? And did the elder Roberto Balducci know the answers to these questions? Maria had said the end was near, and I wondered if he was gone now and with him my hope of finding the Masolino. Of finding Stefano.

Sunday I went again to school and checked for messages. No call from Roberto. I thought about calling him. He said he would call, but if he'd just lost his father I was probably the last thing on his mind.

For some time, I sat at my desk and studied the files, the photos and notes left by Alberto Mazzone, the history sheet initialed *S. L.*

Early Monday I phoned Alberto to thank him for the files.

"Was the material helpful?" he asked.

"Yes, one of the files you copied for me, it's the painting I'm interested in."

"Very good."

"You mentioned that the director of restoration at the Uffizi worked on the recovery after the flood," I said carefully.

"Giuliana Garzoni. Dr. Garzoni. I asked about Stefano Leonetti and she said she wasn't sure where he was now."

I felt a little jump inside as my heart pressed against my rib cage. *She knew him.* Had she worked with him? I had to speak with her. "May I come in and talk with her sometime?"

"I will inquire."

"*Grazie*, Alberto. And thank you again for the files."

Within minutes of hanging up, Alberto called back and said Dr. Garzoni would have some free time the following afternoon. "About one?" Albert asked.

"Yes, perfect."

That afternoon I got a newspaper and checked the obituaries. Roberto Balducci had passed away Saturday. Funeral services would be Thursday afternoon at the Cathedral of San Romolo in Fiesole, the little hill town about half an hour's bus ride from Florence.

I wondered again if I should call Roberto. Would I even have the right words if I called?

I did call, and as I had expected, I got his machine. I left a message telling him how sorry I was about his father's death. "Please let me know if there's anything I can do." The words sounded trite, clichéd, but what more could I say?

I decided to send a card, but then wondered where to send it, having no idea where he lived. It had never come up in our conversations during the several times we had been together. I counted them up in my head. Five times. We had been together five times. The first time we met at the Piazza della Repubblica. The evening we drove to Rome. The day he dropped by the school to apologize. The afternoon he took me to Maria's for lunch. The night of the opera. These events replayed in my mind, the smallest details—the way he smiled, the look in his eyes when he was saying something in a teasing way, the warmth of his hand as he held mine.

Tuesday after my morning class, I went to a *cartoleria* and bought a card. I'd found the address of his clinic online and could send it there. I wrote a brief note—*My heart goes out to you and your family.* I stopped by the post office, then returned to school. Should I go to the funeral? If he wanted me there, would he call? I barely knew the elder Roberto Balducci. Maybe I barely knew the younger Roberto Balducci.

WHEN I MET with Dr. Garzoni in her office, she showed little of the admiration I'd received from both Regina and Alberto when they learned I was a mud angel and had helped with the restoration after the flood.

"They let just about anyone into the libraries and museums after the flood," she said, "amateurs who knew nothing about restoration. Do you know they spread talcum powder on the books? It dried in massive clumps, like blocks of cement. They put tissue paper on the paintings! The young people, some of them I've heard removed pages from manuscripts, taking them out of the libraries under their sweaters."

"There had been no precedent for the handling of such great destruction," I said, detecting a hint of defensiveness in my voice. It wasn't just the students and volunteers, but even the experts who were trying this and that to save the art, using tissue and even toilet paper when they ran out of Japanese mulberry paper. Putting talcum powder, it's true, on just about everything—books, manuscripts, sculptures, even paintings—in an attempt to draw out the moisture. There had never been such a potential loss of art, and no one knew how to handle it, but we did what we were told, we did what we could to help.

Dr. Garzoni shook her head sadly, closing her eyes as if picturing the devastating scene in Florence right after the flood. "Many techniques were developed at the time that are still used today." Her voice now carried a trace of that hope we all felt after the restoration had begun.

Dr. Garzoni was not an attractive woman. Her nose was large, her hair jet black, yet the roots, clearly visible, were a dull gray, her brows flecked with white. I tried to place her as one of the restorers who had worked at the Limonaia, but couldn't remember her. Obviously she couldn't remember me either, but Alberto said she had known Stefano, and this we had in common.

"Alberto Mazzone tells me you are trying to locate some-one you met here in Florence," she said, "a restorer who worked at the Limonaia." She fingered a glass paperweight sitting on her desk among a clutter of books, files, a magnetic paper-clip holder, and a ceramic container of pens. The desk itself was old and worn, just like the woman who sat behind it. I wondered how old Giuliana Garzoni was—she looked at least mid-sixties to early seventies, which would have put her in her late thirties during the flood and restoration, just a few years older than Stefano. She had deep creases along her jowls, lines that ran across her forehead, which made me won-der how Stefano had aged. If he might look like an old man, if I might look like an old woman to him.

"Stefano Leonetti?" she asked, sending a shiver down my spine, as if in hearing his name I was getting closer to Stefano. "A good restorer, very dedicated."

"Do you have any idea where he is now?" I asked, not a trace of excitement or apprehension in my voice.

"We worked together at the Fortezza da Basso during the restoration. I seem to recall he went to Venice, then Milan. But no, I don't know where he is now." She picked up the paper-weight, a colorful millefiori cluster floating inside, and gazed at it for a moment as if it were a fortune-teller's globe that would supply some mystical answer. "I believe I'm familiar with most of the restorers working in Italy at the present." Carefully she placed the paperweight back on the desk. "Per-haps he's relocated. Or retired. I could inquire." The lack of excitement in her voice matched mine, and yet I sensed it was forced. She stared down at the glass globe, then over me as if she were studying something above my head.

"I'd appreciate it," I said.

"Alberto, I understand, has been helping you with the study of a painting for one of your classes."

"Yes, a painting often attributed to Masolino."

"You teach art history?" She looked at me. A filmy glaze lay over her left eye, which even now didn't focus precisely on me.

"Yes, at an American university here in Florence. My interest in art history began to develop when I worked here during the flood."

"It had a great influence on many of us." She nodded approvingly. "We try to keep our doors open to the universities." Her tone had shifted slightly and was almost animated. She hadn't asked why I was interested in Stefano or the painting, and I sensed it was not just her tone that had shifted, but the entire conversation. "We do behind-the-scenes tours in the restoration area for art students, if you are interested."

"Thank you," I replied. "Yes, I would be. I have an enthusiastic group of students, particularly in my upper-division class. I'm sure they would be interested."

She flipped several pages on a daily calendar propped on her desk. "Next week—no, perhaps week after next?" She glanced up, and I nodded. "Thursday or Friday?"

"My advanced class meets Friday at ten forty-five. If we could fit a tour into that time slot it would be fantastic."

"Friday, March third." Dr. Garzoni scribbled something on the calendar. She was left-handed and wrote in that awkward, almost upside-down way many left-handed people do. *Sinistra*, the Italian word came to me. Left-handed, just like Stefano.

"Let me know how many students," she said briskly as she rose from her desk, then walked me to the door. She was much shorter than she had appeared behind the desk, and when she reached out, extending her hand, it was like taking the hand of a child. Our meeting, I surmised, had come to an end. We hadn't even talked about my belief that the painting had been restored, a contradiction to the information in the official Uffizi records. But as Giuliana Garzoni bid me farewell, I realized I wasn't quite ready to share this with her, until I myself had gathered more information.

16

WHEN I PRESENTED Dr. Garzoni's invitation to my class the following day, they were excited about the opportunity to tour the restoration department.

"Will we get extra credit?" Richard Bennington asked with a wide grin. He was a bit of a flirt, and I sometimes felt he was more interested in the six young women students than the Women in Renaissance Art. He even liked to flirt with me.

"Oh, Richard, I've been bragging to anyone willing to listen how dedicated my students are, how they take advantage of any opportunity for enlightenment. I'm not sure I'll give extra credit. Restoration has little to do with our subject matter."

"But aren't they working on Renaissance art? I'm sure there'll be some women in those paintings." He smiled again. Beautiful straight white teeth. His father was a dentist. "I didn't do so great on that last test. I could use the extra credit." He held up his hand, palms spread toward me. "Of course, Professor C., I'd love to go even if there is no credit."

"How many would be interested?" All seven students raised their hands.

After class, I talked with Anthony Randolph to see if any

of his advanced painting students might want to be included. He said he'd check and get back with me.

THAT AFTERNOON THERE was a message from my sister, Andrea, asking me to call. It was early morning back home, I knew Andie was never up at this hour, and we usually communicated by e-mail. Nervously, I punched in the numbers, anticipating bad news.

"Everything okay?" I asked.

"Well . . ." There was a hesitation in her voice. "Actually, no."

"It's not Dad?"

"No, Dad's fine."

"One of the kids?"

"It's Rousseau. Jerry called."

"What happened?"

"Jerry had to . . . well, she was very sick. The vet said she was in a lot of pain and there was no hope. It was the right thing to do—"

"He put her to sleep? Without even calling, without even checking with me?"

"Suzanne, the dog was almost fourteen years old. The vet said—"

"Damn it, couldn't Jerry have called me himself?" I felt a warmth rise up into my cheeks.

"He said it was something that needed to be done right away. With the time change and all . . . and he said he knew it was what you'd want."

"What the hell does the time change have to do with it?"

"You don't even have a phone, Suzi. He couldn't call you at school in the middle of the night. You need to get one at your place, in case an emergency comes up."

As if this wasn't an emergency, I thought. But to Andie it was just a dog.

"Or a cell phone," she said. "Don't they have cell phones over there?"

Something rose in my throat and words wouldn't come. My beloved Rousseau was gone, and we were talking about phones.

"He knew you wouldn't want to see her in that kind of pain."

I wanted someone to blame. "Damn Jerry," I whispered. Then finally I said, "Thanks, Andie, for calling." I picked up a pencil on my desk and clenched it in my fist.

"I'm sorry. I know how much she meant to you."

"What did he do with her?" I straightened in my chair, feeling a deep heaviness in my back.

Andrea hesitated again as if she hadn't understood. "Do with her?"

"Yes, what did he do with her?" I stood and walked the two steps to the window. My office was small with a single arched window. In the late morning on a clear day, a warm sun poured in and onto my desk, giving the room an open feel of space. Now I looked out onto the street in the shadow of the building, and I felt terribly confined, as if the heavy stone walls were pressing in on me.

"Oh, you mean the body?" Andrea asked. "I think they do it right there at the vet's. Like a cremation or something."

"He just left her there?" I cried.

I could hear Andie taking a deep breath over the phone. "He said he saved the ashes. You can decide what you want to do with it—her—when you get back home."

"That was considerate of him." Across the street the driver of a small silver sports car was attempting to wedge the vehicle into an even smaller parking space. I watched as the car bumped up on the curb, in an attempt at parking that was more perpendicular than parallel.

"Hon, I'm sorry," Andrea said; the sympathy was sincere, yet I knew she didn't really understand. With five kids, they'd had a series of pets in and out of the house, and I'm not sure she could tell one from the other.

"I don't mean to take it out on you, Andie." I sat again. "I'm just, well . . . I guess I knew there was the possibility of this happening when I left. Damn." A tightness coursed

through my body. Don't shoot the messenger, I told myself.
"I'll give Jerry a call. Thanks, Andie."

"I do have some good news. Callie and David are engaged.
He gave her a ring on Valentine's Day."

"That's wonderful." I wanted to be happy for her, but I'm
sure Andrea detected the lack of enthusiasm in my voice
now. Callie is Andrea's middle child, a sweet girl, if a bit of a
ditz. She'd had about a million boyfriends, and honestly I
wasn't sure which one was David. Was that the boy I'd met at
Christmas?

"They're thinking maybe the middle of June," she went on,
"after you come home. She's talking about using black for the
bridesmaids. Do you think that's appropriate? Especially for a
summer wedding. It used to be pink or violet, or maybe even
yellow. But black?" Andrea laughed a nervous little laugh. I
knew she was trying to get my mind off of Rousseau. A trick
of diversion she's often used on one of the kids, a child with a
minor, non-life-threatening boo-boo.

"Give Callie my love." I pushed my chair back and walked
to the window again. Several students stood in front of the
building, smoking. A motorcycle zipped by, the rider decked
out in a black helmet and leathers.

"Oh, and your friend Roxie called. I guess I told you that in
my e-mail. I gave her your address. She has some old photos
she wants to send."

"I haven't heard from her."

"Everything still good at school?"

"It's good." The kids were snuffing cigarettes, starting into
the building.

"Great." She didn't ask if I'd made any progress in my
search for the missing painting. I'd e-mailed about contacting
Roberto and told her I hoped his father might be able to help me
out, but I hadn't divulged my growing feelings for him. For a
minute I thought about telling her—about Roberto, his dad, his
dying, the Masolino, Alberto Mazzone, Giuliana Garzoni, the
file—but I didn't. At the moment it seemed too complicated to
explain over the phone.

"I'm glad you took advantage of this opportunity," she said.
"Me too."

"Can't think of anything else pressing, mostly I just wanted to let you know—"

"Thanks, Andie."

After we hung up, I jabbed Jerry's number into the phone, and sat breathing hard, waiting as it rang until his machine picked it up. "Damn it," I shouted, "pick up the damn phone, Jerry." I glanced at my watch—and figured it was quarter to seven in the morning at home. "I know you're there."

"Suzanne," a sleepy voice came over the line.

"Couldn't you call me yourself?"

Silence.

I took another deep breath.

"I knew you'd take it better coming from your sister."

He was right, of course.

"You knew she wasn't doing that well," Jerry said slowly, a hint of accusation in his voice. "Some days she could barely get herself up out of bed. The vet said—"

"But couldn't you have called before, so we could make this decision together?"

"Truthfully, Suzanne, I was afraid you would say wait until you came home, and I just couldn't do that. She was in too much pain. You had to have known this might happen when you decided to leave."

I couldn't even reply to that.

"Look," Jerry said, sounding more awake now, "my alarm just went off. We can talk later."

"No, I want to talk now."

"Look, Suzanne." I could picture him sitting on the edge of the bed, rubbing his mussed hair, then standing, pulling his robe off the chair next to the nightstand ready to head out to the kitchen and put the coffee on. "You're the one who left her," he said with so little emotion in his voice I was thankful once more that we'd split. "Don't come down on me—"

"Did you hold her?"

"You think I just dumped her off at the vet?"

"You'll save the ashes?"

"Yes. Look, I need to get moving."

"Yes. Okay."

After I hung up I grabbed my scarf and coat off the hook on the door and went out for a walk. I needed fresh air, and I needed to feel a cool breeze against my skin. I walked down to the Ponte Vecchio. A shopkeeper, bent over a display case, looked up from inside and smiled through the window—a friendly, come-inside-and-take-a-look smile. I turned away. I didn't want to be forced to smile, I didn't want to let go of this anger mixed with grief, or forgive myself for what Jerry said . . . *you're the one who left her*.

That night I couldn't sleep, imagining Rousseau curled up against my side, her soft, warm coat, even her doggie breath, the rhythm of her heartbeat, her heavy breathing. I would scatter her ashes in the Boise foothills where we often walked. When she was young she loved to run through the sagebrush in the hills above the house. A picture formed in my mind, and then I could smell the Idaho sage, and then I could feel it, along with a deep, throbbing loneliness and longing for home that took me by surprise.

As I lay sleepless that night, I dwelt on every faulty emotional decision I'd ever made in my life, every failed relationship. I thought once more of missed opportunities, missed loves, family and children I would never have. And, as it happened at times in my life when I fell into a state of depression, a memory came back, an event I had so skillfully suppressed over the years that I had almost been able to convince myself it had never happened.

And yet . . . I knew it had.

17

LATE THAT SUMMER, not yet a year after the flood, after Stefano and I had been together almost four months, I noticed the expansion of my waistline, the plumping of my breasts. "The Italian pasta," I told myself. I actually felt very sexy, as I'd given up believing I would ever have breasts. And I'd never had to worry about my weight before. But even after I cut back on the *pasta*, the *pane*, the *dolci*, I continued to grow.

I had missed a period but I wasn't terribly concerned, as my periods had never been regular. I'd skipped two months when Roxie and I first came to Europe, and now I assumed it was the traveling, the change of climate, of diet, extended jet lag.

The first time Stefano and I made love we had not been prepared, and we'd used no protection. My period started just ten days later. After that we always used what Stefano called either an *impermeabile*, which literally translates as raincoat, or a *preservativo*—as if we were going to save it for later—so I knew I was safe.

But as the days passed, a week, and then another, Stefano expressed alarm. He couldn't think of the word in English, but

I knew what he was talking about when he said, "Blood? The last time?"

"Two months," I said, but if something didn't happen in the next few days, it would be three. "This has happened before," I offered. "Oh, no, no, not that," I added when I saw what he was thinking. I tried to explain I'd never been regular, that I'd often gone more than a month without a period.

He was quiet for a long moment, as if hesitant to say what he was about to say. My heart skipped a bit, and for the first time, the reality of it hit me. Very hard. I started crying uncontrollably, and he put his arms around me and rocked me back and forth as we sat on the bed at my *pensione*. I felt like a child, and I wanted my mother, but the thought of my mother sent me into hysterics, my sobbing so deep there was no longer any sound coming out of me. Stefano wiped away my tears.

"You don't have to have this child," he said softly. He might as well have said, You are a child, you can't be a mother.

At first I didn't realize what he was talking about. But then I remembered a girl in my dorm freshman year, the gossip, the stories. We all knew she was pregnant, that she didn't even know who the father was. She left school for a week. When she came back . . . well, she wasn't pregnant anymore. One morning I heard her roommate talking to another girl as we brushed our teeth, standing at sinks before the long mirror that ran along the wall in the dorm bathroom. She spoke softly, but I could make out a word here and there, and when she whispered, "Abortion," my eyes rose and met hers. Then just as quickly I looked down as the water in the sink drained with a big gulping suck.

"No," I told Stefano, "I can't do that." But I didn't know what I would do.

This was the sixties, and although women were beginning to establish some freedoms—well, in the States, not here in Italy—single girls didn't have babies and keep them back then. There was still great shame in being an unwed mother. Weddings were rushed. Eight-pound babies were born two months premature. Or a girl might go visit an aunt, which meant the child would be given up for adoption.

I knew Stefano could not marry me, and I knew I had but one choice—I must give up this child. Stefano said he would help me. He knew a place I could go when I started to show, a place where they would find a family to take the child.

Being tall and slender, this expansion might have been obvious, but the slight rounding of my middle was easy to hide as I'd been wearing a restorer's smock over my jeans and shirts when I worked. I never felt particularly sick. A few mornings, a bit of queasiness, but I kept going to work. I didn't think anyone noticed. Some of the restorers had moved over to the Fortezza da Basso permanently, though Pietro and several others still spent much of their time at the restoration lab in the Boboli Gardens.

My few friends outside the Limonaia—Charley and the others I had met at the National Library, the young people I sometimes went out with in the evenings, had gone back home. American students studying in Florence for the year had returned to their universities in the States.

Pietro was always kind, but caught up in his own little world of restoration, and I was sure he wasn't aware of these changes in me. As Christmas approached, he invited me to have dinner with him and his mother again, but I told him I was meeting friends in Rome, which of course was a lie.

I spent Christmas alone in Florence. It was the second saddest day of my life.

I continued to work until my seventh month, when Stefano took me to a villa in the hills above Florence. It had once belonged to a wealthy family who'd donated it to the Church, and it had been converted into a home for unwed mothers.

My memories of the next two months are so vague I recall little other than the gentle prayerful nuns in white habits, the abundance of food, the fact that it rained almost every afternoon, creating a dark gloom that seemed to come not from outside of me but from within. I got very large, as if I were free to do so now, and every movement, every thought became an effort. Stefano visited at least once a week, and brought letters my mother had sent to my address at the *pensione* in Florence.

I wrote home, inventing stories about the work I was doing, describing the art in the museums I visited in Florence. The tone of my mother's letters became harsh, her expectations unequivocal. She insisted I do what I said I would do—come home and finish school. I wrote and explained the restoration process was long and involved, that I couldn't just up and leave now. I would get my degree when I returned home, but it would be utterly stupid to pass up this opportunity to work with real art here in Italy when I intended to study art history. Of course, my mother did not understand about the art, and I knew she would understand even less if she knew where I really was.

With Stefano's encouragement, I wrote back and agreed that I would return by June or July, with plenty of time to register for fall semester.

The other girls at the convent were mostly Italian. The language, which had always been difficult, became almost impossible when I was tired or depressed, and this had become my normal emotional state. I formed no enduring bonds of friendship in this place where my life was on hold. There would be no good memories.

The nuns and a doctor who had examined me when I arrived, then three times after that, told me what to expect, but I still worried that I wouldn't know when the time came. The doctor spoke English and explained the contractions would start slowly at even intervals then increase. He told me what it might feel like if my water broke, though he explained this didn't happen the same with all women.

But I know now, it is impossible for a man or a nun to describe the pain of childbirth, and no one, myself included, can describe the pain of bringing a child into the world to see him carried away into the arms of another.

I was not brave. I screamed all the way to the hospital. I do remember clearly the thought that God was punishing me, that I had failed to pray with the earnestness the good nuns had encouraged. Surely I was going to die and end up in hell. I was given an injection to numb my body, but the pain I felt that day could not be sedated. I gave birth to a son, who was immediately taken from me.

When Stefano came to see me we had nothing to talk about. He had dark circles under his eyes and I noticed for the first time that he had lost weight. Had this happened as I expanded, and had he suffered too? The following day I was released from the hospital. I got a room at a *pensione* closer to the Limonaia and returned to work. Most of the paintings, as well as the restorers, had moved on to the Fortezza da Basso or other restoration sites, and there was little to do. The workers who remained believed my story—that I'd taken some time off to see more of Europe, since my travels had been interrupted when I got caught in the flood and decided to stay in Florence.

In mid-July, three months after I had given up my son, I returned home.

I told no one. Not my parents. Not my sister. Not Jerry. No one.

18

BY THURSDAY MORNING I had still not heard from Roberto, but I had decided I would go to the funeral in Fiesole that afternoon.

Rain fell in sheets all morning and continued into the afternoon. Dark, rueful funeral weather, I thought as I snapped my umbrella open and hurried down Via delle Belle Donne toward the bus stop. As I stepped off the curb at the Piazza Santa Maria Novella, a car skidded by, splattering my coat with mud. I was running late and by the time I got to Piazza Adua, bus number 7 for Fiesole was pulling out. I bought a ticket and waited for the next bus, standing under the covered bus stop, wondering if I should turn around and go back to my apartment. I was about to leave, when another Fiesole bus appeared. The door opened with a pneumatic swish, passengers got off, others boarded. I helped a young mother fold up a stroller as she juggled the baby in her arms. She nodded a thank-you and hurried onto the bus. I too climbed aboard and found an empty seat.

Fiesole stood at the top of a winding road. Because it was high above the flood plain and filled with gardens and vineyards and beautiful villas, it had been a haven during the flood. But today the sky was dark and gray, and I could see nothing of the landscape or the city of Florence below as the bus twisted round one curve then another. The rain turned to snow. I shivered as I stepped off the bus at the Piazza Mino da Fiesole.

At the cathedral the hearse was parked out front, and several limos and shiny black cars sat empty. I walked in quietly, past columns, over the stone floor of the nave, and stood behind the last pew. Old women in hats and veils with rosary beads in hand, bent-over little men, plump middle-aged couples, distinguished academic types filled the church. The services had already begun. The congregation stood, then sat, then kneeled, then stood again, and I strained, looking over, around the mourners. Six men in dark suits stood in the front pew—pallbearers. I could see Roberto and his large family in the next several rows on the left. I studied them from the back, imagining which daughter was Stella, Anna, Bea, and Luisa. A woman with short white hair stood beside Roberto. His mother, I guessed, and I thought of my own dear mother, the day we had buried her. Maria stood to Roberto's other side. Little Carlo fidgeted and clung to her hand. Leo, in his father's arms, was falling asleep, his head resting on Marco's large, comfortable shoulder. I wondered if one of the men among the women and children in the next few rows was Roberto's brother.

Candles flickered on the altar covered with flowers and wreaths. Three priests in black garments, framed by Romanesque arches, chanted in deep solemn voices. One of them wore a cap like the one I remembered the pope wore when he came to the Limonaia, but it was red rather than white. I wondered if he was a bishop or cardinal and if all Italian funerals were conducted with such pomp and ceremony. The church was freezing, and I shivered as I attempted to listen.

The priests stepped down. The tallest walked around the shiny wooden casket, holding a golden globe on a chain, swinging it back and forth, singing songs of eternal rest. The smell of incense thickened in the air. The priest in the cap read from scripture, words I couldn't understand and yet I knew.

Dust to dust, a rhythmic dirge played in my head. I thought of
my mother, then my father, healthy back home, but someday
I would say my own farewell. *Ashes to ashes*, and it was
Rousseau now, my faithful friend, whose image I could not
release.

Roberto and his family joined the priest in prayer. They
were a beautiful family and a feeling of tenderness, then envy,
coursed through me, so hot and full it made my body ache. I
felt a warmth rise up into my cheeks, a tightness in my throat.
And then, overwhelmed with feelings I knew had nothing to do
with the loss of this man I had met only once, but the grief over
the loss of my cherished Rousseau, the loss of a life, a family I
would never have, tears welled in my eyes. I wanted more than
anything to leave, to get away, to escape. I turned and it was
then that I saw him.

He stood on the opposite side of the church, beside a large
stone holy water fount in the shadow of the last of a row of
massive columns separating the nave and the aisle. In the darkness, I could make out little more than an outline, a tall man in
an overcoat. But there was something about the stance, the set
of his broad shoulders. Or perhaps it was nothing more than in-
tuition that told me I knew him.

He stepped behind the column. I glanced back toward the
altar breathless. The pallbearers were beginning to file out of
the pew. I looked over my shoulder again, the man barely visible in the shadows at the back of the church. Quietly I too
stepped back, my eyes still wet from tears, searching—behind
the water fount, the column, finding no one. Had I imagined
him?

I pushed the heavy wooden door open and rushed out of the
church, heat scorching the back of my neck under my collar,
moisture burning my cheeks. The cold air hit me with a punch.
A single set of crisp, clear footprints appeared in the new fallen
snow, then disappeared as I traced them into the street, where
traffic had obscured any sign. My eyes darted up the hill to my
right, down through the street. I ran across the piazza, a burn-

ing heat radiating through my body. On the far side of the piazza, I stopped, again searching. The man was nowhere.

From the bus stop, I watched as the funeral procession
came down the street, and I wondered if I was losing my mind.
It was an illusion, I told myself. A shadowy vision distorted
through my tears. Yet, I knew there *had* been a man. Footprints
in the snow proved someone had left the church before the services were over. But was it Stefano?

19

AS I SAT on the bus, I felt myself shivering one moment, burning up the next. By the time I got back to my apartment, I knew I had a fever. I lay on my bed and fell asleep, dreaming strange daytime dreams—jerky visions interrupted by the sounds of traffic and voices on the street, the dimmest daylight filtering through the shutters, brightness, darkness flickering in my mind. Rousseau, young and frisky with a shiny black coat, romped with me in the Boise foothills. We ran faster and faster, so fast we were flying across fields and cities, above a dark, shimmering ocean, with Stefano now, the three of us in the Boboli Gardens, splashing in the Fountain of Neptune, cool and fresh, suddenly so warm my skin burned. And then, there was a child. In my arms, floating, sinking. I woke from this dream, a headache piercing my left temple, my cheeks wet with warm tears. The image of this lost child who could exist only in my dreams slipped away once more. Every limb and joint and muscle of my body ached. Feeling nauseous I got up, ran to the toilet, and dropped to the floor, heaving violently. I splashed cool water on my face, took a couple ibuprofen, then lay back down. Again I fell into an uneven sleep.

Again I dreamed. My mother, sitting in the kitchen with my father. She was young, wearing a starched gingham apron. His back was to me and I couldn't see his face. Then the image shifted; my mother was now an old woman. I watched her puttering in the garden. She looked up and smiled and invited me to come into the kitchen and sit with a cup of tea. She pulled two chocolates out of a box hidden in the cupboard, one for me, one for her. I sat down and then she seemed to fade away.

When I woke Friday morning I was too sick to go to school. I pulled myself out of bed, took the elevator down to the ground floor and went out on the street, found a phone, called the school and spoke with Mrs. Potter to let her know I wouldn't be in.

Back at my apartment I curled up under my covers and slept, a blanket of loneliness pressing heavily on my quivering limbs as my fever rose once more. By early afternoon I was vomiting again. When there was nothing left but the raw lining of my stomach, I slept.

Charley dropped by to check on me the next morning. "Need a doctor?" He placed his hand on my forehead like he was my mother. "You feel warm."

"No, it's most likely just the flu. The worst has passed. Should have seen me last night." I smiled a little, knowing I wouldn't want anyone to have witnessed that.

He went into the kitchen and found a single tea bag that must have been hiding somewhere, left over from the Dr. Browning days, and made me a cup of hot tea. Charley stayed until noon as I slipped in and out of a more comfortable sleep, then he went out and returned with a bowl of soup and bread. I ate little but found great comfort in his visit. "Thanks, Charley. I think I'll live. No Last Rites, okay?"

"Okay," he said with a relieved smile.

Sunday morning I felt much better. Regina showed up with rolls and coffee, and I knew I had found a true friend. When I told her about Rousseau she showed just the right amount of sympathy and concern, and when I told her I thought I had seen Stefano at the funeral—even though I could hear the doubt in my voice—she just nodded and said, "You probably did."

That evening a group of my students showed up just after six, noisy and laughing as they came down the hall, then quiet and respectful as they entered the apartment. Several of them sat cross-legged on the floor, a couple on the small sofa. I'd showered and dressed that afternoon, although in my semi-sloppy, comfortable sweats, my hair pulled back in a ponytail.

"We just wanted to make sure you were okay," Richard Bennington said.

"We brought you a little treat." Cassie MacDonald pulled a paper bag from behind her back and grinned. She had a wholesome smile and a sprinkle of freckles across her pale nose. "My mom used to give me ice cream when I was sick. Or Popsicles, but I couldn't find any of those. I hope you like chocolate. I figured everybody likes chocolate."

I got out some mismatched bowls and spoons that came with the apartment rental, and we shared the ice cream, gelato actually, which was very, very chocolatey, but tasted better than anything I had eaten in over a week. Comfort food, and what a comfort to have these young people here with me. It had taken some effort on their part to come check on the ailing professor. Before they left I told them how much I appreciated their visit, and assured them I would be back in the classroom the following morning.

Monday I returned to school and found a small box on my desk. Attached was a note from Charley—*A cell phone for you. Good to have you back.*

BY THE MIDDLE of the week I was ready to admit that Roberto was not going to call. And yet, the memories of Rome, lunch at Maria's, our evening at the opera . . . I wondered if I should call him again. But I'd left a message after his father died and I'd sent a card. If he wanted to talk to me, wouldn't he call? Did our kiss mean anything to him?

I told myself he was going through a difficult time. I tried to put myself in his place, bringing up the memory of losing my mother. She had gone suddenly, without warning, and I remembered little of the days before or after. We hadn't been prepared. Had it been different for Roberto, knowing his father's death was near? I had reached out to others at the time. Maybe our friendship, or whatever it was, was too new. Or maybe Roberto had no feelings for me whatsoever.

As I continued to wonder about Roberto, I also kept thinking of what the elder Balducci had said and the possibility that I had seen Stefano in the back of the church at the funeral. There was more to this mystery; I knew there was more. But what?

A WEEK AFTER her grandfather's funeral, I got a call from Roberto's daughter Maria.

"We're having a birthday party for Papa next Saturday, and I'd like you to come. It's a big event, his fiftieth."

"I'd love to come," I said before I had time to ponder whether I wanted to go, or come up with a reasonable-sounding excuse. "Is there anything I can bring?"

"No. My sisters are all helping out. Papa doesn't know."

For a second, I thought she meant Roberto didn't know they were inviting me, but then I realized—"It's a surprise party?"

"Yes, so don't mention it."

Did she know I hadn't seen her father in almost two weeks? That he might not even want me at his party?

"Come about six. You remember how to get here?" I could hear a kid squawking in the background, Maria talking to him softly. "Let me give you directions again." She gave me the address, a description of where to turn off the autostrada, then off the gravel road—interrupted twice by Leo, whom I pictured sitting on her lap, soothed by her gentle stroke.

"Thanks, Maria, I'll be there." Could I really show up at Roberto's surprise party? Wouldn't that be a surprise for him!

"No gifts. Just come." Another commotion in the background, the two little ones fighting over something. *"Basta,*

Carlo," Maria said, then apologized to me. "Papa, I'm sure, will be pleased."

We'll see, I thought, just how pleased Roberto would be. "See you then." I had no idea how I'd get out to Maria's, but I would, even if I had to walk.

20

TWO RESTORATION TECHNICIANS, one male, one female, sat at a long table hunched over an altar triptych. Anthony Randolph and I stood with our students on an observation deck like doctors on a TV show. Stefano used to say the restorer's role in saving the art after the flood was much like a doctor's. Many of the paintings had been attacked by disease—mold and bacteria literally growing on the wooden panels. We were there to save the patients, working with tweezers and scalpels on paintings patched with bandages of Japanese paper. We often referred to the Limonaia as the *ospedale*.

"An art restorer," Dr. Garzoni said, "must be both scientist and artist. Restoration is an endeavor approached from both the mind and the heart." Her explanation was complete with hand gestures—touching her head, placing a splayed hand over her heart. "A tedious task," she went on, "requiring patience and a love for the creation of the artist. Often a restoration might take longer than it took the artist to create the work." I was surprised that Giuliana Garzoni herself was conducting the tour, as I'd expected one of her assistants, possibly Alberto Mazzone.

Dr. Garzoni explained they were cleaning the painting and went into a long, involved explanation of painting surfaces and the solvents and chemicals used in modern-day cleaning. She pointed out the restorers' binocular magnifiers, allowing them to see the smallest details of their subject while freeing their hands to work. My students listened and observed intently, scribbling in their notebooks.

I was having trouble concentrating, thinking about Roberto's party the next day, wondering if I should call Maria and tell her I couldn't make it. I'd dropped by Charley's office earlier in the week and asked if I could borrow his car for the evening. During our conversation, he'd asked about my plans for spring break and invited me to come along with him, his sister, and his niece. Anna, who was widowed two years ago, felt this trip might provide a nice diversion for her daughter Katie, just ending a second bad marriage. They were going to France.

I hadn't made any concrete plans myself. Regina had invited me to come along on a ski trip in the Italian Alps. She and Giorgio were going with another couple. I wasn't eager to be a fifth wheel, and I really felt I should spend my week seeing European art. I could ski back home. I was thinking about Paris, taking in the Louvre, maybe swinging down to Spain and visiting the Prado, or something up north—the Rijksmuseum in Amsterdam, the Pinakothek in Munich. But I was also considering Charley's invitation.

I hadn't given him an answer right away, and he asked me to think about it.

And I was thinking about it, though I was also trying to pull my mind back to what was going on here in the restoration lab. I had so many things spiraling through my head right now . . . Roberto . . . Stefano . . . a missing painting . . . spring break . . . midterms . . . papers.

We were escorted to a second room, where a man worked on a painting I immediately recognized as Leonardo da Vinci's *Adoration of the Magi*, which perked me up considerably. Dr. Garzoni explained they were doing preliminary tests to determine what steps should be taken, if any, to ensure the preservation of the piece. The man working on the Leonardo looked up and nodded. Quickly, his eyes swept over our little group, then rested on me. His expression was one of confusion, gradually shifting into recognition. Did I know this man? He was in his late fifties, with small round glasses. His hair was sparse on top, a little fringe of black and gray above his ears. After a moment, he returned to his work, but continued to glance up now and then.

As we were being escorted out of the room, he left his post and walked up and over to me.

"Signorina Suzanne, *è L-l-lei*?" he asked. Instantly, I recognized his voice.

"Pietro! Come sta?" It was Pietro Capparelli, little Pietro, Stefano's assistant.

"Bene, bene, and you, Signorina? You stay so young, and here I look l-l-like old man now. No hair." He grinned as he rubbed his hand across the top of his head. "Big belly," he said running his hand over the protrusion of his stomach under the white lab coat. "But you, Signorina, you still beautiful young woman."

"Pietro! What a wonderful surprise!" Our group was starting to leave and I didn't want to upset Dr. Garzoni, but I wanted to talk to Pietro. I had so many questions I wanted to ask him, though I had sense enough that I wouldn't go directly to what I really wanted to know: Did he know where Stefano was? Did Pietro know about the Masolino Madonna? He had been there at Stefano's side as they painstakingly restored the painting. And here he was once more, in the Uffizi standing in front of me.

"Let's get together," I said. "I'd love to hear about what you've been doing the past thirty years. It's been so long!"

Pietro grinned and nodded, taking my hand, rubbing the top of it, smiling as if he'd just discovered a long-lost treasure. "Even more than thirty years now. *Sì, sì,* we must g-g-get together."

"I'd love that. I'm teaching here in Florence."

"You call here at the Uffizi." He pulled out a card and

scribbled something on the back. "Or you call me where I stay here in Florence."

I glanced at the back of the card. He'd written an address and phone number.

"Your n-n-number?" he asked.

I didn't have a card, but I found a scrap of paper and wrote my number at school, then my cell number.

"I buy you l-l-lunch, okay?" Pietro offered.

"That'd be great," I said. "How about Monday?"

He thought for a moment. "*Sì*, Monday."

"I'll call, we'll set something up." I waved his card and nodded as I followed the group out, in somewhat of a daze. Yes, definitely, I would call him.

21

CHARLEY BROUGHT THE car over for me Saturday afternoon.

"How did you meet this birthday fellow?" he asked as we drove back to his apartment to drop him off. He'd always been interested in my social life, as if vicariously he could live through my romances. He met Jerry once, though after we broke up Charley confided he hadn't been impressed and thought I could do better.

I hadn't told him about my interest in finding out what had happened to the Masolino Madonna. I felt the tiniest bit silly, as if I saw myself as some amateur sleuth. Regina was the only one of my friends from school I'd told.

But now, I thought, why not get it over with? Charley would find out soon enough. I'd decided to accept his offer for spring break—and I was sure it would eventually come up if we spent a week together within the confines of his car. So I explained how I'd met Roberto, thinking he was his father, how I was looking for a painting I'd worked on during the restoration after the flood.

"You think someone stole the painting?" He glanced over,

nearly sideswiping a car parked on the street, then veered back into traffic.

My hand tightened on the door handle. "I know it was restored, but it appears to be missing from the museum's collection. There's a young man at the Uffizi who's helping me with some research. And I ran into one of the restorers I worked with years ago. We're having lunch on Monday." For some reason I didn't tell Charley about the notation in the file with Stefano's initials.

"Interesting," he mused, glancing over with a dry grin. "Nancy Drew." His shoulders bounced in typical Charley fashion, a trait I found endearing at times, irritating at others. "So, tell me about this Roberto Balducci fellow. You've been seeing him?"

"Well, yes, I guess."

"What do you mean *you guess*?"

I often felt Charley was the brother I never had. The guy looking out for the interests of his sister. I could tell he felt rather protective of me.

"We've only had one official date," I answered, "and that was interrupted by his father's dying."

"On the date?" Charley laughed.

"Actually, no, we didn't take his father on the date." I had to laugh too.

"Never hurts to have a chaperone." We'd arrived at Charley's apartment. We parked. He got out and I ran around and slid into the driver's seat.

"I'll take good care of your car. Thanks, Charley."

"Have fun," he said. "Don't drink too much," he added with a grin and shake of the finger.

I DIDN'T HAVE any trouble finding Maria's place again. There were several cars driving in when I arrived, and Maria's husband, Marco, directed us behind the large stone barn for parking.

Maria introduced me to Anna, the brunette twin, who

looked very much like her father, then Stella, the blonde twin. Luisa, really the prettiest, rather small and delicate compared to the other sisters, who were quite tall, arrived a few minutes later. Bea had returned to school in the States shortly after their grandfather's funeral.

The little twins, Carlo and Leo, were running around the house with their three-year-old cousin, Teresa, bonking each other on the head with balloons that Stella's husband, Gianni, was blowing up to hang from the ceiling.

Maria introduced me to an Uncle Renato, who I think must have been a great-uncle, then a woman she called Aunt Sofia, and several others. Marco's parents, Nonno Vanni and Nonna Eli, who looked to be in their late sixties, sat on the sofa. With each introduction, Maria called me a good friend of her father's. Good friend, indeed. I wondered what Roberto would think when he saw me pop out from behind the sofa shouting, "Surprise!"

When Roberto arrived, Maria escorted him into the living room, and we all jumped out from behind the furniture. He *was* surprised. His eyes scanned the room, resting on each of his guests, a big grin on his face. And then he saw me and his grin widened even further. "Suzanne!" He walked over and gave me a little peck on each cheek, then turned to Maria and shot her an approving smile and blew her a kiss. "What a very nice surprise." I breathed easier seeing how pleased he was.

Several others arrived throughout the evening. Cousins, aunts, uncles. I visited with Roberto's cousin Antonio and his wife, Claudia, who both seemed interested in knowing more about my school. I met Aldo Balducci, the cousin I'd spoken with on the phone before coming to Italy. He hung around me a good part of the evening, attempting to converse in English. As I'd learned from the confusion over my meeting the wrong Roberto Balducci, Aldo's English was terrible, though this didn't keep him from trying and I admired him for that.

I had little time to speak with Roberto, our attempts at conversation interrupted by family and friends. But he kept looking at me—over a shoulder, around a head, with a smile that told me he was happy I'd come. Yet he also looked tired with dark circles under his eyes, and I wondered if he'd had trouble sleeping, as I had for several weeks after I lost my mother. I noticed he seemed to be a little short of breath. I knew he didn't smoke, but wondered if it had something to do with his post-polio. Didn't they used to put kids who had polio in iron lungs?

I sipped my wine. Marco kept attempting to refill it, and I covered it each time with my hand. It became almost a little game, but there was no way I was going to drink more than a glass when I was driving Charley's car. I switched over to sparkling punch, which Maria had made for the children. Everyone was kind and generous—those who spoke English, even a little, attempting to converse. I tried my best to speak Italian and seemed to have the greatest success with the youngest members of the family.

Another man, Roberto's brother, I thought, arrived with the older woman I had seen at the funeral. I was sure she was Roberto's mother, and after a few moments, visiting with other guests, she walked over and introduced herself, speaking in English, describing herself as a fellow American, though she said she had lived in Italy for over sixty years now.

"You're teaching here in Florence?" She seemed to know who I was and I wondered if she'd been curious about me— this stranger at her son's party—and questioned Maria about my being here.

"Yes, as a visiting instructor for the semester."

"Are you adjusting to life in Italy? A slower pace than you're used to back home I'm sure."

"Actually, with my teaching and visiting the museums and churches, I seem to be on the run all the time." I didn't mention I'd also dedicated a fair amount of time trying to find a missing painting, and at least an equal amount attempting to decode a relationship with her son.

I could see traces of Roberto Balducci in his mother, Grace, though she was a petite, almost fragile-looking woman with a pale Irish complexion, tinted with pink blush. Her blue eyes were flecked with hints of gold, just like Roberto's. When she asked if I'd visited Italy before, I told her about my coming in the sixties, how I'd stayed to help after the flood, how I'd fallen in love with the art and the country.

"Roberto's father was very involved in the restoration too," she said proudly.

"Yes, Roberto has spoken of his father's work." I didn't explain how I'd met her son, and she didn't ask. I noticed she said *Roberto's father*, not *my husband*. "I'm sorry for your loss," I told her. The words sounded awkward even to my own ears. But I felt I should acknowledge the elder Roberto's passing.

She responded with a nod, as a vacant faraway look passed over her face. I was actually relieved when Stella came up and whispered something in her grandmother's ear and the two women excused themselves. I turned to find the man Grace Balducci had come in with standing beside me.

"Angelo Balducci," he introduced himself.

As we visited, I learned he was Grace and Roberto Sr.'s oldest son, Roberto's brother. He looked familiar, but maybe it was because he looked like Roberto—a little older with more gray in his hair. He had Roberto's beautiful smile and the same attentive way of listening. He seemed very sweet and it appeared he had come with his mother—no wife or girlfriend.

"I see you've met the future Bishop of Rome." Antonio came up behind us.

Bishop? And it was then I realized Angelo was one of the priests who had officiated at the funeral, the one with the red cap.

Angelo laughed and placed a hand affectionately on the shoulder of his cousin. "What a weight my family has imposed upon me. I'm expected to reclaim the papacy for Italy."

It came to me then that the Bishop of Rome was another name for the pope. Was I standing here with the future pope? What an interesting family, I thought.

Enormous bowls of pasta, fruit, bread, and chicken were brought out and placed on the large wooden table. And copious amounts of wine. A real Italian feast.

After a big chocolate cake with fifty candles, which Roberto seemed to have trouble blowing out, the guests sat visiting, while Roberto opened gifts. I hadn't brought a gift, as per Maria's instructions, not that I would have had any idea what to get for Roberto—I really didn't know him that well—but I had brought a card. Roberto smiled and nodded when he opened my card. It had taken me over an hour to pick it out, partly because I had difficulty reading the Italian on some of them, but mostly because I wasn't sure what our relationship was all about. I finally decided a "funny card" was generally safe, and had selected one about getting old and wise.

Before he left with his mother, Angelo, who had said the blessing before we ate, offered another prayer, and we all knelt as he blessed the family.

I sat awkwardly in the kitchen as Maria and her sisters cleaned up and the aunts and cousins carried in dishes, silverware, plates, and glasses. I had offered to help, but Maria said, glancing around at the elder members of the family, that as a guest she wouldn't dream of putting me to work. So I sat, observing the women scurrying around, feeling a bit out of place.

Maria's was an old-fashioned kitchen without many modern conveniences, so cleaning up was more than a minor chore— scraping, rinsing, washing, and drying. Every sister had a job. Luisa dried while Stella put dishes away in the cupboards, continually asking Maria where things went, and offering suggestions which, as far as I could understand, were suggestions for more convenient storage—wouldn't it be more convenient to put the silverware here, the mixing bowls there. The girls were all fluent in English, and in between their conversations in Italian, which involved a lot of teasing and laughter, they attempted to include me. Their interaction brought on a little pang of nostalgia, the memories of those evenings spent with my own sister around the sink with our mom in the old days before the dishwasher.

"How did you and Papa meet?" Stella asked. I'd had little time to visit with Stella during the party, but I had already determined that she was the serious one. I remembered Roberto telling me she was studying to be a doctor. She had a husband and three-year-old daughter, and was only twenty-three.

I explained how I'd read something her grandfather had written and had contacted her father thinking he might be able to help me out.

"Suzanne is a professor of art history," Maria said. I think they already knew this, as they had each made an effort to speak with me during the party, but I liked the way Maria announced this. The way she said it, I could tell she was on my side, if there were sides to be on. Was I in some kind of competition for their father's affection? I wasn't even sure how much, if anything, the girls knew about me.

Luisa, the prettiest one, the one who worked in the art gallery in Rome, jumped into the conversation with enthusiasm, asking me what courses I taught. She seemed especially interested in the class on women in Renaissance art. *Score one more for Suzanne,* I thought as I explained what we were covering in the class.

"There was great interest in art at home, particularly with Nonno's encouragement. He always gave us paints, sketch pads, pencils, pastels, canvas, brushes, clay for Christmas and birthdays." Luisa spoke easily of her grandfather and I detected no sadness, just good memories in her recollections. "Even Papa loved to paint and draw. If he hadn't gone into medicine, I think he could have made it with his art."

"I was impressed with your father's drawings, the portraits he did of each of you when you were about sixteen," I told her.

"The ones in the apartment in Rome?" Anna asked. She was the quiet one, the one whose mind was working a mile a minute, but who seldom spoke up. Out of the corner of my eye I could see the exchanged looks, the raised eyebrows on Stella's serious countenance. They were all obviously wondering what I had been doing at their father's apartment in Rome, and I was now wondering about Bea, the little sister in the States. Maybe she would have to be the tiebreaker. I had the feeling that both Anna and Stella saw me as an interloper, while Maria and Luisa rather liked me.

"Yes," I answered. "They're lovely."

This seemed to bring the conversation to a temporary halt, but it soon picked up again when Maria started divvying up the leftovers, putting a little of this and that into ceramic dishes that had come with the various cousins and aunts to the party, pulling others out of her own cupboard. I don't think I'd ever seen so much food in my life, and even after we'd all eaten seconds and thirds, there was enough for at least two more parties.

"For you, Professor Cunningham." Maria placed two dishes in front of me on the table. I looked through the glass lids at pasta and chicken in one, birthday cake in the other. The fact that Maria offered me dishes that would have to be returned made me feel not so much like an outsider anymore, and I was grateful for the gesture.

When we returned to the living room after the kitchen chores, the party was winding down. Uncle Renato was slumped in a big cozy-looking upholstered chair, snoozing with an even rhythm. Two of the aunts sat on the love seat, not really conversing, but exchanging a word or two here and there. One of them was knitting, a bulky blue yarn moving rapidly around two large needles. Several of the guests had already taken off. Roberto sat on the sofa with Carlo asleep in his lap, Leo on one side, his head buried against his grandfather, and Teresa snuggled up against the other, awake, but looking drowsy. The young men sat around the TV watching a soccer game with the sound turned down low.

Roberto looked up and smiled. I knew I should leave soon, as I'd told Charley I would have the car back by nine. Roberto reached out for my hand as I approached, jostling little Teresa a bit.

"I should be going," I whispered, bending down so I wouldn't wake anyone.

"Please, stay," he said, softly. "We've barely had time to talk." We'd managed little other than his apology that he hadn't called—that being interrupted by Uncle Renato, with a good slap on Roberto's back and something said, which he obviously found humorous, but that I didn't understand. Then our second attempt at conversation—"I'm so glad Maria thought to call you"—cut off by little Teresa, asking for a balloon, which Roberto reached up with his crutch to loosen from the ceiling.

"I borrowed a car," I explained, "and I promised to have it back by nine."

"Please, for a moment," he said. He smiled and my heart took a little leap. Clearly my fears about attending the party had been unfounded. "Sit, Suzanne." He patted the sofa next to Teresa, who moved closer to her grandfather.

I sat.

"I know I said I'd call."

"I understand—"

"Do you like to swim?"

His question took me by surprise. "Yes, I like to swim," I answered tentatively.

"How about tomorrow? Do you have plans?"

I shook my head.

"I'd like to invite you up for dinner," he said, the inflection of his voice presenting this more as a question than an invitation.

I nodded yes.

"I'll send a cab. Bring a swimming suit. About four tomorrow afternoon?"

"Okay," I said, a little puzzled.

He touched my cheek and kissed me quickly on the lips.

Teresa, whose curious little eyes had been moving back and forth with this conversation, grinned. Carlo looked up with heavy, sleepy eyes. "Ciao, Cuckoo," he said.

22

WHEN I WOKE the next day, it was raining ferociously. I made a pot of coffee and spent the morning and early afternoon in my apartment, going over test questions for midterms the coming week, then reviewing my information on the Masolino and rereading the article and history file in preparation for my lunch meeting with Pietro. I still couldn't believe Stefano could have been involved in the painting's disappearance, and I wanted desperately for Pietro to tell me something that would make sense of all this.

For lunch I ate the cold chicken, manicotti, and leftover chocolate birthday cake Maria had sent home with me. I was curious about Roberto's invitation for dinner and swimming. Where would we go swimming on a cold, rainy, winter afternoon?

I STOOD IN the covered *porta* of my building looking out onto the wet stone street and waited for the cab, which arrived a few minutes after four. We headed north and drove through the city, up into the hills toward Fiesole. *"Dove andiamo?"*

I asked the driver. *Where are we going?* Was this another one of Roberto's kidnapping schemes?

The driver looked back at me, puzzled, as if wondering what kind of woman gets in a cab not even knowing where she's going. "Villa Balducci," he answered.

Were we headed to Roberto's home? A villa?

I looked back at the city of Florence as we climbed the hill. Unlike my last trip, when I had taken the bus to San Romolo for the elder Balducci's funeral, I could see the city below. Today the rain had created a misty drizzle and a rather romantic view. The large red-domed Cathedral of Santa Maria del Fiore and Giotto's beautiful bell tower reached up into the wet silver sky. I settled back, comfortable, yet curious about what the afternoon held. We turned off the main road, passed a vineyard, then pulled onto a private lane lined with tall cypresses and followed it up to a large stone structure glowing golden in the sun just starting to peek out from behind a cloud. The rain had let up, but there was still a slight pitter-patter against the cab window.

Roberto stood in the doorway. He yelled to the cab driver and held out an umbrella as he leaned on a crutch. The driver ran up to the door, took the umbrella and came back for me, then escorted me to the front door. Roberto kissed me lightly on each cheek. "Welcome," he said.

"To your humble abode," I replied in a teasing voice, gawking as Roberto motioned both me and the taxi driver into the house. I stood in the tiled entry and looked around in awe as Roberto paid the driver. A large living room with exposed beams spread out before me. An Oriental carpet in shades of mauve, plum, and blue covered a good portion of the floor. Several areas of furniture were grouped in conversation-friendly settings. Books and antiques, paintings and drawings were arranged artistically on shelves, tables, and walls.

"This is your home?" I asked, then realized it was probably a stupid question.

He nodded.

"It's beautiful."

"Thank you."

My eyes wouldn't hold still. Roberto didn't say anything more, perhaps aware I had to take a minute to inspect my surroundings.

"I didn't know where you lived," I said. "I mean, I guess we never talked about that." I realized that there were many things I didn't know about Roberto.

"Please, your coat." He motioned to a small closet just inside the front door, took and hung my coat. I set my bag on the floor and we walked into the living room.

"I'm making coffee," Roberto said. "Rather a dismal, wet day out there. Please, let's sit."

We sat in two roomy velvet chairs pulled up close to the big cozy fireplace. It was a real fireplace with real logs. Not the phony gas type I had at home that turned on and off using a switch on the wall.

"I appreciated the card," he said.

At first I thought he was talking about the birthday card.

"And the call," he added, and I realized he was talking about the card I'd sent when his father died. "And thank you for coming to the services."

I felt my face grow warm. He had seen me at the funeral. Had he also seen me come in late and leave early?

I nodded and we sat quietly, our faces turned to the glow of the fire. "Your home is lovely."

"It's been in the family for a long time. I grew up here."

I continued to look around the room.

"We've done several major updates over the years," Roberto said, "and I've added some of my own touches."

My eyes stopped at a portrait of a beautiful blonde woman.

"Paolina," Roberto said quietly.

"Stella looks very much like her mother." I turned and smiled at him.

"Probably more than the other girls."

"I enjoyed meeting your daughters. The party was fun." I thought of Stella, her mother's look-alike. I didn't think she liked me. I wondered, What would Paolina think?

"I want to explain," he said, "why I didn't call."

"It's—"

"No, no," Roberto protested. I could tell he didn't want me to say "It's all right," which was exactly what I was going to say. "I think I need to talk about it," he said. "I really haven't. I feel I can talk to you, Suzanne. Will you let me?"

"Please."

"I knew Papa was going to die. He was very sick, in a great deal of pain. . . ." Roberto cleared his throat and coughed, staring into the flame as it cracked and popped. "It hit me much harder than I thought it would." He looked over at me. "I haven't been feeling well. I'm not sure if it's losing Papa or just this goddamned weak body of mine giving out, or the combination of the two. I've felt very angry." I could hear it in his voice. "I'm trying not to let this anger get the best of me."

I leaned in with an urge to take his hand, to assure him it was okay to feel anger at the loss of a loved one, to feel cheated when life dealt a blow.

"I didn't think it would be this hard," he went on. "When I lost Paolina . . . but it was different then. So many people depending on me. I don't know, but somehow I just wasn't prepared like I thought I was."

"You were very close to your father?"

"No." He shook his head.

His answer surprised me.

"Sometimes I felt I barely knew him. There were secrets, so many secrets. And I don't think he knew how much I loved him, that no matter what he did, no matter what he was, I would always love him."

"I'm sure he knew," I said softly, though I wasn't. I had no idea what Roberto was talking about, but I felt he needed some kind of reassurance. I wanted to tell him we all feel like that when we lose a parent—*If only I'd taken the time to know them better, to say "I love you" more often.*

"When Maria had the party," Roberto said, "it made me realize how much goodness there is in my life right now. It gave me the boost I needed to start living my life again. When I saw you . . ." He didn't finish his sentence. "I think that coffee's ready."

"Please, let me help." I stood.

"I'll put another log on the fire." He reached for his crutches. "I've set out cups, sugar, a pitcher of milk in the refrigerator—you might warm it in the microwave for a few seconds." I could hear the rain on the roof, hitting the tile. It sounded like it was coming down in torrents again.

"The kitchen is just down the hall." He motioned.

I started down the hall, past an enormous dining room that looked out onto a garden. Silk flowers were arranged on a large glass-topped dining table with a suite of heavy wooden chairs. The house seemed to wrap around the garden—a courtyard. I could see that buds on the foliage were starting to green and I realized it was already March, and spring was just around the corner. A fountain that I recognized as a reproduction of *Bacchino*, the little dwarf at the Boboli Gardens, stood in the center of a stone patio that was being hammered by the rain. A plump little man, completely nude, sitting on top of a turtle— this was not a beautiful nude like the classical sculptures or Michelangelo's gorgeous *David*. Ugly, but ugly in a cute way. An image came to me briefly—Stefano and I walking through the enormous gardens, taking a break from our work that first spring when life was coming back to the city, when the trees and flowers were beginning to bud. I had never been so happy, unaware then of how it would end.

I turned left to the kitchen and looked out again on the court-yard, through the wide expanse of glass. The kitchen, like all the rooms I'd seen, was huge, and very up-to-date with double ovens, a microwave, a stainless steel refrigerator with a water dispenser. The counters were cobalt tile, the cupboards dark walnut. Enormous, brightly colored ceramic pots in Florentine yellows and blues were displayed above the cupboards. Copper kettles and pots hung from an iron rack, utensils of every shape and size stuck out of ceramic containers, and glass jars filled with pasta, flour, sugar, and coffee were lined up on one counter. I remembered Roberto's sparse kitchen at the apartment in

Rome and wondered if this wasn't a kitchen designed by and for a woman who loved to cook. I could imagine Paolina and her five beautiful daughters bustling about this enormous kitchen, preparing a fantastic feast together, chatting and laughing and tasting each other's creations. I wondered briefly how it would feel to be included.

I found the milk in the fridge, warmed it in the microwave, poured the coffee, and placed the cups on a tray Roberto had prepared with sugar, spoons, napkins, and a small plate of biscotti and carried it into the living room.

Roberto sat staring into the fire. He'd added a couple of logs. He looked up at me and said, "I feel much better now."

I wondered if that was it—if that little snippet of a conversation had fulfilled his need to talk. I set the tray on the table.

"I haven't been swimming in weeks," Roberto said as I sat again. He stirred a small spoonful of sugar in his coffee. "Are you a good swimmer, Suzanne?"

"Well . . ." I added milk to my coffee. As he had at his apartment, Roberto had made it American style for me, which still seemed to require a good dose of milk.

He grinned. "You are, aren't you?"

"I did a fair amount of swimming when I was a kid. I loved it."

"Tell me—you had a case full of trophies?"

"A few," I said with a modest smile.

His eyes rested on me with an expression that seemed to say, I'm discovering new things about you every day. "You should enjoy the afternoon, then. I love to swim too."

"I assume it's an indoor pool," I said as I picked up a biscotto. "You know it's raining and still a bit cold. It's winter."

"Yes, but spring's right around the corner."

"I noticed the garden is starting to bud."

"It's been a long winter. I'm ready for spring."

"For me, it's gone very fast. Half my semester's almost over. Midterms are coming up the end of the week."

"I should have invited you sooner." I could hear some regret in his voice.

The fire crackled and popped as we sat silently for several moments.

"Your mother," I asked, "she lives in Venice?"

"She moved there several years ago to be near Angelo." Roberto offered no explanation as to why his parents didn't live together, and I guessed it was because of the elder Balducci's health. I also assumed that the parents' separation or divorce probably wouldn't look good on the pope's resume.

"Your brother, Angelo, he's your older brother?"

Roberto explained that Angelo had been named after his grandfather who'd passed away just a month before he was born. "So, I got to be the junior."

"Angelo is a bishop?" I asked.

"A cardinal," Roberto replied. "His official title is Patriarch of Venice."

"And the future pope?"

"It's a possibility. He's risen quite rapidly in the hierarchy of the Church. Politics. Unfortunately there's still much of it in the Church and Angelo is quite skilled at it." Roberto shook his head. "He had plenty of practice calling the shots, being five years older than his baby brother. But a good man, yes, a very good, spiritual man."

"I met the pope once," I said, "at the Limonaia." I told Roberto how I had been homesick, feeling I might have made a terrible mistake by choosing not to return home for Christmas, and then the pope showed up. "He blessed me and I knew I had made the right choice, that this was a confirmation of my decision to stay in Florence. And now," I added, "I've been blessed a second time by the pope."

"I'm not sure if potential popes count," Roberto said with a laugh.

"Good enough for a Protestant girl like me." I laughed too.

"Confirmation that this second trip to Italy was a wise decision?"

It was, I thought as I sat with Roberto Balducci, a wise decision, but something inside me, maybe a tendency to distrust my own emotions and my ability to judge men, made me wonder if I was about to embark on a second ill-fated love affair in Italy.

We talked about the villa, how Roberto's grandfather had owned it, how it was passed down to his father, the oldest son. "By all rights," Roberto said, "the family home should have gone to Angelo because he is the eldest." He paused for a moment as if waiting for me to ask how he had come to inherit the house, which I assumed he had, though I wondered if priests could own property. He continued, "The villa had become rather run-down at one time, after my father left. We made improvements over the years. Angelo will never live here, and so, here we are." He looked around the room. "Perhaps someday Maria will live here, or at some point we'll consider selling it. It's a bit much for upkeep at times, or perhaps . . ."

No sons, I thought. Was this important to a man? Again we sat not speaking for a while. "More coffee?" I asked.

Roberto nodded, and I got up and went to the kitchen.

After I returned and sat, he said, "I'm sorry my father died before he could help you out. Have you had any luck in your search for information on the painting?"

"A little. I've contacted a young restorer from the Uffizi, visited the director of restoration, and Friday during a tour I ran into one of the restorers I worked with at the Limonaia."

"Stefano Leonetti?"

"No." I didn't want to talk about this right now, and I felt myself growing uncomfortable. "Pietro Capparelli."

"You've got to find this Leonetti. I think my father was trying to tell you something when he said that name."

For some reason I couldn't tell Roberto about my discovery in the file, the notation that appeared to be in Stefano's hand. The image of the man in the back of San Romolo at the elder Balducci's funeral flickered in my mind again, and I knew there was some connection between Stefano and Roberto's father. I didn't want to make accusations I couldn't support, and maybe by telling him about Stefano I felt I would have to confess some sin of my past. This seemed ridiculous—I was a middle-aged woman with one very short marriage to my credit, or maybe discredit. Surely Roberto knew if I was remotely normal I had some kind of sexual past. But I didn't think he'd hold me in high regard for having an affair with a married man.

"If you could determine the source of my father's information about the painting being destroyed . . . ," Roberto mused.

"Yes, that would be helpful." I thought again of the official Uffizi file that stated the painting had been destroyed. The obvious source? And yet, I sensed there was more to it than that.

"Well, ready for a swim?" Roberto swallowed the last of his coffee.

"Yes, but where are we going?"

"Follow me." He stood, grabbed his crutches, and motioned me to come along. He showed me to a bedroom down the hall where he said I could change, and then told me how to get to the pool—down the hall, turn right—and said he would wait for me.

"The pool's here?" I asked.

"We had it put in about fifteen years ago."

I know I must have smiled. I liked this place, Roberto's villa.

After he left, I glanced around the room—very feminine, surely for one of his daughters. No, maybe the twins. There were twin beds. A lush white cotton towel and a cozy terry-cloth robe were laid out on one of the beds like in a fancy hotel. I stepped into the adjoining bathroom. Flower prints hung on the walls from satin ribbons, a white and peach color scheme. A big porcelain claw-footed tub sat in the middle of the room and there was a separate shower. I drooled for a moment over that tub. Forget the pool—I could spend the afternoon soaking in that tub. An open door led into another bedroom. A double bed and crib—for the grandchildren, I assumed. Although they were all old enough now, I imagined they were in big kids' beds. There would surely be more grandchildren. I took my time, double-checking myself in the full-length mirror. I wasn't in bad shape for a woman my age, and my suit had a comfortable bra that held things pretty

well in place, but I still didn't feel completely at ease revealing this much of my body in broad daylight. I secured my
hair with a clip, wrapped myself in the terry-cloth robe, and
walked down the hall.

The pool was covered with a high arched glass ceiling. A
wall of glass doors that looked like they could be removed
during warmer weather ran the full length of the enclosure.
Roberto sat at the edge of the pool. I could tell he hadn't been
in yet. He was waiting for me. I dropped my robe on a lounge
chair alongside the towel and sat beside him.

I'd been curious about his body. I tried not to be too obvious, and the thought passed through my mind that he was examining mine too. His legs were thin for a man his size, but
his chest and shoulders were broad and athletic looking. He
had a fair amount of hair on his chest, which I found rather
appealing.

I held my tummy as I sat, sucking it in with a deep breath.

He touched my knee lightly. "Last one in's a rotten egg,"
he said, shoving off the edge.

I slipped down into the water. We were at the deep end. It
was a good-sized pool, the water as clear and clean as if it'd
been poured out of bottles. It smelled of chlorine, but not in an
overpowering way. A beautiful pool—aqua-colored tile, like the
waters off the isle of Capri, which made the water look very
blue. Heated just enough to feel comfortable, it was still cool
enough to get a good workout. As I surfaced, I looked out the
full-length windows that ran along the outer wall, facing out to
the courtyard. Yes, I could really get used to a place like this.

Roberto had started across while I was taking all this in.
He moved quickly, with a strong stroke. I followed. Obviously
we were racing. He had a head start, and was on the other side
before I could catch up with him. He grabbed on to the side
and waited for me, running his hand over his face, pushing his
hair back.

"Fantastic pool," I said.

"We've all enjoyed it. I haven't been in for a couple of
weeks. Feels good, very good. How many laps can you do?"

"How many you want?"

Roberto smiled. He liked this, I sensed, the fact that he could compete with me on this level. In the pool he felt he could be my physical equal, an athletic competitor, and I could tell he rather liked the idea that I'd touted myself as some kind of swimming champion. He pushed off again. I caught up with him and overtook him. He reached the other end of the pool, then shoved off. We did several more laps, swimming now almost in synchronization, then Roberto pulled ahead.

He reached for the side of the pool, then held out his hand and pulled me over beside him. Silently we stared at each other. His face was flushed.

"Ready for a break?" he asked.

"I could slow down for a minute or two." After several moments, looking around again, I said, "This is beautiful." Stone mosaics in the style of those at Pompeii decorated the side of the pool. "You weren't about to give up 'til you pulled ahead, were you?" I asked.

"You'll have to come again. This is good for me."

I wasn't sure if he meant the swimming, or maybe just my company. "I'd like that."

He touched me on the cheek, drew me closer, and kissed me. His lips were warm and wet and tasted of chlorine—clean, yet sweet. He kissed me deeply.

"Thank you for coming," he said.

"Thank you for inviting me."

He ran his fingers along my breasts across the top of my swimming suit, but nothing more.

He pulled himself up and sat, then reached down and helped me out. "Why don't we go ahead and shower."

I thought he was suggesting we do this together, but then he said, "Feel free to use anything you need in the bathroom. The girls have it well equipped—shampoo, rinse, lotion, hair dryer. Take your time. I'll shower and get dinner started."

I wondered if he wanted me to get up and leave, so he wouldn't have to feel the indignation of my watching him struggle with his crutches. I had noticed they were lying on the tile just a few feet from where we were sitting, within his reach, I was sure. I thought about picking them up and handing them to him, but decided he wanted me to leave and deal with it himself.

I stood. "Roberto?"

"Yes?"

"Would you mind," I said, feeling rather silly for asking, "could I take a bath?"

He nodded. "That would be fine."

"It's just that, well, I've only got a shower at my apartment, and I saw that beautiful claw-foot tub." I don't know why I felt I had to explain. If I went ahead and took a bath, rather than a shower, he would never know.

"There's bubble bath. Don't rush. Enjoy the tub. I'll start dinner."

"You don't mind? If you wait, I'll help."

"No, no, you go ahead. I enjoy cooking and I know you don't."

"All right," I said.

I FOUND THE bubble bath, shampoo, and rinse—there were several kinds and I took my time, opening each and sniffing it, before I picked a shampoo with the tangy fragrance of tropical fruit. The bubble bath was pink with a strawberry scent. There were several candles on the vanity. One was brand new, with a clean white wick. The others had been used. I found matches in the drawer and lit one of these. It smelled like peaches. I undressed, hung my wet suit on a hook in the shower, combed through my tangled hair, unpacked my clothes, set them on the vanity chair next to the tub, and started running the bath water. I heard a knock on the bedroom door.

"I've got something for you, Suzanne."

I pulled on the terry robe and opened the door a crack and peeked out. Roberto stood, fully dressed, fresh from his shower, smelling of soap and cologne, his hair still damp. How did he do that so quickly? Somehow, he managed, even on his crutches, to hold a bottle of wine in one hand, a glass in the other.

He handed me the glass, then the bottle. "I thought you might enjoy a drink while you soak."

"Thanks," I said. We stood looking at each other, neither of us saying anything for an uncomfortably long time. "How did you know I don't like to cook?" I asked.

"Your apartment," he answered. "It didn't look like a place where a person did much cooking."

"Oh," I said. "I thought the same thing about your apartment in Rome."

"I seldom cook there. I don't enjoy cooking if I'm alone."

"Oh," I said again, awkwardly. He looked so fresh and sweet and sexy, and I didn't want him to leave. Why had he come to deliver this wine? I wondered. If I hadn't been so slow in choosing my shampoo, and contemplating the candles, I would now be in the bath. Again I wondered about his intentions, and thought of the kiss, then the intimate touch in the pool. "Would you like to join me?" I asked, feeling myself grow very warm.

"More than you know," he answered, then shook his head. "I'm afraid, Suzanne, I find myself with limited energy."

"We could skip dinner," I said. "Would that save some energy?"

He opened the door a bit further with his crutch, then entered the room. He shut the door behind him and leaned up against it. He reached out and pulled me close to him, his lips finding mine, his hand separating the robe, touching my breasts, sending a shock through my body all the way to my toes. We stood there for I don't know how long, the wine and glass still in my hands, Roberto's fingers moving down my body, sending waves of heat through me, when I heard the water, still running in the bathroom. "Oh, no, I left the water running!" I pulled myself away and ran to the bathroom.

I'd added just a capful of bubble bath, but it was already up to the top of the tub. I set the wine and glass on the floor, knocking the bottle over. It rolled under the tub. I turned the water off. Roberto entered the room.

"Oops," I said.

"It's okay," he said. "Tile floor."

I walked over to him. We stood looking at each other for several moments, then I undid the top button of his shirt and ran my fingers along his neck, down his chest. Again our lips met.

I led him to the vanity chair, pushed everything off, coaxed him down, knelt in front of him.

"If I'd planned better," he said, "we could have skipped the swimming." He was breathing very heavy now—not so much from excitement, I thought, but sheer exhaustion, like he'd done at his birthday when he'd tried to blow out the candles. I didn't want him to be embarrassed. I think he was trying to tell me that he didn't have the energy to perform, but I thought we'd come too far now to quit. He reached over and pulled the robe off my shoulders, then dropped it to the floor. "You're a beautiful woman, Suzanne." He pressed his lips to my neck and started working his way down.

Slowly, I finished unbuttoning his shirt and slipped it off, then started on his belt. He stood and removed his pants, then turned and slipped off his undershorts. He walked over to the tub, slowly, without his crutches, held on to the side and got in. Bubbles pushed up, over the side, onto the tile floor. I climbed in front of him, and slid down into the warmth of the silky water.

He put his arms around me, stroking my breasts. I closed my eyes.

"Mmm," he said, "this is very nice. I've had fantasies."

"About this?"

"About you. Us, together. I'm afraid this evening they might be just fantasies."

Again, I thought he was apologizing, warning me.

"In the fantasies I'm whole again, well, with good strong legs. And enough energy to—"

"I just want to be near you," I said.

His hand moved down, along my leg, then stroked my inner thighs, then his fingers moved inside me, his touch, the warm water exciting me beyond belief. I arched my back, pushing into him. He continued to move his fingers inside me.

"Feel good?"

"Oh, yes, good."

"Just relax, Suzanne. Let yourself go. I'm afraid this might be all I can offer you right now."

He continued to caress my breasts with one hand, the other moving inside me, his mouth moving along my neck. I relaxed into his touch, my body against his. And I knew I couldn't hold on much longer as I reached a peak and the feelings, the sensations circled round and through me, finally exploding, touching every nerve in my body.

We lay together in the warmth of the water, Roberto's arms wrapped around me now, not speaking, just being together. I must have fallen asleep. The bubbles had receded, the water was now lukewarm. Roberto shifted a bit, which brought me back out of my reverie.

"Is this getting uncomfortable for you?" I asked.

"No, it's fine, just need to rearrange things." He kissed me on the neck. I leaned forward a bit so he could adjust himself. "You okay?" I asked.

"I'm fine. I'm fine." He coaxed me back again, nuzzling the side of my neck.

"Will you stay tonight?" he asked. "Maybe in the morning . . ."

"Yes."

"Are you hungry?"

"Not so much." I looked down and saw the wine bottle sticking out from under the tub, the wineglass sitting upright about a foot away. I was amazed that neither had broken when I rushed in and dropped them on the floor, and there the glass stood as if waiting to be filled.

"Ready for that glass of wine?" he asked.

"Sure." I tried reaching for the bottle on the floor, stretching. I touched the side of the bottle and, with my fingers, was able to roll it out enough to grasp it and pull it up and hand it to Roberto. I could see the wineglass was too far away to reach. I stood and, bracing with my hand on the side of the tub, reached over, feeling ridiculously naked and exposed. I started to giggle as I slid back into the tub, looking back at

Roberto, who was grinning, then laughing too. "Oh, dear," I said. "How are we going to open it?"

"A corkscrew," he answered. "In my pants pocket."

I looked over toward the vanity chair, where his pants had dropped to the floor. Again I reached, stretching until I grabbed hold of the corner of one leg and pulled it over. Roberto reached into the pocket and dramatically plucked out the corkscrew and held it up. He twisted it into the bottle and pulled out the cork, then poured a glass of wine and handed it to me.

I took a sip. "Very good," I said and held it to his lips.

He wrapped his hand around mine and took a small taste.

"You're not much of a drinker, are you?" I asked.

"I enjoy a good wine, but find it's best to limit myself. There are many things I enjoy, but find I can only do them in smaller ways now." He reached over and touched my cheek. Again, I felt he was offering an apology. Didn't he realize none was needed?

We added more hot water, and cuddled, drinking our wine slowly.

I spent the night. We didn't eat dinner. Roberto took me to the master bedroom, and we snuggled in his enormous bed under a warm feather quilt. In the early morning, the room still dark, I woke and sensed Roberto was awake too. He reached over for me and pulled me close. We made love, taking our time, comfortable and already familiar with one another's bodies. He touched and caressed me tenderly. He pulled a condom out of the nightstand, and I helped him put it on, in no way disturbing the rhythm of our lovemaking, which was slow and sweet.

We fell asleep in each other's arms. When I woke again, he was awake, gazing at me. He kissed me, then whispered, "Ready for breakfast?"

"May I help?"

"No. You just relax."

So I did. In Roberto's bed under his crisp white, freshly laundered sheets, the softest scent of our lovemaking lingering. The headboard was black wrought iron with scrolls and curls. I lay in bed, examining the room in the early morning light. Soft buttery yellow walls with a trompe l'oeil on the ceiling, a dome similar to the Pantheon in Rome with a circle of bright blue faux sky. The design painted on the upper portion of the wall imitated drapery and tassels so real I was tempted to reach up and give one a little tug. I lingered, thinking how good it had felt to be held by a man, to feel the warmth and comfort of his body. To laugh with a man. To have a man fix me breakfast.

I got up, slipped on my clothes, and went out into the kitchen.

"You're a morning person?" Roberto asked with a smile.

"Yes." I was smiling too. I think I had been smiling all morning. "As soon as I get some exercise and my coffee."

"Well, we've had the exercise." He poured coffee and handed me a cup. "And here's the coffee."

What a perfect morning, I thought as I gave him a quick kiss on the neck as he returned to the stove. "I guess we're all set," I said with a laugh.

It was a wonderful breakfast—American-style bacon and eggs with fried potatoes, and tiramisu, the dessert he had planned for last night.

"Do you have some time off at midterm?" Roberto asked as we finished eating.

"A full week for spring break."

"I suppose you've got plans?"

"Yes, actually, I do." I carried the dishes to the sink. "I'm going to France with Charley."

"Charley?" His tone was simultaneously curious and bothered.

"Father Stover, dean of my school." I poured more coffee and sat.

"Your friend the priest."

"Well, not just Charley." I didn't want Roberto to think I was taking off for an intimate week with a priest, though in truth I would rather be going with just Charley and not the sister and niece. "His sister and her daughter are coming as well."

"Are you looking forward to it?"

I laughed. "I'm not sure. I think there's some history of dysfunction in the family."

"In everyone's, I suppose," he replied. "Maybe later, Easter or this summer, maybe we could"—he hesitated—"take a weekend."

"I'd like that."

We sat with coffee in the kitchen, talking about where we might go—Vienna, Barcelona, Prague, London, Amsterdam.

It was a beautiful sunny morning. Roberto pointed out the various areas of the garden, explaining what the different trees, flowers, and plants were, what it would look like when it bloomed in the spring.

"You have a gardener?" I asked.

"The last few years, yes, but I still like to get out and do as much as I can myself. How about you, Suzanne, do you like to garden?"

"I do some potted plants every spring, but I've never really had a garden, with . . ." I started to say with Rousseau, a garden just didn't work out—she liked to dig when she was a puppy and I gave her free run of the yard. But the words wouldn't come, and then, I could feel a warmth and moisture rise up behind my eyes.

"What is it?" Roberto reached for me.

"My dog . . ."

"Rousseau?"

I was touched that he'd remembered her name. I'd mentioned her only once. "My sister called a couple of weeks ago. Rousseau was old, almost fourteen, and they put her to sleep."

"I'm sorry, Suzanne, you should have said something."

"With you just losing your father—"

"You and Rousseau were probably closer than me and my father." It was the second time he'd alluded to the fact that he and his father weren't close, and again it surprised me.

"She meant a lot to me." Roberto held my hand and I liked the feel of his warmth, the slight pressure on my skin. "When I decided to come to Florence, she was my biggest concern. I had to give this serious consideration, I guess because I knew something like this might happen when I was gone. I missed her, and now I still miss her."

"I'm sorry," he said. "But I can't say I'm sorry you came to Florence."

"I'm not either. I'm glad I came."

We sat quietly for several moments, staring out into the yard.

"What time do you have to be at school today?" Roberto asked.

"School? It's Monday, isn't it?" I laughed. I'd lost track of time, here in this little fantasy world in Roberto's beautiful villa. "My first class is at ten forty-five. What about you? Are you going to work today?"

"I'll go in later," he said. "I've been doing just half days lately."

I looked at my watch. It was almost ten. "I probably should call a cab. I need to run back to my apartment before I go to school."

"I'll take you," he said.

"You sure?"

"No problem, but we'd better get moving."

I swallowed the last of my coffee, put the cups in the sink, then went back to the bedroom to gather my belongings.

Roberto had warmed the van in the garage and pulled around to the front. I jumped in and we took off down his private lane and onto the main road.

"Sorry, Roberto, making you rush off like this. I don't know how I could have lost track of the time."

He smiled. "I see how it could have happened. We had a nice time this morning."

I returned his smile. "We did. And yesterday too." I didn't want him to think I had been in any way dissatisfied with what happened last night. Everything about the past two days had been wonderful—the swimming, the bath, our lovemaking, breakfast.

We twisted through traffic, into the city center, onto my street. Roberto touched my hand, then kissed me as I started to get out of the car. "I'll be gone this week," he said, and I thought how strange he hadn't mentioned this before. "But I'll call." He kissed me again, then smiled and waved as I stepped out of the car.

I rushed into the building, wondering why Roberto had waited until the last minute, as if it were an afterthought, to tell me he would be gone. And I had the sensation that I couldn't completely trust him, though I knew there was no clear reason for my feelings.

Secrets. He'd said something about secrets—his father's secrets. Was there something Roberto wasn't telling me? Did the younger Roberto Balducci have secrets of his own?

23

PIETRO WAS SITTING at the trattoria sipping red wine when I arrived. I ordered a glass and we looked over the menu as we visited. I wanted desperately to ask him about Stefano, about the painting, but couldn't bring myself to do it just yet.

"Tell me, Signorina Suzanne, about your l-l-life. You are a p-p-professor of art history?" He laughed with affection. "You surprise me. You knew little about art when you came to us."

"I knew *nothing* about art." I laughed too. "But I learned. I was a student here in Florence. Then I went home and studied from books, but my true classroom was here in your beautiful city. Even with all the destruction, I was able to go to the museums. And you, you and the other restorers, my teachers, my mentors."

He looked up from his menu. "Stefano Leonetti."

There. He'd said it. I felt a warmth rise up the back of my neck and spread into my cheeks. Could Pietro see this? "Do you keep in touch?" I asked lightly, making every effort to steady my voice. "You and Stefano? What is he doing now?"

Pietro shook his head. *"Non so,"* he said. "I do not know.

I do not know what has become of Stefano Leonetti. M-m-many years ago I see him in Milano."

We stared at each other for a long moment. I remembered how Pietro always used to have prints and smudges on his glasses, sometimes little splashes of solvents and chemicals. They were those enormously thick lenses—Coke-bottle glasses—but those he wore now were the modern, light-weight, little round glasses, so perfectly clear I could see a touch of sadness in his eyes. Was this because he knew the mention of Stefano's name brought back painful memories?

"It was such a nice surprise," I said after several moments, "running into you at the Uffizi."

"Sì, sì, a nice surprise."

"Tell me about your work. Have you been at the Uffizi all this time?"

"For a short time I work in Milano on the *Cenacolo*, the restoration of Leonardo's *Last Supper*."

Of course I'd heard about the cleaning of Leonardo's masterpiece. After layers of grimy buildup and past restorations had been removed, the painting was barely visible. The work itself had been an experiment in technique, painted with tempera on a dry wall rather than the traditional fresco on wet plaster. It had been less than successful—Leonardo's masterpiece began cracking and peeling while the artist was still living. Many critics believed the restoration had been a greater failure and there was much contention between these opposing groups.

"There are those who believe the *Cenacolo* should have been left as it was," Pietro went on. There was bitterness in his words and I saw something in his eyes I vaguely remembered from years ago—the pain of one who has been undervalued all his life. "Have you seen it since the cl-cl-cleaning?" he asked eagerly.

"I plan to go up to Milan before I return home. I've always wanted to see Leonardo's masterpiece."

Pietro nodded, as if thanking me for taking an interest in

his work. "Now the s-s-same critics, up in arms, saying the *Adoration* should not be touched. We are in the initial stages of testing to determine what should be done, but already there are those who do not approve, stirring up trouble." He shook his head.

I wondered if the critics weren't right, but did not voice my concern. I knew Leonardo's *Adoration of the Magi* was an unfinished piece, a sepia-colored underpainting with barely enough pigment on the surface to withstand any type of cleaning. "At least there are more advanced methods since the work we did after the flood," I said. "More educated restorers and techniques."

"*Sì.*" Pietro nodded. "So much we didn't know back then. So much was d-d-developed then for the restoration process. Oh, such a tragedy, the flood, but much good came from it."

The waiter arrived, scribbled our orders on a little pad, and returned to the kitchen.

"How is your mother?" I asked, then wondered if she was still alive. I remembered her kindness to me that Christmas Eve when I had dinner in their home, and how very old she was even then.

"My mother, still in good health," Pietro replied. "Ninety-two years old now."

Ninety-two? I did some quick math. She must have been in her late fifties at the time, just a few years older than I was now, though she'd seemed so much older. "How wonderful to have good health at ninety-two," I said.

"*Sì, sì.*" He nodded.

"Do you have family? A wife?" In truth, I'd thought Pietro a bit effeminate and often wondered if he preferred boys to girls. Sometimes I felt he was jealous of Stefano and me, but I wasn't sure if it was personal or professional. I was just a kid, an amateur volunteer, and often Stefano would choose to have me assist him, rather than Pietro.

"For a short time," he answered, "I was m-m-married, but divorced now."

Divorce? Ah, yes, for twenty years now divorce had been

legal in Italy. What would have become of Stefano and me if divorce had been an option in Italy when we met? I knew the Catholics still did not approve, but I had never seen Stefano as a particularly religious person.

"And you, Signorina Suzanne. Still Signorina Cunningham? You do not m-marry?" Again a note of sadness.

"Divorced, but I kept my name when I married. I was in my late thirties, and it just seemed I'd been Suzanne Cunningham for too long, I'd established a career. So . . ."

He laughed in a kind, yet almost sympathetic way. "It is a m-m-modern world now. A woman keeps her name. A woman does not need a man. *È vero?*"

"*Sì, sì,*" I said, "*è vero.* A modern woman does not need a man."

The waiter delivered our meals and we sat and chatted; about our days in Florence long ago, the Christmas we spent together, the pope's surprise visit to the Limonaia to bless the Cimabue, what we had each been doing for the past three and a half decades, marveling over how long it had been.

We ordered coffee and dessert. Pietro pulled out a pack of cigarettes and lit one up.

I told him about the classes I was teaching now in Florence. Then, as if it fit so naturally into the conversation, I pulled the copy of the painting from the Uffizi file out of my bag and unfolded it on the table. "Do you remember this painting?" I asked. "We worked on it at the Limonaia."

He wedged his cigarette in the ashtray, then picked up the copy of the painting and examined it carefully. "A beautiful little p-p-painting," he said thoughtfully. "There were over a thousand paintings damaged. Almost three hundred at the Limonaia, and I worked on at least two hundred myself. Clearly I remember the Botticelli, the Giotto, but this painting . . ." He squinted, then looked up at me.

"I found a reproduction and article in a book as I was preparing for a class I'm teaching this semester. It was identified as a fifteenth-century Italian Madonna. Stefano believed it was a Masolino."

"Sì, sì," he said, nodding, "early fifteenth century." Then he shook his head, picked up his cigarette, and took a slow drag. "I'm not sure. It looks like one from . . . there were so many. Some of the minor works. Every fifteenth-century Italian artist, the good, the b-b-bad, they all did the Madonna with the Christ Child. *Non so.*" He ground his cigarette into the ashtray, then took his glasses off and rubbed the lenses with his napkin, then placed them back on his nose, adjusting them as if a cleaning, a repositioning would jog his memory. "I'm sorry, I do not recall."

"The article said the painting had been destroyed, but I remember, I distinctly remember this painting. I remember working on it at the Limonaia, then seeing it at the Fortezza da Basso."

Pietro cocked a doubtful brow. "M-m-many of these paintings, very similar. It is perhaps a different painting you remember?"

I took a second copy out of my bag, the written history sheet. Maybe if he saw the notation in what appeared to be Stefano's hand he would remember something.

"These words . . ." He looked up at me, his brows still pressed tight. "This is the file from the same p-painting?" He picked up the picture again and studied it. There was no description on the copy of the painting itself, other than what I guessed was an identification or inventory number matching the number on the history sheet. I wondered for a moment if somehow these numbers had been changed—if the history sheet and photo didn't really go together—yet the description on the history sheet matched the description and size of the painting exactly.

"It was over thirty years ago, Signorina Suzanne." Pietro's voice was soft, almost patronizing, as if he were talking to a child or a very old person. "Perhaps you're confused. Memories . . . ah, the mind." He touched his forehead dramatically. "I w-w-wish I could remember something to help you."

* * *

AS I WALKED back to school after my lunch with Pietro, a very intense doubt accompanied me. Could I have been mistaken about the painting? It *had* been over thirty years ago.

No. I had been there. I had seen it. Touched it.

I returned to my office and checked my messages, hoping for a call from Roberto, but finding nothing. I'd given him my cell phone number too. Surely after what had happened between us over the weekend, he would call.

Tuesday morning there was a message from Roberto on my phone at school. He said he was sorry he had missed me, that he would like to get together when he returned, before I left on break. His voice sounded very impersonal—as if he were leaving a message for a business associate. At least he had called, but I was puzzled by his tone and why there was no mention of where he was, particularly after we had come to such an intimate point in our relationship.

Late the next morning Mrs. Potter rang my office and announced a young woman would like to see me. At first I thought she must be a student, and wondered why she didn't come directly to my office. My door was always open. "Maria Pavoncello," Mrs. Potter explained, a name I didn't recognize.

"I'll come out to meet her." I got up from my desk and walked out into Mrs. Potter's office, which also served as a general reception area.

"Maria!" I greeted Roberto's daughter, giving her a kiss on each cheek, realizing I had never heard her last name. "So nice to see you."

"I was in the city and thought I'd drop by. I hope I'm not disturbing you."

"No, not at all. I've been thinking of you." I had—wondering how I should arrange to return her dishes. I didn't want to just hand them off to Roberto. And now I was beginning to wonder when I'd see him again. "I enjoyed the party. I wanted to thank you for inviting me. It was fun."

At her request, I showed Maria around the school. She asked questions about my classes and seemed interested. "Do you have time for lunch?" she asked.

"I have a class at one fifteen," I answered, surprised, but delighted by her invitation. "I'm giving a midterm, but if we leave now and go someplace close we could do it."

We walked to a self-service restaurant on Via dei Calzaiuoli. The place was noisy, filled with tourists and students and local businesspeople. Glass cases with enormous stainless steel bins full of salads and pasta, and plates with roasted veggies and meats, numbered for easy selection, were dished up by college-aged kids cracking jokes with customers. Such a contrast to the traditional Italian restaurants with their dignified, mature waiters, where lunch could take over two hours. I'd eaten here before and the food was good and perfect for someone in a hurry. I got a salad, Maria a plate of bow-tie pasta, and we found a table next to a couple of students, a group of hefty American tourists wedged into the table on the other side.

We talked a little about the party again, Maria's sisters, how much she enjoyed when they were able to get together. She said she was sorry I didn't get to meet Bea, that she was sure we would like each other—a pleasant thought as I added up my points, thinking if Bea liked me I would have a majority of sisters on my side. But then I wondered again what was going on with Roberto, where he was at this moment.

"Have you talked to Papa lately?" Maria asked, as if reading my mind.

I had no idea what she knew about our relationship, and wondered myself if I had any idea what it was all about.

"Not for a few days," I answered. It had been only two since I'd actually spoken with him, but it seemed much longer.

"Papa isn't good about expressing how he feels." She smiled. Her smile was very much like her father's. "But then, most men aren't. They don't always know how to tell us how they feel. Marco . . ." She shook her head. "Sometimes I have to pull it out of him."

I nodded. Here was a young woman, explaining to me about men. Maybe she knew more about men than I did.

"He called last night from Rome," Maria said. "There are

still details to work out, with the clinic, and he's selling the apartment."

I assumed she was speaking of her father now. "He mentioned he was going to be out of town for a few days." I said this casually, as if I also knew he was in Rome, taking care of details on the clinic, the sale of the apartment.

"Papa likes you very much, Suzanne. But, I think he's also afraid of you. He's having a hard time now, with his health. It's just been in the last few years that he's admitted he needs some help. The crutches, this is something new in his life. He started using a cane a couple of years ago, and now . . ." She shook her head again slowly. "The admission that he must slow down, conserve his energy. With proper rest, he's able to do many things, but if he wears himself out too much . . ." She looked up at me, something in her eyes begging me to see her father as the man he was, not as a cripple.

I thought of our night together, the swimming, Roberto's fatigue, his difficulty in breathing, his pride, not wishing for me to see him struggle with his crutches at the pool.

"It is very difficult for a man," Maria continued, "especially a proud man such as my father. He has always been one to lead, to take hold of life, but to find himself in such reduced physical condition . . . it is very difficult for him." She went on and explained in some detail; perhaps being a nurse she used more medical terms—cardiovascular system, motor neurons, muscular atrophy—than easily understood by most laymen, but I listened intently. Basically, she was telling me that, with the proper pacing of his activities, with adequate rest, he was able to do most of the things that he wanted to do, but in smaller ways now. It was very much what Roberto had told me, although he had been hesitant to speak of his inabilities. And I had been reluctant to ask. Perhaps I was as afraid to talk about it as Roberto was. But with Maria, with her knowledge, I realized I wanted to know, so I asked questions, which she willingly answered.

"Is it life-threatening?" I asked.

"It threatens the quality of life," she said. "But it can be managed, and he is learning, finally accepting, that this is the key, the management." She sighed. "It's been difficult, the last few months. He is generally one to have great optimism. When I saw him with you when you came to visit Nonno, I could see how very happy he was again. Then, losing Nonno, he started slipping again. Don't give up on him, Suzanne." She looked deep into my eyes as if she were pleading.

"He invited me Sunday afternoon for a swim. We had fun. He enjoyed himself. And I did too." I wanted to assure Maria that our relationship was moving forward, but I wasn't so sure myself.

"Then you *are* seeing each other?" Maria smiled broadly.

"We're getting to know each other, enjoying each other's company. I like your father very much." I assumed she had no idea we'd slept together. Surely, fathers don't discuss such things with their daughters.

"Good, good. You're very good for my father. You make him happy."

But happy enough? I wondered.

"This has been fun," Maria said as we finished. She told me she enjoyed coming into the city and getting away from the children now and then. She said she had a neighbor with a little girl and they tended each other's children sometimes, though she really hadn't been able to get out much since Nonno had been with them. She ran her finger under her eye. She didn't cry, but I could see she missed the old man.

I reminded her I had her dishes and she said don't worry about it, I could bring them next time I came out to visit, which made me feel both comfortable and uncomfortable at the same time.

As we got up to leave, Maria said, "There's something I feel I should tell you, yet I'm not completely sure it is the right thing to do." She looked me directly in the eyes, as if I might provide some type of encouragement or support.

"What is it, Maria?" I asked, touching her lightly on the arm. We stepped out of the restaurant onto the street.

"It's something Nonno asked me to do. He asked that I tell

no one. But his mind," she continued tentatively, shaking her head, "those last days it wasn't terribly clear, and . . ." Again she hesitated and her pace slowed, as if she couldn't move too rapidly and collect her thoughts or choose the appropriate words at the same time. "I keep thinking perhaps it is information he intended for you."

My heart picked up speed.

"Just after your visit," she said, "in one of his lucid moments, he asked that I contact a young woman—he gave me the address of an antique shop here in Florence on Via dei Fossi."

I remembered the street name, as the *pensione* where Roxie and I stayed was on Via dei Fossi. I had walked down that street several times since my return and had noticed all the high-end antique shops.

"I called the shop," Maria went on, "and asked for the owner. Nonno wished to speak to her father, but did not know where he was, only that the daughter was still in Florence." Maria glanced over at me, almost as if she were trying to gauge my need to know what she was about to reveal. I could see she still wasn't completely sure that she should tell me. "The daughter did call back and told me her father was now living in Greece, but would be visiting soon and she would have him call when he arrived. I had no idea why my grandfather wished to speak to him, as he never told me. But I kept remembering your visit, and I keep thinking it was because of you, and that Nonno would want me to share this information with you."

"Did the man, the woman's father, call?"

"Yes," Maria answered. "He did. Unfortunately it was the day after we lost Nonno."

We were just a block from the school. Maria motioned down the street. "My car," she said, then took a deep breath. "I hope I'm not breaking my promise to my grandfather, but I feel he wanted you to know."

"And the man's name?" I asked Maria.

But before the name was spoken, I knew. And I knew I had seen Stefano Leonetti at the funeral.

24

THE LAST THREE days of the week were set aside for midterms, so I didn't have to present a lecture or class discussion that afternoon, but merely appear to hand out tests, answer questions, receive the finished exams. I sat at my desk, thinking about what Maria had told me.

Now I knew Stefano was living somewhere in Greece. Why had Roberto Balducci attempted to contact him? Had they both been involved in the disappearance of the Masolino, and was Roberto Balducci calling to warn him? About me?

As soon as the last student handed in her exam, I stuffed all of them in my briefcase, dropped them off at my office, ran down the stairs, rushed out of the building, and headed toward Via dei Fossi.

A block from school my cell phone rang. I pulled it out of my bag. *"Pronto."*

"Suzanne, it's Roberto."

"Roberto, hello."

"I'm pleased I was able to catch you."

"Yes," I said, realizing how good it was to hear his real live voice. "It's wonderful to actually talk to you, not just listen to a message."

"I must apologize. I felt uncomfortable leaving a message on your phone at school, but somehow in the rush Monday morning, I misplaced your number. But fortunately I found—"

"How are you?"

"Good. You sound out of breath."

"Cell phones," I panted. "Exercise your jaw and legs at the same time."

He laughed. "Where are you headed?"

"Well, I'm . . ." I'd told Maria I wouldn't tell anyone. Did this include her father? "Just headed home."

"I'm glad you answered. I didn't want to leave another message."

"Me, too."

"I enjoyed the weekend," he said. "I must admit it took me rather by surprise—what happened between us."

"Good surprise or bad surprise?" I needed to sit down. I couldn't have this conversation walking down the street. I leaned up against the corner of a building and pressed my hand against my ear to block out the sounds of traffic and people on the street.

"Definitely good, but rather unexpected, and it's left me wondering what is going on."

"What do you mean?"

"When I'm away from you," he said slowly, "I can almost rationalize that this isn't a good idea."

"This?" I asked.

"You and me." He paused. I took a breath and he continued. "But then, all the rationalizing in the world can't remove the image of you from my mind. But I'm not sure—"

"About us?"

"When I think about it logically," he said, in a very rational-sounding voice, "there are so many reasons this relationship shouldn't go any further."

"Maybe we need to get together and talk."

"Yes, probably," Roberto said, and I could hear a hesitation in his voice.

I hate cell phones, I thought, glancing at a noisy cluster of people gathered at the corner, waiting for the light to change. Several took off into traffic against the light.

"But there's something I need to know now," Roberto added after several moments. "When I look at you, or even imagine you, I see a beautiful, vibrant, healthy woman, and I can't help but wonder"—again he paused—"does it matter to you, Suzanne, my physical limitations?"

I hesitated longer than I wished I had. "I don't really see you as limited."

"Please, I'd like you to be honest." He sounded a little irritated now.

"Okay, yes, in some ways, I realize you are limited. But no, I don't think it does . . . matter, that is." I thought about what Maria had told me about his need to conserve energy, to properly manage his physical activities, and I knew there were some things that Roberto and I couldn't share. "Any relationship, particularly at the beginning, has a lot of unknowns. I know I enjoy your company, Roberto, enjoy being with you." I felt a dryness in my throat and continued cautiously, "I don't see your physical limitations as reason to quit seeing each other. I want to get to know you better. I hope we can be honest with each other about how we feel."

"Thank you," Roberto said, "I would hope for the same, and yes, we do need to get together. There are other things I want to talk about, but yes, better in person. When do you leave for spring break?"

"Saturday."

"How about Friday night? Dinner?"

"I'd like that."

"We'll go someplace special."

"I'll look forward to it." I started walking again. "When will you be back home?"

"Probably not until Friday afternoon."

"Where are you?" I asked, though I knew where he was because Maria had told me.

"Rome, didn't I tell you that?"

"Oh, well, maybe." He was in Rome just as Maria said. Why was I so suspicious?

"How has your week been so far?" he asked.

"Good."

"How about the meeting with the restorer?"

"Pietro Capparelli? We had a nice lunch, talked about old times. He knew nothing about the Masolino, couldn't even remember working on it. He said he saw Stefano Leonetti years ago in Milan, but has no idea where he is now." But Maria knows, I thought. I stopped again as I approached the Piazza Santa Maria Novella. I sat down on one of the stone benches in the square flanking a large marble obelisk. "He thought the file stating that the painting had been lost was probably correct."

"The file?"

"From the Uffizi. The file Alberto Mazzone found for me."

"Oh, yes," he said thoughtfully, and I realized I hadn't actually told him about the history file, the file with Stefano's initials.

"Oh, and I had lunch with Maria," I said casually, thinking maybe I should mention it. Again, I covered my ear to mute the outside noise. The square was covered with pigeons, the flap of wings creating a stir as they took off.

Roberto didn't reply for several long moments. Did this make him uncomfortable? Did he think we had been talking about him? Which of course we had. "You and Maria?" he asked.

A young couple sat on the bench next to me, their arms wrapped around one another, oblivious to me as well as the others sitting in the square. I stood and started out of the piazza. "She was in town and dropped by." For some reason I wanted Roberto to know I hadn't initiated this. "She's a sweet girl, Roberto."

"Yes, she is," he said, then another little pause as if he needed time to think about this. Had I overstepped the boundaries of our relationship? But it was Maria who had come by, Maria who'd invited me to lunch.

"How about you?" I asked. "How has your week been?"

"Trying, but in the end successful. I'm selling my interest in the clinic in Rome. We are moving forward with that, but there are still many details to work out. I'm having second thoughts about letting the apartment go. I'm considering using it as a rental, though that might turn into a tiresome responsibility."

I explained that I had a rental management company handle my house in Boise. I glanced up at the street sign. Via dei Fossi.

"Not a bad idea," he said.

"Good luck with the clinic, the apartment."

"Thank you. I'll pick you up about seven Friday?"

"How about eight? Could I meet you somewhere? I'll have papers and tests to grade, and I want to finish up before I leave."

"I'll make a reservation and let you know."

"I'll see you Friday." I looked up and realized I had arrived at the antique shop. *Antonelli* was scripted in ornate gold letters on the window. Should I say something to Roberto? Should I tell him?

"Friday, then," he said.

"Ciao," I said.

"Ciao."

I pressed the red button on the phone, slid it into my bag, took a deep breath, stood for a moment gathering some courage, then stepped inside the shop.

A little bell rang on the door, and a woman looked over from where she stood arranging framed paintings on the wall. *"Buon giorno."*

Something pushed up inside my throat and for a moment I thought I would not be able to speak. She was so obviously Stefano's daughter. She appeared to be in her late thirties or early forties, which would be just right. Her hair was black, her eyes very dark and close set, her features sharp, much like her father's, not particularly beautiful on a woman. I had always imagined her mother as very glamorous, but the daughter was not. She wore a gray skirt and plain white blouse, looking almost like a modern-day nun.

"*Buon giorno,*" I said casually, picking up a ceramic figurine on a marble-topped table as if I really was a customer. Carefully I replaced it, feeling a nervous moisture on my hand. *You break it, you buy it*—strangely these words went through my head.

"May I help you?" she asked in English now, adept as are all Italian shopkeepers at spotting the American tourists, though I hardly considered myself one anymore.

"Yes," I answered, "I'm looking for a Signora Elisabetta Antonelli."

"*Sì*, I am Signora Antonelli."

I hesitated, attempting to collect the right words. "I recently ran into an old friend who told me I might find you here."

"A friend?" she asked. "Have we met?" She studied my face, trying to place me.

"Oh, no. I knew your father, Stefano Leonetti, many years ago. We worked together after the flood of nineteen sixty-six."

"You are an art restorer as my father?" She seemed pleased.

"I worked as a volunteer then, and I'm teaching art history in Florence, and I thought . . . well, I thought I might . . . Where is your father now?" I asked with what I hoped was the appropriate degree of interest in inquiring about an old colleague. My heart was racing so fast I wondered if she could see it vibrating under my coat. I put one hand in my pocket and held tightly to my purse with the other to keep them from shaking.

"I often have inquiries about my father." She seemed very composed, self-assured, and interested, again so much like her father. "He was a much respected art restorer."

"Does he still work in art restoration?"

"He retired several years ago. He and my mother have been in Crete for several years now, living in a lovely villa on the sea. It's been in my mother's family for many years."

"I'm going to Greece later this spring," I said, wondering where these words were coming from. *Her mother*, I thought, *Stefano's wife . . .* they were still together. Had I really hoped that this would no longer be true, that the woman had died, or that they had finally divorced? "A study tour with my students of the Greek and Minoan cultures and art," I added, sounding very confident. "Perhaps I would have time to look him up."

Without hesitating, she offered me her father's phone number and a description of where he lived. In fact, she actually drew a little map on the back of her business card, explaining the street was not well marked, but the villa itself stood out as it was the largest and most elegant of those along that part of the coast.

"Thank you." I slipped the card in the outside pocket of my purse.

"I'm sure they would enjoy seeing you."

They? I don't think so.

We stood smiling at each other for a moment, then she said, "Please, feel free to browse. If you have any questions or are looking for anything in particular, Nicco or I would be delighted to help." She motioned toward a tall, thin young man I hadn't noticed in the back of the shop. He glanced up from the shelf he was dusting.

I looked around, thinking maybe I should buy something. I picked up a small vase, looked at the price tag and replaced it, then carried a small snuffbox with a mother-of-pearl cover to the cash register. Stefano's daughter had apparently left or gone to a back room. For a moment I thought about putting the box back and quickly making an escape. The young man came up to the counter. He rang up my purchase, carefully wrapped it in tissue, placed it in a bag, and handed it to me with a smile.

"*Grazie,*" I said and turned to leave.

Just as I reached the door—"I'm sorry, Signora," a woman's voice called out, "but I didn't get your name."

Again, my heart raced as I looked back. Stefano's daughter stood next to the young man, and I felt their eyes pressing down on me.

"Suzanne Cunningham," I said. "Professor Suzanne Cunningham."

25

SMOOTH MOVE, PROFESSOR Cuckoo Cunningham, I told myself as I rushed back to school. Why did I give her my name? I didn't want Stefano prepared for my visit. If he knew anything about the Masolino, if he'd had any part in its disappearance, it would be much better if I caught him off guard.

And what was I thinking when I told Stefano's daughter I had a study tour planned for Greece? But maybe that wasn't a bad idea. I'd always wanted to go to Greece. This coming week, I thought. I had a full week for spring break. By the time I arrived back at school, I had decided that was exactly what I'd do—I'd go now. Would Charley be hurt if I canceled on him?

I hurried up the steps, past Mrs. Potter's empty desk toward Charley's office, and ran smack dab into Regina in the hall.

"You look like you just ran a marathon," she said.

"I feel like it too."

"Time for coffee or a drink?" she asked. "I haven't seen you in days."

"I have to go talk to Charley." It came out brusquely, not very friendly. "I'm sorry, Regina, I'm just—"

"You okay?"

"I've got a lot on my mind." I laughed. "Or maybe I've lost my mind."

"What's up?"

I hadn't talked to Regina all week, not since finding out about Stefano, not since I spent the night at Roberto's. "I slept with Roberto"—the words burst out of my mouth—"and I'm going to see Stefano in Greece."

"Whoa, girl," Regina said, grabbing my arm. "We need to talk."

"I can squeeze you in," I said, offering what I hoped was a friendly, if exhausted, smile, "between my last midterm Friday afternoon and my date with Roberto Friday night."

"Friday afternoon?"

"Yes, I'd love to. We've got a lot to catch up on."

"Stefano's in Greece?" she asked, releasing my arm, but steadily holding her curious eyes on mine. I could see she wasn't going to let this go until Friday. "How did you find out?"

"I've promised to protect my source," I said, as if making a joke.

"Roberto?"

I shook my head and thought once more of Roberto, our weekend together, his phone call, my persistent nagging feeling that he knew more than he was telling me.

"I've got to cancel with Charley." I motioned toward his office door.

"Friday then," Regina said.

"Okay," I said with a smile.

Regina hesitated, her expressive face teeming with concern, then she turned and headed into the reception area. I heard her say hello to Mrs. Potter.

I continued down the hall and stood before Charley's door, rationalizing; we'd planned on taking his car, so there weren't any nonrefundable plane tickets to worry about, and my room reservations could be canceled without affecting anyone. I wondered if he would be upset. His invitation had come almost as an afterthought, as if he was feeling sorry for me because I'd planned to travel alone over break, which honestly didn't bother me. But maybe it was important to Charley that I join them.

I knocked. "Come on in," Charley called out.

I entered and he invited me to sit.

"All ready for the big trip?" he asked with an enthusiastic grin.

This might be more difficult than I thought. Better get right to it. "Would you mind terribly, Charley, if I canceled our spring break plans? Something has come up."

He pushed his glasses up on his nose and his brows rose in that inquisitive way of his. "A better offer?" He seemed more interested than angry or hurt, which sent a wave of relief through me. "I was probably asking too much of you to come along," he said. Now I could hear the hurt.

"Oh, Charley, I'm sorry."

"I thought we might have some fun." He sat in a big, padded, comfy-looking swivel chair, almost regal in size. My chair was stiff with a straight back. He sighed. "Oh, well, probably serves me right. I guess in all honesty I had hoped you might act as a buffer. I'm not sure how this will go with my sister and her daughter."

Maybe his invitation had nothing to do with altruism. "Oh, you'll have fun."

He responded with a little snort that seemed to say don't count on it.

After a few moments, attempting to gauge Charley's true feelings, I said, "I've got some information that might help me find the Masolino. I don't want to let you down, but I feel I have to see what I can find out now."

"Before the evidence cools?" His voice was tinged with an irritating condescension. *If he calls me Nancy Drew again, I'm going to deck him.*

We stared guardedly at each other, and then Charley pulled his chair up close to his desk, folded his arms on top with a hint of resignation, and asked, "Where are you going?"

"Greece."

"That should be lovely this time of year. Probably more interesting than tagging along on this little family outing." He sounded disappointed, but I thought he was okay with my reason for canceling out.

"Charley, I'm sorry, but—"

"Hey, it's okay," he said, holding up his hand. "It's okay."

"You sure?"

Slowly he offered me a smile. "Yes, it's okay."

"Forgive me?"

"Yes, of course." He nodded as if giving me absolution.

"Thanks, Charley," I said. "You're a true friend." I reached over and patted him affectionately on the hand, then stood.

"You've discovered something?" he asked, any trace of hurt in his voice now replaced with curiosity. I could see he wasn't going to let me go so easily.

"I don't know for sure. I'll let you know when I get back. Okay?"

"Okay," he replied reluctantly, and I turned to leave.

"Be careful, Suzanne."

I glanced back. "I will."

As I walked out into the hall it struck me that this was the first time anyone, myself included, had even considered there might be something dangerous in what I was doing.

FRIDAY MORNING, MY last day before break, I met with my upper-level course. Students handed in their papers and some of them hung around for a while, mostly just talking about where everyone was going and of course, as a good instructor of art history, I suggested what they might look for in terms of art in the various places they were visiting. A group of them were going to Greece, and I said, "Well, I might run into you. I'm going to visit an old friend." *Old friend?* Who was I kidding?

Before rushing off to meet Regina for coffee, I checked my mailbox for the last time, noticed an envelope from Roxie, and stuffed it in my briefcase along with my other mail.

I spent more time than I probably had to spare with
Regina, filling her in on the latest—visiting Roberto at his
villa, my plans to find Stefano, though I kept Maria's secret. It
was nice having a friend I knew I could trust to share my recent adventures with. I could feel her excitement, about what
was going on with Roberto, what might possibly happen with
Stefano.

"And here I am, going off on this little ski trip for spring
break," Regina said with a mock sigh.

"You'll have fun," I said.

"Oh, I know I will. I'm looking forward to a little time off.
But I can't wait to hear what happens with you."

"I'm rather eager to see what happens too," I said with a
nervous laugh.

"You be careful," Regina added, patting me on the arm,
and I knew her warning was very different from Charley's.

I RAN HOME, graded more papers, hopped in the shower.
While towel drying my hair I got my mail out and opened
Roxie's letter. Inside I found a brief note and a second envelope. She apologized for taking so long, explained these were
the pictures she'd found at her mom's. She thought I might enjoy seeing them. I threw the towel over a chair and tore the inside envelope open and started going through the photos.
Several were taken at the Limonaia—a couple of Pietro with
another volunteer, a student from England whose name I remembered was John. A photo of Charley that made me
smile—a pretty blonde looped through each arm.

Then one of Stefano.

I sat on my bed, which I hadn't bothered to make or flip
back into the wall for the past two days. I needed something
under my legs.

He was facing directly into the camera, a startled look on his
face, not particularly flattering. The next two were blurry, Stefano at a workbench in the Limonaia. Then one perfect shot,
Stefano as I remembered him—young and handsome and

proud. He was standing in front of a workbench and smiling into the camera. My stomach tightened as I held this image, one I had carried in my head and heart for over thirty years. I examined the photo carefully. Then I turned it sideways, then almost upside down. Although the painting on the workbench behind him was distorted by the angle of the camera, and the photo faded with age, my heartbeat increased and the hairs along the back of my neck stood up.

The painting on the bench was the Masolino Madonna.

26

THE PAINTING HAD not been destroyed in the flood. It had been taken to the Limonaia for restoration and the photo was proof.

I got out my copy of the Uffizi file and compared the photo with the reproduction in the file. The painting on the bench was blurry and distorted, still patched in places with mulberry paper, but I was sure it was the same as the one in the file.

Quickly, I finished my hair and put on my makeup, my hand unsteady as I attempted to brush on mascara. I dressed, slipped the photo into my purse, left the apartment, and took off for the Piazzale Michelangelo.

Roberto was sitting by the window with a fantastic view of the city below, surely the most romantic table in the restaurant. The Duomo and bell tower were silhouetted against a deep blue sky, and lights from the buildings along the Arno reflected on the river below. He looked up and smiled.

I bent over to kiss him. His cheek was smooth and warm and smelled of spicy aftershave.

"You look stunning tonight," he said.

I had dressed in such a state of shock and excitement, this

was nice to hear. I wore the black dress I'd bought for the opera. I'd recently purchased a silk shawl from a shop on Tornabuoni and it was absolutely gorgeous—brilliant colors with dreamlike floating figures that reminded me of a Marc Chagall. Anyone wearing this shawl would look *stunning*.

"Thank you," I said as I sat. "So do you." He was wearing the Gustav Klimt tie I liked so much.

"Did you finish grading your tests and papers?"

"Almost," I replied. "I've been running all day—tests, coffee with Regina, rushing back to school to finish reading papers, home, getting ready."

"You look lovely." He reached across the table for my hand.

I glanced down and saw that my hand was shaking.

"Are you cold?" he asked. "Should I ask for a table away from the window?"

"No, please, this is fantastic."

A waiter approached with menus and a wine list. Roberto angled the wine list on the table so we could study it together. He pointed out several selections he thought might be good. "What do you think?" he asked.

"An Italian Chianti, *naturalmente*," I said. We picked an Antinori Chianti Classico. Roberto waved at the waiter and ordered a bottle, requesting our *antipasti* be brought to the table right away along with the wine.

"What time do you leave tomorrow?" he asked.

"Late morning for Rome. Then I'm catching an evening flight out."

"I thought you were driving." He stared at me, confusion in the lines around his eyes.

He still thought I was going to France with Charley. "There's actually been a change in my plans. I'm going to Greece."

"What brought this about?" His eyes widened in surprise.

"So many new discoveries since we last talked." Now I weighed just how much I wanted to tell him.

The waiter brought our wine and poured a glass for

Roberto to taste, then one for me. He placed a plate with olives, prosciutto, and salami between us.

"Tell me about your discoveries," Roberto said.

"Well, I found out that Stefano Leonetti is in Greece."

"How did you learn this?" he asked.

I avoided answering by pulling the photo out of my purse. "And another, maybe even more important discovery." I placed it on the table in front of him.

"This is Leonetti?" he asked, staring down, his eyes narrowing.

"The painting," I said, directing him to the small panel on the workbench.

Roberto stared at it, then looked up at me as if he didn't understand. I wondered if it was wishful thinking that anyone other than myself could see this tiny faded image as the Masolino.

"It's the painting claimed to be destroyed in the flood," I explained.

Roberto's brows knit as he studied the photo.

"I know, a little blurry, but you can make out the shapes of the Madonna, the Child"—I ran my finger over the small figures—"the pink, white, and blue garments, the gold-leaf background. And the size. It was—*is*," I corrected myself, "a small painting. I know this is the Masolino and this photo proves it was taken to the Limonaia for restoration, that it wasn't lost in the flood."

"Where did this come from?" He picked up the photo.

"Roxie, the friend I came over with. She had this little camera, and I borrowed it from her when she left. I took this picture. When I returned the camera, I guess the film was still in it. She was going to finish the roll, have it developed, and then we didn't get together much that summer. I took off for school. She stayed home to work. This is the first time I've seen the photo. It came in the mail today."

"You think someone took the painting from the Limonaia?"

I nodded, thinking of what Dr. Garzoni said about young

people at the library slipping pages from manuscripts under their sweaters, how little security there was, how volunteers came in and out of the work areas freely. How very small this painting was. Then I thought of Dr. Garzoni being at the Fortezza da Bazzo. "But," I answered, "not from the Limonaia. The painting was taken over to the Fortezza da Basso. I saw it there when I went with Stefano."

Roberto's eyes rose up from the photo and locked on mine. His chin lifted at the slightest angle, his back stiffened. Something in his body language had shifted, but he said nothing, and I thought once more of secrets. I felt close to Roberto, yet there was something, something I didn't fully understand.

"At that time the painting's restoration was near completion," I continued carefully, "soon to be returned to the Uffizi."

"But it wasn't?" There was accusation in his eyes, the way they held mine, and it sent a little shiver through me.

"No. I don't believe it was."

"You said the documents from the Uffizi stated it had been lost in the flood. Was there anything indicating who had written the notation?"

"Yes." Little goose bumps spread over my arms. My shawl had slipped and I pulled it up around my shoulders. "It was initialed." My voice quivered.

"Stefano Leonetti?"

I bit my lip and nodded.

"You're going to Greece alone?"

Without words I answered yes.

Roberto studied the photo again. For several moments he said nothing. The waiter approached the table. Roberto dismissed him with an abrupt wave of his hand, and the man smiled and backed away.

Roberto tossed the photo on the table, again the gesture disturbingly abrupt.

I stared down at it, Stefano gazing up at me, then my eyes rose to Roberto's, and I could see hurt and a sense of betrayal in them now.

"What a fool I've been," he said. He took in a deep breath and slowly released it as if blowing out puffs of smoke. "It's not the painting you're after, is it, Suzanne? You've been using me and my father to locate Stefano Leonetti. You and he were lovers. How could I have been so gullible? This was the man"—he waved a hand toward the photo—"the man I saw you with all those years ago at Santa Croce, the man you watched with such passion in your eyes."

I fought to find the right words. "You recognized Stefano from this photo?"

"No," he answered, a roughness in his voice I'd never heard. "I have no memory of what the man looked like. But I know now this was the man. Why did you put me through this? When you first came to me I had no stake in this, but you've used me. I've developed real feelings for you, and now . . ." He rubbed his head, then ran his fingers over his lips. "Is it too much to ask for honesty? You were in love with this man, and you are using me to find him."

"Roberto, no," I whispered, reaching across the table for him, but he pulled his hand away. "That was never my intention. I want to find the painting. It wasn't destroyed in the flood. It was rescued. It was restored. I want to know what happened to it."

"But, Stefano Leonetti, you were in love with him. You think he took the painting? You want to find him and warn him?"

"Warn him of *what*?" I laughed with a disturbingly wicked edge. "Your father's article, the Uffizi file, both refute what I believe. Pietro Capparelli, who was there, tells me I'm mistaken, that I don't remember what I saw. And *what* would I have to *warn* Stefano about? No one other than myself seems to be looking for this painting that was claimed to be destroyed in a flood over thirty years ago." My voice rose to a pitch that seemed to pierce the air. Diners at the next table glanced over.

"But why," he asked, "why couldn't you have been honest with me about Stefano?"

"Maybe I *was* trying to protect him. I don't know." I shook my head, my eyes dropping to the table, the photo, Stefano. "I can't believe he took the painting or was involved in any way. I think someone else forged the notation in the file."

"Who?"

"I'm not sure. Maybe Dr. Garzoni." I looked up at Roberto.

"The director of restoration?"

"Yes."

"You think if you talk to Stefano, he will confirm what you feel? That you'll finally have someone on your side? That you might be able to figure this out?"

"I don't know. I don't know who took it or why. I don't know if it was Garzoni, Stefano, or"—I hesitated, my eyes on the photo again, and then I looked up at Roberto—"your father."

"You think it was my father?" He didn't seem surprised by this accusation.

"Surely you have some suspicions. Or maybe you're trying to protect someone too. Maybe *you're* holding out." My voice was so intense now, the people two tables over stared. I glared back.

Roberto motioned for the waiter. I thought he was going to ask for our bill, but instead he turned to me and asked what I'd like. I pointed to an item on the menu under *secondi piatti*, but I might as well have been blindfolded, throwing darts at a corkboard. My stomach lurched and I didn't think I could possibly eat anything. Roberto ordered us each a pasta dish and himself a *bistecca alla fiorentina*. After the waiter left, he picked up a piece of prosciutto, then another, eating them slowly, saying nothing.

"We're going to have dinner?" I finally asked, attempting to calm my voice.

"I'm hungry," he said, "and we're not finished with this conversation." He picked up an olive and offered me the plate. I took a piece of salami, bit into it and chewed slowly, then washed it down with a swallow of wine.

Roberto stared out the window at the city below. Lights from the traffic moved on the Lungarno. For the longest time he didn't speak and I felt awful. I wanted to say something, to assure him that I never intended to use him or hurt him, but I didn't know if he would believe me.

"I often traveled to Rome alone." His voice was low. "Paolina seldom went with me. The girls were still in school. I'd taken a box to the apartment with drawing paper, pencils, charcoal, and pastels that I found at the villa in Florence, with the intention that I would do some drawing. But, then," he sighed, "I never even opened the box, until . . ." He turned and looked at me now. "I started thinking perhaps this was supposed to happen, our meeting again. This beautiful young woman from my past."

"You're a romantic, Dr. Balducci," I said, offering him a tenuous smile.

He smiled but didn't reply.

"And now," I said, "you've discovered I'm untrustworthy, not at all the image of the sweet, innocent girl you had in your head."

"I suppose you're just real, and I can understand why you might want to find Stefano, but involving me—why were you not honest about your relationship with Stefano?"

I picked up my wine and took a slow drink, now staring out the window myself. "You want honest?"

"Yes, I do."

I turned to Roberto. "I didn't feel *I* could trust *you*."

"Didn't or *don't?*"

I shook my head, wishing I could disappear. "Your father. I think you would want to protect him."

Roberto sighed. "I love my father, but I would want to know if he was involved. *I'm* not a person to hide from the truth."

An honorable man, I thought, but his comment stabbed me—his accusation was clear. I was a person who hid from the truth. "I felt you were holding something back," I said. He waited for me to continue. "You said there were secrets. You said there were things your father did, but you would have loved him anyway despite what he did. What were these secrets?"

Roberto blew out a puff of air, then said, "My father left my mother. Several times. When he was in Rome at the university. They never divorced. Neither of them believed it was right, but there were times, years, when they didn't live together. He tried to stay close to the family, but there was much anger. At times I hated him, desperately hated him."

"These secrets, they had nothing to do with his work?"

"No, nothing to do with his work."

"He left your family?"

Roberto nodded.

"For another woman?" I could see this was painful for Roberto.

"I grew to understand that my father did love my mother," he said softly, "but it was not in the way a man loves a woman."

I felt very sad for Roberto. I had grown up in a family with parents who loved each other deeply. I wished that it had been so for Roberto.

"When I finally accepted who and what my father was, I began to forgive him." Roberto stared out the window again. The lights flickered in the city below. "We couldn't talk about it. I know he couldn't help who he was. Maybe if we had talked, it would have been better." Roberto turned to me. "Yes, there were others." Again he hesitated. "Other men."

My body lurched forward in surprise. I hadn't expected this at all and didn't know how to reply. I wanted to say the right words, but Roberto's revelation had stunned me. I knew there was something hidden, some mystery about the elder Roberto Balducci. I had assumed it had something to do with the painting, maybe because this was what I'd wanted it to be.

"I'm so sorry, Roberto," I said.

"Things aren't always the way we want them to be."

I nodded in agreement.

The waiter delivered our meals, and we ate dinner with few words at first.

"The garden at the villa is starting to bloom," Roberto said. "You'll have to come up when you return from Greece."

"You still want to see me?" I asked, my caution mixed with incredulity.

"I want to know how all this turns out. You've involved me in this mystery—the missing Masolino. And—" He paused, studying me, then continued, "I have a feeling that even if you see Stefano, confirm that he wasn't involved, you'll discover what you had before can't be revived."

"Why do you say that?"

"Because you are a different person now."

"Yes, I am," I answered. "You're wrong about my using you, Roberto. That was never my intention. And I do have real feelings for you. I would never purposely hurt you."

"So, where are we to go from here?"

I took a deep breath, trying to compose the words in my mind. I truly didn't want to hurt Roberto. I knew that I cared for him, that my feelings, though mixed and jumbled, were sincere. "I have to find Stefano," I said. "Because of the Masolino . . ." I couldn't finish.

"And because you are still in love with him?"

I shook my head. "I know there is still something unfinished between us."

"What happened?" he asked.

I looked at him blankly.

"With you and Stefano?"

"I was very young."

"You went home, found someone else?"

"No." A long, uncomfortable silence filled the space between us, until a waiter arrived with a large silver tray delivering meals to the diners at the table next to us.

"You don't want to talk about this?" Roberto asked.

"You'll think much less of me if I tell you." I took in a deep breath. I wanted Roberto to trust me, but I wondered if after this he ever would. I exhaled. "Or, maybe you couldn't possibly think any less of me."

"Tell me," he said calmly.

"Stefano was married." My back stiffened now, preparing for the onslaught to come.

"He no longer is?"

I couldn't answer.

Roberto stared at me for a moment, but I couldn't tell what he was thinking. "What would you like for dessert?" he asked.

27

FEW WORDS PASSED between us as Roberto gave me a ride home. He pulled up to the curb and parked, the motor still running. "Good luck," he said, turning to me. "I hope you find out what happened to the painting."

His eyes held mine without wavering and I knew he was sincere. "Thank you." I forced myself not to look away.

"There's something I want you to keep in mind, Suzanne."

"Yes?"

"Everyone comes with a past. It's not the past I'm concerned with, it's the future."

I nodded a thank-you—for his confirmation that what was going on between us hadn't ended this evening, that there was more to our relationship than the Masolino. I leaned over and kissed him on the cheek. "I'll call when I get back."

I went up to my apartment and graded papers, struggling to concentrate. Roberto and I had just had our first fight. I noted the word *first* prefaced the word *fight* in my mind. Yet hardly a fight, a clearing of the air perhaps. Nothing compared to the fights Jerry and I used to get into. We'd fought over everything from what to name the dog to what to have for dinner, to who would cook. Stefano and I had never fought. I'd never questioned anything he said or did.

I finished reading papers, then pulled my suitcase out of the closet and tossed it on the bed. I would take the smaller carry-on, with a pull-up handle and wheels—best bet for a woman traveling alone. I threw in two pairs of jeans, three T-shirts, and sandals, and then wondered if I should take warmer clothes. It was still March. Maybe it would be cold. I put in a turtleneck, a long-sleeved shirt, and a jacket, then realized Greece would be warm. I took the turtleneck out, then put it back in— evenings might be cool. I tucked in walking shoes. I'd need another pair of shoes. Which ones? I looked in my closet, and couldn't decide. Why was this simple little task of packing so difficult? Maybe I shouldn't go. Maybe I should call Roberto and tell him I wasn't going. I stuffed in my swimming suit, a pair of capris. He could go with me! The bag was getting too full. I sat on it and zipped it closed, then realized I'd have to add cosmetics and toiletries in the morning, and I hadn't yet put in a stitch of underwear. What was I thinking?

I sat down on the bed next to the suitcase. I breathed in, then out, in and out. I couldn't even decide what to pack for my trip let alone make any big decisions.

I couldn't sleep. My thoughts spiraled back to Stefano, forward to Roberto, colliding over and over, one image, one feeling tumbling into another like a circus of confused acrobats. When I closed my eyes, colors and images appeared—the pink, blue, and gold of the Masolino, then the soft yellow of Roberto's bedroom at the villa, the faux dome opening to a painted sky. I sat up in bed. Roberto was a man who slept under a circle of blue sky.

I did care deeply for Roberto; maybe I was in love with him. Why had these feelings been so clear in my youth, and why had I come to distrust such emotions now? I didn't want to hurt Roberto, yet I knew I had to see Stefano.

I rose early the next morning, dressed, finished packing, and walked over to the train station. The wheels of my small suitcase bumped up and down on the cobblestones. I traded my ticket in for an earlier departure, though I'd now arrive in Rome with six and a half hours before my flight to Athens.

I bought a cup of coffee, drank it quickly, and headed out to the train platform where passengers were already boarding. I got on and found my seat. The train pulled out and picked up speed as it moved through the old city, then past dingy brown and gray buildings blurring into one another, and into the countryside. Two Italian girls and a sixtyish American couple sat in the compartment with me. I didn't want to visit. I didn't want the Americans to know I understood everything they were saying. They argued over an umbrella that he—*no, she*— had left behind in the hotel room. I stared out the window.

An hour passed. The American woman was reading a travel book. The man, head against the window, snored quietly. The girls giggled and chatted, the words flying so quickly I could only catch one here or there, but I knew they were talking about boys.

I opened my purse, took out the photo of Stefano, and studied his beautiful young face, trying to imagine what he might look like now. What would he think of me? Would he see any of the young woman I had once been? And it came to me how very different I was now. Roberto was right. I wasn't the same person.

As I studied the photo, it took me back in time—to the Limonaia, then to my *pensione*, the tiny bed where we made love. I thought of the last time Stefano and I were together. Our lovemaking that afternoon was filled with passion near anger, as if we wished to consume one another.

After, as he held me, I cried and he asked if he had hurt me. It had been just two months since I'd given birth, and we didn't talk about it—ever—and this was the first time since then that he'd touched me. Sometimes I felt that he wanted me to go away, to release him from the memory of what we had given up.

"Did I hurt you?" he asked again.

"No," I told him. But he had. By allowing me to fall in love with him, by failing to tell me about his wife and daughter until it was too late to turn back, by giving me a child I couldn't keep. "I don't want to leave," I cried. "I want to stay with you. I'll be anything, do anything you want. I'll be your mistress," I sobbed. I had never used that word before. It was a word from books and movies.

"Ah, *carina, carina,* you must return home, but someday—"

"Do you love me?" I asked.

"Sì," he said as he touched my damp face.

Before I left for home, I gave him my address in Idaho. He told me to write him at the Uffizi. On that long-ago journey home as the train rumbled through the Tuscan countryside and into Umbria, I fantasized that we would be together someday. I imagined Stefano and me in a beautiful little Italian farmhouse with a grove of olive trees, a garden where we could pluck fresh lemons from the trees. I never considered he'd let me slip away as easily as he eventually did.

And here I was again on another train, making the same trip, but this time heading toward, not away from him.

I wrote him at the Uffizi, and he wrote back once. It was a poetic, tender letter, yet strangely impersonal, as if he had taken the words from a book of sadly romantic poetry, a tragic drama of ill-fated love. He wished me a good life and said he knew I would fulfill my destiny. I should have understood the finality of the letter; it was hardly necessary to read between the lines. Yet I persisted.

My letters after that were returned. I continued to write. There were never replies. Eventually, I gave up, but still couldn't admit what should have been evident. I made up possible scenarios, contrived excuses: he'd accepted a new position at a different museum; someone was not forwarding his mail; my mother, who had no idea of my real relationship with Stefano or the fact that he was married, was tossing his letters out.

I threw myself into my studies, my causes. I *would* fulfill my destiny. With or without him, I would move on. I'd never been a particularly dedicated student, but now my studies and social causes became my life. At the time campuses were filled with a rage, not unlike my own, and I found an outlet fighting to correct injustices: protesting the war in Vietnam, speaking out for civil rights, demanding fair and equal treatment of women. I admit I was angry with men in general. What did I need a man for anyway? I could almost hear Helen Reddy's "I Am Woman" roaring in my head as these memories came back to me.

My anger toward men turned into hunger. I threw myself into one relationship after another. But there was always something holding me back, something going bad, a lack of commitment, either on his part or mine.

Eventually I came to believe that it was because Stefano loved me that he'd sent me home. In giving me up, he had allowed me to go on with my life. Isn't that what you do for those you love, release them for a chance at a better life? Isn't this what I had done for our child? And now, knowing I would see Stefano, I had lost my ability to chase these thoughts away. And yet another thought kept prying itself into my mind, one so filled with grief and guilt that it could make me tremble—the real reason I had given up my own child. Because I was afraid.

I arrived in Rome and called the airline to get an earlier flight to Greece. The woman spoke English with a heavy accent and didn't understand what I was telling her. I attempted to switch to Italian, while she held stubbornly to English. Finally I became so frustrated I slammed the phone down. I left the station and walked, pulling my little suitcase behind me. I had over six hours to kill. The sun was shining brightly in Rome, accommodating weather for a stroll, but not to feed my inner turmoil. After several blocks, I took my sweater off and tied it around my waist. My stomach growled with hunger. I stopped at a bar and bought a tomato, mozzarella, and lettuce sandwich and a Diet Coke in a bottle.

I found a piazza with a fountain—lusty naiads frolicking with enormous sea monsters. I sat, unwrapped the sandwich, and ate slowly, watching the traffic on the street, pedestrians coming in and out of the square, a little postcard kiosk on wheels like a hot dog stand, a toddler chasing pigeons. He appeared to be about a year old and still unsteady on his feet. His little face tightened as he kicked at the cooing birds, lost his balance, and fell down on the hard stones. He cried and his mother scolded him gently, then scooped him up and kissed him on top of the head.

I studied the woman, who was plumpish with a wisp of faded dark hair peeking out from under a silk scarf. Maybe his grandmother, rather than mother—she looked older than I'd first thought. Older than me.

She took the child's hand and they walked over to stand in front of the fountain. The woman crouched down and whispered in his ear. He pointed up at the enormous gush of water coming from the middle of the fountain, then the smaller donutlike circle with thin arches of water spraying out like a sprinkler my grandmother used in her garden on the farm.

After several minutes, they started out of the square, hand in hand. The little boy squatted to pick something up off the ground, then turned and hurled a stone at the pigeons. Wings flapped and they took off with a gust and clamor. The most amazing grin spread over the child's small innocent face, proud yet terrified to have such power.

I watched them as they walked down the street and slowly disappeared. *I am a mother too,* I thought. *Could my child have a child now?*

I had often wondered what my mother would have done if I'd come home from Italy with a baby. Would she have been ashamed? Would she have disowned me? But I knew, as I had for many years now, that my mother loved me, and that she would have also loved this child.

When I realized I was crying, I pulled the napkin out of my takeout bag from the bar and dried my eyes. I tossed the last crust of my sandwich to the pigeons gathered again in the square, then placed my empty bag and bottle in the trash can as I left the piazza.

I walked back to the train station and caught a bus to the airport.

On my evening flight to Greece I slept, emotionally and physically exhausted. When I woke I felt surprisingly calm. What a little cry, a little nap can do to clear the mind and soul.

At my hotel in Athens that night I went over the information I had gathered—the copies Alberto Mazzone had made from the Uffizi records, a copy of Roberto Balducci's article in *The Madonna in Italian Renaissance Art*, and the picture of Stefano at the Limonaia. Would I discover something in Greece that would bring me to the Masolino?

Lost but not destroyed.

28

AFTER BREAKFAST AT the hotel buffet, I went out and walked, the weather as sunny as it had been in Rome, the sky a deeper, truer blue, the air much warmer. I found a travel agency a block from the hotel and asked the agent, a nice-looking man with a bushy mustache flecked with silver, about a flight to Crete.

"Everything appears to be booked for today," he said, his fingers moving rapidly over his keyboard. "Perhaps you would consider the ferry?"

"How long would that take?"

"About nine hours, six on one of the high-speed fleets."

I shook my head. I was too keyed up to be confined that long.

"Let's check tomorrow." His eyes darted across the computer screen. "Aha," he exclaimed, "tomorrow morning, a cancellation." He studied the screen, his mouth slowly turning down with disappointment. "Just one." He looked up at me. "Would one be sufficient?"

"Perfect." I pulled my credit card out of my purse. "I'll take it."

I continued down the street to the Acropolis. Last night from the hotel room window I was able to see the outline of the Parthenon high on the Acropolis, and it had sent a little shiver of pure delight through me. Now I had time to take a closer look, and something to keep my mind occupied, to keep from thinking about what might happen when I finally met Stefano again.

I climbed the hill. For over two hours, I was able to forget the ultimate purpose of my journey. I studied the Parthenon, working my brain, constructing a puzzle, mentally replacing the original missing pieces of the frieze, the metopes, the pediments, with those I'd viewed in London, carried away by Lord Elgin. I'd seen them at the British Museum twice, the first time when I came to Europe with Roxie and we had no idea what we were looking at, the second time many years into my teaching. Now here I was for the very first time going back to the original source, and I wished for a long moment I had someone to share this adventure with. The image that came to me was that of Roberto.

I spent the afternoon at the Acropolis museum, viewing more pieces taken from the temples, thinking once more of the Marbles in Great Britain, called the Elgin Marbles by many, always the Parthenon Marbles by the Greeks who wanted them back. Once more I thought of stolen art—Marbles and Madonnas.

I slept surprisingly well that night, and when I arrived at the airport the following morning and boarded my plane, I felt an adrenaline-like rush. Ten minutes into the flight it morphed to near panic. Against my better judgment, I had a drink to relax.

As we began our descent, I stared out the foggy window. "Oh, you foolish, foolish, woman," I whispered. I pressed my fingers to the glass and rubbed off a clear circle. "What in the hell are you doing?"

Everything—the sky, the water—was the most brilliant blue I had ever seen, and as the island came into focus, I could see why someone—Stefano—might want to retire to such a spot.

But why away from Italy? From the art he loved? His daughter
said the home had been in her mother's family for many years,
and I remembered Pietro, the day after I learned Stefano was
married, rubbing his thumb and fingers together, telling me
without words that Stefano's wife came from money.

At the airport, I rented a car, a little golden Hyundai. I
asked the pretty young woman who helped me, who spoke
beautiful English, for a map of the island. I pulled out the
card on which Stefano's daughter had drawn her own perfect
little map.

"About six kilometers from Elounda, two from Agios Niko-
laos," I explained to the agent. Elisabetta Antonelli had told
me her parents lived on the northeastern coast of the island,
between these two cities, and she'd given me a rather detailed
and elaborate description of the location, as well as of the
house, which seemed as much about bragging as directions.

The rental agent drew a line with a bright yellow marker on
the island map to show me my route and marked the spot with
a yellow star. "A beautiful area, lovely private homes. You are
visiting friends?"

"Yes." The lie was becoming easier.

Later that afternoon as I drove along the coast, I placed the
open map on the passenger side of the car, consulting it at
first, then just enjoying the drive. The road narrowed and rose,
the view below practically taking my breath away. Rugged
cliffs jutting from a sea, shifting in color from a deep royal
blue to a crystal clear aqua. Whitewashed homes—squares
and rectangles—hung on cliffs, a church appeared here and
there with a domed steeple tiled in orange.

At Elounda, a picture-perfect resort town with little shops
and tavernas and white sandy beaches, I checked into a hotel,
splurging on a very nice one with a view of the bay. I spent the
rest of the day walking around the city.

The next morning I ate breakfast on the patio, looking over
layers of blue—across a tiled aqua pool, the sea, the distant
mountains of the Spinalonga Peninsula, the morning sky, tinted

with a hint of pink. The Bay of Mirabello—named by the
Venetians, Italian for "beautiful view." Ah, the Italians had
been here before!

Then I went shopping. Why not? I was on vacation. But I
knew, now that I was actually here, I was terrified of going on
with my plan, that I didn't even have a plan. I thought about
what Charley, and then Regina, had said—be careful. I knew
my fear had nothing to do with the threat of physical danger.

I bought a big straw hat, sunscreen, bottled water, and fresh
fruit, then took off. Driving along the coast, I kept a steady
eye on my odometer. When I had traveled the exact number of
kilometers designated by Elisabetta Antonelli, I parked and
got out to walk. The coastline was dotted with sandy beaches
and rocky cliffs. The sand was warm, the temperature perfect.
I walked, looking up along the row of white stucco villas and
large homes, some set back from the beach, others perched
along the rocky coastline. I picked out the largest and nicest,
the one with terraces on every outcrop. The one that had been
described so perfectly. Yes, this would be Stefano's.

I spread out my towel and sat on the beach below, a fair distance from the house. I pulled my book out of my bag. Day at
the beach, I thought. What was I doing? Had I become a stalker?

Seagulls glided overhead, shrieking. A light wind pulled in
a fishy smell. A family set up a bright yellow umbrella. The
children ran to the water, giggling, flipping their towels at
each other. A couple with a frisky golden retriever walked
along the beach. The woman carried her sandals in one hand,
stooping now and then to pick up a pebble or shell and stick
it in her pocket. The man wore shorts and enormous, thick
rubber-soled shoes, his pale skinny legs rising out of them like
toothpicks. The dog ran over to me, sniffing with curiosity as
if to say, *What are you doing here?* I reached out to pet him
just as the woman called and he darted back toward the couple. She shrugged a *sorry*, said something I could not hear. I
would have been grateful for the dog's company.

I ate my fruit slowly, a fresh sweet pear, half a banana. I

drank a swallow of water, closed my eyes, the sun warming me. I must have dozed off for a moment. I woke suddenly as a group of teens ran by tossing a Frisbee. I attempted to read, glancing back up to the villa, having great difficulty concentrating.

It was midafternoon when I stood, picked up my towel, folded it, and stuffed it in my bag. If I wanted to see Stefano, I should behave as a rational adult and give him a call.

And then I looked up. A young man and woman walked out onto one of the terraces and sat with another man whose back was to me. An older woman carried a tray. The man was reading a newspaper now, sipping a drink. I was too far away to make out the faces, but when the man stood and walked out to the rail that ran along the back of the terrace and looked out, my heart nearly jumped out of my chest.

The tilt of his head, the movement of his shoulders, so familiar. He was heavier than he had been those many years ago, but I knew it was Stefano. Was it also the man I had seen at Roberto Balducci's funeral, hidden in the shadow of the column in the back of the church? My heart now sent a spark of electricity pulsing through me, then did a little leap and pushed up throbbing into my throat.

The younger couple walked toward the beach. The older woman unlatched a door on the stone fence running along the property. Two children bounded out and ran ahead of the adults. As they got closer, I could see the boy was about seven, the girl I would guess to be ten or eleven. He carried a plastic pail, his long thin arms swinging it back and forth by the handle. They both wore swimsuits, towels draped over their shoulders. The older woman wore large round dark glasses, à la Jackie Kennedy, and white loose-fitting pants with a sleeveless turquoise shirt over tanned arms. Her hair was short and sleek and white. I was sure this was Stefano's wife, though I had never seen her. I guessed her to be in her late fifties or early sixties, a woman who, even in middle age, would be described as beautiful. She carried herself with a regal air. Once a princess, now a reigning queen.

Stefano followed several moments later. His hair still thick, more gray now than black. Still handsome, an aging movie star. He wore khaki shorts and sandals and a tropical print shirt, dark sunglasses hiding his eyes.

When he reached out and took her hand, and the two of them chatted and laughed as they continued toward the beach, I felt a knot twisting tighter and tighter in my stomach. This was the woman he had married, the woman he'd betrayed, yet never left. Did she know about me? Perhaps I was one of many. In their touch, their shared laughter, I could see so clearly what I had wanted so much to deny those many years ago. *This* was the woman he loved.

I pulled my straw hat down over my face, then turned and hurried down the beach, back to my car. I should leave now, return to Florence, and forget this whole stupid idea of seeing Stefano.

I got in my car and started back toward my hotel. As I drove I wondered if he'd talked to his daughter, if she'd said something about my coming to see her. I'd given her my name, implying I was a professional colleague. And here I was showing up on his beach, like some kind of weirdo spying on him and his wife.

When I got back to the hotel, I started throwing everything back in my bag—off the vanity in the bathroom, out of the dresser drawers, where I'd placed my clothes as if I'd planned to stay for a while. Then I sat down on the bed, breathing deeply, placing my hand on my chest to calm my thudding heart.

I should leave, but I knew I couldn't bring myself to go when I'd come this close. I pulled the card Elisabetta Antonelli had given me out of my bag and picked up the phone. Trying desperately to focus my eyes on the number she'd written on the back, I punched it into the phone.

A man answered, greeting me in Greek. My heart hammered violently. His voice had not changed at all. Even with the single unfamiliar word, I knew his voice. For several seconds I hesitated, thinking it would be best to hang up, as it seemed impossible that I could speak. My throat constricted. I took a deep breath, then another.

"*Pronto,*" he said impatiently, speaking Italian now.

"Hello," I said. "It's Suzanne, Suzanne Cunningham."

29

FOR A MOMENT it seemed the line had gone dead.

"Suzanne?" he said.

"Yes."

"You are here on the island?"

"*Sì*, yes, I am."

He didn't reply and I gazed down at my hand, twisting the cord of the phone, as if it wasn't even attached to my body.

"It's been many years," he said finally.

"Yes."

And then to fill the void, I started speaking so rapidly my words tumbled one over another. "I'm here on a study tour, studying the Minoan art. I'm teaching now, and I always feel it's better, more believable for the students, when the instructor has actually seen and gathered firsthand knowledge about the art she is describing, and what better place than the island of Crete, well, actually, I know much of it has been removed to museums, but, and I, well, I just thought . . . I met your daughter in Florence." God, this sounded so phony. Though I had rehearsed what I might say, with several possible scenarios, I sounded ridiculous and this wasn't at all the way I'd intended to say it.

"Students? You're a teacher?"

"Yes. Art history. I'm spending the semester in Florence at a year-abroad program for a university out of Portland, Oregon. We're on spring break right now." I wondered if he remembered when I told him I wanted to teach art history. I wondered if he remembered how he had laughed, as if it were the remotest possibility.

"How long will you be here?"

"A couple more days," I said vaguely.

A long hesitation. Wasn't this where he was supposed to suggest we get together?

"I'd like to see you," I said.

"This is not a good time," he replied slowly. "My son and his family are visiting."

His son and family? The young man, the woman and children I had seen on the beach? He had a daughter in Florence, and a son? No, I thought, with a flash of anger, *he has two sons*.

"Perhaps tomorrow," he said. "Perhaps I could arrange time tomorrow. Will you be free in the evening?"

"Yes, tomorrow would be fine."

I ROSE EARLY, unable to sleep, and spent the morning hiking up into the hills above the village, wondering as I trekked what Stefano thought. Did he think I used Cunningham as my professional name? Did he think I hadn't married? I wondered if he ever thought about me, if he wondered what had become of me.

That afternoon, to fill that enormous empty time until evening, I drove along the coast, then turned off and visited the temple of Knossos. I walked through the remains—mostly reconstructed—studying the architecture, the frescoes and mosaics, remembering more than once my comment to Stefano's daughter that I was studying Minoan culture and art, wishing I could have brought some of my favorite students along, wishing that I could better concentrate on what I was seeing. I returned to my hotel and sat on the patio, staring into the blue sea, drinking a glass of wine to calm my nerves. For a moment I thought how nice it would be to talk to Roberto.

STEFANO AND I had made arrangements to meet at a restaurant several blocks from my hotel. It was a nice restaurant, not a seedy little joint where a married man and a wanton woman might meet to contemplate an illicit love affair. I got there five minutes late, but Stefano hadn't yet arrived. The waiter escorted me to an outdoor table, and I thought, *Here we will sit for the world to see.*

The waiter asked if others would be joining me and I said yes, one more. I requested water, bottled without carbonation, two glasses.

The waiter delivered the water and poured me a glass. I sat drinking, wetting my parched throat. I checked my watch several times, and after ten more minutes, I thought, *He isn't going to show up.* Is this how it would finally end? With him standing me up? I was about to ask the waiter for my bill when I looked across the street and saw him walking toward me.

I took a quick gulp of water. He smiled a familiar smile as he stood before the table, but he didn't reach for my hand, or plant a kiss on my cheek, or touch me lightly on the shoulder.

"Hello, Suzanne." When he said my name, it almost sucked the air from my lungs.

He sat across from me at the small round table, and I noticed a slight tremble in his hand. He was nervous about our meeting too.

He wore a tan summer sport coat and dark glasses, which he removed and slipped into his pocket. Now I could see his eyes—eyes that could still send a shiver down my spine, still deep and dark and serious, changed only in the lines that fanned out from the corners.

"You look well, Stefano. It's been awhile." That was the most original thing I could come up with?

"You look well also, Suzanne."

The patio was not crowded. A few people sat at tables, most of them enjoying predinner drinks.

"Are you hungry?" Stefano asked.

I nodded. I'd eaten little since breakfast—fruit and water on my hike, a handful of nuts and pretzels with my glass of wine.

He motioned for the waiter to leave menus, then retrieved the sunglasses from his pocket. I didn't put on my reading glasses. The print was large enough that, with a slight squint, I could see just fine. We sat staring down at our menus. Stefano adjusted his chair, metal scraping against the stone of the patio. He held up a hand, an attempt at apology for the harsh sound, then returned to his menu. Even through the tinted lenses, I could see he was studying me, his eyes rising, glancing over.

"You are enjoying the island?" he asked.

"Yes," I answered. "The drive along the coast was beautiful. I visited the temple of Knossos, went for a nice hike into the hills this morning." I explained I'd spent a day in Athens at the Acropolis, which opened up the conversation a bit as we discussed the position I'd taken at the school in Florence. I told him I'd be in Florence just for the semester.

Then the conversation lapsed once more into an uneasy silence.

Stefano took a deep breath and set the menu aside. "How the years have slipped by. You are a teacher. Art history. I remember, this was your dream."

"You laughed when I told you."

"No, no, I never laughed. Well, perhaps." He laughed now and there was something so familiar in the resonance, I felt a tightening in my chest. "Not unkindly, though. No, never unkindly," he added. "You were such a determined little thing, eager to learn, enthusiastic, and inquisitive." He looked intently at me, still examining the changes I knew were quite evident. "You studied art history? You finished school?" He smiled approvingly.

"You were my first teacher," I said.

"Yes, your first." There was something almost sad in the

way he said this. I knew we were both thinking of something else. I knew he thought he had been the first—the first of *everything* really. I had never corrected this misconception.

The waiter returned to take our orders and Stefano picked up the menu again as he spoke in Greek. He turned to me, pointing to the menu. "You will enjoy this, very fresh on the island this time of year."

I read the English translation on the right side of the menu—*catch of the day.*

"No," I said. "I'm not fond of fish." He didn't even remember *I hate fish.*

I pointed to the chicken with herbs and rice, and he nodded as if the memory was coming back to him. He ordered a bottle of wine without consulting me.

After the waiter left, Stefano placed his sunglasses back in his pocket and asked, "Are you a good teacher?"

"Yes," I said, "I am a good teacher."

Again he smiled. *"Bene, bene,"* then, "good, good." He laughed softly. "You are a woman now."

I laughed, not quite so softly. "Yes, I am." And it dawned on me—he had seen me as a child.

"In Italy we celebrate a woman's maturity, unlike America where they worship youth."

I wasn't sure how to react to this. Stefano was certainly acknowledging he could see the years on my face, but perhaps it didn't matter to him.

"How about in Greece?" I asked. "Do the Greeks also celebrate a woman's maturity?"

"Yes, here too," he said with a low chuckle.

"Good thing for me," I said. "Maybe I should hang around." I wished I hadn't said that as soon as it came out of my mouth.

He didn't respond right away, as if weighing it, choosing his words carefully. "Yes, we're both older. And wiser." His smile now carried a hint of regret.

"Hopefully." I laughed lightly.

The waiter brought our wine. He poured some for Stefano, who tasted and approved, then a glass for each of us.

Stefano raised his in a toast. "To the treasures of Florence," he said, "and to the beautiful young *americana* who came to the rescue."

I raised my glass to his and we drank.

Over dinner we talked about my classes, the topics we'd covered, some of the discussions I'd had with my students, particularly those in my upper-division courses.

"You have a course now on women? Women in Renaissance art?" he asked. "In my days at university," he said with a shake of his head, "there was never a class solely on women."

"I've also taught a class dedicated completely to women artists," I replied with a grin. "Two semesters—the first on women through the seventeenth century, the second dedicated to more recent women artists."

"Times have changed," he said.

"Yes, they have."

As I told him about some of the other classes I'd taught over the years, he seemed surprised by my knowledge and understanding, but not, he told me, my enthusiasm. I remembered how much I had craved his approval, how much I had wanted to learn about the art that he loved, the art that seemed to be part of the air he breathed. And I remembered how connected I had felt to this man as we worked together to save the treasures of Florence.

But now a new sensation came over me. He was no longer the teacher.

We chatted about the work we had done at the Limonaia. I told Stefano I'd run into Pietro and he said he hadn't seen him in years. He told me they'd worked together on several projects after the flood. They had both worked in Milan on the restoration of the *Last Supper*. I recalled now, during my lunch with Pietro, he had mentioned he'd worked with Stefano in Milan, though I thought it had been a very long time ago. But then, perhaps it was. According to Stefano, the restoration had taken almost two decades. *Decades*, I thought . . . years counted in tens now. It had been over three since Stefano and I first met.

I told him about the restoration tour Dr. Giuliana Garzoni

had arranged for us. I confessed I didn't remember her and Stefano said she was one of the assistant restoration supervisors at the Fortezza da Basso. I didn't mention Roberto Balducci—not yet. Stefano brought up names of others who had participated in the restoration, several, he said, had passed on. He told me he had stayed in Florence four more years after the flood, then gone to Venice, and Milan, where his wife's family lived, and how they had eventually decided to retire to the island. We had never spoken of his wife before, but now I felt he was confirming what I already knew—that nothing had changed.

As we finished our dinner a young girl with dark eyes, a colorful native costume, and a basket full of roses approached the table. She spoke to Stefano in Greek. She was a pretty little girl, her dark eyes fringed with black lashes. Although I could not understand her words, I knew as she smiled at Stefano, then me, she was giving him the usual sales pitch. "For the beautiful lady, a beautiful rose." Stefano reached in his pocket and pulled out several bills.

The girl handed me the rose with a smile and a slight bow. I held it to my nose.

When the girl strolled to the next table and was waved away, Stefano looked at his watch and said, "I must leave soon."

"I understand," I said; then, "You didn't write."

He looked up at me. "I did."

"Once."

He looked out to the street, now crowded with tourists in sandals and straw hats, cameras hanging on straps or stuffed in pockets. "I thought one day you would understand that I did this because I cared so deeply." He turned and looked at me. "That I wanted you to go on with your life, that I wanted you to be happy."

For several moments I was unable to reply. He had sent me home, and it was only later that I did realize it was because he wanted me to have more than he could offer. He had not deserted me then, or even after I told him I was pregnant. He had taken me to the convent, a safe place to have our child. Did he ever think of our son? Did this loss torment him as it did me? I fought to hold back the tears. "Happy?" I whispered; and then, "Are you happy?"

He looked out toward the street again. "I've settled into a comfortable life."

"Your wife enjoys living here, away from Italy?" I fingered the rose. The thorns had been removed. I wouldn't tell him I had seen his wife on the beach today.

He didn't answer.

"You've been together how long?" I asked.

"Renata and I have been together for over forty years." He picked up his wineglass and took a slow sip, gazing at me over the rim. "There have been, how do you say it, rough spots over the years."

Was I a rough spot? I wondered. One of many?

"But, yes," he said. "We are happy. And you?"

"I enjoy my teaching, being in Florence, having this opportunity to travel, to study some of the art I feel I have known so well, but have never seen."

"Bene, bene," he said, his voice warm and sincere.

I placed the rose on the table and looked directly at Stefano. "What did you tell your wife—Renata?" I had never heard her name before. "What did you tell her about meeting me here tonight?"

His lips lifted into a half smile, I think at my boldness. He had never seen this side of me. "I told her I was meeting a colleague, someone I had worked with years ago, a professor of art history."

"And did you invite her to come along?" I asked with a wicked grin now, my tears no longer on the edge. How brave I was being.

He shook his head. "My son and his wife will be here for only two more days. This time is important to Renata. She would not have come. I told them I wouldn't be late."

"Did she know about me?"

He said nothing, but slowly he shook his head.

"How did you say it?" I asked.

He looked at me puzzled. "Say what?"

"Colleague? In Italian there's a difference, isn't there? *Un colleague* or *una colleague*?" I said exaggerating the sound of the *a* on *una*.

Stefano laughed softly. *"Americano? Americana?"*

"Yes," I said, "you thought I was a boy." I laughed too—it seemed even after all these years we had many memories to share—our first encounter at the National Library, when he chose me to move to the Limonaia. I had never told him Roxie and I had seen him before that as we passed by the Uffizi where he was loading damaged paintings onto a truck. It was probably that day I had first fallen in love with him.

He studied my hands as I ran my fingers over my wineglass. For a moment, I thought he was going to reach over, take my hand in his. These hands that had worked beside his. These hands that had touched him so intimately. These hands now growing old. And then, I could see he was looking at my left hand.

"You are not married?" he asked.

"No."

"I thought you would."

"Oh, yes, I did."

He waited.

"Divorced."

He said nothing. What could a man say, sitting here with a former lover? He did not believe in divorce, yet he had been unfaithful. How were we to judge one another? I knew we wouldn't.

The waiter approached the table. We had decided against dessert, both of us making comments about staying fit— Stefano told me he tried to exercise on a regular basis, that he rode his bike each morning.

We ordered coffee.

"I must leave soon," he said again.

"Yes," I said, "I understand."

And then, aware the evening was about to end, I asked, "Did you know Roberto Balducci?"

"The art historian?"

"He passed away recently."

"Yes," he said. "I know."

Something inside me did a little flip. Somehow I had expected him to deny this, to say he couldn't place the name. "I was at the service," I said, "in Fiesole."

He stared at me. "If I'd only known."

"You were there?" I asked as if surprised.

"Yes, though I left early—I had a train, then a flight to catch out of Rome. With the weather, the snow, I wanted to make sure I was not late."

I didn't tell Stefano how I thought I had seen him at the funeral. But now, I *knew* he had been there.

"You came to Italy for his funeral?" I asked. "You were close friends?"

"I hadn't spoken with him in years. At one time we talked often. As an art historian he was interested in several paintings I had worked on."

Like the Masolino? I wondered.

"His daughter—no, his granddaughter—spoke with my daughter in Florence," Stefano continued. "She told me her grandfather wished to speak with me. But evidently he was very ill. I called when I came to visit my daughter, but he had passed." Stefano shrugged his shoulders. "I never learned why he wished to speak with me. But I was in Florence at this time so, yes, I went to the service to pay my respects."

I wondered if there was more to it than that, if Stefano had gone to lay more to rest than the remains of Roberto Balducci. If he was burying something else from the past. The knowledge of what had happened to the Masolino.

"Did she, the granddaughter, give you any indication why he wished to speak with you?" I asked.

"I'm not sure she knew," he said seriously.

"Could it have had something to do with the restoration?"

He shook his head. "It's been over thirty years. Many of those who worked on the restoration after the flood are gone now." I heard a sadness, a true sense of loss in his voice.

"Sculptures, paintings, frescoes, centuries old, threatened with destruction by the flood, once more displayed in Florence." There was a shift in his somber tone now, the slightest lift. "Masterpieces that will continue to be displayed for generations to come."

I nodded, but said nothing.

"Life," Stefano said, almost a whisper, "as we grow older, it seems we realize how very short it is."

I wondered if he was thinking of Roberto Balducci, or if his thoughts went back to how young we had been. Two middle-aged people now, the gap between us in many ways less than it had been before. And yet, so much we did not share. So much of my life lived without him.

And I realized it was indeed over. Was this what I had needed all these years? To see Stefano one more time? And I knew this would be the last time I would see him. Not his choice alone, but now mine.

"We saved many," Stefano said, "yet, some were lost. And some . . . but oh, the attempts. Have you seen the Cimabue?"

"I haven't." I had not yet returned to Santa Croce.

"You must go," he said.

"I will."

"Such small portions remained of the true Cimabue, but . . ." He rubbed his head, ran his fingers through his hair, a gesture I had seen often, and in his still-handsome face, the same sorrow I had seen when he examined the battered Cimabue that day at Santa Croce. I felt something tear inside me.

"There's something I need to know," I began again slowly. "Roberto Balducci, I contacted him when I arrived in Florence. I believe he wanted to speak with you because of me, because of something I wanted to know."

Stefano looked at me blankly, and then there was something else, something that moved so quickly across his face I was unable to identify it before it was gone.

I opened my purse and pulled out the photo of Stefano and handed it to him. He blinked several times, and I thought I could detect a nervous lump moving up and down his throat. "Ah, yes, so very young."

I rotated the photo in his hand. "The painting on the work-bench. Do you remember this painting?"

His eyes tightened. He reached into his pocket and pulled out his glasses again and put them on. It was dark out now. Tiny lights had come on around the patio, which was now filled with noisy dinner guests. Stefano shook his head, obviously unable to see with the shaded lenses. "The eyes," he said with a quiet laugh as he placed the glasses back in his pocket. He studied the photo again, his eyes tightened, straining for a long moment. "I do not know. There were so many, Suzanne. I know at the time, I thought I would never forget any of them. But do you know there were over fifteen hundred paintings, both canvas and panel? So much damage, and yes, I thought I would remember them all."

"Like old lovers?" I asked.

He smiled as if he wished not to. "As time passes," he said and took a sip of water. "There were many, and yes, we did attempt to save them all."

I pulled out the Uffizi file photo, which I had stapled to the history sheet, on which someone—perhaps Stefano—had written *destroyed in the flood*.

He gazed at the photo then flipped the page. His eyes moved across the sheet. He rubbed his chin, and then looked up at me. "This is a history file," he said, "from the Uffizi?"

"And this photo, isn't it the same painting?"

He did not respond, but studied the file and the photo of himself at the Limonaia.

"This is your handwriting." I pointed.

"It appears, but . . ." He shook his head. "I have no recollection of this. But, yes, some were lost."

I didn't know what I had expected. He either had no memory of the painting—which I found very difficult to believe—or he had been involved in some way in its disappearance. But I knew these words, which he had or perhaps had not written, were not true. I knew the painting had not been destroyed in the flood.

"Is this why you've come to see me?" he asked. "Because of this painting? You do not believe it was lost?" He said this very calmly.

"Oh, Stefano," I said with an audible sigh, "there are so many reasons I've come to see you."

There was a sad look in his eyes now. *"Sì,"* he agreed.

We finished our coffee. Stefano paid the bill. I picked up the rose and we left the restaurant. He asked where I was staying, and I motioned down the street. "Just a short distance."

He was still gentleman enough to escort me back in the dark.

"When do you return?" he asked. "To Florence?"

"School starts again Monday." I realized it was only Wednesday. It seemed like so much time had elapsed since I left Florence on Saturday morning, but I still had four days of my break left.

He nodded, and when we arrived at the entrance to the lobby, I knew he wouldn't come in. Stefano said it was good to see me again, so stiff and formal, but then he put his arms around me and kissed me gently on the forehead. "I'm sorry," he said, "for any hurt. I think this is something I've needed to say. Thank you for coming to see me."

"Maybe we both needed this," I said. He held me, neither of us speaking. Then he released me. I turned to go inside, then stopped and looked back. "Do you . . ." I hesitated. "Do you ever think about him?"

He stared at me for a long uneasy moment. "Yes," he said.

30

I LEFT THE island the following morning on the first boat, headed for the island of Santorini, not my chosen destination, but one of necessity—I had to leave Crete as soon as possible. I'd like to say I dropped the rose Stefano had given me into the Adriatic Sea with dramatic, movie-worthy flare. But I left it on the vanity in the bathroom of my hotel in Elounda, the stem dipped into a drinking glass filled with water. Maybe the maid took it home and placed it in a vase. More likely, she tossed it in the trash.

On Santorini I hiked, I biked, I visited temples and ruins. I pushed all thoughts of Stefano, and all thoughts of my son, out of my head, and filled it with beautiful breathtaking vistas.

On the boat back to the mainland I had no such diversions. The sea was colorless and choppy and thoughts moved in and out of my head with an equally disturbing rhythm.

Stefano had apologized. Yet I knew I had been an equally active participant in what had happened between us, my youth a poor excuse for refusing blame. Was I the Eve of Masolino's fresco in the Brancacci Chapel, naïve and innocent? The woman who, as soon as the artist set down his brush, would turn and pluck fruit from the tree, then with a seductive swivel of the hip present it to the man?

Now I wondered if Stefano and I had finally released each other. I knew in my heart we would always be tied together. There would always be the art and always the memory of the child we would never know, the child I had never held in my arms.

Was it also time to give up my search for the Masolino? Maybe it was time to quit this too—this search in which I was turning up so little.

Yet I couldn't let go of the unanswered questions. Did Stefano have some part in this? His behavior at dinner seemed strange. I didn't believe he could have forgotten the painting. He'd made such a fuss over it during the restoration. I remembered how he'd spoken of further study, how, if proven to be a Masolino, this recognition might influence the historical perception of the artist.

And I still wanted to know if Roberto Balducci the elder was involved. Again I thought of Roberto. Though he said he would want to know the truth, it would surely hurt him if I discovered that his father had taken a part in stealing a painting from the Uffizi. I decided when I returned to Florence I'd talk to both Giuliana Garzoni and Pietro again. Neither of them had been able to help me, but I hadn't shared much of what I knew with Garzoni because I hadn't trusted her. And Pietro hadn't seen the photo of Stefano at the Limonaia—visible proof that the painting had made it at least that far in the restoration process. Surely this would jog some sort of memory.

On Friday in Athens I spent the day at the National Museum.

As I stood before the beautiful bronze Poseidon, I heard a familiar voice behind me.

"What a fortuitous find, our esteemed professor of art history, right here in the National Archaeological Museum of Athens."

Richard Bennington and Cassie MacDonald, from my upper-division class, stood beside me, and I gave them each a hug. Within seconds, we were joined by Heather James and Beau Macey.

"Professor Cunningham, ciao." Heather greeted me with a grin.

"So," Richard said, "ready for the official art tour?"

We walked through the museum together, reviewing the pieces in the collection, my art majors adding a fact or observation here or there, my nonmajors taking an active part in the discussions. Several English-speaking tourists enthusiastically adhered to the group as we moved through the gallery.

Heather, who was in my Intro to Art History along with Beau, said she wished I'd been here last semester. "The art history teacher first semester wasn't nearly as good as you, Professor Cunningham."

"Thank you, Heather." It was fun—seeing their genuine interest, feeling I might have had something to do with it—and I knew this was the true gift that Stefano had given me, the one I could hold on to forever.

"Are we going to have a test?" Beau asked with a grin.

"How about extra credit?" Richard added.

"The pleasure of this afternoon should be sufficient reward in itself," I answered.

"Good enough, Professor C." Richard nodded agreeably.

"Yes," I replied, "good enough."

SATURDAY MORNING I flew out of Athens to Rome, then returned to Florence, arriving late Saturday evening.

I slept until past ten Sunday morning. I got up and dumped all my dirty clothes in a hamper, replaced my cosmetics and toiletries in the bathroom. After a shower, I wrapped myself in a big towel, dried my hair, and then opened the window to let in fresh air, to rid the room of the musty, empty smell that had settled in over the week I'd been gone. I pulled the shutter up and gazed out onto the street. It had rained the night before, and I had a vague memory of the pitter-patter against my window. The cobblestone streets were still damp and a clean smell had settled in the air. The chatter of people gathering at the bar across the street drifted up; the backfire of a motorbike popped in the street. A young man—Italian I was sure— called to a couple of girls as they walked by. They were giggling and whispering and enjoying the attention. Ah, to be young, I thought, realizing I wouldn't want to go back to that for anything.

I pulled a pair of jeans and a T-shirt out of my dresser, slipped them on, left the room, and bounded down the steps onto the street. At my favorite bar, where I stopped for coffee, the padrone greeted me as if I were a long lost friend. We visited for several minutes; I told him about my trip to Greece, and he related a story about years ago when he'd gone with his young wife. *"Romantico? Sì?"* he asked with a grin.

"Sì," I said.

It was afternoon by the time I left the bar. I walked down toward the River Arno. The Ponte Vecchio was crowded with tourists so I strolled down to the Ponte Santa Trinita, crossed the river, and continued on to the Pitti Palace. I had returned twice to visit the galleries in the Pitti since I'd been in Florence, but had yet to venture into the Boboli Gardens, which were rather drab and cold during the winter. Now throngs of tourists filed through the palace, overflowing into the gardens, and I followed.

I strolled along the lane, turning right as if by instinct, tracing a familiar path. Soon I stood before the Limonaia, a long gray building with a tiled roof. Garlands of fruit carved from stone hung over the arched, open doorways. The grounds were gated and locked, and I peered through the slats of the black iron fence into the wide entry at orange and lemon trees that were being housed inside during the cooler weather. Soon they would be coming out into the sunshine.

I continued on through the gardens, stopping for a moment to sit at the fountain of Neptune. A family—a young mother and father with a child about three and a little one in a stroller— sat eating sandwiches. The father cut and peeled a pear, then handed small slices to the baby as she cooed and smiled.

An hour later as I headed out of the gardens, I passed the *Bacchino* in the square just before the exit, and once more my mind turned to Roberto. He'd told me the gardens were starting to bloom up at the villa. Maybe he'd turned on the fountain.

As I left the grounds of the Pitti Palace, I turned east and walked along the river, then up toward Santa Croce. When I reached the piazza, surrounded by the little shops, bars, and restaurants, I stood for a moment gazing about, remembering the square in front of the church as it had appeared when I first came with Stefano—the muddied, foul-smelling mess, the piles of rubbish, the soiled, ochre stucco of Florence.

I walked into the church, and after spending almost an hour studying the frescoes, reading the inscriptions on tombs and walls and floors, I headed to the church's museum, where I knew the Cimabue crucifix was once more displayed.

The room was long and stark and cool. Large padded chairs ran along each side, and I sat. The Cimabue hung on the wall to the right of the entry. The afternoon sun slanted through one of the three Romanesque windows, falling upon the face of Christ.

My mind held an image of the crucifix—first from the back as I stared up at Stefano climbing to gaze upon the damaged panel; then at the Limonaia, resting on a bed of wood and metal, slowly drying, the smallest fragments of original paint clinging to the wooden surface. The face of Christ, no more than a lowered eyelid, a half face, dropped to a blank space of shoulder. And then, the pope, who had come to bless it on Christmas Eve. And memories of my own blessing.

I had never seen the Cimabue before the flood, yet later I had studied reproductions in art history books. I knew what the original looked like—the elongated figure of Christ nailed to the cross. Arms stretched, head bowed, and the anguished countenance. A bridge from Byzantine to Renaissance, a masterpiece from the brush of Cimabue, Cenni di Pepo.

It hung now from three heavy chains. I'd read about a system of pulleys to raise the crucifix if necessary, as well as an alarm installed to protect this treasure from future floods.

In a sense a resurrection, I thought as I studied the painting. Imperfect as it was, the restoration had taken over a decade. It wasn't until Holy Friday of 1977 that Cimabue's crucifix was returned to the museum of Santa Croce.

Chips of flaking, bubbling paint had been completely removed from the wooden panel. These, along with small fragments that had been dislodged by the force of the river and retrieved floating in the lake of Santa Croce, were dehumidified, cleaned, and restored, then slowly and painstakingly reapplied to the treated surface of the panel. The methods used were new and considered revolutionary at the time, discoveries developed because of this tragedy that would be used in future restorations. Even now there were large sections of the crucifix that were forever lost, and no attempt had been made to reconstruct these portions. A neutral color had been applied to preserve the wooden panel in these areas. Yet, the original remaining colors appeared more vibrant than in the photos of the preflood painting, tinged with a greenish hue brought about by hundreds of years of grime and dust and poorly done cleanings. Yes, an imperfect resurrection. The full artist's rendering, forever destroyed by the raging waters of the Arno.

I left Santa Croce and started back to my apartment.

Stefano had often told me that although the flood brought great destruction there were also treasures uncovered because of it. The revelation of preliminary sketches providing new insight into the work of ancient artists; the removal of old, dirty restorations and varnish, showing for the first time in centuries the artists' true creative intent; sketches beneath the frescoes of Giotti in the Bardi Chapel; the revelation of the flesh tones and gold on Donatello's Mary Magdalene after layers of dark brown paint were removed to show the gilded wooden carving.

Back then, I saw myself as one of these revelations. Layers cleaned away to reveal the real me. Now as I walked, I laughed out loud—I had been much too young to have had layers peeled away. Layers had been added. Would I continue to add more—disappointments, regrets, lost lovers, found lovers, new lovers?

Was it time to peel away some of the old, to finally find myself hidden beneath it all?

Strangely I knew that to do this I had to find the Masolino. I would not be satisfied until I knew the truth.

And I also knew—to strip myself to the core, there was something else I must find.

I knew now that I must find my son.

31

THAT EVENING I called Roberto on both his home and cell phones. The greeting on the phone at the villa said he would be in Rome until Monday afternoon.

I could hear a nervous lilt in my voice as I left a brief message. "I'm home! I missed you! Call me!"

I felt excited about seeing Roberto, but my excitement was wrapped in a nervous tension. I had missed him and I wanted him to know that finally I had reached some kind of understanding with Stefano. Maybe not even with Stefano, but within myself. Some kind of personal peace. But I also wanted Roberto's help. As an infertility specialist, he'd worked with couples who had difficulties conceiving. Surely he had some knowledge of the system of adoptions in Italy, and maybe he'd have access to records. Yet I was uneasy about asking for his help. Would he feel again that I was using him? I wasn't even sure I could do this. I'd never told anyone about the child Stefano and I had given up.

* * *

MONDAY MORNING BEFORE and after my first class, my students were full of stories about their travels, reporting on the art they'd seen, asking about my own discoveries. When I checked my box at school, I found a letter from Andrea, and one from my dad, which I tore open right away. It was newsy—he'd visited Andrea and Michael, gone on a fishing trip with a buddy. Not very emotional or revealing, but that was Dad, and I'd learned to appreciate him that way years ago.

There was also a note from Charley asking that I come see him. I wondered if he had truly forgiven me for not going with him on break.

When I knocked on his office door, he yelled for me to come in. He was on the phone, and motioned me to sit while he finished the call—his sister, I guessed, as he said he was glad they'd made it home safely, and he'd had fun too.

"My sister," he said as he replaced the receiver. He looked refreshed and relaxed, as people are supposed to, but never do, after a week's vacation. He had a redhead's tan—more pink than tan, with a sweep of freckles across his nose.

"You had a nice break then?" I said. "Got a little sun."

"French Riviera." Charley grinned, and I had to work to push a vision of Charley in a Speedo out of my head. "Yes, we had fun and even worked out some family misunderstandings, which might have been impossible if you'd come along."

I was especially grateful now that I hadn't. "So it worked out better without me?" I asked with mock disappointment.

"It worked out just fine," he said with a cheerful nod. "How about your trip?"

"I didn't discover anything more about the Masolino, but Greece was absolutely beautiful, and I spent some time at the Acropolis, Knossos, several museums and temples, did some hiking, some biking. It was a good trip."

"Wonderful," he said; then, "I spoke with Dr. Browning before I left Florence."

"She's doing well?" I asked.

"She's doing much better, but she's decided not to return next year. I'd like to offer you the position."

I was touched, but also completely unprepared.

"I'd like to know by the middle of next month," he said.

"I'll take it," I answered quickly.

Charley smiled again. "Well, good. We're pleased with the job you've been doing, Suzanne. Very pleased."

I fled out of Charley's office, wanting to tell someone, when I ran into Regina.

"How was Greece? Did you find what you were looking for?"

"Yes and no. Did you and Giorgio have fun?"

"We had a great time." She was carrying a large bag of clay balanced on her hip. "You saw Stefano?"

"Yes."

"And . . . ?" She motioned a *come on* with her head, and we started up the stairs to the third floor.

"We talked about the painting, I showed him the file—"

"He denied it was his handwriting?"

"Actually, he didn't. He said he couldn't remember the painting, which I find extremely difficult to believe. He said paintings *were* lost."

"Does he know you think it was stolen?"

"He was aware that I didn't believe it was destroyed, but the way he reacted to my questions was, well, odd. If he'd had anything to do with the painting's disappearance, I had expected him to be defensive. If not, I'd expected some concern, some curiosity, but he showed neither."

"You think he did—take it?" She adjusted the bag on her hip.

"Honestly, I don't know what was going on with Stefano. Like Pietro, he seemed to accept what was written in the file, what Roberto Balducci wrote in his article."

Regina wrinkled her nose like she was beginning to doubt me too. "And so, what about Stefano?" We'd arrived on the third floor. We stood together in the landing. "How did he look?"

I just nodded and bit my lip. Regina got the message.

"Before I asked about the Masolino we had a nice visit."

"And?"

"We parted on good terms."

"But no old spark rekindled?"

I laughed. "Oh, sparks were flying everywhere. But the fire of passion was not reignited."

Regina didn't seem to know quite how to take this. I think she was a little disappointed.

"Oh, something else—Charley offered me the position next year."

Regina squealed, dropped the bag with a thump, and threw her arms around me. "You took it?"

"I did."

LATER THAT AFTERNOON I called Pietro at the Uffizi, and got a puzzling recording that said the number was no longer in service. I called Dr. Garzoni's office. Her assistant told me she wasn't in and if I wanted to schedule an appointment, I should call next week. When I asked about Pietro, she said he was no longer with the Uffizi. Could this be a mere coincidence?

"Do you have a forwarding address or number?" I asked.

"That's confidential information," she replied abruptly.

I called Alberto Mazzone, the young restorer who'd helped me with the information on the Masolino.

"I thought perhaps you knew," he told me. "Pietro is no longer here at the Uffizi. He became so, how do you say it, fed up, with all the controversy over the restoration of Leonardo's *Adoration of the Magi*."

"Do you know how to get in touch with him?"

"Pietro always kept to himself. I know nothing of his personal life or where he lives in Florence."

How very strange that Pietro hadn't mentioned he would be leaving, I thought as I thanked Alberto. Maybe this was something that happened suddenly. I remembered the conversation we'd had about the restoration of Leonardo's *Adoration of the Magi*, how Pietro seemed upset that his work was not being well received, how there were some in the art community who thought an attempt at restoration or cleaning would be a tragedy.

I felt a nervous energy push and tug inside me as I sat staring down at the calendar on my desk where I'd written myself a note to call Dr. Garzoni. I wanted to talk to Pietro again before I met with her. I got up and walked to the window, gazing out. It was a clear, warm day. Students stood outside in shirtsleeves.

Poor Pietro. He loved his work. I wondered if there was anything else in his life. He had no family. He told me he had married but was now divorced. I thought about how kind he had been to me when we worked together long ago, how he had invited me to his home on Christmas Eve, how pleased his mother had been to share their meal with me. She was still alive—did Pietro live with his mother? Her home was somewhere in the Oltrarno close to the river. I remembered the dank smell of the Arno's leavings still pungent inside on Christmas Eve, a month and a half after the flood.

I walked back to my desk and rummaged through my top drawer, trying to find the card Pietro had given me the day of our restoration tour. I remembered he had written an address and number on the back. I'd keyed his office number into my phones, but I couldn't recall what I'd done with the card after that and it wasn't in my desk.

I looked through my Masolino file, thinking I might have put Pietro's card in with my materials on the Madonna. It wasn't there. I glanced over at the bookcase. The phone book. I flipped through until I came to the Cs. No Pietro Capparelli. There was no Capparelli listed with what sounded like a woman's name. Maybe his mother had remarried—I thought Pietro's father was dead, but I wasn't sure. We'd never talked about that. In fact we'd never talked about much of anything other than our work. Alberto was right—Pietro was very private.

My phone rang. It was Roberto.

"So good to hear your voice," Roberto said, echoing the words in my own head—what a comfort to hear the sound of his voice. "Tell me about your trip."

"It was absolutely beautiful in Greece. I visited the

Acropolis, the National Museum, got some exercise, biking and walking. The weather was beautiful." I knew this wasn't what he wanted to hear. "Could we get together?"

"Yes, I'd like that." I detected a bit of nervousness in his voice, which surely he could hear in mine. "Did you find Stefano?"

"I missed you, Roberto, and yes, I did see Stefano. . . ." I didn't want to talk about this over the phone. "I missed you," I said again.

"I missed you too," he said with a trace of tentativeness.

"When will I see you?"

"Unfortunately I'm still in Rome. The contract signing was set for this morning, but there are details to work out that we thought had been resolved. It's been reset for tomorrow morning. I should be back by early afternoon. You don't have class Tuesday afternoon, right?"

"I have office hours, but I doubt I'll have anyone come in since we just got back from break."

"May I come by as soon as I get into town?"

"I'd like that."

"Did you find anything more to help you with the painting?"

"Not really. We've got a lot to catch up on."

"We do."

"You were right, Roberto. I mean about my not being the same person. Well, you were right." I wanted to give him at least that much now.

"I'll come by as soon as I'm back in town." I was grateful he wasn't pushing for a detailed, intimate conversation over the phone, that he wasn't asking for specifics on Stefano just yet.

"Maria told me she was the one who discovered Leonetti was in Greece," he said.

"You knew?"

"Not until late last week. Maria is sorting through my father's papers." He sounded almost casual now. "You are very good at keeping secrets," he added lightly.

Secrets? "Yes, I've always been a good secret keeper." I could hear a nervous twitter in my laugh.

"Maria's invited us for dinner tomorrow night. Mother's coming from Venice to help her go through the papers. The university in Rome has expressed an interest in archiving some of his work."

Maria had invited us? I wondered if she had any idea what her father and I were going through, that a little family get-together might not be the best idea until we'd sorted through a few things. And then, another thought passed through my mind—could these papers reveal something more about the Masolino, the article he'd written on the painting?

"She thought you might want to take a look," Roberto said, again as if my thought had been out loud, "maybe find something that could help you."

I'd never mentioned anything about the painting to Maria. "Roberto," I said, picking up a pencil on my desk, twisting it, and then starting to doodle little circles on a notepad.

"Yes?"

"Does Maria know that her grandfather might be involved in the disappearance of a Renaissance painting? Does she know that's the reason I came to see him?" I remembered she had left the room when I visited with Roberto the elder, and Maria hadn't heard that conversation.

"We discussed it when she told me my father had wanted to talk with Stefano."

"If I discover something that might incriminate him, how will she—you—handle that?"

"We'll deal with that when the time comes. I'd rather we find this information than someone else, an outsider."

I felt a small throbbing warmth on the back of my head. A moment of distrust flickered again. Did he include me in the *we*, or was I an outsider? *No, no,* I told myself, Roberto was inviting me to look at the papers. He was counting on me to work with the family to find the painting. Yet protect his father? Was this what he was implying?

"I'll give you a call," he said, "when I'm on my way from Rome tomorrow."

"Sounds good. Please, tell Maria I'd like to bring something.

They have wonderful pastries at the bakery where I stop every morning."

"Very thoughtful. I'll let her know."

"And, Roberto, there's something else I need your help with." I wanted to work up to this gradually, and I wanted to be very careful that he didn't perceive my asking for help as my using him, that he understood I trusted him with something I'd never shared with anyone.

"What is it, Suzanne?" His voice softened—so perceptive.

I took a deep, slow breath. "We can talk about it when we get together." Yes, I could do this. Roberto could help me. "And, I've got some good news," I said, my voice shifting brightly. I hoped he would see this as good news—my accepting the offer to teach the following year. I didn't want to tell him over the phone. I wanted to see his face when I told him. I glanced at my watch. Ten after one. *Saved by the bell.* "My class starts in five minutes. We'll talk tomorrow."

"Well," he said with the slightest hesitation, and then, "it sounds like we do have much to talk about."

"We do."

"I look forward to it," he said; and I said, "Me too."

HE CALLED AGAIN the following morning.

"The closing has been delayed. We've rescheduled for two o'clock this afternoon, so I won't make it as early as I'd hoped."

"Oh," I said, hearing my own disappointment.

"If there are any further delays, to hell with it." He sounded vaguely angry. "I'm coming home. I want to see you, Suzanne. I'll be there as soon as I can. My mother's looking forward to tomorrow, but I'd much prefer some time alone. Perhaps I should cancel the little family dinner. We'll see how quickly I get out of the city. I'll call again."

He called later that afternoon to tell me he was on his way. He'd pick me up about five.

I stood outside my apartment building with Maria's two ceramic dishes, which I'd filled with desserts—little chocolate crème-filled cakes, flaky pastries with nuts and raisins, and buttery cookies—and placed inside a sturdy cloth bag.

He arrived at a quarter after. I hopped in and gave him a clumsy kiss before we pulled out into traffic.

"Let's go get a drink," he said.

"Okay." I'd almost been grateful for the family dinner, a little buffer, but I knew this was better. I had so much to tell him. The sooner, the better.

We found a bar on the outskirts of the city where parking was no problem. It looked fine from the street, but wasn't the cleanest place inside. Roberto shot me an apologetic glance as we walked in. I doubted he'd been here before. "It's fine," I said, touching his arm.

The linoleum floor was scuffed, and our worn Formica table slick and sticky in spots, granules of sugar adhering to the surface. I brushed crumbs off the padded vinyl cushion of the chair and sat. A sixtyish man in a stained apron, the padrone I guessed, took a quick sweep over the table with a damp towel before asking us what we'd like. We each ordered a glass of wine.

"You look beautiful," he said, "soaked up some of that Greek island sun?"

"Thank you. I did spend some time on the beach. The weather was beautiful. And the islands. Well, gorgeous." *Enough of that,* I told myself. I'd already filled him in on the insignificant details of the trip briefly in the van. We'd talked about the difficulties he'd had in finally closing on the clinic in Rome.

"I loved Stefano," I burst out, surprising myself. This wasn't at all what I had expected to say, but for some reason it just came out, and I realized I wanted Roberto to know this. "I don't know why, but it's important that you know this. It wasn't a tawdry little affair. . . ." I bit my lip and took a deep breath. "Well, okay, maybe it was. Even after I learned he was married, we continued to see each other." I looked at Roberto, directly into his eyes, and I could see he wanted me to continue. "There was something magical about the time we spent together, something almost unreal. I was nineteen years old,

I had never done anything of significance, and here I was saving some of the most valuable paintings in the world, masterpieces from the Renaissance, beautiful, priceless works of art. I had never felt so useful, never knew my life could have such meaning. Maybe it wasn't even Stefano I was in love with but what we were doing together." I picked up my paper napkin and ran it through my fingers, then placed it back on the table, smoothing it. "I don't know, I just wanted to share this with you. How important this time in my life had been, how it connected me to Stefano in such a significant way."

"He was your first love?"

I nodded.

"How did you feel when you saw him again?"

"Very weird, at first. We talked about our work. I told him about my teaching. I would never have become an art history teacher if it hadn't been for Stefano. But as we visited, I knew, I knew it had been a moment in time, not to be repeated. And I also knew we were different. I'm not really even sure if he is that different. But I am. He had been an adult, and I, legally an adult, but in so many ways a child. Seeing him again, talking with him, I knew he could no longer be my teacher. I had moved beyond what he could give me. There was a difference in the balance of our relationship." I took a deep, relieved breath, then slowly exhaled. "Does that make sense?" I asked.

Roberto nodded, continuing to look at me intensely with no anger, no regret, but an appreciation for this openness.

Then I laughed. "And he didn't even remember I hate fish."

"You hate fish?" Roberto asked with eyes wide, and we both laughed, maybe because it was the first interruption he'd made in my long-winded monologue. "I didn't know that either," he said.

"Well, now you know, and I don't want you to forget it." I shook my finger at him. "Even thirty years from now."

He reached for my hand, and playfully folded my finger into his fist. It was a strange, wonderful feeling, and it seemed we both realized the possibility of a future together. A middle-aged couple talking about thirty years from now.

"It's good we can talk about this," Roberto said. "It's important that I understand how you feel. They say no matter how many times you fall in love, there's something unforgettable about the first."

"Who was your first love?"

"Paolina."

He still held my hand, but it felt like another hand had reached inside my chest and taken hold of my heart, squeezing it so hard there was nothing pumping through my veins. This frightened me beyond anything he could have said. Roberto had loved one woman. The first. Till death do us part.

He released my hand with hesitation. I adjusted myself in my chair, fingered my napkin again, took a gulp of wine. "I'm not good at this, Roberto. You have to understand that. One true love years ago to a married man, then one relationship after another."

"What about your marriage?"

I'd told him about Jerry very early, when we went to Rome, but we'd never really talked about my marriage. Now we were laying it all on the table right here—this sticky, old, worn Formica table. Maybe it was necessary. "I was thirty-nine at the time," I said, "grasping at my last chance for family." I took a hard slow swallow of air, then washed it down with wine. "After we married, I learned it wasn't that important to Jerry. I felt he had been dishonest, and I felt terribly, terribly betrayed, as if he had robbed me of something precious and irreplaceable. My last chance."

"No, never say last chance."

"Oh, Roberto, it was. I know that part of my life, that opportunity is gone forever." I stared down at the table, then looked up at him. Could I possibly tell him now—that I'd had my chance, that I'd given up my own child?

He said nothing, but looked at me deeply, as if he could see my pain and wanted to take it away. And I realized how much he wanted to help me. Had he thought at any time that I would seriously consider having a child at my age?

"I don't want you to think I don't respect and admire you

for your work, Roberto. I know you've helped many women, older women who have wanted children. But that's not for me." I shook my head slowly. "No, not for me."

We stared at each other for a long moment, and then he said, "I'm quite relieved to hear you say that."

I laughed. "I'm relieved that you're relieved."

He smiled. "Are you still up for dinner with the family?"

"Absolutely," I answered and he motioned to the waiter for our bill.

As we drove out to Maria's, I told him about Stefano's reaction to my showing him the Uffizi file and the photo taken at the Limonaia. Roberto agreed with me that his reaction was strange. "Don't you think it implies guilt?"

"I'm not sure."

We pulled into the lane at Maria's and drove along the row of tall cypresses. Roberto asked, "Was there something else you wanted to talk about?" He was being gentle. I could hear the doctor in his voice.

My heart again did a little leap. *Not yet,* I thought as I caught sight of the house. The children were out front playing with the dog.

"The good news you promised to share?"

I glanced over to catch his reaction. "I've been offered the position on a permanent basis next year."

"You've accepted?"

"Yes."

He looked at me with a grin that conveyed just what I had hoped for.

32

CARLO AND LEO came running up to the car. "Nonno, Nonno," they shouted as Roberto got out, then shyly, "Nonna Cuckoo." I couldn't help but smile. They were still calling me Grandma, although now Grandma Cuckoo! Carlo grabbed for my hand and the dog jumped up to greet me.

"Per favore, mi aiutate?" I asked the little boys. I reached in the car for the pastries I'd picked up from the bakery.

Carlo's eyes widened as I handed him the larger dish. *"Dolci,"* he said, taking it carefully, peering through the glass lid. I handed Leo the other dish, hoping this wouldn't incite a quarrel, his being entrusted with the smaller. I was grateful when he offered me an elated grin. We walked slowly toward the house, the two little ones proudly balancing the dishes, glancing up at me now and then.

Roberto joined Marco, who greeted us as he rose from his lawn chair on the small patch of grass between the barn and house. A table with a bright yellow and blue Provence-type fabric cover was set up on the lawn, and it appeared we would be eating outdoors. I went inside and found Maria and Roberto's mother in the kitchen.

"Dopo pranzo," Maria told the children when they asked for *dolci.* "How thoughtful. Thank you, Suzanne." She set the dishes on the counter, gave me a quick kiss on each cheek, and shooed the little ones back outside.

Grace Balducci and I visited as we washed and cut vegetables for a salad. I felt much more comfortable than I had the last time I'd come to Maria's when I'd been banned from helping in the kitchen. I wondered if Roberto's mother had felt excluded at one time too—an American woman forging her way into an Italian family. She asked about my trip to Greece and told me about a visit she'd made with her husband years ago. It was a good memory, and I could sense she had no idea her son had told me the truth about their relationship. Then she said, "Maria tells me you are interested in an article Roberto's father wrote, that there might be notes you'd possibly find helpful."

"Yes." I looked over at Maria, knowing now that she and her father had shared what they each knew. I wondered if they had shared any of this with Roberto's mother. Grace Balducci was a small woman, almost frail, though, as we visited, I didn't think she was emotionally frail. Yet I wondered if her family kept things from her—knowledge of her husband that might hurt her even more.

"We've been going through the papers," Maria said. "They are stored in the barn. There isn't room in the house. Grandmother and I have been attempting to determine what might be valuable to the university. We'll go out after dinner."

"Thank you," I said, "I'd appreciate that."

We carried bread, salad, and bowls of pasta outside. It was a beautiful, warm spring evening, with the slightest breeze. The yard was sparse with little grass and, like the road up to the house, bordered with tall trees that whispered as they caught the wind. Maria and I returned to the kitchen, and I carried out more bowls, Maria a large pot of what she called Tuscan stew.

Both Carlo and Leo picked at their food, sharing a bite now and then with the dog, who obviously knew where to position herself if she wanted a handout. Maria excused the boys, speaking so rapidly I could only catch a few words, but

I thought she told them she would call when dessert was served. They bounced down from the table, the frisky Border collie taking off after them.

Maria served cheese and fruit, and then I helped her with coffee and brought out the pastries. Carlo and Leo appeared instantly for their *dolci*, then once more took off to play. We adults sat and visited, Roberto's mother asking me about my teaching. I told her I would be going home for the summer, then return next fall. I caught Roberto's eye as I said this, and I could see that he wondered why I hadn't told him I would be leaving, though I assumed he knew.

I enjoyed Roberto's mother. Perhaps we had other traits in common besides our nationality—poor choices in men. Was I to have another chance with her son?

After we finished, Maria led me out to the barn. The smell reminded me instantly of my grandparents' farm—hay or straw and chickens. We walked past several wire coops, the cackle of hens, wooden shelves laced at the corners with filmy spiderwebs.

"Here," Maria said, pointing to where stacks of cardboard boxes sat. "We cleaned out Grandfather's apartment in a hurry. Luisa took some of the file cabinets to her place in Rome, and Stella took the desk to her office. The files were stuck haphazardly in boxes. Unfortunately some of them separated. They're not in easily accessible order."

I looked around, my eyes bouncing from one stack to another, my heart bouncing inside my chest with anticipation.

"These," she said, pointing to a half dozen set apart from the rest, "are papers he used in teaching at the university. I believe those over by the garden tools are academic papers. As far as I can tell, some of the articles and additional papers are in these boxes. I couldn't find anything about the Masolino, but you are free to look."

I took a deep breath, looked around again, and wondered how I would find anything. So many boxes! I started through a small one in the pile Maria had described as articles and papers. I had to keep myself from stopping to read some of the papers that I found particularly interesting, though they were in Italian, which severely taxed my brain. I doubted the file with the section on the Masolino would be labeled *Masolino*. The article was one in which Roberto Balducci had used several paintings to illustrate his point—some of them well known—so I tried to keep my mind on that, focusing on the other paintings that had been included in the article.

Finally I found a box that had about fifteen or twenty thick files that all appeared to be on studies of the Madonna. I rummaged through it. There was faint light in the barn, though Maria had brought out a lantern.

"It's getting late," she said. "Please take whatever you think might be helpful. The whole box if you want."

"You're sure?"

"Make copies of whatever you need and return the files when you are finished."

It was dark with a slight chill in the air by the time we joined the men in the yard. Roberto was saying his farewells to his mother. Marco had tucked the children into bed. Maria sent him to the barn for the two boxes I'd specified.

As we drove out, Roberto asked, "You're going home this summer?"

"My niece is getting married. And Jerry saved Rousseau's ashes for me, and I feel . . . well, I know it might sound silly, but I need to say my own farewell to her."

"I understand." And I knew he did.

"I'll be back."

"Good."

We drove a little farther, then Roberto said, "You've shared the good news, that you'll be coming back next fall, but there was something else, something you said you wanted my help with."

Even though I had resolutely decided I would ask for Roberto's help in finding my son, I knew this request would be difficult, and I'd had such a wonderful time at Maria's, then her offer of the files, the possibility of finding something. Maybe I had enough to consider right now.

"You're not sure you want to ask for my help?" he said. "You think I might perceive this as your using me?"

I nodded. Damn, that man was perceptive.

"You know you can trust me."

"Yes, I know that, Roberto." I thought back over the past few months. Had I really known Roberto for less than three? There had been doubtful moments since we'd met, seriously doubtful. This was nothing new. Maybe I had never truly trusted a man. But I knew I had to trust Roberto if I wanted his help. "There's something else I haven't told you about my relationship with Stefano, something I've never told anyone."

"Something more than his being married?"

"Yes."

Roberto waited, and several long moments passed without conversation.

"Did you ever cheat on Paolina?" I asked.

Roberto looked surprised by my question. So much for reading my every thought.

"People make mistakes," he said.

My heart did a little jump.

"Do you want me to say yes? Would that make us even?" I could see I was trying his patience. "Would you feel better if I said yes?"

"I'm so terribly flawed. And you, Roberto, you are perfect."

He emitted a faint sound, part laugh, part snort, and motioned with his head back to his crutches on the seat of the van.

"Oh." I actually laughed, and so did he. "Well, see, I guess this proves I don't see any disability. Here I am calling you perfect."

"Nobody's perfect, Suzanne. Do you want me to list my flaws?"

"No. I'd like to discover every one of your perfect flaws on my own."

"That may take some time."

"I've got plenty."

He smiled now, pleased with my reply.

"No," he said softly. "That's my answer to your question,

I didn't cheat on Paolina. I was tempted. At times I actually thought about it. There were opportunities, but no."

"So, it wasn't a perfect marriage?"

He shot me a look, not annoyed really, but I could see I was getting close.

"Okay," I said, "I know. Nothing's perfect in real life. Yes, of course, I know that."

He nodded. "It was good—very good, on a good day. Not so bad on a bad one."

"You loved her very much?"

"Yes, very much."

"Could you . . . could you ever love that way again?"

Once more, he answered with a simple, "No."

My heart sank.

He looked over at me. "Could you ever love someone the way you loved Stefano?"

I was touched by the fact that he did not make light of my love for Stefano, that he understood it was not the cheap affair it might appear to be. "Thank you for saying that. And yes, I know that too. I know that every love is different."

He nodded. "Now, what is it that you want to share, but are so hesitant to tell me?"

"It's . . ." I couldn't finish. In fact, I couldn't even start. I knew I was about to cry.

Roberto pulled over to the side of the road. He looked at me, but said nothing. He reached over and took my hands. His were very warm. Mine were cold and trembling. In fact, my entire body was shaking.

"Take your time," he said softly. "When you're ready."

I straightened myself. Looked at him deeply. "There was a child."

He touched my face, lifted my chin, wiped a tear from my cheek, then pulled me into him and held me with a force and physical strength I hadn't known he possessed.

"I've never told anyone."

"It's all right," he said. "It's all right." He rubbed my back, softly, tenderly, soothingly.

"I need your help, Roberto. I want to find him." I pulled back now, looking him in the eyes again. "Can you help me?"

"Yes," he said, "I'll do whatever I can."

ROBERTO STAYED WITH me in Florence and held me through the night.

In the morning, at my request, he dropped me off early at school. I wanted to take the papers Marco had loaded in the van to school where I could make copies if I found anything.

We pulled up in front of the school. I jumped out and lifted the boxes onto the sidewalk, then glanced toward the entry to the building. Two of my students, Beau and Brian, were just going in. I let out a shrill whistle, two fingers in my mouth just the way my cousin Mickey taught me years ago. That made them jump. Roberto laughed. I stuck my head in the driver's-side window and gave him a quick kiss. "Thanks, for everything."

Brian and Beau ran over and picked up the boxes. I introduced them quickly, then Roberto pulled out, a big grin on his face. The two young men and I started into the school, each of them carrying a box up in the elevator.

I sat in my office before my first class, pulling out files, sorting through them, again reading those that I knew had no value in helping me find my missing painting, but I couldn't help myself. I wished I'd had the opportunity to know this man better.

About an hour into my search I came across a file that referred to one of the other paintings Roberto Balducci had used in his article. This was followed by several on a completely different topic. Maria was right; it appeared files had been stuck haphazardly into boxes with little organization.

Then I noticed a file labeled *Madonna #255431*. A familiar number? Yes! This was the number that had been used in the Uffizi records. Eagerly I placed the file on my desk and opened it. The same photocopy I had obtained from Alberto Mazzone sat on the top of a pile of loose papers. Again the only identifying mark was the number. I lifted the sheet off the pile and looked at the second. A copy of the history sheet. My heart thumped wildly. Here again Stefano's—or was it?—handwritten history sheet. There were several other sheets of typed notes, which I examined and translated carefully. Historical information on the artist, Masolino, and then handwritten notes, what appeared to be a chronology of the research the elder Roberto had done for the article, dates included, all in 1982, a year before the article first appeared in the Italian art journal.

Leonetti no longer at restoration department. I translated the words from Italian. Proof that Balducci had attempted to contact Stefano. To question him on the false notation in the file? Had he spoken with Stefano?

And then, something that made my heart nearly jump out of my chest as I put the words into English. Roberto Balducci had written, *Pietro Capparelli, meet at 4 P.M. Thursday to discuss false notation in file.*

And here the notes in the file ended.

33

I WAS DONE entertaining the possibility that Pietro and Stefano had no memory of the painting. And I knew now that the elder Roberto Balducci was aware the painting had been restored. What had taken place at the meeting with Pietro? Why, knowing it wasn't true, had Roberto Balducci claimed the Masolino had been destroyed in the flood?

After my first class I skipped lunch and walked toward the river, crossing over the Arno at Ponte Santa Trinita. I had a vague memory that Pietro's mother had lived somewhere in the Santa Maria del Carmine area. I headed west and walked through one neighborhood, then another. Two boys in short pants played soccer in the street. An old woman bundled in a heavy wool coat, despite the warm spring weather, pulled a small wire shopping cart, bumping along the cobblestones.

Everything looked familiar—narrow little streets, ochre stone, green shutters, red tile, and I thought I might actually find the building I was looking for. But as I continued walking, everything began to look strange and unfamiliar. It had been almost thirty-four years, and I had visited Pietro only once. How did I expect to find it, and what were the chances that he still lived in the same place with his mother?

I returned to school and frantically ripped through my desk again, trying to find Pietro's card. I gave the top drawer a good yank, pulled it out, dumping everything on my desk, and combed through paper clips, single loose staples, rubber bands, and plastic file label tabs with my fingers searching for Pietro's card. Then I reached into the very back of the top of the desk where the drawer slid in, and felt a small rectangular paper hanging from a gap in the top! I pulled it out—it was a card from a shop on Lungarno Corsini. Another Dr. Browning leftover? Reaching back again, running my fingers over the wood I felt the gap open wider. Large enough for something to fall through to the file drawer below?

I yanked the lower drawer open and reached back over the hanging folders. Stuck along the top, I felt a small stiff paper. Another card? I tugged it out, scraping my wrist against the metal of the hanging folders. *Ouch.*

It was Pietro's card! I flipped it over and looked at the address he'd handwritten on the back. *Via San Giovanni.* I glanced at my watch, and then—evidence that I am truly a dedicated teacher—I went to my afternoon class, though I must admit my mind was on anything but symbolism in *Arnolfini and His Bride* by Jan van Eyck.

As soon as my class was over I rushed toward the river, searching for a cab. Finally one appeared on the street. I flagged it down and hopped inside. "Via San Giovanni," I told the driver.

The cab zipped through town, along the Lungarno, over Ponte Amerigo Vespucci, through several narrow streets. We pulled up on Via San Giovanni next to a row of Vespas. A man hurried out of a building, hopped on one of the tiny motorbikes, and sped down the street. I scanned the row of doors until I found the address written on Pietro's card. The building looked vaguely familiar. An arched doorway, grated windows, the requisite pale stone front. Yet even as I paid the driver and got out of the cab, I wasn't sure this was the same place Pietro had brought me on Christmas Eve.

As I knocked on the door I realized I had no idea what I was going to say.

It opened slowly and a very old woman appeared. She was short and plump and so wrinkled the skin around her eyes nearly concealed them. She stared out through the heavy lenses of large rectangular glasses. There was something deeply familiar in her face, and I knew instantly it was Pietro's mother. He had told me she was ninety-two now. I wondered if she had any memory of my coming to dinner on Christmas Eve, and I felt a strange stirring of sadness. She and Pietro had been so very kind to me, and I had in no way repaid their kindness. I wanted to find the Masolino, yet a wave of regret swept over me and I wished that my growing belief that Pietro was involved in the painting's disappearance would prove to be false.

"*Buona sera, Signora Capparelli,*" I said. "*Come sta?*"

"*Bene, bene.*" A warm, toothless grin wrinkled her flesh, folding it down around her mouth.

I introduced myself, and explained that I had worked with her son after the flood, that I had come for dinner on Christmas Eve.

A glimmer of recognition flashed in her eyes. "*Signorina Suzanne.*"

"*Sì, sì,*" I said with a smile. After all these years she remembered me, and I felt once more a pang of regret, of hope that I could be wrong, that Pietro had no part in the Masolino's disappearance.

"Pietro," I asked, "*è qui?*"

The old woman took my arm in hers, the other hand grasping a cane. With slow careful steps, tapping the cane against the wooden floor, she led me into the dining room, which I now remembered was merely an extension of the living room. It smelled of onions and garlic, and the table was set as if a meal had just been consumed, as if my knock on the door had interrupted her cleaning up after. Two plates, I noticed.

"Pietro?" I asked again.

"Non è qui," she replied. *"È andato a comprare le sigarette."*

Pietro had gone out for cigarettes?

She offered me tea, as if I'd come for a social call, and memories came again of that Christmas Eve when the smell of the flood still lingered in the air, when Pietro had invited me into his home to share with him and his mother their meager meal.

We were just sitting down when Pietro opened the door and stepped into the room.

He looked at me, his eyes wide behind his glasses. "Signorina Suzanne," he said, "you have come to v-v-visit!"

"Sì, sì."

His mother retrieved another cup and saucer from the cupboard and poured water from the kettle on the stove. She placed it, along with a tea bag, before Pietro as he sat. He looked at me, a touch of confusion around his eyes.

"You've left the Uffizi?" I asked.

He nodded. Neither of us spoke for several long moments as if we were each waiting for the other. A dog barked outside.

"Oh, I am growing weary," he finally said. "I work to b-b-bring the paintings back to how the artists intended. The Leonardo—do those who object think I do not love this work as much as they?" He dunked his tea bag with a jerky rhythm, then placed it on his saucer. "I would never do harm to it. I want only to restore it. To bring it back to life." There was anger in his voice, and then his mouth settled into a thin, tense line as he stared down at his cup.

And again I saw something that I had noticed when we met for lunch, how very insignificant he might appear to others. Was this a man who had been underappreciated his entire life?

"I saw Stefano," I said finally.

"Where?" he asked casually as if he was not surprised.

"He's in Greece."

"Oh, you ask him about your pretty little p-p-painting?"

"Yes."

"And he also believed it was lost?"

"His memory was about as reliable," I said cautiously, "as yours."

He nodded, as if choosing not to hear the accusation in my voice.

Pietro's mother continued clearing the table, moving slowly, dishes in one hand, cane in the other. I picked up the last plate and carried it to the sink. She motioned me away with her hand and a smile, then started running water, squirting in soap.

A warm smell now laced the air. She was baking something in the oven.

"Such a small p-p-painting," Pietro said, glancing up as I returned to the table, "but it makes such trouble for you, Signorina Suzanne." There was something almost taunting in the way he said this now.

"But surely not an insignificant painting," I said as I sat. "Stefano treated each painting that we restored as if it were as valuable as a Leonardo, a Botticelli, a Masaccio."

Pietro nodded and silently we sipped our tea.

Suddenly, something came to me . . . *your pretty little painting*? The file photo I showed Pietro that day at the restaurant was the same I'd received from Alberto Mazzone, the same I'd found in Roberto Balducci's papers. The only identification on it was the number. The description, the measurements of the panel were all on a separate history sheet. And I remembered, even before he saw the history sheet, he had called it "your pretty little painting." He would have had no idea it was a small painting. For all he knew, it could have been any size. *Unless* he had seen and remembered it.

"Do you know where it is?" I asked now.

He didn't answer, but a smug satisfaction flickered on his face, and I was sure my hunch was correct.

"The painting was restored," I said, my inflection unequivocal.

"So many years, no one inquired . . . no one missed it."

I looked directly at him. "Did you take it?" I felt my heart jump. I hadn't intended to make this accusation, and I thought he would deny it and tell me once more that the painting had been destroyed in the flood.

But then, slowly, looking up into my eyes, Pietro said, his voice little more than a whisper, "It was not something I had p-p-planned."

I took a deep gulp of air. Not fear, but a different sensation—discovery, excitement—spread over me.

Pietro reached into his shirt pocket, pulled out a pack of cigarettes, slowly unwrapped it, then tapped the pack and pulled out a cigarette, and returned the rest to his pocket. He took a lighter from his pants pocket, the movement so unhurried and deliberate this whole scene seemed unreal. He lit the cigarette and took a long, slow drag, blowing the smoke into the air above us.

I could almost feel my heart vibrating now, but I wasn't really afraid. We sat, a strange sense of calm gradually enveloping the two of us.

"It was early nineteen sixty-nine," he said as if telling a story, "and there were several paintings scheduled to return to the Uffizi. All m-m-minor works that had been stored on the ground floor, no major pieces displayed in the upper rooms, but as you know none of those paintings were injured." He looked at me now as if he wished me to confirm this—that the paintings, those on display in the museum, had not been damaged.

He pulled a plastic ashtray from the center of the table and tapped his cigarette on the edge. "They were loaded in the van, carefully. The interior had been constructed in such a way that the paintings fit into padded slots for protection. All history files were to be sent b-b-back at the time. The Masolino's among them."

I held my breath now, barely able to breathe. He was calling it the Masolino. As if it had a known creator, rather than *early fifteenth-century Italian artist*, as the history file stated.

"The paintings were all taken over and dropped off at the Uffizi. The van was returned to the Fortezza where we used it to run supplies, for trips between the restoration locations."

"But the Masolino, it was not returned to the Uffizi," I said.

He shook his head.

I was filled with an odd mixture of triumph, sadness, and curiosity. *Why, Pietro?*

"This was not normally a task I performed, but the young man who had been assigned this duty, he was ill that day. So I went along with his assistant, who drove the van. He was very young and somewhat unreliable to have such a responsibility put upon him. But, as he was unloading the van, somehow . . . well, you know the painting is small." Pietro held his hands out now, as if he were a fisherman describing a catch—twelve inches. A respectable-sized trout. "Of course, the paintings had been removed from their frames," he continued, "and somehow, being so small, it had been overlooked. N-n-normally, we would have discovered this when we did the checkoff with files to be replaced in the museum's records." Pietro shook his head. "I know this sounds, oh, how to describe this—there was not the concern, the security, the c-c-care that might have been required for such an undertaking. It was late and the young man said we could return the following day and do the files." Pietro's eyes met mine. "I know, particularly to an American . . . well, sometimes we might seem, oh, too casual, too unconcerned about our treasures. So many wonderful paintings here in Florence, so many. Like the members of a large family, where a small child might wander off unnoticed and become lost."

"But surely someone would search for this child?" I asked.

Pietro shrugged. "The young man had a date and wanted to leave early, so I told him yes, I will finish. While I was cleaning out the van, I discovered the small p-p-painting and decided I would carry it over."

"But you didn't?"

"There are times," he said slowly, "one step in this direction, another step in that direction, will change—" He laughed, emitting a soft little sound both sad and evil all in one chortle.

For the first time since I'd arrived I felt the smallest trickle of fear.

Signora Capparelli walked to the stove, tapping with her cane, picked up the teapot, came back to the table and filled our cups. She smiled at me. The smell of whatever she had in the oven overpowered the room, now drifting in the air and mingling with the smell of Pietro's cigarette.

"Grazie," I said.

She returned the pot to the stove, and then continued drying the dishes and replacing them in the cupboard, the sound of plates placed on plates resonating in the quiet of the room.

"As I w-w-walked to the Uffizi," he continued, "I don't know . . . I was thinking of the painting, of Masolino. How much time and energy we put into the restoration. What a lovely little painting this was. You know Masolino was always overshadowed by Masaccio. He has not been given the credit he deserves. The tourists go to the Brancacci and it is always Masaccio, always Masaccio." Pietro's voice rose into a much higher pitch, thin and wiry. His hands went up into the air. An inch of ash on his cigarette appeared as if it might fall, and then it did—to the floor. He squashed it with the heel of his shoe. "Do you know it was Masolino who was the teacher of Masaccio? *Tommaso*. Two Thomases." He laughed. "Masolino—the little. Masaccio—the big and clumsy."

I nodded. Stefano had told me this. Both Masolino and Masaccio were named Tommaso.

"Something rose up inside me," Pietro said, again a tinge of frenzy in his voice.

I felt another little shiver of fear.

"This painting," he continued, "it will be returned, I thought. Again it will be stored and no one will see it. What a waste, what a t-t-terrible injustice to the artist as well as those of us who spend so many hours, so much time dedicated, so much devotion. By the time I realized it, I had p-p-passed over the bridge, carrying the little Madonna and Child at my side. I had passed over to the Oltrarno."

"You didn't return it?"

"It was my intention to take it b-b-back. But the next day, no one inquired. No one missed it."

"But the file? It was written that it had been destroyed?"

"The next day I simply removed the file."

"But the file was eventually returned."

Again he nodded. He snuffed out his cigarette in the ashtray and with a swift movement produced another and lit it up.

"And the false notation, written by Stefano?"

"Suzanne," he said softly as if a warning, but to this he added nothing more.

We stared at one another. I could hear sounds outside—a motor starting, the high-pitched squeal of a child playing in the street.

"And the elder Roberto Balducci?" I asked, thinking of his words as he lay dying. "He knew you had taken the painting. Yet he wrote an article stating it had been destroyed. Why?"

Pietro took a sip of tea, the cigarette balanced in his stubby fingers. "He was researching for a paper, and he remembered the p-p-painting he had seen at the Limonaia, then the Fortezza, and he had wanted to know more, to study it. He called asking for access to the painting, and of course it was not there. But he knew it had been saved." Pietro chuckled a little and took another dainty sip of tea, a small puff off his cigarette. "Just as you did, Signorina Suzanne." He smiled now, the curl of his lips touched with satisfaction. "Yes, there were those who missed the little painting and who valued it for what it was. A treasure."

It struck me once more what a powerless little man Pietro was. Yet he had taken this painting. Was it the power, more than the painting, he had craved? Had it given him great satisfaction all these years, particularly when his work was not well received, when he was undervalued, underappreciated? Did it give him a feeling of satisfaction to have taken this pretty little painting, undiscovered until . . .

"But why?" I asked. "Why did Roberto Balducci write that it had been destroyed?"

"Secrets," Pietro said. "We all have our secrets, now don't we, Suzanne?" He looked at me so deeply, it gave me another little start.

"And what were Roberto Balducci's secrets?" I asked cautiously, though I was sure I already knew.

"Roberto Balducci was a man who loved men." There was nothing disgusted in the way he said this.

"But he put up a pretense. He had a wife and two sons."

"Ah, yes. But the truth. How powerful, how hurtful the truth." He sighed, and I wondered again if Pietro also shared Roberto Balducci's proclivity, also his fear of being discovered, if this gave Pietro one more reason for wanting some power—power he might have gained by keeping hidden for decades one small fifteenth-century Italian painting.

"The eldest son," Pietro began.

"Angelo Balducci? The priest, the cardinal?"

He nodded. "*Sì*, the priest, the pride of the Balduccis. Even as a young man, Angelo Balducci had political ambitions within the Church. To have a father . . . well—"

"You blackmailed him to keep this secret?"

"Oh, Suzanne, we all have secrets, truths about ourselves that we wish to keep just that." He stared at me for several moments, and then he took another long, slow draw on his cigarette. He snuffed a long stem of ash in the ashtray.

"The painting, the Masolino, what did you do with it?"

Pietro gazed out toward the street through a small window covered with streaks as the afternoon sun slanted into the room.

"You didn't sell it?" I asked.

He turned abruptly and looked at me now for the first time as if I had offended him. "No, no, never." He stood, pushed the last of his cigarette into the damp tea bag, then placed it in the ashtray, said something very rapidly to his mother, and motioned me to follow.

I felt my heart thumping, my throat constricting, an intense fear finally grabbing me. But my desire to know the truth impelled me as I followed Pietro up the narrow stairs, down a dark hall. We entered a room that contained a brass bed with a white chenille spread, floral print paper on the walls. Mama's room, surely, though I wondered how she managed those steep stairs.

Pietro motioned and I turned. On the opposite wall, partially hidden by the open door, hung the Masolino Madonna.

He closed the door, allowing me a full view.

An unlit candle sat on a low table in front of the painting, and a bouquet of small purple flowers stood before it in a crystal vase. An altar of adoration.

I felt something squeezing tightly inside me, then a familiar combination of excitement and anxiety warming my body as I walked closer. My head felt light and dizzy as I stood and stared at the painting, taking in the vibrant colors—the pink, blue, and white, the rich gold-leaf background. The lovely face of the Madonna, the innocent Child reaching up to touch her. And once more it struck me, the sweetness of this portrait. For a moment I felt again that odd sense of calm.

"It's lovely," I whispered, then turned to Pietro. "It's been here all along?"

"Over thirty years," he said, a hint of pride in his voice. "When I brought it home I had every intention of returning it, but then a day p-p-passed, another. No one inquired."

"But Roberto Balducci?"

"Well, yes, but I took care of that." Again he chuckled. "My mother, you can see she adores the painting. The Virgin has brought her great comfort. She is a good, religious woman, my mother."

"What did you tell her?"

"A good woman, but she knows little of art. She said it is a p-p-pretty little picture. She did not know where it came from. She thinks her son bought it for her in a shop in Firenze, a reproduction of a painting from the famous Uffizi museum. A gift from her good son."

Yes, I thought, a good son, but a thief nevertheless. I studied the painting again, touching it only with my eyes, tempted to run my fingers over the ancient strokes of Masolino da Panicale, to feel the texture of the paint. I remembered the many hours I had spent with Stefano bringing this tiny painting back to life. I could see now the colors were not as clean as after we had finished the restoration. There was a light patina of soot, probably the result of hanging here with a candle lit before it in adoration. Not thirty years' worth, I thought, and I wondered if

Pietro had cleaned it during this time, if he had treated it with the great respect we both knew it deserved.

I turned and looked at him again and I could see a sad resignation in his eyes. "It must be returned," I said quietly.

He hesitated for no more than a moment, and I wasn't surprised when he said, "Yes, I know." But then he added, "Please, Signorina Suzanne, may I m-m-make one request." I thought he would ask that I return it without implicating him, which I felt I could certainly attempt. "My mother is an old woman, ninety-two. She is in remarkable health, but might I ask that you w-w-wait . . . until . . ." He didn't finish. He lowered himself, sat on the bed, and ran his fingers tenderly over the soft white chenille, then gazed about the room, his eyes moving from a small chintz-covered chair to the dresser, where bottles of lotion sat on a mirror, a small statue of the Virgin perched on a lace doily.

Was he asking that I wait until his mother died? That he would not wish his mother to see him shamed? "You want it to stay here until your mother is gone, then you will return it?"

"*Sì,*" he said. He stared down at the floor, polished wood, a pair of scuffed slippers peeking out from under the bedcover. I could see Pietro transforming back into the man I knew—timid, meek, and accommodating. If I decided to take the painting now, he would not stop me. It was my decision. Again, I studied the Masolino, my eyes moving slowly along the rhythmic lines of the figures of Mother and Child. How easily I could take it from the wall, walk down the stairs, through the house, past Pietro's mother, onto the street, across the river. I had found it! It was mine to return to the Uffizi. I would be hailed as the heroine who had returned the lost Madonna. But questions would be asked. Where had it been? How had I found it?

"Pietro," Signora Capparelli called from downstairs. "Signorina Suzanne." A sweet, comforting aroma entered the room and swirled around us as if it had been carried along with her voice.

I remembered again the night they had welcomed me into

their home, the kindness they had extended to a young American girl without family to celebrate the Christmas holiday. I thought of the sparkling wine, the laughter, the fish and cake we ate that evening. I shivered now, recalling the chill of the winter night when Pietro and I ventured out and walked together through the streets of Florence, hoping to catch a glimpse of the pope. We had found him unexpectedly at the Limonaia where he had stopped to bless the paintings, Masolino's lovely Madonna and Child among them. And here it was again, this ancient painting, over five hundred years old, hanging in front of me in the intimacy of this small room on San Giovanni. Mine to take and return.

"Signorina?" Pietro said, his voice tapping me on the shoulder, bringing me back. "The p-p-painting? You will w-w-wait?"

After so many years, what would it matter now, I thought, if I waited until his mother was gone? "Yes," I said, "I'll wait."

Pietro let out a sigh of relief. *"Grazie,"* he whispered.

He rose from the bed and together we walked back downstairs. His mother had taken the cake from the oven and cut a piece for each of us. She motioned us to the table. Pietro and I sat. The situation seemed surreal. Here I had found the painting, and I had agreed I would do nothing about it. Pietro's mother poured more hot water for tea and brought us each a new tea bag.

We sat, eating, smiling guardedly at one another. The tea and cake were warm, and I no longer felt any fear. I had found the painting. I had found the thief. And now we had struck our deal. I had agreed. The painting would eventually be returned.

I finished my cake, set the fork on the plate, and took a final sip of tea. I knew there was one more question I must ask.

"Stefano . . . he had nothing to do with your taking the painting?"

Pietro didn't answer right away, and I knew from the downward shift of his eyes that there was yet more to this story. "Stefano had nothing to do with my taking the p-p-painting," he said.

"Who wrote the words on the history sheet?" I asked.

"Do you really w-w-want to know?" He looked up.

I nodded.

He hesitated, waiting, I think for me to say I was satisfied—I had found the painting, it would be returned, there was no need for more.

"Please," I said, "I want to know. The handwriting, was it Stefano's?"

He didn't answer.

"But why?" I asked.

"Oh, Suzanne, let this go. You saw Stefano. You are not to see him again, sì?"

"Should I?" I said so loudly Pietro's mother turned with alarm. I smiled and nodded at her.

Pietro scraped the crumbs on his plate with his fork, raised it to his mouth. Carefully, he wiped his lips with his hand. He pushed the plate aside, then again pulled the cigarette pack from his pocket, withdrew one and lit it. I could see his hand tremble as the flame ignited the cigarette, and now reluctance in the confession in which he had taken a curious pride. There was something Pietro did not wish me to know. "We all have secrets," he said quietly.

"Yes," I replied. "What was Stefano's?"

Pietro stared at me and again I nodded.

"He had a wife," Pietro began again slowly, "and a daughter."

"Yes, and a son."

"Yes, a son." A lump like a large cold stone moved from my heart up into my throat.

"It was difficult," Pietro said, "for him, this son. A man always wants a son, but sometimes it does not come easy. Oh, the jokes, the chatter, the men at work. They t-t-talk about these things. Is a man's virility proved by his m-m-making a son?" He stopped for a moment, his eyes unfocused, moving as if along the wall. "The men at the Limonaia, we all knew he wanted a son, but his wife she could not conceive. For many years, they try." Pietro took in a small swallow of air. And once more looked at me.

I said nothing, and he continued. "You are innocent, young, when you come to Italy, but you want to learn. We see, you begin to change. You grow. You learn. Then changes in your heart. You are in love. Oh, with the art, with this man! And then . . ." Pietro took a deep, deep draw on his cigarette, tilted his head back, and blew out a puff of smoke. He looked toward the window again. The sun had shifted, no longer falling into the room. "Then other changes. These in your body." His face reddened with embarrassment, he took another slow drag on the cigarette, and waited as if he wished me to speak.

I couldn't.

"You go away," he continued. "You tell us it is to travel. This is a g-g-good explanation. But you come back. Again you have changed. You are very sad." Pietro picked up his cup and brought it to his lips, then placed it back in his saucer. "You are different."

"Different?" I asked, urging him on, but I wanted him to stop.

He nodded. "There are some things, a sadness, a loss, which one cannot hide." Pietro lifted his cup to take another drink, but I could see it was empty. "Then you go home to America," he said. "One day, Stefano, he comes with his new son, his proud wife. 'He is our gift,' she says. I don't believe she knows." Pietro's voice was barely a whisper now. "I don't believe . . . but it is his son. It is his son."

"B-but?" I asked. "His son, and she didn't . . ." I couldn't finish, couldn't find the words, because I knew, now, Stefano's secret. His ultimate betrayal.

34

I REMEMBER CLEARLY the smallest details from that enormous gap in space and time before Pietro called Roberto. The vibration of little Pietro's chest as we sat staring at each other. My stiff rigid posture as I attempted to keep myself from collapsing. My blinking away the tears. The smoky smell of the room, now tinged with a hint of sweat. The scent of Signora Capparelli's cake barely clinging to the air that seemed to have been sucked out of the room. I recall Pietro's inability to comfort me, his searching for words, unable to find them, stammering and stuttering, and then finally giving up as the moments of silence stretched between us.

When he finally asked if there was someone he could call, and I said, "Yes, Roberto Balducci," I could no longer look at Pietro. I knew my eyes were so filled with anger he must have felt some remorse for his part in this betrayal.

"Roberto Balducci?" He asked it as if I were asking him to call a dead man back to life.

"His son," I said firmly. "His son, Roberto Balducci, Dr. Balducci." My voice was hoarse, as if I had been screaming, but there were no screams, only the tears that I was forcing myself to hold back. I gave Pietro Roberto's cell number, then asked to use the bathroom while he got up to phone. I noticed now his mother, who stood by the sink, working busily, becoming almost invisible as she had witnessed this intimate scene taking place in her kitchen. She glanced at me with a mixture of embarrassment and confusion, then shuffled over, took my hand and led me to the bathroom, handed me a tissue, and then left me alone.

In the bathroom, my tears fell, and I wiped at them as I stared in the mirror. My son, I thought. That day at the beach, I had seen him. His wife. And his two children. My grandchildren.

I didn't leave the bathroom until I heard Roberto's van pull up in front. I didn't speak to Pietro or his mother as I walked through the dining area and out onto the street.

I opened the door on the passenger side of the van, the motor still running, and climbed inside, instantly motioning for Roberto to drive.

He pulled out onto the street.

"I know where it is, the painting," I said. "I saw it. It's there."

"Pietro?"

"Yes. It was Pietro. He's had it all along."

"Has the Uffizi been informed?" Roberto kept glancing over at me as if trying to decide what to do.

I shook my head.

"Would you like me to call the authorities? He didn't threaten you?" Roberto's voice was soft, but pulsing with both confusion and concern. Clearly he was aware that I'd been crying. Surely he wondered why Pietro had let me go, free to announce to the world that he was a thief.

"There were no threats," I answered. "No, he didn't . . ." I was about to say he didn't hurt me, but I couldn't. I wondered if Roberto could possibly understand what I had done. I took in a deep breath, then released it, putting my hand on my chest to hold in the emotions that I knew might explode again at any time. Then I told Roberto about the agreement I had reached with Pietro. He said nothing, implied in no way that I might not want to trust the man.

As we crossed over the Arno I gazed down into the dark waters. Roberto asked, "It will be returned?"

"Yes, eventually." I explained very calmly, in some detail, about the Masolino, about Roberto's own father's part in all this. And then suddenly, the floodgates broke loose and I was sobbing again.

Roberto slowed the van. "There's more to your discovery? There's something more you haven't told me."

"Yes." I motioned him to continue driving, wanting to get home as soon as possible. I ran my hand across my damp cheek. Then I told him what I'd learned from Pietro about my son as I stared out the window at a sunny blue-skied day that could not have been more beautiful and more out of sync with the dark, betrayed feelings that surged within me.

I glanced at Roberto now and caught a calm, almost knowing look in his eyes.

When we arrived at my apartment, he asked if I'd like him to stay and I said yes. He pulled the bed down and I fell immediately into a jerky, exhausted sleep, but could not hold on to it. I woke and found Roberto asleep at my side. Quietly, I got up and walked into the bathroom for a drink. I splashed water on my face, then went back and sat on the edge of the bed. Roberto reached out and stroked my back. "What do you want to do?" he asked. "How can I help?"

I turned to him and touched his face. We both knew we were no longer talking about a lost painting. Roberto would accept my decision, my agreement with Pietro. "Thank you for being here," I said.

He reached for my hand and held it to his lips. "There's something I should tell you, something that confirms what you learned about your son."

"You knew?" My body, my voice, were both shaking.

"No, no, not until late yesterday afternoon," he reassured me. "After you gave me the birth date, the name of the convent, I made some inquiries and was able to locate a copy of the adoption papers. There was no name listed for the birth father. But the adoptive father . . . at first I thought it was a mistake, that the name had been entered on the wrong line, but then I realized—"

"Stefano?"

"Yes."

"Why didn't you call me?"

"I was still trying to sort it all out, gather additional information, and by then I got your call."

"This confirms what Pietro told me. Did you learn anything more?"

Robert nodded. "His name is Gianni, Gianni Leonetti."

"Gianni?" He seemed real now. He had a name. I shivered with a new excitement. "Anything more?"

"I also learned that he plays in the European soccer league for Milano."

An athlete, I thought and smiled, overcome with the realization that he really was my son, that I had found him. "I want to contact him," I said, "but first, I want his father to know." I took a deep ragged breath. "I can't speak to Stefano again. Not now. Maybe never. I'm so filled with anger toward him. I think I hate him."

Roberto said nothing, for which I was grateful.

"I want to know if my son is aware that he is adopted, if he knows anything about me. I hate to ask you, Roberto, but will you call Stefano for me? Will you ask him if our son knows he was adopted? I want to make some kind of contact, but I don't know if he will want to see me. I will leave it up to him."

"That's very generous, to let Stefano know what you are about to do."

"Generosity?" I snorted. "Anger maybe, but I don't want this anger to carry over to my son, if there is any chance . . . I want to leave it up to him, whether he wants to . . . to know anything about me. You'll call Stefano?"

Roberto nodded. "Yes, I'll call Stefano."

"Thank you." I kissed him, then settled my head against his broad shoulder.

* * *

LATER THAT DAY at school, I looked him up on the Internet on the site for Milan's soccer team. And when his face came into focus, the image slowly appearing on the screen from top to bottom, I cried. He didn't look at all like his father. I barely remembered the young man I had seen that day at the beach, but I had the vaguest recollection that he was tall. Now that I could see his face, the set of his jaw, his thin resolute lips, I could see his resemblance to my cousins, Mickey and Trace Jr. In the full-body shots, I could see his athletic build. Not so thick through the shoulders as his father, but tall and slender, yet muscular.

And, in his eyes, he also looked like me.

I met Roberto for lunch and he told me he had called Stefano. My new lover contacting my old lover? I didn't want him to relate the details, just to tell me what my son knew. I trusted Roberto with this.

Stefano understood that I would make an effort to contact my son. And he had told Roberto that Gianni Leonetti was aware that he was adopted, though unaware that his father was his biological father. Would he wish that I not reveal this to my son should we meet? Just as Pietro wished that his mother not know about the painting?

I would make no promises here.

Must we always feel we protect those we love by hiding the truth?

"Was he angry?" I asked.

"I think he knew, particularly after he met with you. He realized that someday this might happen. That his son, your son, might even want to know more."

ROBERTO ALSO THEN wrote a letter to Gianni Leonetti. I'm not even sure how he knew where to write, but he found an address, maybe from Stefano. It was a simple letter stating that his birth mother would like to make contact if it was his wish. That she would abide by his decision, whatever it might be. Roberto used his address at the villa for a reply. I didn't want Gianni Leonetti to know I was in Florence if he chose not to contact me.

Weeks passed. I did not hear from either Gianni or Pietro. Roberto and I did not talk about the painting. If he suspected that I had found it only to lose it again, he didn't share this with me. He knew the knowledge of what had become of my son was now what consumed me. I did think about the Masolino, often I thought of the painting, and always I believed Pietro would be true to his word. It would be returned to the Uffizi.

I still didn't know exactly what Pietro's threat consisted of. Was it a threat to tell Stefano's wife that the son they raised was his—Stefano's own flesh and blood—that the mother was a young, naïve American girl who like so many others had been caught up in the destruction of the flood, that she had become involved in the restoration, and in an ill-fated love affair that had resulted in a child? Or maybe the real threat was that Pietro would reveal to me that Stefano had kept our son.

And it was still unclear to me why Roberto Balducci had included the Masolino in his article. Wouldn't it have been better for Pietro to erase any trace that might bring about suspicion? Or maybe he was trying to drop a clue here and there. Was he deriving a gleeful gratification from all this, a taunting satisfaction? Did he want someone to read the article, to see the notation in the file? To say, "I know this isn't true"? Maybe discovery was what he wanted.

Easter came. Roberto and I traveled to northern Italy. We went to see Da Vinci's *Last Supper* in Milan. Both Pietro and Stefano had helped with this restoration. As I had read, the images were very faded. But it was not the Da Vinci that brought me to Milan. I now had another, far more intimate connection with the city of Milan. My son.

I saw him play in a soccer game. I felt very proud, and joyful, and yet at the same time very sad. How much I had missed. My son, a grown man now. I would not force him into meeting me, but I knew it was what I wanted.

Roberto and I drove up through Switzerland, into Germany.

During the trip, each day I wondered if there would be a letter when I returned. Roberto said he could have Maria check and call, but I said no. I would wait.

When we returned, there was still no word from Gianni, but I had reconciled myself to this—if he did not wish to contact me, I would abide by his decision.

And nothing from Pietro.

My anger toward Stefano soared, then ebbed. At times I could understand what he had done; at times I truly felt I hated him.

Gradually, over those final weeks at school I told others about the child I had given up many years ago. Regina, then Charley. They were both very understanding and nonjudgmental. Charley especially was so very kind in helping me deal with my anger—toward myself, toward Stefano. Sometimes I even teased Charley about how helpful all that training in seminary could be in dealing with us sinners.

The weather was beautiful in Florence. The tourists came. We had finals; the students, with tears and fond farewells, left. I would return home to Idaho and stay through the middle of August. My niece was getting married the third Saturday in June. And I also wanted to say a proper farewell to Rousseau. Yet I was hesitant to leave Florence—Roberto, the possibility of a call from Gianni Leonetti, a call from Pietro Capparelli.

I spent the two weeks after the students left cleaning up my apartment, packing boxes to store at school, running up to the villa to visit Roberto. My lease ran through the middle of June. The landlord could get a much better return on short-term rentals during the summer months. I had signed a lease beginning again in September. *My* apartment now, not Dr. Browning's.

I sent a note to Pietro at his address on San Giovanni, telling him I would be leaving for the summer, that he could contact me through Roberto. Maybe I was just testing him, reminding him of his promise. I prayed that the letter wouldn't be returned undeliverable.

I did not hear from my son.

Roberto took several days off. Each morning we packed a picnic lunch and went for a drive—one day to Pisa and Lucca, the next to the lovely villages of Volterra and San Gimignano with its medieval towers.

Roberto's youngest daughter, Bea, came home in early June. She was much younger and more innocent than I had imagined. I liked her and I sensed that she liked me. She too had taken off for an adventure in a foreign land. Yet, it was not a sisterly type of affection I felt for this young woman. There was still something in her that needed a bit of mothering. She even asked me what I thought about a young man who came up to the villa to visit. She had met someone in the States and she was confused. Could I possibly tell her to *follow her heart*? Yes, wasn't I the wise old woman seasoned in romance? Should I tell her the truth—that love often hurts, that following your heart isn't always the best choice? That life is more complicated than that?

A week before I was to return to Idaho, a letter arrived at the villa. I was spending the day with Roberto. Without words he placed it in my hand. I sat on the sofa, my hand shaking, my heart pounding. I studied the script on the outside of the envelope—handwritten. Not left-handed like his father, but a blocky, European-type script, with the little slashes through the sevens on the address. I attempted to open it, the sharp flap of the envelope cutting into me. I pulled my finger to my lips, my hand trembling. I placed the envelope on the coffee table and stared at Roberto, who sat on the chair opposite me.

"I'm almost afraid to open it," I said. "A birthday present that turns out to be not what you wanted at all." I laughed softly. I knew what I wanted it to say—that he wished to meet me. Yet the thought terrified me.

Finally I slid the letter out and began to read.

Dear Suzanne Cunningham, it began very formally.
I am not sure how to start this letter, or what to call you.
I have known since I was very young that I was adopted.

I have had a very good life with good parents and an older sister. I often wonder about you, also my father.

My heart jumped. He still didn't know Stefano was also his birth father. I continued reading.

There are many ways in which I have felt different. I do not look like my parents or my sister. Even as a small boy I enjoy sports. No one in my family is an athlete, though they, especially my father, has given me much encouragement. I wonder if this gift for sports comes from my birth father.

I laughed through my tears. Had he ever considered this might have come from his mother?

I play on a professional soccer team. I am married and have a son and daughter.
I am hesitant to write this letter. I do not wish to hurt my parents and I have not told them of Roberto Balducci's letter. But I am curious to know more about my birth. Roberto Balducci has written that you are an American. Were you here in Italy as a student? I know that I was born in Florence. Do you have a family? Do I have other brothers or sisters?
Please write to me and tell me something of yourself.
Gianni Leonetti.

I sat running my fingers over the script, then looked up at Roberto. "He wants me to write."

His own letter seemed so uncertain, so vague. Maybe he didn't speak English well, but he knew I was American—Roberto had told him that—and he was writing me in English.

I spent the next two days attempting to compose a letter. I decided I would not mention his father. I would not reveal this information unless he asked, and even then I wasn't sure how I would reply. His father had obviously said nothing about Roberto's call. Had he hoped I was bluffing?

My letter also was very brief. I told him that I was a professor of art history, that I had worked on the restoration after the flood, and this is where my love for art began. I told him I was not married and had no other children. I said I too enjoyed sports. I didn't suggest that we meet. I would let him lead on this.

I waited anxiously for his reply, but I would be leaving in just days, going home for over two months before coming back to Italy, and I doubted I would hear from him before then.

I received a little note from Pietro on the back of a postcard, a photo of the Uffizi taken from the Piazza della Signoria. He was either taunting me or reassuring me. *Enjoy your summer,* he wrote, *I will be in touch.* I had to believe it was his promise that he would be true to his word, that one day I would get a call or maybe another note, telling me that his mother had passed.

The day of my departure Roberto drove me to Rome to catch my flight home, and I cried when I left him—so filled with a jumble of emotions. I had arrived in Florence knowing I was at a crossroads in my life. Looking for something new, searching for something old. And now I had found both. But there was still so much unfinished business.

35

VISITORS TO BOISE expect it to be surrounded by trees. *Les Bois*. But the hills shimmer not with the deep green of pine, or with leafy foliage shifting colors with the seasons, but with the soft green of the sage. The smell is exquisite.

To some these hills might appear barren, yet I know they teem with life—the flora, the fauna. Sometimes I see a small red fox. One year I spotted a deer, though they seldom come anymore as homes encroach and move up the hillside.

Early on the morning of my niece's wedding I walked up into the foothills with Rousseau. Jerry had lovingly placed her ashes in a golden vase. I was surprised that such a small container could hold the remains of my big old puppy. I climbed to the top of a small ridge, opened the vase—it had no lid, but Jerry had secured a piece of plastic wrap over the top with a rubber band. I stuck the rubber band and plastic wrap in my pocket and then released the ashes, letting them flow downwind. Some of the gritty powder found its way onto my jeans, a little on my arm. I brushed it off.

The past will always cling, if not physically, emotionally.

Charley had told me this, during a discussion of sin, penance, and forgiveness.

It was Charley who had helped me most with the spiritual healing, my understanding of forgiveness. Forgiving oneself. Forgiving others. God's forgiveness, he told me, comes much easier. We talked about the social aspects of sin, how the wrong we do does not exist within a void, that it touches one, then another. In a conversation that became a bit too Catholic for me—but then, he was a priest—we talked about the concepts of penance, restitution, and restoration.

"A child?" I ask. "How could a child ever be considered part of the sin?"

"Never," Charley said. "A child must always be viewed as a gift."

I laughed uneasily. "Is this God's idea of irony? The woman who might have been hurt most reaps the benefits of the gift?" I thought often of the evening I had dinner with Stefano, how he told me this time with her son was so important to Renata, how Gianni Leonetti himself had told me he had good parents.

Charley smiled. "I don't think that's how God works."

I'm not sure how God works. But I know we create our own world of hurt and deception.

After I told Roberto, then Charley, then Regina, I knew when I returned to Boise, I would tell my sister about my child.

Andie came to pick me up at the airport. We gathered my bags, headed out to short-term parking, chatting as we drove, mostly about the wedding, family visiting, a group of Callie's college girlfriends in town for the big day.

"There's something important I need to tell you," Andie said, almost as if she meant to steal my thunder. And I was thinking in terms of thunder—a bit of a storm surely when I got around to my own revelation.

"What?" I asked.

"Don't be surprised if Callie looks, well, a little plump."

"Oh?"

"She's three months pregnant."

I realized this must have happened shortly after they'd decided to get married. It wasn't as if it was a shotgun wedding. "Are she and David happy about it?"

"Kids these days," she said with a shake of her head. "She's got two girlfriends with babies, neither married. With all the birth control available now, well, you'd certainly think these things wouldn't happen." She gave the steering wheel a good jerk as we turned into her subdivision. "One of them lives with the father, and Callie says they're getting married. She wants to wait until she loses a few more pounds before the wedding—baby fat." Andie shot me an annoyed look and laughed. "There doesn't seem to be any shame in it anymore."

"Maybe that's not so bad."

"Maybe not," she said, resigned. "Callie isn't showing all that much, though we had to let the dress out over an inch. It's not like we're going to announce it at the wedding, but I thought you should know."

"Are *you* happy about it?"

"What's not to be happy about a new baby?" She smiled. "Thank God Mom's not still here. Dad doesn't know yet. Maybe he won't notice when the baby is three months premature."

We both laughed.

What an opening for my own announcement, I thought, so I asked, "What do you think Mom would have done if that had happened to one of us?" I'd planned to bring this up later, after the wedding, but hadn't she just presented me with the perfect opportunity for what I had to tell her?

"It was different then," Andie said without a clue. "She would have freaked out."

"Do you really think?"

"Oh, I don't know. Mom surprised me now and then. And, well, it didn't, so . . ."

We pulled onto Andie's street. I was staying with her and Michael. I'd extended the lease on my house for another six months.

She hit the remote for the garage door.

"It did, Andie."

"Did what?" She glanced over as she turned off the ignition, opened the car door, and started to get out.

"Happen. It did happen."

She turned and stared at me with confusion. Then she put her hand to her mouth and her entire face seemed to twitch. Her eyes blinked and her lips moved without producing a sound.

"When I was in Italy. The first time. I got pregnant. Stefano and I had a child."

I thought she was going to either slap me or burst into tears. For a long moment she did neither.

"Oh, Suzanne, no." Her lips quivered, her eyes glistened. "Oh, my God, what happened to the baby?" She stopped, her upper teeth digging into her lip.

"I gave him up for adoption. He just turned thirty-two." I'd ease into the story about Stefano and Renata raising the child, because we were both crying now.

Andie reached for me and, awkwardly over the gearshift, put her arms around me. "I'm so sorry, Suzanne. I'm so sorry that you didn't feel you could trust me with this."

"I'm sorry too, Andie. Please forgive me. I was so frightened. I didn't tell anyone. Jerry didn't even know."

I had sensed this would be her reaction, that she would be upset not so much with what had happened, but that I hadn't told her, that I hadn't trusted her with this. Now I told her everything. About Stefano—she knew the basics, that I'd fallen in love with Stefano, even that he was married, something she'd found quite scandalous. I told her now about Pietro, about the Masolino, how I learned of my son, how I learned he had been raised by Stefano and his wife.

"Have you seen him?" she asked, wiping a tear.

"Yes." I told her about my day at the beach on the island of Crete, about going to the soccer game with Roberto. I explained how Roberto had made contact with him for me. "He's aware he was adopted, but he doesn't know that his adoptive father is his birth father. He wrote. I wrote back.

We're taking it slow. My original intention was just to know that he was okay, but I think now, yes, I hope someday we will meet."

Callie came running out to the garage to greet me. I got out of the car and gave her a hug.

"Auntie Suzanne, I'm so happy you're here. Mom told you the good news about the baby?"

Andie rolled her eyes, and I just said, "Yes, congratulations on your marriage, and the baby." And I truly felt happy for her.

NOT HAVING MY own place in Boise wasn't that great, though Andie and I had some fun together, and I enjoyed the wedding, seeing family. It was amazing how opening up about the truth can free one, though I asked Andie not to share this with the rest of the family just yet. I was working up to the public announcement.

I missed Roberto more than I could have ever imagined. We spoke or e-mailed often, and always, I asked, "A letter?" And always, "Not yet," as if he knew there would be another soon. Roberto, so hopeful and optimistic.

I left for Florence in the middle of August. Again Andie drove me to the airport, and I couldn't help but think of the last time she'd taken me on this first leg of the journey. I'd been worried about Dad then, about Rousseau. Now Rousseau was gone. Dad was doing fine, but I still hadn't told him about my son. I wasn't sure if I was protecting him or deceiving him, and I couldn't help but think of Pietro when I thought about the secret I was keeping from my dad.

Andie, being the efficient, take-care-of-things type, a list maker who checked off finished tasks, couldn't understand how I had agreed to let Pietro keep the painting. "I don't know how you can survive with so many unresolved issues, so much unfinished business, trusting people who are obviously unreliable. The man stole a valuable Renaissance painting, and now you are letting him have more time?"

Maybe I'd just lived my life with too many loose ends and

too much unfinished business to live it any other way. But I had given Pietro my word. I had to trust that he would be true to his. "It's a five-hundred-year-old painting," I told Andie with a nervous laugh, "lost for the last thirty years. What's a little more time?"

She shrugged and said, "I suppose you've got to do it your way."

She was definitely curious about Roberto. I knew he was not part of unfinished business. He was the newness, the brightness, the future, and I missed him immensely during my visit home.

The lease on the apartment in Florence didn't start until the middle of September, so when I returned to Italy I stayed at the villa with Roberto. Despite the uncertainties swirling about me concerning my son, and also Pietro Capparelli and the painting, that time with Roberto was filled with a wonderful contentment.

Maria had convinced him to get help with the day-to-day upkeep, the cooking and cleaning. He'd had someone coming in just once a week, but now that he had full-time help, it was almost like being on vacation for both of us. Good meals, clean sheets and towels, fresh coffee every morning without raising a finger.

Roberto continued to go into Florence for three half days. I got together with Regina for lunch several times, for a game of tennis early one morning before the heat was overpowering. I hiked in the hills around Fiesole on mornings when I was alone, up to the amphitheater and monastery. One morning I wandered into the chapel and sat listening to the harmonious chant of the monks as if they had scheduled a concert just for me. How peaceful I felt.

Each morning I woke in Roberto's bed. Sometimes we'd have breakfast brought in on a tray. His housekeeper, Margherita, was a wonderful cook, often making fresh pastries, hand-squeezed orange juice, and wonderful rich, dark coffee. Sometimes we'd have breakfast in the garden. One morning I studied him as he read the paper, and I thought—I am fifty-three years old, and just now I am learning what it truly feels like to love a man, to love a very good, kind, giving man.

In early September as Roberto and I lay in bed together, contemplating what we would like to order for breakfast, I laughed and said, "I'm not sure I want to go back to my little apartment in Florence. I'll miss the room service here."

"Then don't," Roberto said. "Don't go back. Stay here. There are other things you might miss too."

I sat up and looked at him. What was he asking? That I move in with him? Or was he just joking? "School starts in a couple of weeks," I said.

"It's a short drive down to Florence."

He stood, slipped on his robe. "What shall I tell Margherita we'd like for breakfast?"

"Are you asking me to move in with you?"

"I love you, Suzanne." He sat on the bed beside me. "I'd like something a little more permanent than that." He took my hand.

I was stunned by his words, not that I hadn't realized that he loved me, that I was in love with him, but it was the first time either of us had said it.

"Is this a proposition," I asked, "or a proposal?"

"If I were to propose to a woman, I might do it in a more romantic way, though it would be helpful to know how she might reply."

I pulled him closer and kissed him quickly. "I love you too, Roberto."

Three days later, at a restaurant in Fiesole, with a beautiful view of Florence, Roberto presented me with a lovely ring and asked me to marry him.

I said yes.

SCHOOL STARTED AGAIN. All new students, mostly juniors. Once more I felt that familiar mixture of uneasiness and excitement. Did they realize how lucky they were to be here in Florence? Easily I slid back into the rhythm. I seldom spent the night at my apartment, and when I did Roberto stayed with me.

One day slipped into another. September to October to November. Roberto and I were married in a quiet civil ceremony in Florence the first week in November.

The following week, when I was just beginning to accept that I would not hear again from my son, another letter arrived. Again it was short. He told me more about his own family, his children, and then, he wrote, *for my children, I would like to meet you. I want them to know more about their heritage.* There was nothing definite—no meeting set up—and I knew we would continue to take this slow, but there was now hope.

I wrote back and told him I would also like to meet.

I hadn't spoken to Pietro since the day I found the Masolino and discovered the truth about Stefano and my son. He had sent the postcard, and I clung to that as his promise. I did not wish his mother dead, but I must admit to a certain anxiety in waiting.

Then, late one afternoon, almost two weeks after Roberto and I were married, I got a call at school from Pietro. My first thought when I heard his voice was that his mother had died.

"She says she must s-s-speak to you." He asked that I come, explaining the doctor said she would be gone before the night was out. She was at home, where she wished to die.

This request made me very uneasy. I wanted to return the painting to the Uffizi, but I didn't want to take it while the body was still warm.

"I don't understand, Pietro—your mother asked to see me?"

"Yes."

Would I deny a dying woman a last request?

Roberto was apprehensive too, but he drove me to San Giovanni.

I knocked and Pietro came to the door. He looked frail. He

was a short man, but it seemed he had shrunk since I'd seen him last spring and the fatigue was evident in his eyes.

He invited us in. Roberto waited downstairs. With Pietro I climbed the narrow steps to the second floor. His mother was in bed. An ancient-looking priest with a shock of thick white hair sat on a wooden chair beside her. Pietro motioned me into the room, but did not enter himself. Warily, I stepped into the bedroom. The scent of death and incense hung in the air, and I guessed the priest had performed a final anointing. But why was I here? Why did she wish to speak to me? The priest greeted me without words and then rose. He held out his hand, a gesture inviting me over to the bedside. He left the room, joining Pietro, who remained out in the hall.

She looked small and pale and withered as if the last tiny fragment of life clung to her body. Was she waiting for me? Her eyes were closed. I couldn't bring myself to sit. I said a quick wordless prayer, for myself as much as for this woman who lay dying. She opened her eyes, and though she was unable to focus on me, I knew she was aware of my presence when she whispered, "Signorina Suzanne."

I knelt down beside the bed. "*Sono qui,*" I said in a low voice.

She took in a low, ragged breath that carried a dry, stale scent when she exhaled. "*Mio figlio,*" she said in a voice much stronger than I had expected, "*un buon uomo.*" My son, a good man.

"*Sì,*" I told her, "*lo so.*" I know.

Then, so quietly I had to draw near enough that I could feel her labored breath on my cheek, she said, "*L'Arno . . . ha rubato la Madonna.*"

The beat of my heart quickened. I remembered clearly the first time I had come to visit on Christmas Eve—she told me, with a little laugh in her voice, that *the Arno had stolen all the furniture.* What was she saying now? The Arno had taken the painting? I forced myself not to look back, and then I heard

steps behind me. When I turned, my eyes met those of the
priest, who nodded a gracious thank-you.

I stood and glanced to the wall, the small table, the altar of
devotion. Even though only a portion of the painting was visible behind the open door, I could see the small picture in the
gilded frame was not the Masolino Madonna.

36

November 2006

IT HAS BEEN forty years now, forty years since the flood of 1966.

When the heavy rains come—always in November—I notice a certain tension in the air, people gazing at the river. Sometimes I join them. It is always the older citizens. The young people of Florence, the students who flock to the city, the explorers, the adventurers, they have little knowledge of what happened those many years ago, the great destruction, the coming together of so many for the rebuilding, the restoration. And I wonder, do we learn from our mistakes? Have any further precautions been taken to prevent another tragedy? The walls around the river have been raised and reinforced. But could it happen again?

Often I think of something one of the students, a mud angel, said about art being forever, about people fading and dying. And with this comes the realization of how truly vulnerable we are, how easily broken. And yet, we too can be restored.

Do I ever regret the agreement I made with Pietro? I've

learned not to look back with regret. Perhaps it is from Roberto that I've learned to enjoy each day as it comes.

Often as I walk along the Arno, I imagine I catch a glimpse of it floating in the river. Some days, my imagination carries me further. I see a group of children playing on the bank, digging in the damp earth, constructing little roads and villages the way children do.

A boy yells, "What is this?" as he yanks at something hard and stiff, a corner protruding from a mound of rubble in the bank, twisted fishing line, paper cups and cans.

The others join him, pulling up handfuls of dirt, yanking at tangled filament, brushing the filth from the wooden panel.

"Look!" one of the girls shouts. "Look at the gold!"

"It's mine," the boy cries. "I found it."

"We have to share it," the smallest girl says.

The oldest boy grabs the panel, now released from the earth. "This is Christ and his mother. This is a sacred picture."

There is no further discussion. He starts up the bank and, one by one, in single file, they march proudly following the boy carrying the painting, an icon in a religious procession.

The oldest boy takes it home and presents it to his mother. She cleans the remaining mud from its surface, then hangs it on the wall and admires it. "What a pretty little picture!" she exclaims.

Some time later, a visitor to the home sees the painting. He knows something of art and suspects it might be valuable. He suggests it be taken to an antique dealer he is casually acquainted with. The dealer is simply amazed, as he thinks it is possibly a fifteenth-century painting. He asks that it be analyzed. He takes it to an appraiser who refers it to a friend who works for the Uffizi. Eventually it is identified as a painting that was thought to have been lost in the flood of 1966. The director of restoration agrees that it has some water damage, but surely it has not been in the River Arno for almost forty years. It will be restored and returned to the Uffizi collection.

I continue to hold on to this belief, that eventually the painting will be found and returned.

* * *

I WENT TO see Pietro in the spring after his mother passed away and was not surprised to find he was no longer living on San Giovanni. I have no idea where he is.

I'd gone to the funeral services for his mother. A small group gathered in the intimacy of the Brancacci Chapel in the Church of Santa Maria del Carmine. How fitting that Signora Capparelli would have her last prayers here at the Brancacci, under the beautiful frescoes of Masolino and Masaccio. I smiled a little as I looked up at Masolino's lovely Eve, whose face so closely resembled our Madonna. I was sure Signora Capparelli knew full well where her pretty little painting had come from.

After the services, Pietro came to me. "You must believe me, Signorina Suzanne, I did not take the Masolino. It was my intention that you return it. My mother . . . I came home one day and it was gone. She would not tell me. You must believe me, Signorina." The look in his eyes, a sadness, a loss, told me that he was telling me the truth. He didn't know.

But strangely, I did. Because a dying woman told me. The River Arno had taken the Madonna.

But why had his mother shared this with me, and no other? Not even her son? I thought about what Charley said regarding sin and penance and reconciliation, that there was an obligation on the sinner's part to make things right, that a mere absolution offered by the priest would not forgive the sin. Was this why Signora Capparelli told me—to release her from the burden of her sin? If she confessed to me, did she believe this would gain her entry into heaven, as well as protect her son?

Mothers and sons.

The Madonna and Child.

Often my mind produces an image of Masolino's Madonna and Christ Child, gloriously restored after the flood. The gold leaf shimmering, the rich dark blue, soft pink and white, the delicate fine-lined halos. The child, reaching up so tenderly to touch his mother's face. Mother and son—this is the true beauty of the work. Not the divinity, but the humanity. A mother's love. Did she know as she held that tiny child that he would one day be called to sacrifice his life for the sins of mankind?

Often I think of a mother and son, two thousand years later. A mother who was not willing to give up her son.

And one who had given up her son, and then found him again.

EPILOGUE

November 2000

THE WOMAN STEPS out onto the slick cobblestone street, lowering her head against the wind and rain. She adjusts the stiff wooden panel under the bulk of her coat, holding it against her side, moving with small steps. Her cane taps a slow, careful rhythm, muted by the moisture that glazes the street and puddles in crevices between the stones. It is early morning, still dark. Lights from lampposts and buildings reflect off the street. The rain has fallen for days now and a familiar scent—the hard, cold, lifeless smell of November—permeates the air. So unlike the fresh, earthy scent of spring showers, she thinks as she moves toward the river.

It is just two blocks to the Arno River, but it takes great effort to make it that far. She has always been a strong woman and taken great pride in her health, yet she knows it is but a gift from God, and pride is a deadly sin. All things of the body will pass. She must go now, before her strength is gone. She takes a deep, labored breath and hears a faint rattling in her chest.

She slept little this past night, tossing and turning, contemplating what she knew she must do. A long-ago November came once more in her dreams. She remembers those days clearly, as if the past is closer than yesterday.

Thirty-four years ago, Thursday evening, the third of November, 1966. The city was draped in green, white, and red Italian flags. The Florentine banners, red lilies on white, were raised in anticipation of the holiday on November fourth commemorating the Italian armistice of the Great War. It had been raining for days and continued through the night. And then the river came bursting through the streets. Oh, beautiful little city of Florence, the Arnò gently meandering through, but then such rage, such great anger as the river tossed about the life of the city—priceless paintings, sculptures, and ancient manuscripts. Flooding the churches, the palazzos and piazzas, even the humble dwellings of the Florentine people who fled its path. Yet later, many came to the city to save what might have been lost forever.

Today a different task, a different thought. The scarf, which she had so tediously wrapped over her head and tied under her chin, begins to slip and she snuggles into her thick wool coat, the dampness bringing out a smell that reminds her of something else from long ago. Her mother dressing her warmly to go out on a winter morning. These thoughts have been with her often now, her childhood.

Again the woman adjusts the small wooden panel under her coat and stops to rest. Her lungs feel heavy, as does her heart, and she prays for both strength and resolve to do what she knows she must.

She sees little traffic and no one on foot as she moves slowly onto the Lungarno Guicciardini. It will soon be daylight. The wind no longer blows and the rain has let up. It comes down almost gently now as she stops again, looking to the river, admiring the curve and three arches of the Ponte Santa Trinita. This very bridge had been destroyed in the second war, yet rebuilt. Her city, so often destroyed, so often resurrected.

She will go to the Santa Trinita rather than the Ponte

Vespucci, where there is much traffic even at this hour, or the Ponte alla Carraia, which is very plain.

Two statues stand on pedestals welcoming travelers to the Ponte Santa Trinita. White marble—ancient, draped figures symbolizing Winter and Fall. Winter seems to shiver from the cold as he attempts to pull a robe carved in stone about his muscular body, and the woman shivers too. She gazes toward the far side of the bridge flanked with Spring and Summer and thinks how fitting that she be greeted by Winter and Fall.

She steps onto the bridge. A single car rumbles over, splashing the woman as if she is not there. A lone man passes quickly on foot. He carries an umbrella, obscuring his face, and he does not acknowledge her. She feels invisible and smiles at the thought.

She stops to rest, breathing deeply. Closing her eyes, she smells not the rain now, but the river, and even it is filled with the cold, flinty scent of the season. She continues to the middle of the bridge, leans her cane up against the stone rail, adjusts her scarf, then looks about to make sure no one is present. Carefully with gloved hand she reaches beneath her coat. Her hand trembles as she withdraws the small wooden panel. The first light of day attempts to reach through the clouds. The rain is but a damp drizzle now.

She studies the small painting—the sweet face of the Virgin, the precious Christ Child, the soft pink, blue, and gold. The morning light is faint, and the woman's eyes have grown dim, but she has gazed upon these images many times and does not require her earthly eyes to see. She imagines others who might also have found comfort and delight in the artist's creation over the past five hundred years. Perhaps a Medici, a bishop, a cardinal, or even a pope. Surely this little painting was created for private devotion in a small chapel rather than a grand cathedral or church.

"You will understand what I am about to do," she whispers to the Madonna, as if the woman in the painting might reply. "You know I must. The Arno meant to claim you many years ago."

She holds the tender portrait up to the first light, then takes one small step and raises it above the river. "Forgive me," she whispers, lifting her eyes to the morning sky. Her fingers tighten around the painting for a moment, then relax and let go. She watches the panel fall as if in slow motion. It hits with a soft splash, floats for a short distance, and disappears into the darkness of the Arno. The woman stands, staring down into the river. She crosses herself, then reaches for her cane, turns, and starts for home.